Ben seemed remote, but she sensed something seething beneath his composed exterior. Whatever was going on in his head, he had to have something more on his mind than her disappearance.

"You seem upset," she ventured, not knowing what to make of it. If anyone should be upset, shouldn't it be her?

An awful silence met her words. It expanded until it filled the room and pressed in on her.

"Upset?" he said finally, then shrugged. "I'm not upset. I'm just trying to figure out why you'd fall off the face of the earth *exactly* when bad shit started happening."

She licked her lips, not liking what he was inferring. Something else must have happened that she didn't know about. "I don't know what I can say that will make you believe me," she began, stomach squeezing tighter when he didn't even glance at her. Despair filled her. "I called you because I need your help."

He set her BlackBerry on the side table next to him and regarded her dispassionately. "That's nice."

His remote expression jangled her nerves. What had happened to make him look at her like that?

"You want me to trust you, Sam?"

She frowned. "Of course I do."

"You're a bright girl, so I'm sure you can understand why that's not going to happen. But if you want to try to earn my trust, I'm game." He tilted his dark head, pale eyes glittering a challenge in the lamp light. "You can start by taking off all your clothes."

Praise for *OUT OF HER LEAGUE*

"Ms. Cross writes well, with smoothness and polish, and her ability to create sub plots means that she makes a [stalker] theme refreshing. Go for it—this is a super read."

~Between the Lines WRDF Review

"Truly one of the most remarkable stories I have read. Kudos to Ms. Cross for a story well told."

~Graded "A" by Simply Romance Reviews

"*OUT OF HER LEAGUE* is a tantalizing story that has well-developed characters plus lots of mystery, suspense of the ever-present stalker. Ms. Cross' description of settings brings the locations to life and reveals even more about the characters. Her smooth, easy-flowing writing is a joy to read, AND the love scenes are truly love scenes, not just sex—ah!"

~Rated 4.5 books by Long and Short Reviews

"Clearly written with an eye on the commercial potential of today's more explicit romance fiction, *OUT OF HER LEAGUE* is a bona fide page-turner, peppered with profanity and violence, and with a slow, but steady, progression to several steamy sex scenes... Cross' prose is spare, fast-paced and evocative, with enough narrative hooks and violent jolts to snare even those who profess to deride this kind of fiction."

~Peace Arch News

No Turning Back

by

Kaylea Cross

HOPE YOU ENJOY IT!

Kaylea Cross

This is a work of fiction. Names, characters, places, and incidents either are the product of the author's imagination or are used fictitiously, and any resemblance to actual persons living or dead, business establishments, events, or locales, is entirely coincidental.

No Turning Back

Contact Information: info@thewildrosepress.com

Cover Art by *Kim Mendoza*

The Wild Rose Press
PO Box 708
Adams Basin, NY 14410-0706
Visit us at www.thewildrosepress.com

Publishing History
First Crimson Rose Edition, 2010
Print ISBN 1-60154-719-6

Published in the United States of America

Dedication

For my boys,
with the hope you will only know peace
in your lifetimes.
And to all the men and women
serving across the globe to safeguard us all,
you have my heartfelt gratitude.
Thanks to future NYT bestseller Katie Reus
for keeping me on my toes
and lending an empathetic ear when I need one.
Also many thanks to my fellow RWAGVC members
for their unyielding support and enthusiasm.
You guys rock!

Chapter One

Late September, Baghdad, Iraq
Afternoon

When either the CIA or a terrorist cell was targeting you, you were having a very bad day.

Sam was in serious goddamn trouble. The life and death kind.

With an uneasy glance around the hotel room she now knew was bugged, she studied the manila envelope clutched in her damp hands. She'd found it shoved under her usual computer terminal at the internet café fifteen minutes ago. It bore her name on the top, written with a red felt-tipped pen.

Like her day could get any worse?

First, she and her teammate Ben had found the transmitters hidden in her place. Then, she'd relayed her suspicions about their Iraqi informant Fahdi to her boss, legendary CIA operative Luke Hutchinson. A few minutes after that awkward conversation, she'd planted a tracking device on Fahdi and left the office for a badly needed break. She'd headed to the internet cafe for a hot drink while she checked e-mail in relative privacy, and the envelope had been under the keyboard of the machine she'd sat down at. Sam had no idea how it had gotten there or who it was from, but sensed whatever it contained was going to be bad, so she hadn't opened it. Though she hadn't seen anything else suspicious, she was sure someone had been watching her, so she'd high-tailed it home. Not that she was any safer here, she admitted, standing rigid in the middle of the place she'd called home for the past four months.

The thin envelope suddenly felt like it was made of lead instead of paper. She had a really bad feeling she wasn't going to like whatever was inside. Swallowing her dread, she opened it anyway and pulled out the contents. Color photos filled her hand.

Sam laid them on her desk and lifted a shaky hand to her mouth. Dear God. They were all of her, shot with a powerful telephoto lens, from her meeting with Fahdi and his wife. Her eyes skipped to the cryptic note clutched in her nerveless fingers.

We know what you've done. We will contact you with a meeting time and location. Come alone. Tell no one. You are being watched.

The blood pounded in her ears. Her stomach knotted. They knew what she'd done? What did that mean? Panic swirled in her head. Fahdi. Had to be. Whatever he was involved in, they thought she was, too.

Her gaze darted about her cozy living quarters and she wondered if someone was watching her right now.

The place was finished in soothing taupes and creams, and she'd always loved coming home to relax. Not anymore. She and Ben might not have found all the devices. She wasn't safe here. Not with whoever was closing in on her out there, waiting. She had to leave. Right now, even though she had nowhere to go.

Sam stuffed the pictures back into the envelope. Running to her bedroom, she flung open the closet and wrenched her clothes off the hangers, shoving them into the backpack with the envelope. The seconds ticked by like a timer on a bomb. Perspiration prickled her skin as her heart rattled in her chest.

In the bathroom, she cleared the shelf above the sink with a sweep of her arm and dumped everything in the bag, then ran to the kitchen and snatched the picture of her and her cousin Neveah hanging on the fridge. They'd been brought up together and were closer than sisters. Sam wasn't going to leave that behind, especially after Neveah's letter had mysteriously disappeared. She'd noticed that this morning, along with the fact that someone had been into the hard drive of her laptop. Add in the transmitters and she had every right to be paranoid. But the envelope of pictures changed everything.

The sudden shrill of her cell phone made her jump, but she didn't dare answer it. As of right now, she had to cut contact with everyone until she figured out what was going on.

The crawling sensation on the back of her neck was an ominous warning as she ran for the door, snagging her laptop on the way. She had sensitive information in it, and couldn't leave it behind in case it fell into the wrong hands. Someone had been into it once already.

You are being watched.

The menacing words sent a shiver down her spine. She'd first detected the surveillance weeks ago while walking home from the market one night, but had convinced herself she was being paranoid. Now that someone had followed her to the café and left the package, she wished she hadn't dismissed her intuition so quickly. Whoever was after her had to be close.

Whether it was the CIA or a terrorist cell didn't matter a damn right now. Gut instinct told her if she stayed where she was, they'd kill her.

Get out. Now.

Heart pounding like a jackhammer, Sam rushed out of the room. Her shaking fingers fumbled with the key in the lock as she turned the dead bolt in the hallway, then shoved it into her pocket and ran for the stairwell.

Hurry, hurry…

It seemed to take forever to run down the five flights of concrete steps. She wasn't moving fast enough. Whoever was looking for her could be here already. She had to get out while she still could, hide somewhere and decide what the hell to do next. With no other plan, she tore down the stairs and into the underground parking garage. The heavy metal door banged shut behind her and echoed through the cavernous space like a shotgun blast. She cringed at the noise and couldn't help a nervous glance around her to see if anyone was there. Empty.

The sudden silence unnerved her. Her compact, silver rental car sat in its usual spot close to the elevator. Staring at it, her heart tripped. What if someone had planted a bomb in it? The building had security, but it wasn't impossible for someone to sneak around here and not get caught.

Since half the building was occupied by US intelligence staff and civilian contractors, it made for a pretty ideal target. Considering who she worked for, she ranked right up there for interested terrorist groups, and that could also explain why someone had been tailing and threatening her. With anti-US sentiment at an all time high in Iraq and throughout much of the Middle East, it wasn't much of a leap to imagine someone trying to blow her up to make a statement.

Not with the kind of week she'd had.

She eyed her vehicle. Nothing seemed out of the ordinary, but she wasn't going to bet her life on the fact no one had tampered with it. Probably wasn't safe to take her car anyway, even if no one had rigged it. All they'd have to do was tag her license plate and bingo, Samarra Wallace on a platter.

Her mind whirled as she reviewed her options. Going on foot was too risky. Even with her titian-red hair tucked under her headscarf, anyone looking for her would notice the color right away if they got close enough. That left public transit. She didn't want to get on a bus because it would put too many eyes on her. So a taxi it was.

Spinning around, she raced for a side door and exited into the sunlight scorching the parking lot. The heat slapped her in the face and sucked the air out of her lungs. She'd have thought she'd be used to the climate by now, but every time she left the cool of her air conditioned building it hit her. Hefting her backpack strap up higher across her right shoulder, she tightened her grip on the laptop case.

At a brisk pace, she aimed for the sidewalk of the main street in front of her building. She made sure to keep her head up high and tried not to appear nervous, even though she desperately wanted to glance around to make sure no one was following her. Last thing she needed was to draw any more attention to herself than she inadvertently had already.

As soon as she got in the cab, she'd check her BlackBerry for new e-mails. If the same people had broken into her place earlier and accessed her laptop, maybe whoever was hunting her had sent another message. Or maybe someone from the team had tried to contact her. Best she could hope for at this point was a clue that would help her figure out if it was safe to contact her boss Luke—

A sudden explosion ripped the quiet apart.

Sam swallowed a yelp and hit the ground, instinctively covering her head with both arms as the deafening boom tore through the air. The concussion reverberated in her chest and shook the ground.

What the...

Heart pounding, she lifted her head and rolled over to stare at the plume of black, greasy smoke swirling up into the air a few blocks to the west in the militarized Green Zone. Holy hell... Was it a suicide bomber going after US or Iraqi security forces? She clutched her bags, eyes widening as she realized it was close to the barracks where the rest of her team was staying. Far too close.

Ben.

A shock of fear hit her as his handsome face and warm smile flashed through her head. What if he'd been caught in the explosion? Or the others? She stared at the smoke, her stomach twisting. Was everyone okay? She thought of them: Dec, Bryn, Ali, Fahdi, Rhys... But most of all she thought about Rhys's sexy twin brother, Ben.

She liked him. Probably more than she should, under the circumstances. Part of her wanted to call him to make sure they were all right, but the rational part knew she couldn't risk it yet.

If her boss had sent any of them after her, they could trace her too easily. Sam gnawed on her lower lip a moment, caught in indecision. Damn. She wanted to find out if they were okay, but... No, she wouldn't. Wasn't smart right now.

The smoke roiled up like a giant charcoal thundercloud against the bright blue sky. Whatever had exploded, it was powerful and must have done a lot of damage. There had to be casualties. Her hand tightened on her phone, wavering under a rush of self-doubt. What if she was being paranoid about all this? What if the CIA wasn't responsible for scaring her to death?

Truth be told, she'd rather it be them than the other option. Terrorists and radical militias. A shiver rippled over her skin even though the temperature had to be in the upper eighties. What she'd done to gain the interest of a terrorist group, she couldn't say, but she wasn't interested in finding out. All she wanted was to go someplace safe until she could figure out what to do and who she could trust. If it turned out her team was after her, she had some hope Rhys would believe she was innocent of whatever it was she'd supposedly "done". Maybe Ben would, too.

Sam pulled out her BlackBerry and stared at it for a moment. Ben and Rhys would help her.

Don't you dare. Not yet.

The wail of sirens rose in the air as the first responders raced to the scene. Once more her eyes strayed to the plume of smoke boiling into the air. Even if the team had been caught in the explosion, there was little she could do to help. Ben was the team medic; he and the others would take care of any casualties in the immediate area. Her conscience squirmed, but it didn't matter that she wanted to help. At this point she didn't really have a choice.

Move, Sam. Get going. Nothing you can do now anyway.

She forced herself to her feet, legs wobbling a bit as she ran the rest of the way to the sidewalk. Standing at the curb, she hailed a cab. The perspiration beading on her skin made her silk blouse stick to her back beneath the black robes Iraqi women wore.

When the taxi pulled up she wrenched open the door and scrambled inside. Tossing her bags on the seat, she instructed the driver in flawless Arabic to take her to the bus station. Since she had no place to go, that seemed as good as any.

The cab pulled away and stopped at an intersection. The driver met her eyes in the rearview mirror and she quickly looked away, her panic easing a little now that she was on the move. Still torn, she cast another glance out the rear window, and prayed all her friends were safe. In time, they'd all understand why she had to run. Provided she lived long enough to be able to tell them, that is.

Her mind scrambled to come up with a plan. Cash. She'd need cash to stay under the radar. Credit cards could be traced, and banks and ATMs had security cameras. She'd have to stop only once, pull out all the cash she could and hope it was enough to get her by for...well, however long this was going to last. She couldn't just wander around aimlessly, either. Wherever she went, she had to appear like she had a purpose for being there. Otherwise she'd look suspicious, and suspicious drew attention.

Finding somewhere secure to stay was going to be a challenge. She could pay for a hotel room with cash, but they'd most likely demand a passport or other ID, and that wasn't going to help her cause any. She was going to have to do something to alter her appearance, namely her hair—a shade of auburn even a nearsighted eighty-year-old could spot at a hundred yards. Even if she kept it covered with a scarf, she'd have to dye it black in case anyone caught a glimpse of it, plus it would help her blend in with the local population better. Her brows, too, although they were already a few shades darker than her hair. At least her eyes were deep brown, so she didn't have to worry about contacts to disguise their color.

Okay. First thing was to pick up the cash. Then she'd find a pair of scissors and some hair dye, and make her way somewhere to do a quick beauty treatment. Maybe in a washroom at the bus station. Then she'd need a safe deposit box or locker of some kind to leave her passport and other ID in. No way would she carry that around in case someone searched her or stole it.

Sam stared straight out the windshield past the

driver's right shoulder. The thickening traffic slowed their progress. Out the back window, more vehicles closed in. It made the skin between her shoulder blades itch. She wanted, needed, to keep moving, especially during daylight hours.

"Roadblock up ahead," the driver informed her.

Sam swiveled around to peer out the windshield, and made out the uniformed soldiers standing where the traffic was stopped. She huffed out an irritated breath. Great. That's all she needed right now, a security check. What if the military had already been alerted and was looking for her? An American checkpoint was just as dangerous to her as an Iraqi one, since she didn't know who was behind the threats.

The taxi's brakes squealed as the vehicle slowed and inched along as it crept behind the rear bumper in front of it. Sam's eyes darted around them, watching for any threatening movements. About ten cars waited in front of them. She couldn't afford to wait that long.

The soldiers searched each vehicle as it came up to the checkpoint, checking the interior, trunk and under the hood. Her fingers clenched around the backpack strap.

Please let them only be looking for weapons.

Time crawled by as she awaited their turn. The closer the cab moved, the more her heart sped up until tiny prickles raced over her skin and perspiration broke out all over her. The tinny music coming from the taxi's ancient radio scraped across her nerves like a dull knife, as did the driver's cheerful whistling.

Second in line now.

Up ahead, Sam noticed one of the guards glance at her in the backseat. *Stay relaxed. Don't let them see you're nervous.* She schooled her features into an expression of calm.

Yeah, she wasn't that good an actress. Her heart beat a sharp tattoo in her ears, her palms damp as she cradled them in her lap. She struggled not to hold her breath as the driver pulled up and stopped at the Iraqi soldier's command. He was tall and thin, about twenty to twenty-five. As he approached, his eyes swept over the driver, and then her.

Their gazes locked. He stilled.

Her stomach knotted. Did he recognize her? Something about her had caught his attention, because he put one hand on the butt of the pistol at his hip, his body language making it clear he was thinking about drawing it if either she or the driver made a wrong move.

"Hand over your identification," he demanded in clipped Arabic.

Something was wrong. There was no reason for him to be looking at her so suspiciously unless an alert had been issued for her. Her fingers hesitated on the zipper of the pouch that held her ID. She couldn't hand over her passport. *Think, Sam, think!*

Her seat. If she moved fast, she might have time to get it out and slip it underneath.

She swallowed, keeping her eyes on the guard while she inched the front zipper open, praying the front seat shielded her hand. Her shaky fingers found the smooth cover of her passport.

The driver, his profile showing his wide-eyed shock at the turn of events, snatched up his documents and shoved them through the open window, then put up his hands in a gesture of surrender. Sam yanked out her passport, cocked her wrist and shoved it under the seat as fast as she could, then covered the move by smoothing out the folds in her robe, her gaze glued to the soldier who was checking the driver's papers. He handed them back, then focused his full attention on her. She fought to keep her breath from hitching. Frowning, he opened and closed his hand in an impatient gesture.

"Your documents."

Shit, she couldn't just ignore him. Her heart was slamming now, so hard she was sure he must have heard it. It took everything she had to look calm. *Don't panic.* "I have no papers with me."

The soldier stared hard into her eyes.

"The bag then. Let me see it."

Sam gripped the strap of her backpack. He might not be looking for her, but once he found out she had no ID, he might not let them through. That would lead to more soldiers and policemen coming around to question her.

"Give me the bag," he growled and took a step back, spreading his feet out as though he was about to draw his sidearm.

The driver cranked his head around to give her a disbelieving look as if to say, "Are you crazy?"

Wincing inside, Sam lifted the bag and handed it over, glancing out the passenger window to gauge the distance to the intersection. If she tried to run for it, would she even get out of the taxi before they shot her? Doubtful.

Hands clenching and unclenching, she watched the guard rip open the zipper of her beige backpack and rifle through it, and when he raised his head, his dark scowl made her heart sink. No chance she was getting out of this.

"Mustafa," he called out, and another soldier ambled over, shorter and stockier than the first. The guard holding her bag dumped it on the ground and gestured to her with a curt jerk of his chin. "Get out of the vehicle."

Everything in her froze. Her breath, the blood in her veins. Her heart stopped for a beat or two, then made up for the deficiency by going into triple time. Automatically her hands came up, palms out.

Mustafa yanked the passenger door open and palmed the butt of his pistol. In front of her, the driver sucked in a sharp breath and muttered a prayer to Allah. The first soldier opened the driver's door and hauled him out.

Eyes locked on Mustafa's face, Sam inched over the ripped upholstery toward the door.

"What's your name," he demanded.

"Ariah," she blurted, trying not to panic as he snatched hold of her wrist to haul her out of the taxi. In her current state of terror, she didn't know where the name came from or even if it was Arabic.

His grip was almost bruising. As she scrambled out, a rough yank sent her to her knees on the baking hot pavement in front of him. He wrenched her upright and flung the backpack at her feet. "Don't move from this spot while we search the vehicle."

Without thinking, Sam grabbed the strap of her pack, clutching it in her sweaty grip. While the driver wrung his hands and prayed beside her, she stood frozen, watching while the two of them tore the taxi apart, covering a flinch when they got to the back seat. Mustafa opened up her laptop case, lifted the lid of the computer and set it on top of the trunk. Jesus, were they going to check that, too? They went back to searching the taxi.

Keep going, she willed them silently. *Pass over it, come on, miss it, miss it…*

God must have been busy just then, because her silent prayer went unanswered. The tall, skinny one fished under the seat and stared in surprise at the passport in his hand. When he aimed an angry glare at her, her stomach plummeted.

Then he was on his radio, and his words chilled her to the core.

"Sir, you must come here, we have an American woman," he flipped open the front cover, "by the name of Samarra Wallace." He made her surname sound like Wool-ass.

She only had a couple of seconds to digest that before one of the vehicles parked on the other side of the checkpoint threw its doors open, and three masked gunmen popped out, coming at her with their rifles up. Sam jumped. The cab driver dropped to his knees with a high-pitched wail.

Sam cried out too, unconsciously backing toward the building behind her, eyes whipping from side to side to search for an escape route.

Who were these guys? They weren't going to shoot her in broad daylight in front of everyone, were they? Quaking, she sucked sharp breaths through her mouth as the trio approached, looking like some kind of deadly Special Ops team. She should know—she'd worked with enough of them. Her legs shook so hard she had to lean against the building to stay on her feet. The men came up fast and stopped about ten feet away.

The one in the middle, a tall muscular man with light brown eyes said in nearly perfect English, "You are Samarra Wallace?"

She couldn't nod, couldn't do anything but stare into those cold, merciless eyes and wonder if she was about to die.

He stepped forward, got right in her face, and the gleam in his eyes convinced her he was getting off on how terrified she was. His hand came up. She flinched as his fingers seized her chin in a cruel grip, shoving her head back so hard it smacked against the wall.

The sharp crack of her skull hitting the building stunned her for a moment and she blinked to clear her vision. When it did, her lungs constricted in mortal fear.

"I'm not going to ask again."

With her face held in those strong fingers, she

forced out a stiff nod. Dear God, what was he going to do to her?

"You work for the CIA?"

Her head spun. Oh, shit… They were going to kill her, weren't they?

He cracked her skull against the wall again. She yelped, stars dancing before her eyes, and brought her hands up to lock around his thick forearm. There was nothing she could do, he completely overpowered her. Jesus, what had she ever done to them?

"The CIA and Luke Hutchinson?"

Sam stilled. The blood pounded in her head as she stared up at him. He knew Luke's name? How could he know it, unless her boss had sent him after her?

"Sir."

She jerked when one of the others called out in Arabic, but the man holding her didn't break eye contact with her.

"What?"

"We need her password to access the laptop."

The glint in his pale brown eyes intensified. His hand tightened slowly until she feared he'd fracture her mandible. "Your password."

Uttered in that silky voice, the threat sent another wave of apprehension through her. Would they torture her if she didn't tell them? Her mind raced with all sorts of awful possibilities. They might torture her anyway, once they confirmed from her laptop who her employer was, so what difference did it make if they saw what was on it?

Teeth chattering, she opened her mouth to force the password out of her tight throat. "N-Neveah."

"Spell it."

She did, but halfway through, something hard punched into the wall above her.

The man holding her flinched and ducked as a

fine shower of dust rained down on them. Sam's stupefied gaze traveled up in that split second and found the bullet hole in the wall a foot above her head. Someone had *shot* at them?

Oh, God, please help—

Two more sharp cracks followed, one pinging off the taxi. Sam let out a strangled cry, her heart slamming against her ribs so hard it made her dizzy. Another bullet zinged past, so close she felt a puff of air against her cheek. She shrieked. Her captor swore and released her, hitting the ground with the others amidst their shouts, rolling to his front with his rifle up to return fire.

Sam dove onto her belly and landed atop her backpack on the pavement, covering her head with her arms as she cowered into as small a target as possible. Chaos reigned around her. Men shouted in Arabic. The staccato shots of automatic gunfire popped like fireworks.

Yanking the strap of her pack, she belly-crawled as fast as she could toward the corner of the building, intent on getting around it for cover. *Almost there.* The breath exploded in and out of her lungs, muscles screaming as she scrambled to safety. Grabbing the edge of the building, she hauled her body around the edge and shrank up flat against the wall.

What the hell had just happened? Shaking, she sucked in a few breaths of air and squeezed her eyes shut, sending up another prayer that God would be paying attention this time. Cold, greasy sweat trickled down her sides, over her back and between her breasts.

The firing out in the street intensified until a continuous barrage of noise filled the air, deadly projectiles peppering the buildings and vehicles. Over the cacophony, someone screamed as if they'd been hit. She shuddered. Death squads. Had to be.

Two death squads firing at each other. Pressed against the cool, shadowed wall, her panicked brain began to come out of its fog. She was free. No one was coming after her yet. This might be her only chance. Whipping her head to the side, she glanced down the deserted alleyway and back toward the street. Then she took off.

Run. Run!

With the speed borne of terror, she burst from her hiding spot and tore as fast as she could down the alley to the first thing she could hide behind—a dumpster. She waited a few breaths, lungs heaving. Convinced no one was following yet, she darted out again and sprinted on, whipping around the next corner.

With her skin crawling like a sniper's crosshairs were lined up on her back, she ran, heedless of the stares she elicited. She ran until the stitch in her side burned like a hot poker between her ribs, until her quads trembled with fatigue. Sweat poured off her, rank with her fear. Even when she slowed, her lungs about to explode, she kept jogging, zigzagging through the back streets. Every cell screamed at her to get as far away as she could.

She must have run for more than fifteen minutes before she had to stop and collapsed forward, hands resting on her knees as she fought to fill her starving lungs. Still the sense of urgency pushed at her. *Keep going, keep going…*

Sam forced her exhausted body onward, driving it past its limits, fueled by adrenaline and the fierce will to survive.

If she was going to die today, it would be from a heart attack or heat stroke, not an assassin's bullet.

Chapter Two

Two days later
Baghdad, morning

Ben Sinclair stood outside Sam's apartment with a 9 mm Beretta in his right hand and his left curled around the doorknob. His fraternal twin, Rhys, stood ready behind him, a looming presence at six and a half feet tall with a build like a heavyweight fighter.

"Let's do this," Rhys growled.

For an instant, Ben hesitated. They'd already lost one teammate in the truck bombing at their compound, then Dec and Bryn, plus two other members had been injured in the Basra op. Their leader Luke was still in the hospital down there from the same friendly fire incident that had taken Dec and some of his SEALs out. Could Sam have been behind any of that? He liked to think not.

The tension in him ramped up another few notches as he tightened his grip on the knob. He wasn't really sure he wanted to find out what was inside. He didn't want to confirm she'd set them all up to die.

Ben's expression hardened. Screw it, he thought, and twisted it open. Aiming his weapon through the doorway, he stepped in. The place was dark and quiet. With his brother at his back, they swept through the rooms, silent as ghosts.

"Clear," he said.

"Clear," Rhys echoed.

Not that they'd really expected to find anyone waiting for them. Still, both of them were paranoid enough to take every precaution. Holstering his weapon, Ben went back to the desk in the living room and started looking for evidence. Her laptop was gone. BlackBerry, too. She hadn't left any other electronic devices behind except for an iPod she'd put away neatly in one of the drawers, all of its little wires and cables individually wrapped with twist ties to keep them from getting tangled. So very Sam.

Whatever else she was, Samarra Wallace was a neat freak. Daughter of a well-respected American archaeologist, she'd been named after the Iraqi city of Samarra. Ironic that she'd wound up stationed in Baghdad.

Like everything else in her home, the desk was immaculate. Everything was stacked just so, each item in its proper place. The top drawer housed a little tray with dividers separating paper clips and thumb tacks from elastic bands, post-it notes and spare batteries. Not your average junk drawer. She'd sorted her mail into little wicker baskets on the desk and labeled them with a P-touch. Her fricking pens were all capped and standing end down in a little holder next to a color-coded stack of office supplies, also labeled with a P-touch.

Little OCD, Sam?

The devil in him wanted to rifle through the desk and mess everything up, just to get a rise out of her. He smothered the impulse, but even after all his years of military discipline it wasn't easy for him. If he was honest, he owed whatever he'd learned about self-control to his iron-willed twin. Judging by what he saw in front of him, Miss Wallace shared the same control-freak tendencies his brother did.

The meticulously organized way she kept her things made Ben feel worse about this whole situation. It meant they were dealing with a woman who was anything but careless. He already knew she was intelligent and charming. All right, wicked smart and charming. She had an Electrical Engineering and Computer Science degree from MIT, after all. But standing in her living room, he had to wonder if the whole time he'd been looking at her and seeing an efficient, reliable teammate, she was really a cold-hearted, calculating bitch who'd sold them all out to the same terrorists they were tracking. Could she really have duped him and all the others like that?

She'd sent him a text message while Rhys and the others had been out doing the op in Basra that bothered him more than anything else.

Intel leakd. Op cmpmisd. Abort.

If she was up to no good, why had she bothered to warn him at all? To try and clear her name? As the acid in his stomach started to churn, Ben groped in his pocket for the roll of Tums he kept on hand, and popped two into his mouth. Goddamn, he was going to have an ulcer before this was all over. If he didn't already. His friend Bryn had been kidnapped and nearly killed in the op two days ago, and his guts still hadn't recovered. This thing with Sam was making it worse.

"Anything?"

Ben turned his head toward Rhys, standing in the kitchen doorway. Man, the guy could be a giant pain in the ass, but he'd been so glad to see him in one piece after that botched op he could almost forgive him for being such a hard-ass. "No. You?"

"The picture of her and her cousin is missing."

Ben remembered Rhys staring intently at it when they'd come to Sam's aid the other day. When they'd found those damn transmitters.

"Must have taken it when she left."

Ben grunted. That was the thing. Her disappearance seemed carefully planned, and the fact that it was premeditated left him wondering about her involvement. But why would anybody run if they were innocent? If she was in trouble, why hadn't she contacted him or his brother like she had when she'd found the first transmitter? She had no reason not to trust them. So why would she have disappeared off the radar and gone AWOL like this? It didn't feel right. None of it did.

"Like to get my hands on that photo," Rhys continued. "Thought I saw someone in the background I recognized, but it doesn't do us any good now. You checked her room yet?"

"Just about to." They went to her bedroom together.

Neat as a goddamn show home. Not a scrap of clothing on the floor, not a single wrinkle in the bedspread. Only thing that pointed to her hasty getaway was the fact she'd left the closet open a little, and some of the hangers were empty. From the looks of it, she'd only taken a few things, so she was traveling light. Ben couldn't help but notice all the clothes were organized perfectly, too. By color, for the love of God. The hangers were evenly spaced, and he was willing to bet if he took out a tape measure, they'd all be pretty damn close to an inch apart. For interest's sake, he pulled open the drawers and saw even her bras and underwear—most bore Victoria's Secret labels, he noted with approval—were organized by color and folded neatly too.

Jesus, who *lived* like that? Talk about control issues. No wonder she and Rhys got along so well.

"Bathroom's clean."

Well, no surprise there. Ben moved to the connecting bath and peered around Rhys' wide shoulders. Clean was right. Damn, except for a few empty shelves that told him she'd taken some things, the place looked like a photo shoot in a magazine. All gleaming and orderly, no clutter. How could she stand being so damned organized?

"She didn't take much," Rhys added. "Maybe she just wanted to get away until the dust settles."

Yeah, or maybe hop a flight and get out of the country for good. "You still think she might be innocent?" Rhys had a better sense of her character because he'd worked with her before.

"She's not the type for subterfuge. Doesn't play games." Rhys shrugged. "We don't know what happened to her. She might have been threatened."

Yeah, but then why wouldn't she have gone to them for help? Ben scrubbed a hand over his face and scratched the goatee he'd grown in an effort to appear more Middle Eastern, though when he wasn't wearing shades his light green eyes killed any chance of that. "Want to look around some more, or are you good?"

"I'm good. She wouldn't have left anything incriminating behind if she was guilty anyway. She's way too smart for that."

Wonderful. Even Rhys, who knew Sam better than any of them, thought their chances of tracking her were pretty much nil. Since they were all ex-Special Ops soldiers, that said a lot, didn't it? "So what now? Want to check in with Davis?"

The former Green Beret and resident CIA spook was out scouring the city to find whatever intel he could about their darling Sam. At Rhys' nod, Ben dug out his phone and called Davis. While waiting for the call to connect, he thought about Luke back in the hospital in Basra. Dude was going to be out of action for a while yet, and that had to drive him mental—edgy, controlling bastard that he was. At least Dec and Bryn were safe back in the States, but they'd lost Ali in the bombing, Fahdi because of it, and now Sam and Luke too. Their team was down to three members now.

"Hey," he said when Davis picked up. "We're at Sam's place, but didn't find anything. Got any news?" He glanced around the tidy apartment, mindful of the transmitters they'd found planted in the smoke detector, phone and behind a painting. He didn't delude himself they'd found all of them. Someone was probably watching and listening to them right now.

As Davis' words registered, Ben's heart leapt. "*What?*"

He met Rhys' sharp gaze as his jaw tensed. Hanging up, he shook his head. "Apparently Sam was caught at a fake checkpoint yesterday in a cab. Driver said three armed men hauled her off, then a firefight broke out between whoever grabbed her and another militia. Police found her passport next to the bullet-riddled taxi she'd been in. So far there's no match from the blood samples they've collected."

"Jesus. Mahdi army?"

The uncharacteristic worry on his controlled twin's face sent another wave of dread through Ben.

He swallowed. "Looks like." The Mahdi Army were Shi'a. Known to be linked to the terrorist mastermind they'd been hunting.

Ben ran a hand through his short hair. Holy shit, if it was true, then Farouk Tehrazzi could have orchestrated the whole thing, from Fahdi planting the bomb that had killed Ali, to the ambush the team had walked into in Basra. His guts clenched with fear for Sam. She might have been tortured for information. Raped. Christ, if Tehrazzi was behind this, she was probably already dead, and knowing that sick fuck, it hadn't been quick or kind.

Sick to his stomach, he whipped open his phone and dialed Luke, wondering what he'd say. Nothing would surprise him at this point, Ben thought, trying to ignore the deep burn under his sternum. This CIA shit was going to kill him.

****

Basra

Luke Hutchinson eyed the congealed lump of hospital food on his plate with disgust. The package next to the dish said it was Cream of Wheat, but come *on*. With his head pounding and his stomach doing somersaults, you'd think someone would have had the decency to put something appetizing in front of him. Broth. Crackers. A banana maybe. At least bananas tasted pretty good when they came back up again.

He wanted the hell *out* of there. His doctors, though, made it clear they thought that was a piss poor idea. Luke doubted it would sway their opinions any to know he'd been on the verge of killing an incredibly dangerous terrorist two days ago, and every second he spent sitting on his ass in a hospital bed was time he couldn't afford to lose. So his head hurt and he puked a lot. Big deal. He'd survived much worse than that in his lifetime. The physical symptoms weren't the problem anyhow.

No, the thing keeping him in that hospital bed was the very real fear he'd messed up his melon. As in, permanently.

The thought terrified him. His mind, the thing he'd always counted on to get him through whatever situation his job put him in, was broken. Not that he was crazy. At least, not more than he'd been before this operation.

When that Air Force missile had veered off course and exploded too close to him, the crack to his skull had shorted out something in his brain. He didn't remember chunks from that night. Nothing about the op before the strike—not the intel, the briefing he must have given the team, the firefight they'd supposedly been in. Nada. Zip. Whole thing was a blank screen for him.

Luke supposed that was normal enough. He'd suffered concussions before, understood a person generally suffered some memory loss regarding the surrounding events. This was different. This time, he couldn't remember critical events before the explosion, or one of his team members. Sam. Samarra Wallace, a CIA communications specialist he'd enlisted to work this op. She'd gone AWOL the day Ali had been killed in the bombing at the compound and hadn't surfaced since, except to text Ben saying the op they'd planned in Basra needed to be aborted. Now here Luke was, lying stuck in the hospital, while Tehrazzi was out there plotting his next move, and Sam was gone. For the life of him, Luke hadn't been able to remember what she looked like.

That ate at him because he'd always had a photographic memory. He never forgot anything, let alone something that significant.

The only things he knew about Sam were from the picture he'd accessed in the CIA database using his phone. She was a twenty-seven-year-old redhead, five-feet-six-inches tall and weighed one-thirty or so. He figured she must have been good at her job, too, for him to have hired her. The black hole where the rest of her portfolio should have been was what kept him from sleeping. Even if it turned out she wasn't involved with Tehrazzi, it still meant his memory was shot. And with pieces already missing, what else was gone? Sure as shit something else was, because that's just the way his luck went.

His cell buzzed on the nightstand like a dying fly. Recognizing Ben's number, he let out a relieved breath. For a second he'd thought his ex-wife Emily might have been trying to reach him again. On their last conversation he'd unintentionally blurted out that he loved her, spilling the most carefully guarded secret he'd been carrying around for the last twenty-odd years. He wished the hell he'd puked and passed out like a pansy before he'd said it instead of afterward.

"Hey," he said to Ben. "What's up?"

"You sound chipper."

Ben's familiar Boston accent was a welcome sound. "Can't complain."

"Good, then I'll get right down to it. Davis reported in. Sam went missing at a fake checkpoint the afternoon of the Basra op."

Luke's hand tightened around the phone. "Who was it?"

"Cab driver that was with her thinks they were Mahdi army."

Shit. "Any intel as to what they did with her?"

"Looks like she got away somehow. Davis is still digging." Ben paused. Cleared his throat. "Thing is, if it was Tehrazzi's crew... She's probably dead by now."

Luke let out the breath he'd been holding ever since the mention of the Mahdi army. If they had taken Sam, for her sake he prayed they'd killed her quickly. He'd found some of their dead captives in the past and knew firsthand what kinds of horrors Tehrazzi's bodyguard could perform with his knives. Sick bastard loved his work, to the point where even Tehrazzi could hardly stomach him. That in itself was scary.

Luke tried to puzzle it all together. Sam was a contractor for him. A techie. Not even an operative. What possible use could she be to Tehrazzi, other than the intel he'd already gotten about the op in Basra? There had to be something more to it.

Ben cleared his throat again. "I'll uh...keep you posted. If we hear anything we'll act on it right away."

"Good. I'll meet you up there as soon as they let me out of this place." That had better be soon.

"Roger that. Later."

Luke hung up and set the phone next to his disgusting breakfast. He wasn't sure what was making him more nauseous, the food or the fact that Tehrazzi might have one of his team members. And a young, attractive female at that.

Chapter Three

Baghdad

Deep in the shadows of the alley where she'd spent the afternoon, Sam sighed as she counted the remainder of her dwindling cash supply. Only enough to see her through a couple more days, if she ate sparingly. Her stomach let out a harsh growl. She was so damned tired and hungry. How much longer was she going to have to keep running on her own? The past few days hadn't changed her situation any. She was still in danger, and knew for sure the Mahdi Army was looking for her. Whether or not it was because the CIA had sanctioned it or because someone higher up the terrorist food chain wanted her, she still didn't know.

Thinking about everything that had happened, Neveah's missing letter bothered Sam almost as much as the rest of it, because the letter detailed Nev's arrival in Kabul with her Doctors Without Borders team. Why *that* letter, unless someone would use her cousin against her? She didn't want her cousin to get caught up in any of this. Her secret fear was that her job would endanger someone she loved, and she loved Nev more than anyone in the world.

Digging in her bag, she pulled out her phone and stared at it in indecision. The last text she'd sent had been to Ben, warning him to abort the op in Basra. That was days ago now. She wished she knew what had happened out there, but had been too afraid to contact anyone from the team. Given that she'd cut herself off from everyone that knew her, she needed to check and see if the people who'd threatened her had sent any new messages. Trouble was, as soon as she fired it up, anyone looking for her could track her.

She'd left her custom made device in it to act as a beacon in case of emergency. Right now, it switched on and off with her phone, and as soon as she turned on the power, it broadcasted a signal to the guys back at the Tactical Operations Center so they could follow it. She'd programmed the thing and she could disable it at any time, but something made her hold off. Sam wasn't quite ready to cut that lifeline back to her teammates.

At times she wanted to contact Luke and the others so badly she almost risked an attempt, but knew she couldn't. Not yet. Not until she knew what the hell was going on and who was setting her up. She'd seen way too many movies where the CIA lackey wound up dead to cover up someone else's mistakes. Or secrets.

Sam wasn't interested in fulfilling that role. But damn, she'd love to hear Luke's Louisiana drawl right now, telling her everything was okay.

Deciding to leave the device activated for the time being, she took a breath and turned the phone on, waited agonizing seconds for it to reset, and then dove into her e-mail. Funny how good the Internet and cell service was here, considering Baghdad was essentially a war zone. But then, no one used technology like the US military.

As the e-mail loaded, her heart began to pound. Knowing the activity in her account would alert her old teammates made her feel terribly exposed.

When it was ready she opened the file, and her stomach dropped as she saw the text and the attached photo.

We have something that belongs to you. Everyone has a price. This is yours.

Her muscles went rigid. *Oh, shit.*

No signature, no clues for her to figure out who'd sent it. Expelling a deep breath, she clicked on the photo. And saw her personal nightmare.

Neveah. Hands tied behind her, surrounded by three masked men holding various weapons. Her face was white, eyes wide, mouth pinched. Terrified.

"Jesus!" Sam closed the file and shut her eyes, fighting off the fear and anger warring in her soul.

Terrorists. Had to be, and it explained why the letter from Nev had gone missing. They'd been the ones threatening her, the ones following her. Now they had Neveah, the most precious thing in the world to her. Sam fought the rise of tears. Why had they done this? She was only a communications contractor. What could they possibly want from her that they would go to the lengths of kidnapping her cousin? It didn't make any sense.

Sam forced herself to take a breath and think logically. At least now she could be reasonably sure the CIA wasn't after her. They might be watching her, would certainly be trying to find her since she'd disappeared without a word, but maybe they didn't have a hit team after her. She prayed that was true, because right now she needed their help. They needed to know about Neveah, and maybe they already had details she didn't. If anyone could help her now, it was Luke.

She typed out a quick text message, intending to send it, then shut it down and move away from her location. Attaching the e-mail she'd received, she set her thumb over the send button. Then she hesitated, considering the possible repercussions of the action. What if the kidnappers found out she'd been in touch with a CIA team and killed Neveah as punishment? They hadn't told her what they wanted from her yet.

You know you can't handle this on your own. Send it.

Before she could change her mind she hit the send button, transmitting it to Ben. She didn't know why she chose him instead of Luke or Rhys, but it had to do with her gut, and didn't bother wasting energy worrying over it. The instant the message sent, she shut off the phone.

Ben would help her. She didn't doubt that for a second, and yet she'd hesitated to contact him before now. He'd been so kind to her, warm and funny, working the communications equipment with her after Luke had brought him to Baghdad. Whenever she was around him she felt…safe. He was the kind of guy you could rely on when things got tough, and she needed him more than ever. But for now she had to wait until she was in another secure location to check her phone again. Tomorrow, maybe.

Since she'd just given them and the people holding Neveah the means to track her, Sam had to move. Immediately. No matter how exhausted she was, no matter how alone and afraid she was. Dragging herself to her swollen feet, she turned out of the alley and wound her way through the quiet market, moving south away from the river, wishing with every step she had Ben there to keep watch over her.

****

Ben sat at his computer terminal at the Tactical Operations Center where Luke had set them up when they'd arrived in Baghdad a couple weeks ago. On either side of him, more computers monitored terrorist chatter and analyzed surveillance video they were keeping tabs on. He was good with computers and electronics, but nowhere near as talented as Sam. The irony didn't escape him that she would have been the most useful person in tracking herself.

Ben shook his head. With the amount of technological equipment in the building, you'd think *something* about her would have turned up, but they hadn't found a single piece of data on her since she'd disappeared. They had no idea where the hell she was or if she was even alive. He had to face the facts. At the end of the day, all the technology in the world wasn't enough to find her if she'd chosen to cut herself off. Thing was, none of them knew if it was because she wanted it that way, or because she'd been murdered.

The only thing they knew for certain was that her cousin Neveah had been kidnapped by a group attached to Tehrazzi outside Kabul. She and the rest of her Doctors Without Borders team were the first to re-enter the country since 2004, when their predecessors had been kidnapped and killed by the Taliban. Some Einstein in the Afghan government had decided that security had improved adequately since then, so they'd stupidly approved the humanitarian mission in Kabul. Well, guess what? Things hadn't improved. If anything, security had deteriorated over the past few months. The Taliban and other militias were gaining strength there and Ben had a real bad feeling history was about to repeat itself with this new group of American hostages. The proof was playing on the monitor in front of him.

Security cameras in and outside the cinder block clinic had recorded the brazen daytime kidnapping. The first members to be taken were an orthopedic surgeon, a geriatric specialist and an oncologist, all men in their fifties. The pediatrician was next, a guy in his early thirties. But it was Neveah's capture that most interested Ben because she was Sam's cousin, plus it gave the best view of the attackers, and thus the best information to nail them with.

He played the video back one more time. A

camera mounted above the exterior door outside the examination room Neveah occupied showed a booted foot lashing out. After two solid kicks, the door flew open and crashed against the wall.

Neveah and her half-naked female patient jumped as three men wearing black masks stormed into the room, armed with handguns, AK-47s and knives. The patient screamed and scrambled to cover her face and breasts while Neveah stood pressed against the wall. Women and children wailed in distress outside, cowering in the dust.

The tallest of the men came at Neveah, his weapon aimed dead center in her chest. He seized her arm and whipped it behind her, shoving her face-first into the wall. Ben paused the tape to tighten the focus on the guy's face as she tried to fight out of his grip. Damn. Nothing, except that his eyes seemed to be a light brown.

Ben hit play, determined to find something solid to go on.

Pinning her against the wall, Neveah's attacker leaned around so he could see her face. The camera angle showed his light brown eyes, gleaming from behind the slits in his mask. Though Ben couldn't see the rest of his face, he knew the bastard was smiling. His hands itched to reach through the monitor and permanently remove that taunting smile from his face.

On screen the man leaned in closer, and the audio was clear enough for Ben to hear his words. "We've been expecting you, Dr. Adams," he purred in flawless English. "Welcome to Kabul."

Evil bastard. Ben stopped the video and leaned back with a sigh. Great. A pale brown eyed Middle Eastern man who spoke English without an accent had taken Neveah. Could be any one of a million men.

He ran a hand through his hair. What a fucking

mess. Sam's cousin was in deep shit, but so far nothing more about the hostages had come in. Wherever Sam was, did she know what had happened? Was that why she'd disappeared?

He and Rhys had been monitoring the situation for the past twenty-four hours, and they'd both been sure the kidnapping would bring Sam out of hiding. That was the scary part. The fact that she hadn't resurfaced put a lot of weight behind the theory she was already dead. If by some miracle she was still alive, sure as hell she knew about her cousin, and would do whatever she could to get her out. Ben didn't like to think about the possible ramifications of that.

The lingering uncertainty upped the burning beneath his sternum to an eight on a zero-to-ten pain scale. He put a hand there and pressed, hoping to ease it. Nothing seemed to help, least of all his Tums, which temporarily masked the heartburn episodes he'd been suffering more and more frequently. But heartburn was merely an irritating side effect of what was really going on with his digestive tract. His attempt to smother his worry and emotion behind a super-cool mask over the past few weeks was finally taking its toll by eating a hole through the lining of his stomach. That's what he got for trying to be like his Teflon-skinned brother.

Ben rubbed at his tired, burning eyes. Damn, he'd have killed for a smoke, but he didn't dare start that shit up again. He dug in his pocket for a stick of Big Red instead and popped it in his mouth. The burst of cinnamon on his tongue helped quiet his busy mind.

If Sam was out there somewhere, she must have known the U.S. State Department and the CIA were in contact with the team about the kidnapped Doctors Without Borders group. Because Luke had so many connections within the Agency and the Spec

Ops world, anything to do with Tehrazzi put him in the thick of the intelligence and operations concerning him, so he'd been one of the first people alerted. After what their team had already been through, Ben couldn't wait for the chance to nail the terrorist's ass.

The office door opened and Rhys strode in, short black hair damp from a recent shower. They might not be identical, but with their similar builds and a few days' growth of stubble on their faces, they looked more alike than ever.

Rhys came right over to the bank of computers and even though he was only two inches taller, somehow still managed to loom over him. Unyielding bastard couldn't even let him have the height advantage between them, Ben thought sourly.

His brother took a cursory glance at the illuminated screens. "Anything?"

"Nope. Nada." The sick feeling in Ben's gut told him Sam was probably dead. The chances of her surviving this long on her own with terrorists on her tail were slim at best, and she was no field operative. The thought of her dying was bad enough, but the possible methods of her demise kept him awake at night. To keep from thinking about it, he turned his attention back to the monitors showing live feeds coming in from a team searching the streets of Baghdad for her.

"All we need is one lead," he mused with a shake of his head. "One lousy piece of intel."

Suddenly his cell phone beeped, signaling a text message was coming in. Fishing it from his belt, he flipped it open and froze. The message made his pulse spike. "Jesus, it's Sam." Rhys came up behind him to look over his shoulder, remaining characteristically silent as he read it.

Need help. N hostage A-stan. S.

Sam was still alive. The incredible thought kept

running through Ben's head. Where the hell was she? How did she know about her cousin if she'd cut contact with everything and everyone?

Unless she hadn't.

He ran through the possibilities. Maybe she *was* in contact with someone. Someone on the other side of this. He might be acting like a paranoid nut job, but he couldn't help that. Every Special Ops soldier had that trait. It's what kept a man alive in enemy territory when he only had a utility knife and his gut instinct to keep him that way.

"We don't know it's her sending it."

Ben aimed a scowl at his brother. Damn, could Rhys be any less emotional? "We don't know it isn't, either." And he was going to think positively until he found out otherwise.

"Just don't want you getting your hopes up."

Too late.

Ben stared at the digital image of the photo attachment icon on the tiny screen for another second. Part of him dreaded seeing it. What other surprise did Sam have up her sleeve? *Ah, screw it.* He opened the picture file she'd attached. The breath hissed out between his teeth when it showed Neveah tied up and blindfolded, surrounded by armed militants. *Son of a bitch.* The kidnapping had been bad enough, but it enraged him that anyone would terrorize an innocent woman that way. They'd purposely sent it to Sam for maximum effect.

"Call it in to the boss," Rhys said.

The rare note of urgency in his deep voice had Ben swinging his head around to look at him. Rhys was staring holes through the screen, his mouth so tight the edges of his lips were white.

Whoa. Seeing his twin display even that amount of emotion was a shock. Then Ben realized what it was about. Rhys knew Neveah, because he'd met her in Paris after an op he'd worked with Sam. Gauging

Rhys' dark expression, Ben had to assume she'd made enough of an impression on him that his brother wasn't able to stay completely detached from this.

As far as Ben knew, that was a first for Rhys. "They won't touch her," he offered by way of consolation, lame as it was. "She's worth way more to them alive."

Rhys pivoted around and headed for the door, shoulder and chest muscles straining the seams of his extra large, army-issue-brown t-shirt. "I'll get Davis."

Ben let out a breath and turned his attention back to the screen. With her cousin in their custody, the kidnappers were going to squeeze Sam for whatever information they wanted from her. Unfortunately for her, she had a lot that might be of interest to them because of her close contact with Luke. "Where the hell are you, Sam?" he muttered, dialing Luke and shoving the phone between his ear and shoulder so he could keep typing. How had she received the photo before they did, unless the terrorists were in direct contact with her? Another dangerous possibility for him to worry about.

Ring number three droned in his ear. *Come on, answer.* He didn't hold out much hope that Luke would fill him in on anything else he knew. The guy was a living God in the Special Ops world, and tight as a fricking vault. Probably less than a handful of people really knew him, and fewer yet had his trust. Ben understood that part all too well. Aside from his brother, he didn't trust easily. Everyone else had to earn it. That went double for all these intelligence agents and operators. All of 'em were professional liars to some degree.

As the phone rang for the fifth time, his fingers flew over the keyboard, typing in commands to trace the signal from Sam's phone. With any luck, they'd have a location to start a new search from. "Hey," he said when Luke finally picked up. "We've got a situation."

****

Basra, afternoon

After talking to Ben, Luke set his phone down on the lap table he'd pulled across his hospital bed. So, Sam might still be alive and wanting to talk. Her timing made him suspicious, but he wasn't going to leave her out there on her own for two reasons: One, she might get killed if he didn't bring her in, and two, right now she was the best means of tracking Tehrazzi.

They couldn't be sure she wasn't setting up a trap, of course. Tehrazzi could literally be holding a gun to her head, or he could have sent the message himself from her phone once he pried it from her cold, dead hands.

Since Ben was the one to receive the message, he was going to set up a meeting with her while the others provided surveillance and security. Once they confirmed she was alive and got her back into their custody, they could find out exactly what had happened the last week she'd been off the radar. For now, Luke had to get his ass up to Baghdad ASAP.

His phone went off, and he glanced at the call display. Davis, the best he'd ever found for counter-insurgency and intelligence gathering. He picked up. "Hey. You heard about Sam?"

"Yeah, but you gotta see this."

Luke's guts clenched. He knew that flat tone, and braced himself for bad news. "See what?"

"Package came for you this morning with a video tape. Tehrazzi sent you some fan mail."

A quick surge of something close to excitement raced through his veins. "What kind?"

"I'm sending you a video file right now."

Luke hung up and a few minutes later opened up the file on his BlackBerry. He turned the volume up and waited while it loaded, his heart pumping hard in his chest. The clip started, showing a grainy film of Tehrazzi sitting cross-legged on a prayer mat in front of a green martyr's flag.

Luke sucked in a sharp breath and jerked upright so fast a blinding pain shot through his skull. The room seemed to sway a moment until he got his equilibrium back, and he had to swallow repeatedly to keep from throwing up.

Tehrazzi was wearing white robes. The symbol of his intention to martyr himself.

Fighting back the waves of nausea, Luke listened to the soft, clear voice deliver the message in Arabic. An Islamic angel of death, calling to his minions.

"My name is Farouk Ahmed Tehrazzi. I am a soldier of Islam, a crusader against the invading American infidels and all who sully the name of Islam. The time has come for me to announce my intention to continue the jihad against our enemies. But now I commit myself to the higher purpose Allah has called me to. I am ready to sacrifice this life in the name of Holy war, and will embrace the glories of the afterlife without hesitation. Allah willing, we will rid the earth of the American people and their allies. I speak to those who have taught me. I pray that my sacrifice will please Him, and that He will reward our struggle here on earth." The image faded to black.

I speak to those who have taught me...

Luke cursed as those words rang in his ears. This was about *him*. He'd trained Tehrazzi. From however Sam was actually involved, to her cousin's kidnapping—all of it was about Tehrazzi getting to him. "You son of a bitch," he hissed, hands clenching into fists.

He hit the call button wound around the rail of his bed and systematically went to work taking out the IV stuck in the back of his hand. He was pulling the plastic catheter out of his vein when the nurse arrived and gasped at the sight of him.

"Mr. Hutchinson," she began in a stern voice, rushing over to stop him.

Luke cut her off with a warning glare. "I need out of here. *Now.*"

Wide-eyed, the nurse shuffled back a step. "Al-all right," she murmured. She went into a cupboard and handed him a bandage and some tape to stop his arm from bleeding.

Luke slapped a piece of tape over the cotton ball on the IV site, his mind racing. Tehrazzi wanted to play hardball? Fine.

Bring it on, you bastard. Bring it on. I'm more than fucking ready for you.

He swung his legs over the side of the bed and stood up, and nearly landed face first on the linoleum. He threw out a hand to grab the side rail, fighting to stay on his feet as the room did a tilt-a-whirl around him. Dammit, he thought, pissed off at his body's weakness. He didn't have time for this.

A doctor stormed in. Luke squinted at the triplicate image of him, trying to focus on the one in the middle.

"Sir, you need to get back in that bed and stay there."

He didn't dare risk shaking his head. "I'm leaving."

"No, you're not." The enraged doctor marched over and grabbed his upper arm.

Fighting down the sudden spike in his temper, Luke merely broke the hold instead of throwing him on the floor.

The doctor's expression turned wary.

"I. Am. *Leaving.*" He straightened, trying to look

down his nose at him.

The doctor's lips compressed in displeasure. "If you leave, it will be against my medical opinion."

"Fine with me."

"You can't even stand up."

The hell he couldn't. Luke let go of the railing, wobbled a bit, but managed to stay on his feet out of sheer force of will. He raised a taunting brow while his stomach did hula-hoops around his ass. *So there, you little puke.*

The doctor glowered. "We still have to run more tests. If you push it too fast, you could end up with permanent brain damage."

"Just get me the release forms."

"Stop trying to be a hero. You're not going to be able to function."

Luke narrowed his eyes. "What the fuck do you know about being a hero?" The doctor blanched, but he just kept on talking. "I needed to be in Baghdad six hours ago. The terrorists you see blowing up people all over the world? I'm this close to nailing one of their top commanders. Every second I sit here on my ass costs lives, so you need to let me the hell out of here. Right now."

The speech, delivered while standing on shaky legs, left him queasy as hell. He gagged, and when the doctor thrust an empty bowl in front of him, vomited up his breakfast. When he finished, the pain in his head almost laid him out flat on his back. Sweating, he wiped his clammy forehead with his shoulder.

The doctor gave a resigned sigh. "You're in no shape to go anywhere, let alone after a terrorist, and you know it."

Luke glared at him and concentrated on staying upright. "Just get me the damn paperwork."

Chapter Four

Baghdad, late evening

Sam crept back to her hidey-hole a few minutes after eleven that night, completely exhausted. She was so tired she almost gave in to the tears clogging her throat, but choked them down. Crying wasn't going to help anything, and it wasn't going to change the fact she was still alone and on the run with the prospect of another sleepless night ahead of her, jerking awake at every tiny noise because it might mean someone had come to kill her. It was definitely not going to free her cousin, or magically make Ben appear in front of her to gather her up in his strong arms and make it all better. She blew out a breath and forced the wistful thoughts away.

The streets were relatively quiet, the marketplace with its tiny shops and restaurants all but empty except for a few male patrons. Keeping her head and face pulled deep inside the shadows of her headscarf, she made certain to keep out of the light, ears pricked for any suspicious sound. Her eyes restlessly scanned for other movement.

Having moved south away from Sadr City and the heavily Shi'a populated areas of Baghdad to avoid any sightings by the Mahdi Army, she'd worked her way into the comparative safety of the Sunni region. She planned to keep traveling southeast until she neared the Iranian border, if she could stay free that long. Her tail was still out there somewhere, but she didn't know who or how many.

As it stood now, she couldn't risk depending on anyone for help until she knew exactly what the Islamic group holding Neveah wanted from her.

The very real possibility that it might be Farouk Tehrazzi made her feel sick.

The light-skinned, green-eyed Islamic militant mastermind had far-reaching tentacles, even into the mountains of Afghanistan where his adopted grandmother had been born. The same grandmother he'd had his bodyguard behead because she'd betrayed Bryn McAllister's location in the Syrian desert.

Right after the bombing of the US embassy in Lebanon he'd orchestrated.

Sam's blood ran cold at the thought. She'd seen the photos of the poor headless woman and her husband. If he could do that to his own family, what could he do to her cousin? Taking Nev and sending Sam the photo of her bound and helpless had the trademark psychological torture Tehrazzi was infamous for. She shivered, feeling very small and alone.

Skulking about in the shadows wasn't easy for her, but if she was still breathing, then she figured she must have been doing a decent job of it. Nearing her safe place for the night—an unoccupied shelter she'd scoped out at the market earlier in the day—she shifted the strap of her backpack on her left shoulder, very aware of the cold pistol muzzle digging into the small of her back at her waistband beneath her robe. She doubted she'd hit what she was aiming at if she had to use it, but a chance was better than nothing.

With a final surreptitious glance around to ensure she was alone, she slipped through the beaten-up door and made her way to the far corner of the tiny room. Inside, she dropped her bag and slid down against the grimy wall with a weary sigh.

Only a dilapidated table and two chairs graced the center of the room, a small counter with a hot plate and kettle on the far side. A tiny, grungy bathroom sat to her left, giving off the foul smells of stale urine and unwashed facilities.

Letting her head fall back, she closed her eyes a moment and took stock of the situation. Six days. That's how long she'd been on the run, alone and looking over her shoulder with every step. She'd only slept about twelve hours total, grabbing whatever she could to eat and drink along the way, which hadn't been much. She was hungry and tired, footsore and scared out of her mind. To be honest, she didn't know how much longer she could keep this up, even if she managed to elude her pursuers a while longer. Her body wasn't going to be able to sustain this kind of stress and deprivation.

Don't think about that right now. You have to eat, get some sleep. You need to stay sharp.

She'd allow herself to sleep for a few hours. Early in the morning, she'd have to try and find another internet café or somewhere she could recharge her BlackBerry in case the kidnappers made contact again. She had to have a way of finding out what Nev's status was. With any luck, she might find a clue or something that would help her figure out who had her, and where they were hidden in Afghanistan.

And maybe Ben had sent her something. She hoped so. Alone in the dark of night with nothing to comfort her, she found herself thinking about him, conjuring up her memories of his smile and the way he teased her. She was attached to him in ways she didn't fully understand, but that didn't lessen her feelings for him. Was he searching for her right now? The thought eased her somewhat.

Her stomach let out an angry growl. She fished in her pack for her compact reading light and set it beside her before turning it on. She pulled out an orange and wolfed it down, then a piece of bread. Man, what she would have given for a plateful of spaghetti with meat sauce, loaded with parmesan and a side of garlic bread. If she made it out of the Middle East alive, that was the first meal she was going to have when she got back home to Virginia.

Squelching a wave of self-pity, she reminded herself things could be way worse. At least she was safe for the moment, had enough food to keep her going, and no one was holding a gun at her head, waiting for the moment to pull the trigger. Neveah wasn't as fortunate. Sam didn't know what kind of conditions her cousin was being held in, but she knew it couldn't be pleasant. She was counting on the kidnappers needing to keep her cousin alive, hoping they would try and use the fact that she was an American doctor to get the US government's attention. For a ransom of some sort, or media exposure for their plight. The alternative was unthinkable.

Sam forced the last bite of stale bread down her tight throat. Pulling a thin sweater from her bag, she extinguished the reading light, plunging the tiny room into darkness and settled on the dirty floor with her lumpy pack as a pillow. Shivering in the cool night air, she closed her eyes and sent out a prayer that all this would be over soon.

Hang on, Nev. I'm coming.

She'd start by getting over the Iranian border someplace and then make her way overland to Afghanistan. Then she'd hit Kabul. That's where she'd start her hunt. On her own, or maybe with one of her teammates if she decided it was worth the risk to contact them. She wasn't sure how she was going to get there, or what she was going to do once she did, but… Somehow, she would get there and find a way to free her cousin. Nev would have done nothing less for her.

****

The next morning, Ben went through the market one last time hoping to find Sam, and had to hold down a growl of frustration when he came up empty. He'd gone to the alley she'd sent the latest text from. She'd left nothing behind except that signal and vanished like smoke. He was disappointed, but not surprised she hadn't left any further clues for him to follow. Although why had she let them trace it at all, if she'd turned it off before they found her? She'd asked for help, he'd answered by telling her they would if she came in, and then hadn't heard anything back. Why was she still running?

It bothered him that she'd disabled the tracking device. It smacked of subterfuge. Since he knew firsthand how good she was with electronics, he had to assume she hadn't done it by accident. They were dealing with one smart lady.

He and Davis had been out here for hours now, trying to find any sign of her, but so far they'd both come up empty. Why wouldn't she have just come to the TOC, or called one of them to meet her and escort her there? Why all this paranoia, unless she was guilty? Even Rhys didn't have an answer for that, and he had an answer for everything. Almost always the right one, too, which annoyed the ever living shit out of Ben.

His phone beeped. He snatched the thing from his belt and waited for the text message to show up. The digital display hit him like a punch.

Will come in. When and where? S.

Thank *Christ.* Letting out a relieved breath, he dialed Rhys back at the TOC. "Hey," he said when his brother picked up. "Sam just texted me. She's going to meet me. Can you trace the signal so I can find out where the hell she is?"

“Just a sec.”

Watching a robed woman pass with three youngsters in tow and a baby on her hip, Ben could hear the keyboard clicking away in the background. His gaze darted around. Come on, he thought. Just one break.

“Got it. Ready?”

“Yeah.” Yet as Rhys relayed Sam’s location, Ben’s heart started to pound. “Christ, I’m about two blocks from there,” he said, already running in that direction. The market was crowded, slowing him down, but once people saw him coming wearing a tense expression they made room real fast. He had to find Sam before she took off and got lost in the sea of people. Surveillance and counter-surveillance were two of his specialties, so if she was out here, he’d find her eventually.

Dodging a truck full of fruit, he tore around the last corner and scanned the alley where she’d sent the text from. No Sam.

Swearing, he whipped down to the next intersection and searched up and down the street. He caught sight of a woman struggling as a man dragged her into a waiting car. His heart hammered. She was the right height, the right build to be Sam, and it was too much of a coincidence she would be accosted in that location. Then she screamed. In English.

“*He-e-elp*!”

“Sam!” he yelled, but she couldn’t hear him.

She flailed against her attacker, but he manhandled her toward the back of the vehicle. Fear for her made Ben’s stomach knot.

“Jesus.” He sprinted down the street, trying to get the license plate as the man shoved her into the backseat and the car took off. Davis’ voice came through the earpiece in his left ear. “I see them. Pursuing on foot.”

Ben kept running, praying he'd catch up at a light, and hit speed dial to contact Rhys. A cab wouldn't help him in this traffic—he'd spend most of the trip sitting at lights. So he kept running. "Track this plate number," he panted and recited it, thighs burning as he raced after the car. "They've got Sam."

Rhys' voice was calm and steady. "Her phone is still transmitting a signal."

"What?"

"I said—"

"I heard you." He moved like a blur, thighs pumping. When would Sam have had time to turn it on? Not in the middle of being abducted. She must have enabled it before. He lost sight of the car as it turned the corner and sped away. Ben stopped, trying to catch his breath. If she'd left her phone on, it meant one of two things. She'd either activated the tracking device intending to contact them but had just been abducted in broad daylight and needed his help ASAP, or she'd deliberately lured him this far and arranged it beforehand, then put on a show for his benefit because she knew damn well he'd try to help. Which meant she was leading him into a trap.

Both options were bad, but he'd rather take the risk of being jumped than leave her with whoever had just taken her. He couldn't abandon her if there was a chance she was innocent. Ben kept going. If it turned out she was trying to get him killed, well…

They'd find out he wasn't an easy target. And then he'd deal with Sam himself.

****

By the time the car slowed and turned into a driveway, Sam's whole body was shaking. Cold sweat dampened her armpits and her breath shuddered in and out. The man who'd grabbed her off the street pulled her out of the car and up the walkway of a sand-colored middle-class looking house with an iron security gate. The driver followed and shut the door behind them with a thud.

The man had taken her gun, first thing after she'd been shoved onto her face in the backseat. He'd searched her bag too, but left her phone in it. That meant the transmitter was still on. She prayed someone was following the signal right now.

Sam glanced around the bright, elegantly furnished rooms, looking for a way out. Were they going to kill her? The man jerked her arm higher up behind her back, and she sucked in a breath at the jolt of pain in her shoulder, automatically going up on her toes and moving forward to lessen the pressure.

"Sit there," he said, giving her a shove.

Sam dropped into the leather chair and kept her eyes glued on her two abductors. What were they planning to do to her? They stood near the doorway to the kitchen, arms folded across their chests, their expressions bored, like they did this every day. She took a quick glance around, noting the sliding glass door that led out to some sort of patio.

You're crazy. They won't let you get two feet before shooting you through the heart.

Well she wasn't going to just sit there, was she?

"Miss Wallace."

She swung her head around as another Iraqi man appeared from the stairway. He was maybe in his sixties, with a round face, a short salt-and-pepper beard, and eyes dark as a shot of espresso. He sat across from her, his manner relaxed and not the least bit threatening. Still, her stomach tightened. What did he want from her, and what was he going to do to get it?

"I have a message for you."

Oh God.

Trying to stop trembling, she pulled herself up straight and gave him her best glare. "Let me go. Right now."

He smiled, his eyes twinkling as though she amused him. "You shall leave after I deliver the message. There is no need to fear, so long as you do not repeat it to anyone else."

Like hell there wasn't.

"No one here will hurt you. I am merely the messenger."

Right. Did he really think she would believe that? Sam raised her chin, narrowed her eyes. She'd be damned if she'd let them see her cower like a frightened animal. "So what's the message?" It didn't come out quite as demanding as she'd have liked.

He settled back into his chair, folded his hands on his portly stomach. "You are wanted in Kabul."

Kabul. Was he talking about Neveah? She waited for him to continue, but he merely sat there, smiling at her. Her jaw tightened. She hated that he was playing with her head. "That's it? That's the message you had to *kidnap* me to deliver?" The fear was fading, replaced by a rising tide of anger.

"I apologize for any distress that may have caused you, but you won't be harmed if you keep our little secret. Your Arabic is excellent, by the way."

Screw this. What the hell kind of game were these people playing? Sam shot up from her chair, darted a look over her shoulder at the two men who'd grabbed her. Neither of them moved, or even glanced her way. She re-focused on the man in front of her. "Who sent this message? Who's after me?"

He shrugged and gave her an annoying smile. "I do not know. I am being paid to bring you here and give you the message, and I have done so."

"Who's paying you?"

"An acquaintance."

Bullshit. "Tell me where my cousin is."

A frown creased his forehead. "Your cousin?"

His genuine confusion threw her. Okay, so maybe he wasn't privy to the details, but something more was going on here than he was letting on. Sam backed away, clutching her bag to her chest, wishing she could amplify the signal coming from her phone. *Come on, beacon, do your thing.* Maybe someone was coming for her—hopefully Ben. He could help her figure out what the hell was going on. But then a terrifying thought occurred to her. She'd seen these men's faces. Were they going to kill her now? Let her think she could leave and then shoot her?

The messenger waved her away. "Go on. You are free to leave."

The blood roared in her ears. *She'd seen their faces.* Knew where the house was. And they were just going to let her walk out of here? No way. She searched around for a weapon or something she could use to defend herself. A large vase lay on the counter, but would she be quick enough to grab it and smash it on someone's head? Doubtful.

Her messenger held up both hands, palms out. "As Allah as my witness, you will not be harmed."

Yeah? Well pardon her for not believing him. She'd already seen what some men did in Allah's name.

Sam took another step back, dividing her attention between him and the men waiting near the kitchen. Her heart thundered against her ribs. She felt like a mouse, running for its life while the cat licked its chops and waited for its chosen moment to pounce. She had no weapon, but if they made a move toward her, she'd go at them with everything she had. It might not be much, but she wasn't going down without a fight.

"Time to go collect my money," the man said, and pushed to his feet. While Sam froze, he and the others filed past her out the door.

She shrank back against the wall, never taking her eyes off them, expecting to be shot or dragged somewhere else where they would kill her. But to her surprise, they left the house and sauntered out into the blinding sunlight, leaving the door wide open and climbed back into the black unmarked car they'd brought her in. The engine fired up, and a second later the vehicle backed out of the driveway and sped down the street.

In the silence, Sam could hear her heart pounding. Its hard, awful thuds vibrated in her head. They'd just...left her. Without harming her. Her fingers slowly relaxed their grip on her bag. Her eyes darted warily around the place and out the door. Was someone waiting outside to finish her off? Maybe they'd activated a bomb, and when she passed through the door it would trigger the mechanism. Or maybe it was on a timer with only a few seconds programmed into it.

Confused enough to be wary, she crept to the front door, paused a moment. Nothing stirred outside amongst the neatly trimmed shrubs and hedges, but snipers were trained to lie perfectly still for hours waiting to take a shot. She couldn't see any evidence of wires or holes drilled in the door frame to suggest explosives might be hidden there. They could have set a timer, though. If they had, she was standing there scrutinizing the possibility when her last seconds could be ticking away.

Her gaze fastened on the open gate at the end of the driveway. Her freedom was right there. She had to make a run for it.

Taking a deep breath, Sam gathered herself and lunged out the door. Relieved when the house didn't explode as she hit the walkway, she sprinted down the drive. Her feet thudded hard on the baking asphalt, blood pounding in her ears, expecting to get a bullet in the back of the head at any moment. She cleared the gate and took off toward the sidewalk, skin crawling with the thought someone was out there watching her, waiting to pull the trigger.

And someone *was* out there. She could feel the weight of their stare between her shoulder blades.

****

Ben's chest heaved from the endurance run as he crouched behind a parked car on the residential street and watched the kidnappers' vehicle pull out. Sam wasn't in it. Had they killed her and left her body in the house because he hadn't gotten there in time? Dread made his guts clamp. He'd thought he'd get here just as fast on foot as if he'd jacked a car someplace, and he hadn't wanted the added attention of anyone reporting their vehicle stolen. He regretted it now.

Shit. He had to go in and look for her. Maybe she was still alive. Maybe he could keep her alive until an ambulance got there—

Sam darted out of the house, her bag thrown over one shoulder as she tore down the driveway and across the street.

Ben's head snapped around so fast his neck cracked. He couldn't believe his eyes. She ran like she was fleeing for her life, and he automatically stood up and aimed his pistol to shoot whoever was after her. But no one else came out of the house.

Cursing under his breath, he shoved the gun in his waistband and took off after her. She was surprisingly quick, but he kept her easily within sight, something holding him back from going up to grab her.

He was no accountant, but things weren't adding up. Why would anyone go to the trouble of kidnapping her, bringing her here, then letting her go unharmed after a couple of minutes? Was she setting him up, knowing someone from the team would follow the transmitter signal? It was the only explanation he could come up with.

What the hell was she up to? He followed at a comfortable distance, watched her slow and finally stop, bending over to suck in some air. It surprised him she'd run as far as she had. She was in good shape beneath those robes. Her head kept turning this way and that, as though she was scared someone was following her. Did she sense him?

An idea occurred to him. He could send her a message to meet him tonight. If she still had her phone and it was on, she would pick up while he watched. Ben pulled out his and typed in the text message, then sent it.

A few seconds later, Sam rifled through her bag, still darting her eyes around the busy street. She dug out her phone and looked down at it, putting a hand to her chest. Her head bowed a little, and Ben was close enough to see the way she closed her eyes, and the relieved expression on her face. She typed something back, and he glanced down at the display on his phone when the message came back.

C U then.

Bet your pretty little ass you will, he thought. Ben shut the phone and slipped it back onto his belt, keeping the same distance behind her as she began to walk away. He wasn't stupid, so he wasn't going to let her out of his sight until it was time for their meeting. Then he'd find out if that relief he'd seen on her face had been because he'd agreed to meet her, or because she was leading him into Tehrazzi's hands.

Chapter Five

Still rattled from the bizarre events of the morning, Sam made her way to the hotel Ben had designated for their meeting. Thank God he'd answered her plea for help. When he hadn't responded right away, she hadn't been sure he would, but the knowledge she was going to see him gave her a renewed sense of hope and energized her exhausted body.

As soon as she saw him, she was going to fling her arms around him and hold on tight, just as she'd imagined doing a thousand times over the past week. She didn't care if he thought she was losing it, because once she touched him she'd know for certain she was safe. Starting tonight, they'd be able to do something to help Neveah and the other hostages she'd read about in a paper she'd glimpsed at the market that morning.

Though she'd be glad to see Ben, she couldn't help the thread of unease that slid through her at the thought of seeing him face-to-face again.

You're being stupid. Ben won't hurt you.

Holding on to that thought, she jogged up the stairwell to the third floor and found her way to the room he'd specified. Pulling out the key that had been left for her at the front desk, she unlocked the door and opened it hesitantly, glancing around in the stygian darkness before stepping inside. Ben wasn't here yet. She was glad, because she could use a little extra time to pull herself together before he arrived. He *was* coming, right? He wouldn't tell her to meet him and then blow her off.

Would he?

She hated the uncertainty. The sound of her even breathing was harsh in the silent room. When the door shut behind her with a soft click, a dim lamp came on across the room. She jerked, blinking in the glare as her heart rate skyrocketed.

"Hi Sam."

The low cadence of his voice almost made her knees buckle. The hand she'd pressed to her heart fell away in relief. Ben was really there. She stared across the room at his large frame, folded into a wingback chair. He was an incredibly attractive man, but she'd forgotten how much so. Tall, muscular, black hair short in the back and a little longer in front, his eyes a startling pale green. The mellow light from the lamp played across his high cheekbones and square jaw, highlighting the pale jade of his eyes and the cleft in his chin. He'd shaved off his goatee, but a few days of growth shadowed his features. Even covered with stubble, his face was still enough to stop the breath in her lungs. But his frigid expression lodged the air in her tight throat.

Any thought of rushing over to hug him vanished. She swallowed. He didn't look all that happy to see her. In fact, he seemed pissed off. "H-hi." Her voice came out as a mere thread. She felt completely off-balance.

Ben was deceptively relaxed in his seat as he studied her, but a coiled energy seethed beneath his calm surface. He could be out of that chair and on her in a heartbeat, and they both knew it. If it came down to fending him off, she had no chance in hell. He was twice her size and a fifth level black belt, in addition to being a former Army Ranger. The way he watched her with those cool eyes told her just how confident he was of his ability to subdue her if necessary. She wouldn't have a prayer against him physically, so the only thing left to use as a weapon was her brain. At least there, they were evenly matched.

First off, she had to find out what had put him into this mood she'd never seen from him before. Her pulse drummed against her throat, dread eroding her joy at seeing him.

He shifted a little, and when his hand moved she realized for the first time he was holding a gun. Sam froze, fear squeezing her dry throat like a fist. She couldn't take her eyes from the pistol, which she had no doubt was loaded.

"I'm not going to shoot you," he said laconically, "unless you do something stupid. Since we both know you're the furthest thing from that, I'm sure you've got nothing to worry about."

She gulped and raised her eyes. What the hell was going on? Ben was holding a *loaded gun* against her.

"Been busy?" he asked in a mocking tone.

She attempted to pull herself together. Why even bother asking? If he'd followed the transmitter in her phone, then he knew exactly where she'd been the past few days. She refused to let him see he'd rattled her. Her chin came up. "I had a few things to take care of." *Like staying alive.*

His short laugh was far from warm. "I bet you did, sweetheart."

His south Boston accent took the R out of the endearment and made her heart ache. A few short days ago, he'd looked at her with warmth and kindness. Now, the expression in his eyes was almost glacial. Speculative and even angry. He had a right to feel that way after she'd disappeared on the team, but why the gun and the hostility radiating from him? She wished he'd let her explain everything. She needed him to believe her, because she had no one else to turn to.

Gathering her courage, Sam took a step away from the door, then another, holding that frigid gaze. He sat perfectly still, a tiger waiting to attack its prey. It unnerved her. This was not the jovial, affectionate Ben she'd come to know. He was a total stranger right now.

She stalled out a few steps from him, scrambling for something to say to ease the tension. "Ben, I—"

"Stop right there and hand me your bag."

She bit her lip and did so, waiting while he emptied the meager contents on the table and went over each item looking for electronic devices. She clenched her teeth. Like she'd even had time to think about bugging anything.

Ben paused at the envelope of pictures and gave them a cursory glance before reading the note she'd received. Then he set the bag beside his chair. "Got your phone?"

She nodded. Wasn't he going to say anything about the envelope? "In my pocket." She was afraid to retrieve it in case it made him aim the gun at her. Her fingers twitched once, then fell still.

He held out one hand, palm up. Her eyes followed it. Ben had such beautiful, strong hands. She'd spent many hours working next to him, admiring them as they moved over the keyboard and the rest of their equipment. Long, lean fingers, the short-clipped nails blunt and clean. The hands of a healer and a warrior. She remembered the feel of them on her shoulders when he and Rhys came to her apartment after she'd called them for help back at the start of this whole mess. Ben's hands had lent comfort and support. Kindness. Now he motioned one impatiently at her.

"Hand it over."

Careful to move slowly in case he suspected she had a weapon of some kind, she dug it out of her pocket and put it in his broad palm, the brief contact shooting sparks of heat up her arm. She snatched her hand back, hating the fact her body didn't pick up on the cold front it had walked in on. Ben seemed remote, but she sensed something seething beneath his composed exterior. Whatever was going on in his head, he had to have something more on his mind than her disappearance.

"You seem upset," she ventured, not knowing what to make of it. If anyone should be upset, shouldn't it be her?

An awful silence met her words. It expanded until it filled the room and pressed in on her.

"Upset?" he said finally, then shrugged. "I'm not upset. I'm just trying to figure out why you'd fall off the face of the earth *exactly* when bad shit started happening."

She licked her lips, not liking what he was inferring. Something else must have happened that she didn't know about. "I don't know what I can say that will make you believe me," she began, stomach squeezing tighter when he didn't even glance at her. Despair filled her. "I called you because I need your help."

He set her BlackBerry on the side table next to him and regarded her dispassionately. "That's nice."

His remote expression jangled her nerves. What had happened to make him look at her like that?

"You want me to trust you, Sam?"

She frowned. "Of course I do."

"You're a bright girl, so I'm sure you can understand why that's not going to happen. But if you want to try to earn my trust, I'm game." He tilted his dark head, pale eyes glittering a challenge in the lamp light. "You can start by taking off all your clothes."

****

Ben barely withheld his cynical smile at the shock in her wide mahogany eyes. Her mouth opened and closed, like she was trying to come up with an argument and couldn't find the words. Other than that she didn't move. Not even a blink.

He hadn't intended to go this route, but the whole innocent routine with the big doe eyes and trembling lower lip pissed him off. Did she think he was stupid? That just because he'd worked with her and she knew his brother he'd jump to her defense after all the suspicious things that had happened in her absence? No way. He couldn't risk more lives. If she proved her innocence, he'd apologize for treating her like a dirty agent later. But for now, that's the way he was going to play it. Hurt feelings could be fixed. Dead people couldn't.

Sam's throat bobbed as she swallowed. "W-what?"

"You heard me. Your clothes. Off. Now. Or did you want me to do it for you?"

Her arms came up to shield her breasts in an inherently feminine move of protection. Her face remained frozen in the dimness. She took a halting step backward, then glanced toward the door behind her.

Don't even think about it, sweetheart.

Her gaze traveled to the double bed against the opposite wall before darting back to him. The color drained out of her face. The sudden peak in her fear ate at him.

He snorted, insulted. "You think I brought you here so I could use sexual interrogation techniques or some shit?"

She blinked at him, wary as a deer confronting a hunter.

Well, shit, wasn't that a kick in the ass? "Come on, Sam. You contact me out of the blue from God knows where and ask for my help. Well, here I am. But I'm not promising you a goddamn thing until I know for sure you're not carrying a wire and I find out what the hell you've been up to the last week." When she hesitated, he pushed. "Don't want to play by my rules? That's fine. Say the word, sweetheart, and I'm outta here." He started to get up.

"I…but— All of them?"

He smiled thinly and sat back down. "Every last piece."

Her mouth tightened.

"I'm sure you can figure out why I'd want to confirm you aren't bugged or wired, since you design shit like that for a living. For all I know, you've been taken captive and sent here by the bad guys to trap me."

"That's not—"

Ben lost his patience. "Off. Now."

Even in the poor lighting he could tell she was blushing, but he didn't care. He needed to know if someone else was listening to their conversation before he got down to business. She must have decided he was her only hope, because she bent down and unlaced her boots, took them and her socks off.

"Kick them over to me," he instructed. When she did, he searched for any signs of a wire or tracking device. The soles of her boots were still intact, the lining solid. So far, so good. Looking up at her nervous face, he motioned for her to continue. She removed her headscarf, exposing harshly dyed raven hair that completely washed her out. It didn't suit her at all, but at least she'd known to change her appearance. Next came the robe that swallowed her frame. She lifted it over her head and let it fall to the floor, leaving her in a t-shirt and cargo pants that hugged every luscious curve of her body. He made himself sit stock still in the uncomfortable chair while she grasped the hem of her snug shirt and started to peel it over her head.

She stopped and met his gaze, as if waiting for

him to say he'd changed his mind. Ben cocked a brow and waited. When she dropped her eyes, her fingers weren't quite steady as she worked the garment up, exposing the pale skin of her flat stomach and then higher over her full breasts encased in a black lace push-up bra. His thighs tightened as he struggled not to react to the sight of her. Man, he'd always thought she was good looking, but who'd have guessed she had a body like that under the robe she had to wear every day?

Sam tossed the robe and shirt to him and he caught them in one fist, unable to tear his eyes away from the sight of her standing there in her pants and bra.

Focus, asshole. He switched his attention to the seams of the garments for an instant, then looked back at her. Her expression wasn't fearful anymore. Now her eyes snapped with resentment. For whatever reason, the rare show of temper made him go rock hard in his jeans. He quickly laid the shirt on his lap. With luck, it would hide the evidence that he liked what he saw a helluva lot more than he wanted to.

"Pants, too." She wasn't wearing any jewelry, so that was one less thing for him to worry about checking.

Sam's elegant fingers moved to the button on her fly and undid it, then slid the zipper down. He shifted in his chair. Knowing her obsession with order, he'd bet anything her underwear would match her bra, and his brain immediately formed a picture of her standing in a pair of lace black panties. The room felt hotter all of a sudden, though the AC was blowing down from the wall above him.

Sam set her jaw and shimmied out of the cargo pants, letting them fall to her ankles until she could kick it to him. Oh yeah, her black thong definitely matched her bra. And her legs were incredibly lean and toned. She was lusciously sensual standing there before him in the dim light.

Her mouth was tight as she glared at him. "Satisfied?"

Ben looked up from the pants he'd been examining and met her angry gaze. "Not yet. Getting there, though." He came out of the chair and she faltered. Fear crept back into her eyes and her posture stiffened in alarm. Her arms came up to shield her breasts again. He stopped inches from where her bare toes curled into the carpet, the nails painted a delicate pink.

Up close he caught the light spicy scent of her perfume and noticed the rapid tremor in her body. She smelled amazing, even after living on the run for the past week. He stomped down the sexual impulse he felt. *So* not the time or place for that. Her breathing seemed shallow, but the uncertainty in her eyes told him it wasn't from arousal. She was afraid. Of him.

He hesitated because his conscience was giving him grief. How far should he push this? The chances of her hiding something in her underwear were pretty slim, but… Seeing her frightened and helpless before him, he didn't have the heart to make her strip it all off. Slim though it was, the possibility still existed that she was innocent, and if that was true, she'd been through more than enough already. "Look at me."

Sam started at the command. Swallowing once, she lifted her gaze. Her eyes were full of trepidation, but at least they weren't wet with tears. Tough as he was, Ben wouldn't have been able to take that. He might be king of the smart-ass remark and have a reputation for possessing a quick temper, but terrorizing a woman went against his code of conduct. While he was paranoid enough to want to frisk the remaining garments, his overriding sense of morality crushed that idea. Humiliating her when he was almost certain she wasn't carrying a wire was a little extreme, even under these bizarre circumstances. He decided to offer her a workable compromise.

"Swear to me, on your cousin's life, that you don't have anything hidden on you right now," he said, keeping his voice low and calm.

"I swear I don't." The melting brown depths of her eyes showed surprise that he hadn't demanded she strip completely, but still held uncertainty.

Yeah, he was such a righteous dude. He had to hope leaving her in her pretty underwear wouldn't get him and the rest of his team killed.

He stepped back, turning his body so she could get past without touching him and jerked his chin toward the pile of clothing he'd dumped on the floor. "Get dressed. Then we'll talk."

Her sigh of relief made him feel like a lecher. Had she really thought he'd force her sexually? He hated the thought that she might have, even as he knew it was for the best she was wary of him. Keeping his eyes off her gorgeously curved figure wasn't easy, but he figured he owed her a little privacy while she got dressed. The whisper of cotton as she pulled her clothes back on made him think of every beautiful naked inch of skin he'd seen.

Ben clenched his jaw. Sexual attraction was the last thing he needed to feel right now where she was concerned. He needed to be remote, clear headed. Detached. Like his twin. Damn, why hadn't Rhys been assigned to do this?

At Sam's soft footfalls behind him, he turned around and met her shadowed gaze.

"Okay," she said, appearing more composed. "Can we talk now?"

****

Sam's heart was still pounding, but she felt

much more in control as she faced him. For a minute there, she'd been sure she was going to have to do the full monty in front of him, but he'd eased off at the last moment. When he'd come up close, the sheer size of him had made her want to shrink away because he'd loomed over her like a giant, shadowy menace. Then she'd smelled the cinnamon gum he always chewed and felt strangely calm.

This is Ben, some inner voice had said. *He won't hurt you.* And he hadn't. While she'd been standing there in her skivvies, she even thought she'd detected a hint of desire in his light green eyes before he'd masked it. Her own body had answered that flicker of male interest with a quick rush of heat prickling over her skin. It shamed her that she could feel attracted to him under the circumstances, but she couldn't deny her reaction. She hoped he hadn't noticed, since it would only make her more vulnerable to him. She didn't know him well enough in this capacity to be sure he wouldn't exploit the weakness, but she intended to find out why he was treating her like a criminal.

Ben cocked his head and folded his muscular arms across his chest. Intimidating as hell, but at least she wasn't *afraid* of him.

"So, talk," he said.

Her arms were already folded across her chest, so she cupped her palms around her elbows. Where should she start? She so desperately wanted him to believe her. Needed him to because he was Ben; because she couldn't do this on her own anymore and had no reason to. "I told you someone had been following me. For a couple weeks now. Then they broke into my place, went into my e-mails and hard drive and I found—"

"The transmitters. Yeah, I know. I was there, remember?"

Nerves grabbed in her belly. She rushed to find

the words to make him understand. "I went to Luke that day, told him I suspected Fahdi was up to something, and planted a device on him." He didn't react to the information other than to nod, and her heart sank in disappointment. "You knew that already?"

"Luke told me."

"But then..."

"Then what? That's it? That's the best you can do to convince me you're innocent?"

She frowned. Innocent of what?

"What about Ali being blown to pieces a few hours after you disappeared? You're saying you didn't know what Fahdi was up to?"

She sucked back a gasp. The explosion on the day she'd run. Ali had been killed by it. "No, I didn't know anything!" Poor Ali. She was horrified Ben thought her capable of being part of that.

"And what about the men he sent after Bryn to kidnap her?"

She gasped. "I didn't know he'd—Is she all right?"

"She's going to be."

"But what happened?"

Ben's hard gaze rattled her even more. "You mean to tell me you had no idea Fahdi'd planned to turn her over for Tehrazzi to torture and execute."

"No!" The blood rushed out of her face. God, poor Bryn. "How could you think that? I would never have done anything to hurt Bryn, or anyone else." Ben was super close with Bryn. No wonder he was so pissed at her. "Is she—did they...hurt her?"

"She'll be okay. She's stateside with Dec, who went in to rescue her. He barely made it through his surgery, by the way."

The blood drained from her face. *The op.* "You didn't get my text in time. Oh, God..."

"Yeah, great timing on your part. He and some

of his SEALs were hit by friendly fire, then the chopper sent in to evacuate them was shot down."

Because of you.

She winced and bit her lip. Ben didn't say it, but she knew that's what he was thinking. Poor Bryn and Dec. As soon as she got her name cleared, Sam was going to contact them and see if there was anything she could do. She rubbed her arms to restore some warmth, growing frantic to find a way to convince him she hadn't been involved in any of it, and was a victim herself. "Ben, please, I swear I wasn't in league with Fahdi, or anyone else."

"Then why run, Sam? Why would you run if you're innocent?"

The reason for his chilly demeanor was suddenly all too clear. "Because they were after me! Someone, I don't know who, maybe even Tehrazzi, had sent me that package of photos," she said, gesturing to the envelope sticking out of her bag, "along with the note saying, 'We know what you've done.'"

"And what was it you did?"

"That's just it, Ben, I hadn't done *anything*!" The pain of it all crashed down on her. To think of all the terror she'd endured, the narrow escape she'd had at that checkpoint and the abduction today. She was exhausted and scared, sick that Neveah was in danger. Sam didn't need this from the one person she wanted to help her. "Can't you see someone was setting me up?"

Ben's expression didn't give anything away. He was about as warm as an iceberg in the middle of the room. "And what about that text message? A little coincidental I got a text saying the intel was leaked about an hour *after* the team had already gone out, wouldn't you say?"

God, what a tangled mess she was in. Sam put her hands in her hair, growled in frustration. "I was running for my life, Ben! They dragged me out of that cab and took my laptop, and would have taken me and killed me someplace if the firefight hadn't started and I ran my ass off to get away. I didn't know who was after me then, it could have been anyone! Luke, some other CIA team, terrorists, all of those. As soon as I felt safe enough I found a place to hide I checked my phone and got the e-mail from Luke about the op. I sent you the text immediately because they had my laptop, and I was worried they might find something about the op. I wish I could have sent it sooner, but at least I *sent* it. If I was guilty, why would I have sent it at all?"

"Oh, I dunno... Maybe to wait until it was too late to abort the mission, with the added bonus it might make you look innocent?"

She stared at him as a hole opened up in her chest. My God, he still didn't believe her. This was awful. She couldn't think of a single thing to add that would take that frigid accusation from his eyes.

Shaking her head, Sam lifted a hand in a helpless gesture, then let it fall against her leg. Despite her vow not to cry, tears stung her eyes. "I—I don't know what else to tell you..."

When Ben didn't move or say anything, she dropped into the chair he'd been in and put her head in her hands. What was she going to do? If he walked out of here without helping her, Nev would die, and most likely she would, too. She'd die, and without being able to clear her name, everyone would think she'd gone rogue.

"The transmitter in your phone. You left in on purposely so we could track you today, but the rest of the time you had it turned off. Why?"

"So the bad guys couldn't trace the signal via the cell towers." In light of the magnitude of his distrust, that sounded stupid even to her, so she could imagine what he must have thought of her answer. This was a no-win situation; anything she said was just making it worse.

“And how about today when they grabbed you off the street and took you to that house?”

Her head jerked up. “How did you know that?”

His expression was cynical. “I saw you. Rhys traced the signal from your phone and I was about a half-block away when it happened.”

The implication numbed her out. “You saw them take me and you didn’t even try and *help* me?” A lump wedged in her throat. Did he not care about her at all? Even just as a co-worker or a fellow human being?

“They let you go without a mark on you.”

“No thanks to you.”

He ignored the jab. “Why is that, I wonder?”

No doubt he assumed she was in on some sort of deal with them. “You think we set that up? That I somehow knew you’d be a half-block away when they caught me and dragged me into that car? You probably think I was screaming and fighting to put on a show for you, too, right?” His expression didn’t change, and the rage ate through the ice in her heart. “Jesus, Ben, you have no idea how scared I was! I thought they were going to kill me!”

“But they didn’t. So convince me, Sam. I’m all ears. Tell me what they wanted.”

She laughed bitterly. Even the truth made her seem like a liar. “The guy at the house said he’d been paid to bring me there and give me a message.”

“Uh-huh.”

The bored tone grated on her raw nerves.

“So? What was the message?”

She hesitated. The man had specifically warned her not to tell anyone, but how else was she going to get Ben to trust her? “That I was wanted in Kabul.”

He angled his head. “That’s it?”

“Yes.”

“You expect me to believe they hauled you away

in that car in broad daylight to take you there and say, 'You're wanted in Kabul'?"

Sam didn't know if she wanted to cry, scream, or hit him. "I thought they were going to kill me," she repeated in a pained whisper.

A long silence filled the room. She blinked fast, tried to keep her breathing steady though her throat was clogged with tears. Crying in front of him right now would just make her look more pathetic. She needed every ounce of strength left to hold it all together. This wasn't the Ben she knew. This remote stranger would sense any weakness and take advantage of it without hesitation. She'd be damned if she'd let him best her.

After a while, Ben finally broke eye contact and sighed, rubbing a hand over his face as though he was very tired. "Davis was the one following you."

Her head came up. She sniffed. "What?"

Ben walked to the bed, sat down on it facing her. "He was the one who took the pictures of you and Fahdi and Hala. He was following orders to track Fahdi, and you were the means to the end. Luke had been suspicious about him for some time before you came to him."

She didn't understand. Why threaten her, then? "So *he* wrote the note?"

"No, Tehrazzi. Or someone linked to him."

Oh, God. "But then... If you know that, why don't you believe me?"

His eyes held hers. "Because even good people are capable of bad things when their life or the life of someone they care about is at stake."

Sam shook her head in adamant denial. "I admit I'd do whatever I could to save Neveah, but dealing with Tehrazzi?" It was unbelievable. "I worked with Ali for more than five months, and I loved him to bits. Do you really think I would do anything to hurt him, let alone kill him?"

“I don’t know you well enough to answer that.”

That hurt. “Fine, you don’t really know me, so I guess I can understand how suspicious all of this seemed, but Rhys, *he* knows me.” Well, sort of. “He’s known me longer than Luke has. Didn’t he at least stick up for me?”

“Yeah, but he also knows exactly how much Neveah means to you.”

Sam let out a weary sigh. This was all too much. She couldn’t think straight anymore. “Take my phone. Analyze it. Go through my e-mails, my account history. Christ, polygraph me if you want.” Abandoning any pretense of pride, she let her desperation show on her face and reduced herself to begging. “Please, Ben, even if you don’t trust me, please help me get my cousin out. She hasn’t done anything wrong.”

He didn’t say anything for a few moments, just studied her with those incandescent eyes until she felt like a specimen under a microscope. “You realize that if you’re telling the truth it means Tehrazzi’s after you.”

“Yes.” The implications chilled her.

“He’s targeted *you,* not just your cousin. He specifically chose to get to you by using her.” Ben tilted his head. “Why is that, do you think?”

Her anxiety drained away, replaced by a swift anger. “I have done nothing—*nothing*—to aid Tehrazzi, if that’s what you’re implying. The only reason I can come up with is that he wants Luke. That’s got to be the point of it all. I’m a way to get to him, or at least information about him.”

More silence. Then Ben took out his phone and punched in a couple numbers, put it to his ear. “Hey, it’s me.” He held her gaze the whole time he listened to whoever was on the other end. Luke? Rhys? “Yeah, that’s affirm. Sam’s going to need a secure location to spend the night.”

A trickle of hope seeped into her heart. So he finally believed her? Had she proven her innocence?

Whatever was said on the other end brought a rueful smile to Ben's lips. "Roger that. See you in a few."

Sam licked her dry lips. What now? What was he going to do with her?

"You took a picture of you and Neveah from your fridge. Still got it?"

He wanted the picture? She wanted to ask him what for, but thought better of it. Right now she wasn't exactly in the position to argue. "Yes, in my book."

He sorted through the contents of her bag, opened the paperback and pulled it out, along with the envelope that had started her hellish journey. "I'll give these back once we've analyzed them."

"What do you want with—"

"Verdict's in about your sleeping arrangements, by the way." His eyes were cold enough to make her shiver. "You get to spend the night in the cell next to Fahdi's."

Chapter Six

Ben shoved the door to his hotel suite open with his forearm and aimed a dark look at the three men gathered around the rectangular table set next to the TV. Rhys, Luke and Davis glanced up from the papers they were studying, their closed expressions so alike it set his teeth on edge. He was already in a piss poor mood from leaving Sam locked up like an animal in that shit hole of a prison, and his conscience was eating at him like sulphuric acid. He kicked the door shut behind him, locked it and stalked over to join them.

"Things went well, I see," Rhys observed.

Ben sent him a don't-fuck-with-me-right-now glare and planted his ass in the empty chair, ready to face off. Forcing down his temper, he slapped Sam's BlackBerry onto the table's pale wooden surface, then the envelope and photo of her and Neveah next to it. He met his brother's level gaze. "Happy now?"

"Ecstatic." Rhys passed the phone to Davis, and set the picture between him and Luke. "She had this on her fridge, and the gesture this guy in the background is making caught my eye," he said, tapping on a slightly fuzzy image of a man standing behind them. "I thought he looked a bit like—"

"Shit," Luke breathed, snatching it up and staring at the thing.

Ben lost some of his aggression and leaned forward in his chair with a sense of urgency. "What?"

Luke shook his head in disbelief. "Son of a *bitch*." He turned to Rhys. "She tell you when this was taken?"

"Cairo, last year. You know him?"

"Yeah. Here," he said, setting it back down for the rest of them to see, "take another look. Picture him with a scar in the middle of his chin."

Because the guy was upside down, Ben couldn't tell anything. But Rhys and Davis must have recognized him, because they made identical incredulous sounds. "Christ," Davis said. "Mohammed Assoud."

Ben jerked. Tehrazzi's bodyguard? He snatched the picture from his twin's hand and squinted at it. His stomach dropped. Oh yeah, it was him all right. Assoud was standing in the background behind Sam's left shoulder with one arm crossed over his chest, and—was his finger drawing across his throat in a slitting motion? Everyone knew the fucker's penchant for knives. "Guess it's too much to hope it's a coincidence he's looking straight at the camera with an evil smirk on his face, right?"

The monster was infamous for the hideous things he did to his prisoners and people who crossed his boss. He was one of the men responsible for the bombing at the US embassy in Beirut that had wounded Bryn and her father. Then the bastard had dragged them miles into the Syrian desert and left them all but buried alive in a suffocating cellar to die without any food or water. If Dec and his SEALs hadn't gotten her out, Bryn would have died along with her father.

Luke pressed Rhys. "Anything else?"

"We worked together the last half of March and first week of April. I knew they were going to Egypt after Sam finished the job in Paris, so I'm going to assume it was mid or late April."

"It fits," Luke mused. "I hired her while she was

still in Paris."

Ben didn't like where this was leading. "You're saying Tehrazzi knew about Sam way back when you hired her, and had his bodyguard follow them in Cairo?"

"It's possible. One of Tehrazzi's major financiers is an Egyptian living there. We know Tehrazzi was there sometime in late spring for meetings. It all fits."

"So how the hell would he have found out about Sam, and why would it interest him?" Ben demanded.

Luke's dark eyes gleamed with anger. "That's something we need to find out ASAP."

Okay, the fact that his god-like boss didn't know already was disconcerting in itself. "You think he might have gotten to her way back then? Used her as a plant?"

"It's a stretch, but yeah, it's a possibility."

Ben sat back in his chair and rubbed a hand over his eyes. They were burning because he was so tired, and this new angle wasn't helping his stomach any. He wasn't going to pop any Tums in front of present company, though. No sense letting them know how keyed up he was over Sam.

"What'd you find out from her?" Davis asked.

Ben sighed. God, where to start? "She claims she's innocent, that she's been set up this whole time. I gotta tell you, she seemed desperate for me to believe her, so if she's lying, she's one hell of an actress." The others stared at him dispassionately. "Look, the facts are she knew she was being followed, knew someone had bugged her apartment and broken in to go through her computer. A letter from her cousin was missing, and trust me, it's not because she lost it. That woman's an organizational freak, so it's no wonder she knew right away it was gone."

He crossed his arms over his chest. "She suspected Fahdi was up to no good, told Luke and then planted a tracking device on the guy. Went out to an internet café on her way home, and found an envelope with the pictures you'd taken," he said to Davis. "Plus a note saying they knew what she'd done, and that she'd be contacted for the time and place of a meeting. She freaks, packs a bag and takes off, hasn't even made it to the street when Ali goes up in smoke, and then she's hauled out at a fake checkpoint."

Man, she must have been scared to death. "A firefight starts up, but she manages to run to safety. She gets Luke's e-mail about the op our team was executing, and realizes something might be on her laptop hard drive, so she texted me that the intel had been leaked."

If she was telling the truth, she was the unluckiest woman he'd ever met. If she was lying, she could make millions acting on the silver screen. "Then because she still doesn't know who's behind all this, she stays on the run four more days until she gets e-mailed photos of Neveah tied up and gagged with four masked guys holding AK-47s standing behind her in front of an Afghan flag. That tells her it's terrorists, not us, so she admits she's in over her head and contacts us."

"She contacted *you*," Luke corrected, "and you alone. For the second time."

Well, whatever. "Point is, her story's plausible. Right up until her abduction today." He had Luke's full attention now. Ben drew a deep breath, knowing the next part was highly suspect. "She claims they took her into the house to deliver a message."

Something changed in Luke's eyes, like a switch had been flipped on. The intense focus was almost eerie. "And what was the message?"

"That she was wanted in Kabul."

"Anything else?"

"No."

Luke exhaled, and his shoulders seemed to relax. "She's clean, then."

"Excuse me?"

"She told you the truth. It was a test, to see whether she'd give the information to us or not. She passed."

Ben was indignant. "You set that up? Had her abducted off the street at gunpoint as a *test*?"

"That's right."

And Luke hadn't bothered warning any of the rest of them. Ben glanced at the others, who were watching Luke with interest, and fought down the spike in his temper. "And what was she supposed to happen if a gunfight erupted? I almost went in there to get her out."

"But you didn't."

Shit no, because he hadn't been sure if she was trying to get him killed. Even then, he'd almost gone in after her. The hell of it was, he'd *wanted* to believe her. That made it doubly important he stay immune to her big brown eyes until they validated whether she was telling the truth about the rest of her story. "So you're telling me she really could be innocent?"

"Yeah." Luke rubbed the back of his neck. "Damn, I never thought sending Davis out to watch her would make her bolt. He's one of the best I've ever seen. If she sensed him following her, she's a hell of a lot more observant than most."

Great. "Why'd you send him out, by the way?"

"Sam was acting suspiciously. Jumpy, on edge. Rhys thought so, too."

Ben shot a glare at his brother. Why the hell wouldn't Rhys have said something to him in the first place if he'd thought something was up with her? Tight-lipped bastard.

"Might not have been Davis she noticed," Rhys

put in. "Could have been one of Tehrazzi's, or someone else."

"Yeah," Ben agreed, "and how did those pictures Davis took end up at her computer in the internet café with her name on the envelope? Who else had access to them?"

Davis' deep brown gaze was unflinching. "Me, Luke, Ali, you two, Fahdi."

Ah yes, Fahdi. The back-stabbing bastard locked in the cell next to Sam at that very moment.

Ben did the math. Ali was dead, so obviously he was absolved of any wrongdoing. Rhys and him were both clean, and he was sure Luke wasn't involved. That left either Davis or Fahdi, and since Davis was pretty much Luke's right hand man, logic dictated that the culprit had to be Sam's current neighbor in cell block C.

Luke planted a hand on the table and stood, pausing a moment to take a couple of breaths. When he straightened, he did so almost cautiously, and Ben thought he saw him wince a little. "I'm surprised the doc discharged you," he said. Guy looked like hell, all pale and pasty.

Luke ignored the comment. "I'll pay Fahdi another visit in the morning. And I'll take these," he said, slipping Sam's photo and BlackBerry into his pocket, "back to the office for further analysis, see if we come up with anything."

The low-grade anger churning in Ben's gut burned hotter. "What about Sam?"

"What about her?"

He narrowed his eyes. "She's stuck in a cell next to Fahdi, remember?"

He'd hated leaving her there, even if he did have reservations about her. She'd been curled up on her hard bunk with her feet tucked beneath her, dull black-dyed hair pulled into a high ponytail and her arms wrapped around herself as if she was freezing.

She had no privacy from anyone, let alone if she had to use the stainless steel toilet against the wall. Though the security guards were on special orders to look after her, she was still locked up with a bunch of male hard-core criminals.

Luke regarded him with a raised brow. "That a problem for you?"

Damn right it was. But he refused to take the bait and curled his hands into fists beneath his armpits. "You're going to spring her tomorrow and find her somewhere else to stay, right?"

"I might if you volunteered to watch her."

That shut him up.

"Look, whatever her reasons, she wants your attention. You giving it to her would only work to our advantage. I'm sure you could get what we need from her without any trouble."

Ben popped his gum and set his jaw. He didn't like the implication embedded in those words. "You want me to seduce information out of her."

The ghost of a smile touched Luke's mouth. He barely glanced at Ben as he gathered up his jacket and tucked a pistol into his waistband. "We'll see what Fahdi has to say first. And if she's innocent, she's safer there than anywhere else in the city."

Like hell she was, and Ben didn't appreciate the idea of being whored out just to work Sam for information. Would he take her to bed? Sure. Would he enjoy it? Hell yes. But would he use it as an interrogation technique? Screw that. He opened his mouth to blast Luke, but Rhys cut him off with a warning look. Ben clenched his jaw so hard his teeth ached, and waited until his boss and Davis left. The door clicked shut behind them.

"Dammit, I can't believe this," Ben barked, surging out of his chair and running his hands through the back of his hair.

"Calm down."

"Don't tell me to calm down—weren't you listening? The guy all but told me to fuck the information out of her. In case you didn't realize it, this is *Sam* we're talking about. Your friend, remember?"

Rhys rolled his eyes as he took a fresh t-shirt. "He didn't say that."

"Close enough, and the prison thing is just as fucked up. I goddamn hated leaving her there—I almost didn't. It's no place for a woman, let alone her." He could still see the nerves and fear in her big brown eyes as he'd turned to go.

Rhys pulled off his shirt and put it away in his duffel, exposing the broad expanse of muscles across his back and the tattoo of a partial infinity symbol wrapped around an up-pointed dagger inked into the skin across his right shoulder blade. Ben had the other half in the same spot on his left side. When they stood shoulder to shoulder, the two halves became a whole. The infinity symbol represented their eternal bond as twins, and the dagger their service in the military, back in the day when things had been black and white and made sense. Orders came, they carried them out. Not like the shit they dealt with working for Luke, which was a world filled with endless shades of gray. At least, for him it was. During his years as a Delta Force operator, Rhys had worked closely with the CIA, doing their dirty work and black ops, so he probably wasn't fazed.

Rhys tugged on the clean shirt. "She'll be okay, man. Sam's tougher than she looks."

"Screw that, she looked about twelve years old sitting there locked up behind those bars."

Stretched out diagonally across his queen-sized bed so he'd fit on the thing, Rhys studied him. "Luke said she might be innocent. What do you think?"

Ben thought about it. Did he believe her, in spite

of all that had happened? It seemed so unbelievable, but, "Yeah. Fuck me, but yeah, I think she might be telling the truth." At least, he hoped she was.

Rhys nodded. "Good. She's gonna need someone to have her back through all of this."

"What, because you're not in her corner all of a sudden?"

"Doesn't matter to her what *I* think." His brother picked up the remote, turned on the TV. "Luke's right." Ben nailed him with a glare, but Rhys raised a hand, asking him to hear him out. "This way she's got a twenty-four hour guard to look after her. And about the other? She could've contacted any of us. I've known her a couple years, worked with her before, but you're the one she reached out to. You're the one she wants to believe in her. You'd be stupid not to capitalize on that."

The weight of responsibility pressed down on Ben's chest. Damn. The thought of using her that way made him uncomfortable. He'd seen the plea in her face before he'd walked away from her cell, gazing up at him with eyes as gentle as a golden retriever's. *Why are you doing this to me? Don't leave me here, Ben. Help me.*

"Who are you, and what have you done with my twin?"

Rhys' navy eyes met his. "Meaning?"

Ben snorted. His twin was a freaking Boy Scout, with a set of morals so high no one but him could uphold them. "I can't believe you, of all people, would condone something like that. Christ, last time I so much as *swore* in front of a woman in your presence you cuffed me upside the head."

Rhys shrugged. "I'm not worried about you mistreating her, because I know you better than that. And let's be honest, we've both seen the way she looks at you. If it came down to taking her to bed, I doubt it would be a hardship for either of you.

So while I don't condone *it*, per se, under the circumstances it could come in handy. That's all I meant."

"Whatever." He huffed out a breath, grabbed a shirt and a change of underwear from his bag. Maybe his shower would help wash away some of the sensation that he was covered in filth. "She's completely out of her depth on this." He twisted his clothing in his hands. "Think she's going to be okay?"

Rhys looked up from his channel surfing. "Like I said, she's tougher than she looks. You'd better not forget that. She's been out there for what, six days by herself? With us, the Mahdi Army and Tehrazzi tracking her. How many women do you know that could evade all of us and live to tell about it?"

Rhys had a point. Until now, the only other woman Ben had ever considered strong enough to take something like that on was Bryn, and then only in a worst case, end of the world apocalyptic scenario. She and her father had been kidnapped after an explosion at the US embassy in Beirut. While he'd been helpless to prevent it, he still blamed himself. *He* was head of her father's security team, and had tortured himself by going over every second of video footage from the embassy, trying to figure out what he'd missed. After all, he'd dropped them off and left them there. If he'd stayed, maybe he could have made a difference.

Dec's SEAL team had gone in to rescue them, but Mr. Daoud had died later in the hospital. Dealing with his own head fuck after that was hard enough, but when Luke had brought her onto his team to go after Tehrazzi, there was no way Ben could say no when he'd been asked to help protect her. Then Rhys had signed up, no questions asked because Bryn meant the world to him, too. Working the last op with her, then finding out she'd been kidnapped—for the second time—was the worst thing Ben had ever experienced, and for damn sure he didn't want to go through that again.

Man, he'd had a thing for her for years, but she'd wanted Dec, and he'd been forced to let the idea of her go. When he'd met Sam in Baghdad, he'd been dealing with that reality and hadn't expected to feel anything for his new teammate. But he had anyway.

Something in the way Sam looked at him resonated deep inside him, like an echo. The light in her intelligent mahogany eyes seemed almost familiar, and her good looks hadn't hurt, either. She was a hard worker, he'd seen that much himself, and calm under pressure, which made her an ideal communications specialist. Sam might not have Bryn's physical strength or fighting skills, but she was brilliant with electronics and evidently resourceful enough to survive being on the run from one of the most lethal terrorist cells in the world. Her quietly confident demeanor was sexy as hell.

Then there was the mysterious effect she had on him. It might be crazy, but Sam calmed him somehow. She was the only person he'd ever met who could quiet the static in his head so he could breathe easier. Just being in her presence for five minutes was better than any relaxation technique he'd ever tried, and he'd test-run more than a few in his years on earth. Damned if he understood how she did it, but it was there whether he wanted to admit it or not.

He shook his head at Rhys. "I don't want to see her get hurt." He couldn't watch another woman he cared about go through what Bryn had, no matter what the circumstances.

****

Sam couldn't believe he'd actually left her here. Right up until the moment the guard had locked her in the cell, some part of her had still expected Ben to grin and say "Kidding," like it was just another of his pranks, and then get her out of there. It had taken a full minute after he'd gone for reality to sink in. This was no joke. Far from it. Did they think she'd tell them something more if they left her here long enough?

On her hard-as-concrete bunk, Sam tucked her knees into her chest and stared at the cinderblock walls. She didn't dare look anywhere else in case someone was watching her. The weight of the stares coming her way made her want to curl into a ball and shut her eyes to block everything out.

Ben mistrusted her enough that he'd abandoned her here. Hadn't even looked back once she'd sat down and the guard had shut the cell door with a resounding clang and locked her in. Now she was alone in a CIA holding facility, the sole female prisoner, surrounded by male guards and men who'd done any number of violent things to land them here. Including her former friend and teammate Fahdi, who was in the cell next to hers for murdering Ali.

Just then, he banged on the wall between them, for the fourth time. She gritted her teeth. His treachery was part of the reason she was stuck here. Nothing he could say would interest her.

"Miss Sam," he called in a loud whisper. It hurt that she could picture his handsome face, so familiar and once dear to her. He'd been one of her only friends since coming to Iraq. "Please, Miss Sam." More plaintive this time.

"What?" she finally snapped.

She made out the sound of him shuffling around next door. Then, "I am glad to see you."

Well, the feeling was definitely not mutual.

After another minute of dead air, he asked, "What happened to bring you here?"

She almost didn't answer him, but her temper,

usually dormant, rose as she thought of the torment she'd endured these past few days. "They think I'm working with you."

"I am sorry."

Yeah, I just bet you are, buddy. "What did you tell them, Fahdi?"

"The truth."

"Oh, *please*!"

"I never said you were involved. I will swear to Mr. Luke you are innocent when he comes next."

Sam was dumbfounded. "You think he or anyone else will listen to a single word out of your mouth after what you did?"

Another silence stretched out. "I... I suffer for that. Ali was my friend." His voice was thick, and she imagined the tears flooding his dark eyes, tangling on the incredibly long, thick lashes that had no right to belong to a man.

"Yeah, so much that you blew him to pieces." She couldn't believe he'd done it. Not in a million years would she have thought Fahdi capable of something so despicable. How could he live with himself?

"I had no choice," he said in a choked voice.

Her hands clenched into fists. "We always have a choice."

"Not so. They would have killed Hala and the children if I did not. And Ali... He was not my intended target."

No, Luke had been, with as many of the others as possible. It might just have easily been Ben he'd blown up. "There must have been another way."

"If there had been, you must believe I would have done it instead."

"You should have gone to Luke for help." Even as she said it, a terrible pang of guilt struck her. She was one to talk. She hadn't contacted Luke either until she knew for sure the CIA wasn't going to kill her. And that was before she'd known Nev's life was at stake.

Maybe her circumstances weren't all that different from Fahdi's. Wouldn't she do whatever she had to in order to ensure Neveah's release? And Fahdi had five children to think about. Six lives, including his wife. Nev was only one. Sam frowned. Did she have it in her, if it came down to it? Could she trade one life for another? She wanted to say she wouldn't, but the only way she'd know was to be confronted with that terrible choice.

She'd contacted Ben and the others for help, despite being terrified whoever had sent her the e-mail would find out. She'd made the choice to risk her cousin's life because she knew she needed help. Thinking of what Fahdi had done made Sam wonder what she would have done if she'd been ordered to sacrifice someone from her team. Some of her anger toward Fahdi faded. He'd been forced to make a terrible decision. Now he had to live with his actions for the rest of his life.

The desolate sound of his quiet weeping from next door hurt her heart.

Curling up tighter and laying her head on her arms, she supposed she should be grateful she hadn't been put in the position of having to choose one life over another. She'd hate to have her loyalties put to the test, because she could already guess what her answer would be.

Chapter Seven

When Rhys strode into the TOC office with Sam in tow the next morning, Ben was completely unprepared for the jolt of physical awareness that hit him when she met his gaze.

"Morning," she said, then glanced away abruptly as though she couldn't stand looking at him.

Considering where he'd left her last night, Ben couldn't blame her, but he was glad Luke had taken her out of that prison.

"Morning." She looked like she hadn't slept at all the night before. Her eyes were puffy, with violet shadows beneath them, dark beneath her porcelain skin. She was pale, too. The light scattering of freckles across the bridge of her nose was more prominent than usual. His conscience squirmed. Dammit, *he'd* been the one to put her in that cell and walk away. It was his fault she'd been awake and probably afraid all night, not feeling much safer than she had for the week she'd been alone and on the run. He doubted it would make her feel better to know he hadn't slept either, thinking of her locked up.

Sam nodded at the computer screen in front of him. "Rhys said you have footage of Nev." Her voice was husky. God, had she been crying in her cell all night?

"Yeah." He looked at his twin, raised his brows. Was she going to be up to this after all that had happened? And what about her security status? Luke hadn't said a word about her case since last night's meeting.

"She's all right," Rhys said.

It wasn't his show so he didn't get to call the shots, but if it had been up to him, Ben wouldn't have let her anywhere near the rest of them until her innocence was proven. "Call the boss and Davis in. Let's do this."

Rhys disappeared, leaving them alone. The room seemed cramped all of a sudden. Sam stayed where she was, leaning a shoulder against the wall near the door, looking everywhere but at him, fingers playing with the veil covering her hair. The black dye in her brows was too harsh for her coloring, made her look pale and washed out. Or maybe it was because of what she'd been through and the fact he'd abandoned her in a high-security *prison* last night.

It made him feel an inch tall. "Fahdi give you any trouble?"

She met his gaze, the silent accusation there adding to his discomfort. "He spent a couple hours pleading his case, trying to get me to understand why he planted the bomb that killed Ali. He felt he had no choice."

Pleasant bedtime conversation for cell neighbors. No wonder she hadn't slept. "And what did you say?"

"I told him we always have a choice."

Ben flinched inwardly, but was saved from more awkward conversation because the others returned and filled the void. Luke and Davis acknowledged Sam with polite nods and gathered around the computer. Ben started up the video clip from the hostage takers' website. An image of Neveah came on screen. Sam gave a tiny gasp.

Since he'd seen it a few times now, Ben kept his attention on Sam's face. Her eyes were wide, and her tightly laced fingers pressed against her mouth as she stared at the video. Traitor or not, watching the footage was not going to be easy for her.

"My name is Neveah Adams. I am a surgeon with a Doctors Without Borders team in Afghanistan..."

Ben watched Sam's expression. Her gaze never wavered from the image on the screen. She didn't move, seemed almost frozen as she stood there, studying every nuance of the clip. He could almost hear her brain hum as she analyzed the thing. Sam thrived on data.

"You have twenty-four hours from the time this message is posted to meet the captors' demands." On screen, Neveah swallowed hard, her Adam's apple moving visibly. "If you do not comply, one hostage..." Her voice shredded, and she took a moment to compose herself.

Ben glanced at his brother and saw the lethal rage burning in that deep blue gaze, the tension in that square jaw. Rhys knew Neveah understood what the men holding her were capable of. No wonder his stoic twin looked ready to commit murder.

She regained her composure and continued. "One hostage will be executed every twenty-four hours."

Ben watched the color drain out of Sam's face as she did the math. If they didn't get her out before the deadline, Neveah had somewhere between one and four days to live.

Fighting the urge to go comfort Sam, Ben forced his attention back to the monitor.

Nev's sapphire gaze moved to something or someone off screen, then back to the camera. "Sam, if you see this, please do whatever they tell you. I love you."

The fear and plea for help embedded in those eyes would have softened the hardest of hearts, and must have torn Sam to pieces inside. Ben stopped the video, his chest like concrete.

"It was scripted," Sam blurted. She had both arms wrapped around her waist. Her face was pale as snow.

"Of course it was," Luke said. "It's all a front. Through them, Tehrazzi demanded money and the release of prisoners in Kabul, Guantanamo and Baghdad." He folded his arms across his chest, leaned back in a deceptively casual pose to assess her reaction.

"Then why Nev? What's she got to do with—"

"Because they know your background with her, and that getting her guarantees your cooperation."

"My cooperation for what? What does Tehrazzi want with me?"

"We think he targeted you and your cousin in Cairo after I hired you."

Sam gave him a confused look. "What do you mean?"

"He knew I'd hired you. He happened to be in Cairo for a meeting the same time you were, and saw you as a way to get to me. You know our history. This is about him and me, but he saw an opportunity to play on what he considered to be the team's weakest link."

"Me."

"You," Luke agreed. "The timing of Neveah being in Afghanistan played right into his hands. He's using her life as a bargaining chip, knowing you'll do whatever he asks of you to get her out, and he's betting on me stepping in to help. He knows I'd never let you go on your own, just like he knows how bad I want him."

A hopeful expression came over her face. "So you believe that I'm innocent?"

Ben secretly winced at her naïveté.

Luke gave a cold half-smile. "Bottom line, Sam, Tehrazzi is using you to get to me. Beauty of that is, it also means I can use you to get to him."

Even as Luke said it, Ben's insides clenched in angry denial. Sam was not equipped to deal with an op like this. Hadn't they already dragged Bryn through a similar disaster? He for one was sick to death of putting innocents in danger to try and trap Tehrazzi. The hell of it was, the terrorist had masterminded this whole thing. No doubt they were playing right into his hands. There had to be another way.

To her credit, Sam didn't react other than to raise her chin a notch. "So this is some sort of test, right? Dangle me out like a shiny lure in front of him and see which side I'm loyal to?"

Luke shook his head. "You've made it abundantly clear whose side you're on."

That was a no-brainer. Her cousin's.

Sam huffed out a frustrated breath. "So what, I'll come along in handcuffs until you're ready to throw me to the sharks and see what happens?"

"I doubt we'll need to cuff you. I think the boys can take care of anything you might dish out."

Her face tightened.

"And you don't need to worry about being dangled alone. One of us will be with you at all times."

"But not because you want to protect me," she said in a voice that wobbled despite her brave posture. "It's because you don't trust me."

Luke shrugged. "Trust is relative in this business, Sam, and ultimately pointless."

She squared her shoulders. "But you're going to get Nev out no matter what you think of me, right?" Ben shifted in his chair, and she turned her eyes on him. "Right?"

"Yeah. We'll get her out," he promised, feeling the impact of her gaze deep in his gut. If this went down, he was going to be on her like a second skin the whole time, and not because it was what Luke wanted. Ben might not trust her completely, but he still cared about Sam and wasn't going to let anything happen to her if he could help it. Plus, he could make sure she didn't pose any further threat to the rest of them.

"You got informants in the region?" Rhys asked Luke.

"Yes. Tehrazzi's in tight with the local population, but I have my ways."

Yeah, stacks of American hundred dollar bills tended to loosen poverty-stricken people's lips when they were facing a hard winter and the threat of starvation.

"If we're under CIA contract, we're considered civilians. Who've we got for backup?" Rhys asked.

Davis spoke up. "The Night Stalkers will provide insertions, extractions and close air support if possible."

If possible. Meaning they might be busy helping the military when the team needed backup. Great.

"Once we get a lock on the location, we'll go over the logistics of the op. You'll handle the hostage extraction with the rest of us as backup," Luke said to Rhys. "Ben, you'll be with Sam on coms and then on the op with us."

"Sounds good." Bonus was, he could keep an eye on Sam himself. Far as he could tell, he and his brother were the only ones that truly gave a shit about her well-being.

Luke pushed away from the wall, and Ben swore he covered a wince. He'd bet his next three paychecks Luke had left the hospital against medical advice. Head injuries were dangerous, and the effect of multiple brain lesions was cumulative. He hoped the hell it wasn't going to affect Luke's judgment or decision making ability, because if it did, people were going to die.

"Let's break into teams and get our equipment together." Luke turned his gaze on Sam. "We're going to be in rough country, so pack light but make sure you've got enough to keep you warm at night."

A tiny frown formed between her brows. "And what about the CIA? They're letting me go with you, just like that?"

Luke gave her a bland look.

Ben did, too. *Sam, honey, look who you're talking to.*

She flushed a little. "Who am I working with, then?"

"I thought you'd appreciate being paired with Ben, since you seem to prefer his company to the rest of us."

Her eyes flashed to his, and Ben caught the secret dread there.

An ironic smile tugged at his lips. "Cheer up, sweetheart. Look at it this way: Time spent with me is less time spent in your cell."

****

Tribal region, Afghanistan
Late morning

Farouk Tehrazzi entered the warlord's camp and headed straight for the largest hut in the middle of the fortified compound. Villagers stopped what they were doing to watch him pass, staring as though the prophet Mohammed had appeared amongst them. Dressed in his white robes, Tehrazzi supposed he must look the part to them. With the money and weapons he'd given them, their standard of living was worlds better than anyone else's in this bleak region of Afghanistan.

Because of him, they had a few trucks, generators, gasoline, a well and chemicals to treat the water, and refrigerators to store food. Yes, they were far better off with him, and that kind of support was exactly why they provided such excellent protection for him. He furnished the means for them to grow their opium poppy crops. The local warlords protected them. Their share of the money from the crops allowed them the weapons to protect, clothe and feed the people. The additional funds Tehrazzi gave them bought their loyalty. Every man, woman and child would die defending him if necessary.

Loyalty was a rare commodity in today's world, he thought bitterly.

That was the lesson he would deliver. He wanted his teacher to feel the bitter sting of betrayal before he killed him. Turning one of his own against him and making him question the loyalty of another repaid his teacher for his original betrayal and the deceit of Tehrazzi's adopted grandparents and his former mentor. Their treachery still pricked him like sharp knives, and even their deaths had not assuaged his anger. Nor would he forget that his teacher had caused the death of his favorite mare, the only living thing Tehrazzi had ever truly loved.

Behind him, his bodyguard sneered in disgust. "These people live like pigs."

He aimed a glare at him over his shoulder. Assoud was a few inches taller than him, about six-three, and wider through the shoulders. Every inch of him was honed to lethal perfection, not an ounce of fat on his body. His skill with weapons was legendary, as was his lack of conscience when it came to his victims. The perfect killing machine. Tehrazzi had never known anyone to enjoy their work as much as his bodyguard did. The pleasure Assoud received from torturing his victims surpassed even Tehrazzi's religious zeal.

While his services proved useful, Tehrazzi secretly loathed him.

"Do not insult our hosts," he warned. "We may

need them to provide refuge in the coming days."

Assoud grinned, and the chilling gesture pulled the scar through his chin and lower lip tight. A souvenir from his time at Guantanamo. "Only twenty hours left until the first deadline."

Tehrazzi turned away to cover an annoyed frown. His bodyguard was like a feral pet, one he could only control with money and by allowing him to do his gruesome work. Assoud was not the same quiet, devout man he had known in Beirut years ago. When the Americans had taken him prisoner, the transformation had begun. Something had happened to him in Guantanamo Bay during the endless months of interrogation and torture. From the rank hatred Assoud conveyed toward women, Tehrazzi assumed it had something to do with a female guard there. Probably sexual in nature. Whatever had happened in Cuba, they'd succeeded in breaking Assoud's mind, and made him even more dangerous and unpredictable in the process. Now free, he posed even more of a threat to them. There was a certain irony in that, but then, Americans always created their own monsters, didn't they? Tehrazzi was living proof.

Women clad in burqas shooed children out of their path as they neared the warlord's hut. Young boys stared at him with worshipful eyes. Their host rose from his place by a table laden with cheese and bread, and greeted him warmly. A wide smile creased his face through his thick graying beard, and a turban covered the thinning hair on his head.

"We are pleased to accept your hospitality," Tehrazzi responded in Pashto.

"Please join me," the warlord said, gesturing to the table where a servant laid out cups of chai tea. Once they were seated, he titled his head at them in curiosity. "The infidels—they have come?"

"They will be here very soon."

"Not soon enough," Assoud remarked with a grin.

The deadline again, Tehrazzi thought in irritation. That's all his bodyguard thought about. If he continued to be that obsessed about killing their captives, something would have to be done to curb his enthusiasm.

"Will you require some of my soldiers? Arms?"

"Perhaps, though I think the American force coming will be small." His teacher preferred working that way. He operated fast and quietly under cover of darkness, and only with hand-picked special-ops soldiers who were highly disciplined—something Tehrazzi increasingly feared his bodyguard was not. Those men knew how to make a kill and then vanish into their surroundings like ghosts. A larger force would hamper mobility, and any movement would leave tracks a child could follow. His teacher would never be so careless.

The challenge sent a thrill shivering through him.

"You are sure they will come?"

Tehrazzi's hand tightened around his cup. "Yes." He knew it without a doubt. By targeting the female doctor, the CIA already had international pressure on it to secure her and the others' release. Her being cousin to Samarra Wallace ensured his teacher would be the one to spearhead the effort. He might have suffered a head injury in Basra, but Tehrazzi was sure his teacher would come. He would never let one of his operatives go on such a dangerous mission alone, especially not a female he didn't quite trust thanks to Tehrazzi's recent efforts.

A peculiar phenomenon, how American soldiers protected their teammates regardless of whether it endangered their own lives. They would even go back and retrieve their comrades' bodies while under fire. And if that was true of what they would do for the men, it was even more ingrained in them to protect a female. Having a woman on their team was an advantage for Tehrazzi, because they would go to impossible lengths to ensure her safety.

The seeds had been sown. All he had to do now was wait. Sooner or later, Miss Wallace would lead his teacher right to him.

****

Baghdad, evening

How did you go about re-earning someone's trust?

Sam secretly studied Ben's profile as he drove her back to the prison for the second night. She'd been thinking about that question all day and still had no good answer, but it mattered to her what he thought of her. Way more than what any of the others thought.

Despite the gulf of suspicion that lay between them, her feelings for him were growing by the hour, and being next to him in the confined space of the vehicle heightened her alarming physical awareness of him. Her body was like a Ben radar. Whenever he came in the room, her senses went haywire. Sweaty palms, accelerated heart rate, nose hypersensitive to the evergreen scent that clung to him. Goose bumps covered her body if he so much as brushed her shoulder on the way past. Trying to hide the reactions all day and still stay sharp so she could be an asset to the team had left her completely exhausted.

They'd worked together going over the communications equipment and packing their gear so they could leave for Afghanistan with a moment's notice. He'd been professional and cordial enough, but distant, and she still sensed a chill from him. Was she any closer to gaining his trust? He hadn't said one word to her about whether or not he believed she'd told him the truth, and he hadn't told her anything about the work Davis and Rhys were doing to find where Neveah and the other captives were. She tried to be calm about it. With all the crazy things going on, she supposed it was only logical for the others to be wary of her, but she'd hoped to win them all over by now.

"Need anything before I take you back?" Ben asked without taking his eyes off the road.

"No, thanks." She studied his hand, wrapped around the steering wheel, and thought about all the times she'd imagined him touching her in her daydreams. All right, fantasies then. She couldn't help herself when it came to him. She'd never experienced such a strong attraction to a man before. Over the years she'd dated here and there, but nothing serious because she'd never found anyone that didn't bore her to tears after a few weeks. Until Ben had suddenly appeared in her life, she hadn't understood the meaning of the word desire.

She *so* got it now.

From the first moment she'd seen him, something had gone hot and fluttery inside her, but with all that had happened since then, she doubted she'd ever have a chance with him. Plus, he'd never once indicated an interest in her, other than friendship. For all she knew, he didn't even find her attractive. Especially now, since he thought she was an evil, conniving traitor. The knowledge made her feel slightly nauseous.

Sam drank the sight of him in. Both the twins were gorgeous, but there was something about Ben that stirred her up deep inside. She felt like she'd known him forever. That was Rhys' fault. When they'd worked an op in Paris together, the stories he'd told her about Ben had peaked her interest. She'd already formed a picture of him in her mind—

a bad-ass Ranger with a gigantic chip on his shoulder, a prankster with a wicked sense of humor, and a loyal brother and friend that had your back when you needed him, no questions asked. Meeting him in the flesh and then working beside him for those few weeks had only strengthened her interest. She admired everything she'd seen in Ben.

He'd been both considerate and protective of her, even though they'd just met. She'd come to love his easy affection and teasing manner, secretly basking in the way he'd put an arm around her shoulder or call her "sweets." He was completely comfortable in his own skin, and unapologetic of who he was and what others thought of him. She liked that, and wished she had even half of his confidence. Thicker skin would have been handy right now, too. Knowing he didn't trust her hurt like hell.

The few times he'd brought his twin up, Rhys hadn't painted Ben as any of the things she'd come to see in him. Guys didn't say things like that, let alone Rhys, who wasn't one for small talk. He was the quiet, dependable type, and if she wasn't mistaken, felt responsible for keeping his brother in line. Maybe that's why he was as big a control freak as she was. Sam knew how that worked. She'd grown up having to look after everyone, too.

Ben was the more emotional of the two, but then, compared to Rhys, that wasn't hard to accomplish. Ben let his feelings show in his expression, unless he had his 'game face' on, like now, when he didn't want anyone to know what was going on in his head—a defense mechanism of sorts.

Having worked with both of them, she could understand why Rhys had gone on to serve in Delta Force while Ben had left the army after his tour with the Rangers ended. Being in that elite unit must have been both exhilarating and wearing for Ben. Keeping all that emotion under control in the worst of circumstances couldn't have been an easy feat for him. Yet he'd done it. He'd served his time in one of the most highly trained and disciplined units in the world, and stuck it out until his enlistment expired before moving on to private security work. She was proud of him for seeing it through, and admired the skills he'd exhibited on the last op.

Sam shot him a sidelong glance, running her gaze over his ripped arms, following the bulge of his biceps to his wide shoulders. Ben was dependable, capable, and good at his job. But he was high strung. She'd noticed the way he popped Tums when he thought no one was looking. He chewed his Big Red constantly as a form of stress relief. She bet his mind never shut off. Inside he was a constant whirlwind of thoughts and emotions, his secret anxieties worsened by the fact he tried so hard to hide them.

When he was jacked up inside, he hid it well enough from his team. He even got along with his brother, whom she could tell he secretly idolized. But Ben didn't work the same way his brother did. Rhys did everything with a stoic, businesslike manner. Ben didn't function like that. Things got to him, and she suspected that bothered him even more.

Sam turned her attention to the buildings flying past her window as they drove, thinking about that.

Like the night Luke and Dec had taken Bryn out on an op and ordered an air strike on a building when one of their teammates confirmed Tehrazzi was inside, she'd seen Ben struggle with himself. The incoming missile had leveled the building and everyone in it plus two young children, and the terrorist had escaped unharmed. When Ben heard what had happened over the radio, his body had tensed hard as steel in his chair next to her. His face had been gray, eyes glued to the computer screen feeding live video from the team's night vision goggles. He'd been worried sick about Bryn, had practically worn a hole in the office carpet as he paced and chomped on his gum.

Sam figured he must have strong feelings for Bryn to react that way. She knew Bryn was deep in love with Declan McCabe, and since they were together stateside now, Ben had to know any hope he'd had of being with her was gone. It might be pathetic that Sam didn't care if she was his first choice, but did that open up a chance for her? Gauging Ben's unreadable expression now, she had no idea.

She withheld a sigh as she snuck another glance at him. Other than that spark of heat in his eyes the night he'd made her all but strip down, he'd never given the slightest indication he saw her as anything more than a coworker, and now a possible traitor. What would he do if she kissed him? The tantalizing thought took root in her brain. She had vivid fantasies about pressing against all those hot, hard muscles and nibbling at his full lower lip.

Though he didn't fully trust her, Ben treated her with respect and consideration, and he was still protective of her. Those were good signs, right?

He was so damn beautiful to her. She loved how quick he was to smile, how fast he could focus on something and how easily he took charge of any given situation. Man, she had to be careful, or she could easily slide from being attracted to him to something altogether more emotionally damaging. She could see herself falling in love with him if he even met her part way.

She'd have to be pretty damn stupid to open herself up like that, wouldn't she?

"You're quiet tonight."

"Got a lot on my mind." Most of which she would only admit to under torture.

His eyes slid her way for a second. "To be honest, I don't like you having to stay in prison, but it's as safe a place as any until we get a lead on your cousin and start moving."

Yeah, plus then they didn't have to spare anyone to keep an eye on her while she was locked up, and the guards could report anything they considered to be suspicious. Like her conversations with Fahdi. What an awful feeling to know someone mistrusted you that much.

Ah, the hell with it. Being direct was her preferred method anyway, which was what made his suspicion of her all the more tragic. She'd just come straight out and ask him, then see how he responded. "Ben?"

"Hmm?"

"After all that I've told you and the things you've found out, do you trust me at all?"

He hesitated a moment. "More than I did."

But not completely. She couldn't stop the sigh from escaping. If all went well, she'd be going with him to Afghanistan to help free Neveah. How awkward was that trip going to be if he didn't trust her further than he could throw her? What was he planning to do, duct tape her wrists and ankles at night to keep her from running away to warn the terrorists? She was so tired of trying to win him over.

"Hey." He reached over and laid a hand on top of hers.

She jumped in surprise, but the contact sent a jolt of electricity right up to her shoulder. His touch was warm, almost comforting.

"I'm going to help you, okay? That's all I can promise for now."

A tentative hope bloomed. "Okay."

He frowned, rubbed her hand. "You're cold. You getting sick?"

Was that concern she detected in his voice? "I'm okay. Just tired and…nervous." What harm would it do to let her guard down and tell him how much she hated the thought of spending another night there? Being in the prison made her feel like a trapped animal. She didn't want to go back there.

Rather than pull away, Ben wrapped his long fingers around her hand, the heat of his skin and the action itself making her belly do a somersault. Slowly, afraid he'd let go, she uncurled the fingers she'd squeezed into a nervous fist, and he surprised her again by shifting his grip to engulf them. When his thumb swept over her knuckles, her heart squeezed. For a panicked instant she thought she might cry.

"We're not going to let anyone hurt you, Sam, and we're going to get your cousin out."

Sudden tears pricked her eyes despite her struggle to contain them. "Promise?" she whispered past the lump in her throat.

His pale green gaze ran over her face for a moment. "Swear it on my honor."

God, she was going to cry. Even after all that had happened, he was so sweet to her. It almost broke her heart. She wanted to crawl into his lap and cuddle up to him so badly her muscles strained with the need. She would have given just about anything to have his strong arms around her for ten seconds, but she was too raw to suffer being rebuffed, and too afraid of ruining the fragile truce between them to try it. Something else she wished were different with her. Her brain always overrode her heart. Practical, not brave. She'd really love to be brave.

They drove the rest of the way in silence, and every atom in her body tuned to him. The spicy cedar notes in his cologne teased her nose, but anxiety dulled all that as the prison gate came into view. Her heart started to thud.

Another night trapped behind those unyielding

bars, lying on her hard bunk, unable to sleep despite her exhaustion because of all the eyes watching her and Fahdi wanting to talk next door. She hated it in there, hated feeling like a criminal when she was innocent.

A block away from the main entrance, Ben pulled the Suburban to a stop and parked against the curb. He killed the engine.

She glanced at him, nerves skittering in her stomach. What now?

Letting out a deep breath, he met her eyes. "All right, I *hate* sending you back there," he admitted. "I've been trying to think of somewhere else to take you, but I can't think of any place you'd be as safe, except...with me and Rhys."

Her breath caught. Would he really let her stay with them?

"Truth is, I can't stand the thought of you alone and scared in that cell, and I'll be damned if I'm leaving you there for another night."

She didn't dare say anything, prayed he'd take her with him.

"I can keep an eye on you as easily as a prison guard, and you'll be way more comfortable in a real bed for a night or two. Besides, you're going to need to be sharp when we go into Kabul." The concern in his gaze touched her. "I bet you haven't had much sleep the last week, have you?"

"Not really." Understatement of the year.

"That's what I figured." He shook his head as he studied her. "You're lucky nothing happened to you out there."

"I know."

"I wish you'd contacted one of us right away instead of taking off by yourself."

"I wanted to call you, but I didn't know who I could trust."

"For the record, you can trust me."

Sam glanced down at her lap and blinked fast to stem the tears gathering in her eyes.

"Do you believe me?"

She met his eyes. "Yes." With all her heart.

"Good. Now let's get you to the hotel so you can get some sleep."

Holy crap. He was going to take her back with him. "So do…you *do* trust me a little?"

Ben looked down at their joined hands, kept moving his thumb in that hypnotic, almost tender, motion. "My gut says you're telling the truth. My brain's ninety percent on board with that."

But he wasn't positive.

"Here's the thing, Sam. I want to believe you. So if you have anything else to get off your conscience, tell me now, before it's too late, because the one thing I won't forgive you for is lying." He held her eyes. "Don't ever lie to me, Sam. On this mission, people's lives depend on the others and me being able to trust you. So don't you ever, *ever* lie to me. Okay?"

She sensed some deeply buried pain beneath his words. This wasn't just about the upcoming op, this was because someone in his past had hurt him terribly by lying. She was certain of it. God, she wished she knew what to say to make him believe her, but she'd just have to earn his trust back somehow. "I understand."

He sighed. "Okay."

Without thinking, Sam leaned over to throw her arms around his neck and held on. "Thank you," she whispered, eyes squeezed shut.

Ben went stiff for a moment, as though she'd startled him. Then his hands slid up her back, making the skin tingle everywhere they made contact as he drew her close in a gentle hug. Sam melted against him, shuddering with relief. All the fear, all the tension and strain she'd been under disappeared within the circle of his strong arms.

She'd needed this from him so much. God he felt good, and he smelled fantastic, a mix of soap and subtle cologne. She drew in a deep breath, exhaled as she buried her face in his throat. The stubble on his skin abraded her pleasantly. His pulse throbbed strong and steady under her cheek. She lay against him, somewhat surprised he hadn't pushed her away yet.

She might as well savor the moment while it lasted, because it might be the only time she ever got to feel his arms around her like this, and she intended to make the most of it.

****

Ah, Christ.

Ben's heart squeezed as Sam clung to him, all warm curves and vulnerable softness. Her hair felt like cool satin against his palm. He'd known she was nervous, but he'd had no idea how scared she was to go back to the prison. Add in her question about him believing her, delivered with her heart in her eyes, and... Well, it would take a man a lot harder than him to stomp out that spark of hope.

Until now he hadn't understood how desperately she'd wanted him to believe in her, but the way she'd pressed against him, like a frightened child, made him want to gather her up in his lap and tuck her in close. That was not a good move, though. Not with the way his body was reacting to the feel of her. Already his erection strained against the fly of his cargo pants.

Instead, he concentrated on stroking her hair from the crown of her head to where it lay between her shoulder blades in soft black waves. He missed the titian color, but was glad she'd had the brains to dye it as soon as she'd gone into hiding.

Sam made a tiny nestling movement and sighed as though she'd wanted to be in his arms forever and just been granted her fondest wish. His already strong protective feelings toward her intensified.

Christ, he hated the thought of her on the run, alone and scared, not knowing who to trust or where to go. It amazed him she'd lived long enough to contact him. Yet she'd managed to keep herself alive, using her brain and her wits to evade capture, then had the sense to call him for help when she realized she couldn't keep going alone. He admired the hell out of her. Especially since she'd done all that, plus tried to warn the ops team while on the run, the whole time knowing she was innocent.

Ben was almost positive she was innocent. But he'd missed signs once already, and Bryn had paid the price. He was not going to make the same mistake twice. No matter how much he liked Sam, he had to rely on his gut and brains this time and not let his emotions get in the way.

But man, he goddamn hated the idea of her going with them into Afghanistan. It was like the op with Bryn all over again, only worse, because this time he knew exactly what could happen to her if he and the others couldn't protect her, and they had other innocent American lives at stake. Plus, all Tehrazzi had to do was pull the right string, and Sam could be the greatest threat to them all. He was messing with their minds, and they were letting him, probably playing right into his hands.

Ben hoped Luke knew what the hell he was doing. The fact that he'd trained Tehrazzi was helpful, but the head injury made Ben damned uneasy, and so did the way Luke hinted at using him to be Sam's keeper. He was already emotionally attached to her because he liked her and didn't want anything bad to happen to her, plus he was naturally protective of her because she was a woman. Okay, an insanely attractive woman, which only made that instinct stronger. He suspected Luke knew this, and was using it to his advantage to keep a close watch on Sam.

Ben hated lies or deception of any kind, so whatever the real deal was, he'd have preferred to find out from Luke and not have to analyze it on his own. And as far as his growing feelings for Sam were concerned? He'd just have to keep them from interfering with his judgment. Wouldn't be a problem, though. If he messed up, Rhys would kick his ass back to reality and tell him like it was.

He didn't know why Sam had chosen him above all the others, but Ben hoped it wasn't because she saw him as the most gullible of the group or the easiest to manipulate. She didn't seem capable of it, but that didn't mean it wasn't possible. If he wanted to do his job properly he'd have to maintain some sort of barrier from her regardless, because if Luke intended to use her as bait, then her life depended on them all being razor sharp. None of that changed anything, of course. He still wanted her on the first flight home to Virginia.

Yeah, Sam was wicked smart. Yeah, she was brave. But she was too gentle, too innocent of how these assholes worked to take this on. In his opinion, using her to get to Tehrazzi wasn't nearly good enough motivation for placing her life in that kind of jeopardy. They'd already tried it with Bryn, and look how that went. They'd all freaked when she'd been in danger. Well, he and Dec had. Luke and Rhys were different animals. They didn't freak about anything. As for Davis, Ben had yet to see him even break a sweat, so he could probably be lumped in with the other two. But Sam... She was in way over her head on this one. She was going to need all the help she could get.

Damn, she felt good all up against him like this. He *so* wanted her to be telling the truth. He wasn't sure how he'd deal with it if it turned out she wasn't.

She was beautiful and bright and quirky, so full of warmth and determination. He'd seen the iron will inside her, and how tightly controlled her life was. Man, he'd love to be the one to loosen her up and get her to let go. His cock leapt at the thought.

When he tightened his arms, she shuddered. Closing his eyes, Ben kissed the top of her head because he couldn't help himself. Poor baby. She was exhausted and worried to death about her cousin, the one person she loved most on earth. He wanted to ease her anxiety somehow. Because he was thinking about kissing away the shadows he'd seen in her big brown eyes, he set her away from him. "Tired?"

She settled back into her seat and did up the belt, her grateful smile tearing at his heart. "A little."

He fired up the engine and turned the vehicle around, then drove straight to the hotel where he and Rhys were sharing a room. When he helped her down from the truck in the underground garage, he couldn't help notice again how tiny she was compared to him. He was six-three and two-twenty, give or take. The top of her head came up to his collarbones. She had to be five-six at the most, maybe one-thirty. How the hell had she made it this far on her own? She knew next to nothing about anti-surveillance, hand-to-hand combat and weapons. Sure, she was a wizard with computers and electronics. But how was that going to help you in the ass end of Afghanistan while you fought for your life against one of the most powerful terrorists in the eastern hemisphere? His heartburn started up again.

With a guiding hand on her back, Ben led her to the stairs and up to the sixth floor, down the hall to his suite. He unlocked the door and let her in, stepping in behind her and met Rhys' gaze.

"Sam's going to stay with us."

True to form, his self-contained twin only nodded, his dark blue eyes betraying not even a hint of surprise. It was damned eerie, how much control he had over not showing what was going on in his head. Ben regretted not inheriting that gene.

Sam tried a brave smile. "Hi, Rhys."

"Hey. How's it going?"

"Good. I appreciate you letting me stay here."

"No problem. You eaten yet?"

"No."

Rhys went over to the mini bar, cracked it open and put some crackers, nuts and bottled water on the table for her. "I'll take the couch," he offered.

"No," Ben said. "I'll take it. She can have my bed."

Sam looked at him, then at Rhys. "I'll take the couch. It's the least I can do, and I'm a heck of a lot smaller than both of you."

No way was Ben going to make her sleep on the couch, especially when she'd spent the previous night in a prison cell. He wanted her safe, warm and comfortable, and for her to know she was behind a securely bolted door with two former Special Ops soldiers to guard her from any threat Tehrazzi and his evil minions could dish out. And that was only for starters. If it would ease her mind, he'd gladly stay up all night and watch over her with a gun in his hand. And he was *so* not going to analyze the reasons behind that. "You're taking my bed. I've got work to do anyway."

She opened her mouth to argue, but he stopped her with an upraised hand.

"Grab a shower if you want. There's a robe in the closet. After you've cleaned up and had something to eat you should try and crash for awhile. Once we find out where your cousin is, we'll be moving fast."

"Okay." She pulled the strap of her backpack up higher on her shoulder and went into the bathroom.

As soon as the door shut behind her, Ben let out a deep breath. Christ, he was never going to sleep knowing she was curled up in his bed. He'd be up all night remembering how amazing she'd felt flattened against his chest with her head tucked into his shoulder and the hero worship in her eyes when she'd gazed up at him.

"You sure about this?" Rhys asked.

Ben regarded his brother warily. He didn't know what the hell to do next, but he didn't want a lecture right now. "Yeah, why? You got a problem with her staying here?"

Rhys cocked a coal-black brow. "I wasn't the one that thought she was lying in the first place, remember?"

****

Ben's cell rang a little after midnight. He tossed the radios he'd been checking aside and grabbed it. "Yeah."

"Got a lead on the hostage location," Luke said. "Flight leaves from the airfield at oh-six-hundred."

"Roger that." He glanced toward the bedroom at the back of the suite. "Sam coming?"

"That's affirm. Bring all the com equipment with you."

When he hung up, Ben dragged a hand over his face and stared at the phone in his lap. So much for that. Pushing to his feet, he paused. He should tell Sam, but he hated to wake her. Expecting to find her asleep, he was surprised when she answered his faint knock in a clear voice.

He pushed the door open. Sam raised up on an elbow. The sheets fell to her hips, the tank top revealing her bare shoulders and the alluring curves of her high, round breasts. The blood rushed out of his brain and into his groin. He shifted his stance to make himself more comfortable and hide the damning evidence from view.

"Everything okay?" she asked, hair spilling over one shoulder in a gorgeous waterfall of black waves.

Ben pulled himself together. "Luke called, said he has a lead on Neveah. Nothing solid, but it's a start. Our flight leaves at six."

She sat up a little more, giving him a view of her full breasts as they strained against the thin cotton top. His abs clenched in reaction. Holy hell, she was stunning. Disturbing thing was, the reaction was far more complicated than being merely sexual. He liked her. Admired her. He wanted to protect her and do whatever he could to shield her from all this ugliness.

Whoa. He gave himself a mental shake. Hadn't he just done this? Hadn't he felt the same thing for Bryn a few weeks ago until she'd given him a variation of the "I just want to be friends" speech? Like he needed another dose of that shit right now. What the hell was wrong with him?

You know damned well Sam wouldn't turn you down.

Whatever. He still wasn't going there.

Sam stared at him with her liquid brown eyes. "So I'm…still coming with you?"

Unfortunately. "Yeah." He studied her a moment, trying to ignore how erotic she looked stretched out in his bed like that. "Unless you've changed your mind." Though if she wanted out, he wasn't even sure they'd be able to find a way to make it happen.

"No. If Luke thinks I can help him get Neveah out, then I'm going." She swallowed. "But I'm—I'm glad you'll be with me."

Ah, shit. "I can only do so much, Sam."

"I know. But Bryn did it—"

"Yeah, and look how well that turned out for

everyone involved. She and Dec both get to spend the next year in counseling to contemplate how lucky they are to be alive."

Sam pressed her lips together a moment, then said in a quiet voice, "Nev's all I've got, Ben."

No she's not, he wanted to say. *You've got me*. He managed to choke down the words before they flew out of his stupid mouth. He wasn't sure how she'd done it, but Sam had wormed her way inside him good and tight. That soft, vulnerable expression on her face almost did him in. He almost gave in to the need to sink to his knees next to the bed, take her face between his hands and kiss the unspoken fear from her eyes.

He made himself step back. "Sleep if you can." His voice was gruffer than he intended. "I'll wake you at five if you're not already up."

She flashed him a shy smile. "Thanks."

"Sleep well." He let himself out, shut her door, and stood there a moment, fighting the urge to go back in and stretch out on top of her. He'd been with enough women to know when one wanted him. She was more than willing.

Would be a dumbass thing to do, though. That was not a complication they needed while they were on this op together.

He made himself turn around and head for a lukewarm shower.

Chapter Eight

When Ben came back into their room the next morning, Rhys took one look at him and announced, "You look like shit."

Nice greeting, Ben thought with a glare. "Morning to you, too."

"Rough night?"

"Nope. You?"

"Nothing too exciting."

Ben grunted in reply.

"So. How's Sam?"

"Fine. Fell asleep about one thirty." He knew, because he'd checked on her. "She's in the shower."

Rhys ran his tongue across his front teeth as though considering the wisdom of his next question.

Ben raised a brow. "Got something you wanna say to me?"

"Everything, uh, okay with you guys?"

His stomach knotted. "Yeah, why wouldn't they be?"

Rhys shrugged. "No reason."

"Then do me a favor and stop sitting there with that smug, all-knowing look on your face."

"Smug?"

All right, no one could ever accuse Rhys of being smug. Detached and unfeeling, maybe, but never smug. God forbid he let even that much emotion show through his untouchable I-am-an-island front.

Ben yanked the zipper on an equipment bag shut with barely controlled violence. "You know damned well nothing happened with her." Or did he?

Rhys had split when Sam had come out of the shower. Ben narrowed his eyes. “Is that why you stayed out all night? So I could get it on with her and pump her for information while I was at it?”

“Jesus, calm down.” Rhys dropped his gaze back to the table and resumed cleaning his sidearm. “Luke asked me to do some recon.”

Uh-huh. “All night.”

“Yup.”

Ben wasn’t buying it.

Rhys checked his gun over one last time before putting it in its holster. The silence stretched out between them.

Ben was already out of sorts as he stalked over to the window and pushed the curtain aside to gaze down at the streets below in the dawn half-light. His feelings for Sam were nobody else’s business, and if anything happened between them, he didn’t want it to be front page news for the rest of the team. Not even his brother.

Rhys glanced over at him with a watchful expression. Ben could almost hear the gears turning in his twin’s brain, and sighed.

People might accuse Rhys of having as much feeling as a computer chip, but only because he let them think that. Ben knew better. They were tight; always had been, right from the start. They’d had their moments over the years, but even during long separations when they’d served overseas and Rhys had worked off the grid behind enemy lines, they’d still managed to keep in contact. Rhys might be a pain in the ass, but his twin didn’t like seeing him suffer. Not unless he was the one dishing out the punishment.

Ben braced himself for the lecture he sensed was coming.

“Listen,” Rhys finally ventured, testing the waters in the verbal equivalent of waving a rag on the end of a stick to find out if the pissed-off Rottweiler would tear it to shreds. "She's going through a lot. You need to give her time."

"I told you, I'm fine. Let it go already."

Ben thought again of the "It's not you, it's me" speech Bryn had given him a few weeks back, and was glad he'd walked away from Sam last night. Didn't matter how it was delivered, or in what variation, the end result was the same. Nothing like mortification to wither a guy in his size fourteens. Of course, the evil eye he was giving Rhys was mostly due to the fact he was upset about Sam going to Kabul with them. Rhys couldn't be too thrilled about it either, but there wasn't a thing they could do to change the current circumstances.

"Okay. Just making sure your head's where it should be. Like on the mission and the new threats to Sam's safety."

Ben cast him an arctic glare over his shoulder. Like he wasn't aware of the situation? If he was so stupid, how the hell did Rhys think he'd landed the job as head of security for Bryn's father? "You know what? You're only six minutes older than me. That hardly qualifies you to be my father. You need to stop trying to be my parent and humble yourself by just being my brother. I can handle myself."

He might as well have jabbed Rhys with a red-hot branding iron.

"Bullshit," his brother snapped, eyes sparking. "All my life I've had to step in and finish what you started with your mouth when it flapped before your brain could catch up, and it was usually with my fists." Rhys hit him with a hard glare. "You know what, little bro? Talk is cheap. You want me to believe you're not the hot-headed punk I grew up defending my whole life? Then *prove* to me you can handle yourself and I'll happily stop riding your ugly ass. Until then, suck it up and take it like a goddamn man for a change."

For an instant, Ben almost went at him. His whole body tensed, ready for it, but then as he held his brother's glare, his mouth started quivering because he was trying not to smile at the situation. A second later, he burst out laughing. He laughed so hard he leaned against the window frame.

With his anger vented, Rhys grinned back. "What?"

Ben chuckled some more, gazing at him fondly. "Who knew you were capable of stringing all those emotional words together? And how the hell long have you wanted to say that to me, anyway?"

Rhys tilted his head as he thought about it for a second. "Twenty years. Give or take."

Ben gave another crack of laughter, fished in his pocket for a piece of gum and popped it into his mouth. His jaw worked as he considered the answer. "I deserved that."

Rhys' eyes narrowed. "Huh. Never thought I'd hear you say that."

"Yeah, well, I've grown up a lot. You just never noticed."

Rhys rubbed his jaw. "Well, shit. If I'd known you'd take it that well, I'd have told you years ago."

Ben sauntered over and clapped a brotherly palm on his shoulder. "Wouldn't have listened. I'd just have clocked you instead."

Rhys held out the holstered pistol he'd cleaned. "Here. Take this and go get our girl. I'll meet you in the lobby with the others in five."

Ben rolled his eyes, but took it anyway. "Yes, *dad*."

"Bite me, punk."

With a grin, Ben flashed him the middle finger on the way out the door.

****

Arriving in Kabul, Davis left them at the airfield

and went to snoop around to see if he could dig up any info on the hostages' location. With the rest of the guys, Sam headed to the clinic where Nev had been taken. She sat wedged in the back seat between the twins, feeling like a midget. And a weak one, at that. Their upper arms were about as big as her thighs. She had to be crazy to take this on.

Yeah, she worked for the CIA, but she wasn't a field agent. She barely knew anything about self-defense or withstanding interrogation, or even firearms. She'd taken minimal training in those things because her bosses had decided she would never need it. And look at her now, heading into one of the most dangerous war zones in the world and about to be dropped into the lap of a terrorist whose name made folks' blood run cold.

Their driver, a twenty-ish Afghan male who served as an informant for Luke, navigated their vehicle through the dusty, tangled streets.

The poverty was every bit as bad as she'd seen on TV. The markets were ramshackle and the sanitation was third world bad. Children dressed in filthy rags played in the streets. Beggars crouched in the dirt at the side of the road, holding their hands out as people passed by.

"Just up there," the driver announced in accented English.

Sam craned her neck to see past Rhys' massive shoulders as the clinic came into view out his window. The concrete building wasn't much to look at, but it was in better shape than a lot of others they'd passed. Situated smack in the middle of one of the poorest areas of town, it was strategically located to serve those in most desperate need, especially women and children. She could almost picture the excited gleam in her cousin's eyes when they opened the clinic the day she'd been taken. Nev had such a big heart. It was so unfair that this had happened to her when she'd only come to help the people of Afghanistan.

The driver pulled up to the building and shut off the engine, and they all piled out. A policeman met them at the entrance to unlock the door. The place was deserted and eerily quiet considering how crowded this part of Kabul was.

The officer unlocked the padlock and let them in.

"The gunmen came in here," their informant said, gesturing to the shattered wooden front door that sagged on its hinges. "Here, and around back."

Where Nev had been working.

Sam swallowed and trailed after Luke, hyperaware of Ben's presence behind her. The clinic's interior was surprisingly modern, with new carpeting and a computer terminal set up on the reception desk. Three well-equipped exam rooms and an O.R. were to the left.

Luke ducked his head inside each room, then said, "Where was Miss Adams at the time?"

"This way." The guide led them down a narrow hallway to the rear of the building, past some sort of staff room to the last door, swung it open, then stepped back.

Sam's stomach tightened as she glanced around the tiny room. Nev had been here. Right here where she was standing, probably working with a patient when the kidnappers barged in and dragged her away. From the state of the room, Nev had put up a fight. The carpet was strewn with papers and equipment. Tongue depressors littered the floor, their glass jar shattered nearby.

"They came through this door."

Luke strode over and opened it, examined the dented metal and splintered lock. "Kicked it in." He studied the ground a moment. "Assault boots."

Sam's gaze went to the ruined door and the boot

prints embedded in the dirt beyond the threshold, imagining someone kicking the door with such force they dented it. She wrapped her arms around herself. God, how terrified Nev must have been.

"Any new information about the attackers?" Luke asked.

The Afghan shook his head. "Nothing other than what the police have released. Witnesses said they drove off to the northeast."

Toward the tribal regions in the mountains and the border with Pakistan, Sam thought. Nev and the other captives could be anywhere in that rugged terrain. How were they ever going to find them before the deadline passed? What would happen if they didn't? If Luke's theory was right and Tehrazzi had done this to get to him, then she was responsible for what happened to Nev. It was her fault her cousin had been abducted. Her fault Nev was being held captive and facing an uncertain fate, maybe death, in any number of hideous methods.

Sam glanced up when Ben laid a hand on her shoulder, surprised to see they were alone. She'd been staring so intently at the ruined door she hadn't noticed Luke and the others leave the room.

"Come on," he said gently, "let's go."

He guided her out to the front entrance with a hand on the small of her back. The gesture was reassuring and commanding at the same time. All the same, she was grateful for the warmth of his palm and the anchor his touch provided. Seeing the crime scene had shaken her more than she would have believed possible.

"Nev wouldn't have made it easy for them," she said to him, fighting the burn of tears. "I bet she put up one hell of a fight."

Ben rubbed his thumb across her spine. "From the looks of that room, I'm sure she did."

This was good. She needed to focus on how

strong her cousin was. Nev was physically and mentally tough. She'd weathered medical school and years of residency in a male-dominated environment, so she wasn't easily intimidated. She was incredibly intelligent and resourceful. If anyone could get through captivity, Nev could.

Sam blinked when the sunlight hit her eyes as they exited the building and headed straight to the vehicle where Luke was holding the door open for her. His fathomless gaze rested on hers as she approached.

"Doin' all right?" he asked.

Even after working for him all this time, he was a complete enigma to her. He could turn his emotions on and off like a switch, and she never knew which side of him would appear in any given situation. Like right now, he was still the consummate professional, but he was letting her know he was concerned about her.

"Fine," she answered, because it was the expected response, and climbed into the backseat next to Rhys, who gave her hand an affectionate squeeze. She returned the pressure and pulled away, linking her hands tightly in her lap so as not to betray her emotional turmoil.

As Ben slid into the seat next to her, the engine whined to life, and the driver sped back toward the city center. Minutes later, they pulled up to a heavily guarded compound that housed some government buildings.

"Where are we?" she asked.

Luke handed over his ID to the armed guard at the gatehouse, flicked a glance at her. "Remember Hank Miller?"

The CIA station chief she'd met in Paris. "Sure."

The corner of Luke's mouth went up. "He got transferred to Kabul."

"Oh." Goodie. What a happy reunion this was

going to be. When she'd first met him in Paris and told him she was going to work for Luke, his treatment of her had gone from friendly and professional to clipped and closed-mouthed in the blink of an eye. Miller resented Luke with the most severe case of sour grapes Sam had ever seen.

Luke not only had the adoration of the Special Ops world and the CIA, he had the job Miller really wanted, out in the field tracking terrorists instead of reading cables about it. To make things worse, as a contractor Luke operated with considerable flexibility, able to cut through all kinds of bureaucratic bullshit and do what he wanted more often than not, while Miller was stuck following rigid protocol and spinning in place like a hamster on a wheel.

She eyed Luke doubtfully. "You think he'll be of any help to us?" If Neveah was further endangered because of friction between the two men, Sam would lose it.

A dry chuckle escaped him, his eyes crinkling at the corners. The sparkle in them betrayed a hint of the warmth she'd come to know. "Only one way to find out."

She tensed. He'd said those exact words to her the day she'd come to him with her suspicions about Fahdi. Look how *that* had turned out.

"Care to fill the rest of us in?" Ben asked in Luke's wake, nudging her along in front of him.

"You'll see soon enough," she muttered and trudged along. They went inside and took the stairs to the fourth floor, then to the office at the end of the hall. Once admitted, Luke strode in like he owned the place, and Sam reluctantly went in behind him to see what would happen.

Miller was stretched out behind his desk, hands behind his head. "Well, well. And here I thought you were dead all these years."

"How you doing, Hank?" asked Luke.

Miller's shrewd blue eyes held a cool glint. "Never better." He glanced at her. "Miss Wallace. How nice to see you again."

"Thank you. I wish it could be under better circumstances."

"Yes, I understand you and your cousin were close."

Are close, she corrected mentally. "Closer than sisters, sir." Her phone beeped, and she groped awkwardly through the folds of her robe to retrieve it.

While Luke and Hank talked business, she checked the incoming e-mail, aware Ben was watching her. She clicked on the file, frowning at the unfamiliar sender name. As she read the message, a shock jolted her. Her fingers froze around the device.

I have a job for you. You will meet with one of my contacts tonight. Alone. You will take the money he gives you and deliver it to another man in Kabul. Fail to complete the mission or bring anyone to the meetings, and your cousin will die while you watch.

The two names and address for the delivery blurred for a moment. The kidnappers, or Tehrazzi. Was this the meeting the note had told her about? How would they know—

Ben popped his gum, and she glanced up into his face. "I..."

"What's wrong?" he demanded, and took the phone from her numb fingers. Rhys peered over his brother's shoulder, and Luke and Miller stopped talking. They all watched her as Ben read the e-mail. When he lifted his gaze, his pale green eyes seared her face. "How the hell do they know you're already here?"

"I don't know," she said defensively. "I don't know who sent it." Her gaze darted around. Someone had to be watching them, following them. They were standing in the middle of a guarded, reinforced building, but were they really safe here?

"Let me see," Luke said, and took it from him.

She gnawed on her lower lip and waited for Luke to say something. "Think it's from Nev's kidnappers, or Tehrazzi?"

He handed the phone to Miller, whose brows shot up beneath his carefully styled bangs. "Could be either," the station chief allowed. "Either of those names in the message familiar to you?"

She shook her head. "Should they be?"

"I hope not." His gaze slid from Luke to her. "The first one's a big time drug trafficker in a group linked to Al-Qaeda. Second's an arms dealer for the Taliban we've been trying to nab for two years." His eyes narrowed. "What the hell's going on?"

They didn't believe her. Their stares weighed on her until a greasy film of sweat coated her body. Her heart clattered against her ribs. "I-I don't know..." God, she sounded pathetic and helpless. "Maybe they're testing to see if I'll comply." In despair, she looked to Ben. Was she actually going to have to go through with this and meet with those men alone? "Ben?" Her voice wobbled precariously.

"Take her outside," Luke said to him. "Give her a minute."

Ben took her by the hand and tugged her out the door. He shut it and faced her, and she immediately started babbling, intent on making him believe her.

"I swear I haven't done anything wrong, and I haven't been in contact with them. I don't know who sent that, but—am I going to have to do it? They said I have to go alone or they'll kill Nev. I have to meet with a drug trafficker and an arms dealer. My God, how do I know they won't just kill me and then Nev anyway?"

"Stop." He took her by the shoulders, gave a tiny shake. "Calm down."

She squeezed her eyes shut and took a deep breath, fighting back the edge of fear.

"There's no way Luke would send you out to do this alone."

Her eyes snapped open. "So I do have to go?"

"I don't think you've got much choice, Sam."

A cold knot formed in her belly. How was she supposed to run a wad of cash through a poor area of Kabul at night, deliver it to those kinds of men, and live to tell about it?

"But it said they'd kill Nev if anyone went with me."

"We're all Special Ops trained," Ben reminded her. "We can be close enough to give you protection and still stay invisible."

Maybe. But did he believe she hadn't had previous contact with the kidnappers about this? "I just want my cousin safe," she whispered miserably.

His expression softened. "I know." He slid his palms down her arms and took her hands between his, rubbed them to get them warm.

The door opened. Rhys stuck his head out and looked at her. "You okay?"

She forced herself to nod.

"They've got more intel."

She glanced up at Ben, hardly able to believe this was happening.

"Come on. Let's find out what the deal is."

Her legs were stiff as she went in and faced Luke and Miller, appearing strangely at ease with each other since she'd last seen them.

Luke held her gaze. "We've just spoken with a DEA agent stationed here who's been after the first contact for a long time. He's big. Bigger than anyone else in Kabul, with a loyal following. He'll be heavily guarded, lots of electronic eyes and ears. As far as we know, he's never dealt with Tehrazzi before. But the second contact has." His gaze was frigid as he maintained eye contact. “He’s Tehrazzi’s main supplier in Afghanistan.”

“So Tehrazzi sent the message?”

“According to early analysis, yes.”

Sam closed her eyes a moment. When she opened them, she glanced between him and Miller, still seated behind his desk. “So what, I’m supposed to go waltzing through Kabul with a suitcase of cash all by myself?”

“Essentially,” Miller answered. He steepled his fingers together. “Whoever goes with you will have to stay out of sight, and the only way for us to know what’s going on in the meeting is to either send a translator along, which isn’t an option, or plant a bug on you.”

“No way,” she blurted instantly. “If they strip or sweep me, they’ll kill me and my cousin for sure.”

“Not if they don’t find it,” Luke said.

She made a scoffing noise. “And where do you suggest I hide it?”

“You’re the expert, Sam. I bet you’ll come up with something.”

She stared at him. “Starting from scratch in less than five hours?”

“I’ll help you,” Ben said.

She glanced over her shoulder at him in surprise.

He offered an encouraging smile. “Two heads are better than one, right?”

“Yes, but—”

“Hank will see to it you get whatever supplies you need,” Luke added. “Tell him what you want so you can get started while the rest of us come up with a security plan.”

This was a nightmare. Not only did she have to pull this off, she had to come up with her own surveillance device that couldn’t be detected by pros. And the clock was ticking.

"Okay." She ran her hands through her dyed hair and tried to clear her head enough to decide what supplies she'd need. The transmitter would have to be tiny—ideally something that could fit into a piece of clothing that seemed ordinary. A button, maybe. They would almost certainly sweep her, so it would have to be composed of non-metallic components.

Would they strip her as Ben had done? Perhaps not, if they were devout Muslims. She could try to hide it in her hair, but that seemed too obvious. Jewelry was out. So were her shoes. That left internal insertion, and while she would do it, she didn't have time to come up with something complex enough to pick up sound through that kind of interference.

About the only thing she could think of was her underwear. Most of her stuff had bows or some other kind of embellishment on them. What was she wearing? She pulled the robe out from her body and took a peek down her shirt. Black bra, fastened in back. Could she hide something in the closure or in the underwire? Maybe, but it wouldn't conceal the device well enough.

The thing did have a tiny crystal nestled between the cups, though. It was round, and just smaller than a pea. Could work if she camouflaged it well and the components were mostly plastic.

"Need some help?"

She twisted her head around to look at Ben, sent him a glare when she saw his wolfish expression. "I'm contemplating the possibilities of where to put the thing," she snapped.

"Yeah, that's why I offered to help."

It was sweet of him to try to distract her, but now was not the time. Still, his boyish grin almost had her smiling in response. "Not funny." Her mind made up, she listed the required items off to Miller, who wrote them down and got on the phone.

"And I'll need a workspace with good lighting," she finished.

He covered the mouthpiece. "You can use the boardroom down the hall. I'll have someone bring you everything."

"What about you?" she asked Ben.

"I'll stay here until we've figured out what's going to happen, then I'll come help you."

****

More than an hour later, Ben turned away from the computer screen to watch Sam working across the table. She expertly wielded a pair of needle nose pliers, her brows pulled together in a frown of intense concentration behind the magnification goggles she wore.

Her black lace push-up bra lay spread on the surface in front of her while she fiddled with the tiny crystal sewn between the cups—the same one she'd been wearing the night she'd stripped down in front of him. Evidently, Sam wore Victoria's Secret even during covert operations in a dangerous foreign country. He remembered all too well how amazing it had looked on her. Since he knew her breasts were bare under the voluminous robe she wore, he couldn't help but let his eyes drift to that region and picture their naked glory in his mind.

The transmitter she'd fabricated was pinched in the grip of the pliers as she meticulously fit it to the crystal with a dab of Krazy Glue. You had to admire a woman who could come up with something like that and actually make it work. And you had to admire her even more when she was the one that was going to be wearing it during a risky mission later that night. That took guts.

He watched her delicate fingers press the bug into place. She set the pliers aside and lay the bra down. Without breaking her rhythm, she removed her goggles, picked up a plastic tube with a spray nozzle on it, about the size of a perfume tester, and began fixing it to some sort of hair clip.

"What's in there, nerve gas?"

Her lips quirked. "I wish, but I had to settle for pepper spray."

The mind boggled. She was a female MacGyver. He shook his head. "You're a dangerous woman, Sam."

The laughter in her eyes faded before she lowered them. "Only to the bad guys, Ben."

He hadn't meant it to sound like an accusation. In spite of this latest incident, he was still betting on her innocence. They all were. Their lives depended on it. "Want to test the transmitter out?"

She didn't look up. "As soon as I'm done with this."

He glanced at his watch. Less than an hour before she had to get going. They'd all gone over the plan several times. He and Luke would follow her as closely as possible undercover, while Rhys waited at their rendezvous point with a vehicle in case they needed a quick getaway. Miller and another team of CIA and DEA agents would do their own sting once Sam was clear, and an undercover agent who'd infiltrated the drug dealer's ranks was going to be at the meeting with her. In addition, they'd all been warned to expect a surprise attack targeting Luke. That's who Tehrazzi really wanted, so they couldn't rule out the possibility. Sam was simply the human lure tonight.

She seemed calm enough. Her hands were steady as she worked. Having tasks to complete appeared to have settled her. After all, she was in her element with this. He was in the presence of a master. Still, she had to be scared of what was coming. If he was worried, she had to be freaking. Ben cleared his throat. "Want to talk about it?"

She squinted as she maneuvered the vial into place. "No."

He knew exactly what she was doing. She was burying herself in her work so she wouldn't have to think about it. "I'll be as close to you as I can the whole time."

Sam paused, pressed her lips together for a moment, but didn't meet his eyes. "Yeah, but not close enough."

No. Not nearly close enough. Especially since she had to do the meeting and exchange by herself, while he and Luke waited outside in the shadows. If something went wrong and her life was threatened, it would take at least a few seconds for them to get to her, and by then it could be too late.

Because he couldn't let himself think like that, he refocused on her face as she tucked the vial of pepper spray beneath the spring mechanism of the hair clip. She was so beautiful, and talk about smart. When was the last time he'd seen her give a real smile? Before all this had happened, she'd been full of smiles and laughter, but he'd hardly seen her crack a grin since she'd met him in that hotel the night she'd contacted him. It bothered him. He wanted—no, *needed* to reassure her.

"Sam."

"You're not going to let this go, are you."

"Not a chance."

With a sigh, she put the clip down and finally looked at him. "What?"

"You're going to be okay."

Her lashes lowered. She managed a nod.

Ben slid a hand across the desk and covered one of hers. Her skin was cold. "We'll be able to hear you at all times." She didn't seem consoled by that. "Nothing's going to happen, but we'll all be standing by, ready if you need us."

"Thanks."

He searched for something to take away the fear he sensed in her. "It'll be over before—"

"You don't have to say anything. I've monitored enough ops to know what to expect."

Yeah, she had. And because of that, she knew how sideways an operation could go in the blink of an eye. "We're going to be right there the whole time, Sam."

"God, Ben." She covered her eyes with her hands, shook her head. "Can't we just drop it? I'm barely holding it together as it is."

A heavy pressure settled in his chest. She needed him to hold her, but wasn't going to ask. Without debating the wisdom of it, he got up and rounded the desk to hunker down beside her. "Come here."

She shook her head harder. "Can't."

Rather than argue, he pulled her out of her chair and gathered her into his arms. A shudder rippled through her and she pressed hard against him, burying her face in his neck. Her hair smelled so damn good.

"I know you're scared, sweetheart, but it'll be okay."

She raised her head. Her eyes glimmered with unshed tears. "You can't promise that."

"Sure I can." And he'd keep it.

Her bottom lip trembled a moment. Then she sank her teeth into it, the edges digging into that soft flesh.

Christ, he was done for. Ben cupped her face, brushed his thumbs over her damp lashes, and touched his lips there. Sam pushed closer and grabbed fistfuls of his shirt, the furthest thing from a *stop*. Her doe-eyed gaze lingered on his lips. The long lashes swept down. She trembled in his arms. He shouldn't kiss her, he really shouldn't, but damn...

With a sigh of defeat, he leaned down and brushed his mouth over hers. A shockwave of heat blasted through him at the feel of her lips under his, and only got worse when she angled her head and kissed him back. She was all firm curves and tremulous vulnerability in his arms, awakening every possessive male instinct he had. Ben tipped her head back and settled in, stroking her parted lips with his tongue to taste her. She opened instantly and he dipped inside, savoring her incredible softness until he had to bite back a moan.

God, just kissing her was enough to set him on fire. He had to stop, before things got out of hand. Though he wanted more, he broke the kiss but kept hold of her face, waited while she blinked dreamily and focused on him.

"I've wanted you to do that since the day I met you," she said softly.

"Yeah?" A grin spread over his face. "Was I worth the wait?"

"God, yes."

He tucked her under his chin, falling deeper under her spell while he dreaded what could happen tonight. "You can think about me doing more of that if you need a distraction tonight."

"If I do that, I won't be able to concentrate at all."

He set her away from him, smiled in encouragement. "You can do this, Sam. I know you can." But it didn't matter what he said. She was the one who had to believe it.

He was so damn proud of her when she straightened and stood up to collect the transmitter. "Since I don't have a choice, let's make damn sure this thing works."

Chapter Nine

Being in a bad neighborhood was nothing new to Ben.

Having lived through a childhood like his, Kabul didn't seem all that scary to him. A little foreign maybe, but he recognized the empty expressions in people's eyes. He identified with their hunger and distrust. None of that was what had him on edge. No, right now the thing that made him most nervous was the woman next to him.

Sam kept fidgeting and wiping her hands on her burqa. She tugged at the hood to adjust the veil of netting over her eyes. The thing looked damned uncomfortable.

"I can hardly see with this thing on," she grumbled. "How do they stand it?"

"Because they don't have a choice." Women didn't have much of a choice in anything here. Just like Sam didn't have a choice in going through with these meetings tonight, and he didn't have a choice in letting her go.

She grunted and fiddled with the veil again, clearly juiced. Seeing her so rattled didn't help the acid level in Ben's stomach, but for her sake he made sure he appeared calm and completely in control. "Sooner we get this done, the sooner you can take that thing off."

He led her deeper into the crowded slum, then paused in the shadow of a market stall to grasp her wrist and bring her next to him. Keeping a trailing piece of his turban wrapped around his face, he dropped his voice to a low murmur so only she could hear him.

"Hand signals only from here on in," he said. "I'll let you know which building it is and then get in position." He squeezed her wrist, the only show of comfort he could give her, because to anyone watching it looked like he was towing her. "Just remember you're not alone." He punctuated the last word with more pressure. No matter what happened, he wouldn't leave her behind.

Sam nodded, but he couldn't see her eyes through the burqa. Her fingers were icy when she grabbed his hand.

With a heavy heart, he waited until she gathered herself, maintaining that simple link because it was all he could do while his eyes never stopped scanning the dusky street. He steeled himself for what would happen next.

The mission, asshole. Focus on the mission, not Sam.

When she let out a long exhalation and released him he started forward, sensing her following in his wake. His pulse drummed in his ears with each footstep. This had to work. She had to get through this and be okay. He wouldn't accept anything else. Luke gave a curt report over the earpiece Ben wore, letting him know everything was ready and that the DEA team was waiting in the wings for Sam to do the drop and leave.

Winding through the maze of streets and alleys, they finally approached the location and he adjusted his turban—the signal for Sam to enter the building. With every ounce of self-control he had, he forced himself to keep walking and not look back.

****

Sam hesitated in the darkened doorway, quaking inside. Her limbs were stiff and her heart was in her throat. Sucking in a deep breath, she gathered her nerve and raised an unsteady hand to knock on the heavy steel door. The raps echoed in the stillness. A few seconds later the door swung open, revealing a strip of dim light coming from inside.

"Enter," a deep voice commanded in Arabic.

Resisting the urge to look over her shoulder to see if Ben was there, she slipped inside, feeling more alone than she ever had in her life. Her legs were like wood as she moved deeper into the room to face the unseen threat. With each step, the light got brighter until she could see three figures up ahead.

Two tall men flanked a white-bearded man seated behind a desk. He had to be the drug runner. Her eyes skittered between the other two. Was one of them the undercover DEA agent? Neither of them gave any sign of acknowledgement.

"You are the American woman sent to me?" the old man demanded in Arabic, letting her know he was well aware of her background by not using Pashto.

She swallowed, nodded. The guards had to be armed, but she couldn't see any weapons on them.

"Come here."

She followed his beckoning fingers and stopped at the desk, assessing them through the veil of her sky-blue burqa.

"You have the money?"

Again, she nodded.

"Speak up."

The sharp command made her jump. "Yes."

"Hand it over."

The gruff order threw her. Weren't they going to search her or something? She reached one hand into her sleeve to retrieve the envelope given to her, but froze when one of the men cocked a pistol and aimed it at her. Her heart throbbed as her gaze fixed on the muzzle.

"Put that down," the old man growled impatiently. "I hardly think she came here to assassinate me."

The bodyguard pinned her with his hard gaze and lowered the gun, but his reluctance showed how willing he was to use it on her.

"Continue."

Breath coming in gasps now, Sam slid the envelope from her sleeve and laid it on the desk, then immediately retreated a few steps.

Without looking at her again, the old man tore it open and examined the contents, pausing to count the money before nodding in satisfaction. "Good. Now take this," he said, producing a duffel bag from under the desk, "and take it to your next meeting."

Sam curled her chilled fingers around the strap, and took the risk of speaking without permission. "Where am I to go?"

The man's eyes narrowed. "You will find a map in the front pocket."

She scrambled to undo the zipper, then pulled out the paper. Whatever was in the bag was heavy, so it had to be more than money. Unless it was in gold.

"There is a GPS tracking unit hidden amongst the cash. If you go anywhere other than the appointed place, I will know. And you will be eliminated."

Her chest tightened.

Then in English he said, "I have eyes all across the city, so do not think you can fool me. Do we understand each other?"

She nodded, hoping Ben and the others were getting every word of this. If the DEA squad waiting to spring didn't give her enough of a head start—

"Go." He waved his hand in sharp dismissal.

One of the guards opened the door to let her out and she emerged into the darkened street with her heart pounding in her ears. Everything was silent except for a few cars moving somewhere close by. No shouts. No gunshots.

Relieved the DEA had held off so far, she took out the map and used the bare bulb in the lamp at the next corner to get her bearings. If they were going to the trouble of tracking her, they would probably have a timeframe in mind too. She didn't plan on finding out what that was.

Choosing a route, she started out at a brisk clip, ears straining to make out the sounds of footsteps or voices. Nothing. Maybe the DEA team had aborted their sting. Was her team still in position? She felt very alone. Winding through the back alleys, a sick feeling took hold. What if they'd left her? Laid her out as bait hoping she would lead them to Tehrazzi?

No. Stop. They wouldn't abandon her to the likes of the arms dealer she was about to face. But she was too chicken to do a voice check to confirm it. She didn't want to risk tipping anyone off that a team was shadowing her.

Please be out there, Ben.

She imagined him following in the shadows at a safe distance, watching her every move, protecting her from harm. It gave her hope and courage. Her shoes scuffed along the dusty street. The weight of the backpack bumped against her ribs and spine with every step.

An old man passed her, his back bent beneath the weight of the sacks he carried. Sam turned right, moving swiftly to the next light source and perused the map again. *Had to be close. Keep going west.* She studied the buildings she passed. The sensation of eyes tracking her from the darkened windows sent a shiver up her spine. Lots of flat rooftops here. Rhys might be positioned on one of them, acting as sniper. The thought gave her an added measure of nerve. She'd seen him in action. He was a lethal shot and moved like a ghost. Ben must be that good, too, or Luke would never have brought him on board. She wasn't alone out here. She had guardian angels watching her from somewhere.

One more left turn. She faltered. The alley was pitch black. How would she ever tell which address it was? Her heart sped up. *Move, Sam.*

Her steps were loud in the blanketing silence, echoing off the steel and concrete facades she passed. A metallic clunk broke the stillness. She froze. Trying to control her breathing rate, she scanned the darkened building the sound had come from. A metal door squealed and shrieked as it swung open. Slowly.

"You're late." Pashto.

Her eyes shot to the right at the rough male voice.

"Get inside."

Her belly pulled tight, but she obeyed and went up to the door. A strong hand grabbed her by the upper arm and yanked her inside before she had time to do anything but gasp.

She flung an arm out to push away, thought about the pepper spray in her hair, but then the door slammed shut behind her and someone shot the beam of a flashlight into her eyes. She flinched and pulled her head back.

"Don't move."

She didn't dare, and stood there shaking as someone pulled off her veil and ripped the bag out of her clenched fingers. "I am unarmed," she blurted.

"This way." He grabbed her by the back of the neck and dragged her further into the building, around a corner in complete darkness but for the beam of his flashlight.

God, the team would never be able to see in here even with their night vision equipment, it was dark as a grave.

She winced. Bad word choice.

The slight glow from the flashlight showed her guide to be a tall, well-built man wearing military-style cargo pants and a snug t-shirt, but his head and face were covered with a headscarf. She had no choice but to follow, even though every instinct urged her to run like hell in the opposite direction. The building was solid, built like a bunker, with nine-foot ceilings. Lots of steel and concrete. Dread slid through her. Would her transmitter be able to broadcast through that kind of exterior?

Another man was waiting beside a safe in the next room. Not as tall as the first, but his expression was twice as menacing. As was the fact he'd allowed her to see his bearded face at all. A sense of foreboding filled her.

What if they weren't planning on letting her leave alive?

The man wasted no time in addressing her. "You are American?"

Right now, she wished she were Swiss. "Yes." She could barely get the word out.

He jerked his chin at the guard. "Search her."

Sam squeaked when he grabbed her robe and yanked it over her head. She instinctively covered herself, though she wore cargo pants and a tank top beneath it. Bracing herself, she withstood the impersonal brush of his hard hands over her body, over her bra where the transmitter lay against her pounding heart, across her quivering stomach and grabbed the thick wrist as he kicked her feet apart and put his hand between her thighs. He stilled a moment.

Refusing to let them know how frightened she was, she gritted her teeth and held absolutely still. He gave an impatient grunt and finished his examination by sliding down her legs to her socks and shoes.

As he stood, he studied her for a moment, then reached for her hair.

The clip, she thought, allowing him to remove it. He turned it over in his fingers, opened and closed it a few times, then thrust it back to her and stepped away.

The man seated next to the safe turned his attention to the knapsack and began rifling through the contents. Apparently satisfied, he reached out his hand to turn the dial on the safe. The sleeve of his robe pulled up, revealing a tattoo. A black scorpion with its stinger raised over its head, in position to strike. A flare of recognition hit her. She remembered that design. She'd seen it during a search of a terrorist group database when she'd worked with Luke in Paris. It was the symbol of the Islamic Resistance, a dangerous militant group operating in northeast Afghanistan.

Where Nev probably was.

Her heart hammered. Did this man know where her cousin was? Was he connected to the plot? He had to be.

He turned his head. Sam met his stare and held it while the blood ran out of her face.

Oh, shit, he knew she'd seen it. Somehow he knew she'd figured out what it meant.

A bolt of fear zinged through her as she gazed into those icy eyes.

His mouth twisted beneath his heavy beard. Then he shocked her by speaking perfect English. "I was warned you were more intelligent than most."

She cast a glance over her shoulder. The door seemed so far away. Too far.

"Not that it matters to me." He swung the safe door shut with an echoing thud and spun the combination dial. When the soft buzzing noise stopped, he settled back in his seat. "But it will matter a great deal to you."

She could not let him bully her. The question crowded her throat, pushed out of her mouth before she could stop it. “Where is my cousin?”

His eyes flared at her boldness. He was probably surprised anyone would talk to him the way she just had. That made two of them. His black gaze held hers for a moment. “I believe I have given you too much information already.”

Like his eyes, the words were devoid of emotion. Her heart sank. He wasn’t going to tell her anything. Then his icy demeanor changed completely. A cruel smile twisted his mouth. A raw slash in the middle of his beard.

“Do you know why Tehrazzi and I work so well together?”

She backed up a step, shook her head. She didn’t want to know why. With each second her chances of her leaving the meeting alive dropped exponentially.

He gestured to someone out of her line of vision. Another hulking male came forward, carrying something in his hands.

She retreated another step, then pivoted on her heel to flee. Everything in her screamed she had to run, and yet she couldn’t bring herself to do it.

The arms dealer held her in place with his soulless eyes. “I only use a meeting location once.” Not even a flicker of emotion played in the onyx depths. A shiver passed down her spine. “And I only use a messenger once.”

His meaning penetrated her screaming brain. She panicked, spun to flee. The guard who’d brought her in grabbed her arms to stop her.

A hoarse shout of denial rose up her tight throat. The team. They had to have heard her. They were her only chance.

The grip on her arms tightened. Bruising her. Something in her snapped. She whirled, wrenching her arms free, hand automatically reaching for the clip in her hair. Her fingers closed around it, found the nozzle on the tiny bottle. She ripped it free of her head and flung it into his face, holding the button down. The spray hissed as it shot out.

The guard shouted and threw his hands up to shield his eyes. She ran.

The thud of her heart was loud in her ears, drowning out the yelling behind her. Footsteps pounded after her, coming closer. Her muscles strained with the effort to go faster. She tripped, falling into the darkness, and hit the floor hard. The breath whooshed out of her lungs. Her aching eyes stared into the blackness. The door. The door was there somewhere. She had to get to it before they caught her, or shot her. If she could fling it open and yell for help, Ben might be able to save her.

Shoving to her feet, she made a desperate lunge. Rough hands seized her and wrenched her arms behind her. A heavy weight settled on her back, crushing her into the cold concrete. She thrashed, turning her head to bite the arm pinning her. She tasted dry cotton as her teeth fastened onto the flesh beneath and sank in like a pit bull. The man howled and struck her hard across the jaw. Her head snapped sideways, neck cracking with the force. Lights flashed in front of her eyes.

Stunned for that instant, her attacker seized the opportunity and hauled her to her feet by her upper arms, nearly dislocating her bones from the sockets. She cried out and rose onto her toes to relieve the pain. His snarled threats floated through the haze of pain and terror.

"Hold her."

The deep growl made her breath snag.

The beam of a flashlight blinded her for a moment, then swept away. A man approached, carrying something in one hand.

The other guard stepped further into the light,

and she finally saw what he was holding. Her eyes bulged.

Her raw scream was swallowed by the cavernous building.

****

Hunkered deep in the shadows, Ben kept his eyes pinned on the door Sam should have walked out of five minutes ago. What the hell was she doing in there? She'd been in there almost seven goddamn minutes, and all of it in total fucking radio silence. Her custom made bug, the one he'd seen her fashion with her own two hands, had mysteriously stopped transmitting the moment that steel door had slammed shut behind her.

How goddamn coincidental.

"Rhys, you got a visual yet?" he whispered into the radio microphone, trying to chill.

"Negative."

The single word answer shouldn't have surprised him. "Anyone else?"

"Negative," Davis and Luke both parroted.

Jesus Christ, was he the only one to see they had a serious fucking problem here? He waited, muscles cramping as he stayed in position fifty meters to the east of the doorway Sam had gone through. His brain whirled with possible explanations. The transmitter going dead *could* be a coincidence. But there were a lot of those going on lately where Sam was concerned.

They had no eyes and no ears. No fucking clue what was happening in there. Was she all right? He hadn't heard any gunshots, but maybe she was in trouble. These assholes were more than capable of killing her. His guts cramped.

All his focus shifted as the locking mechanism on the door squealed.

He raised his rifle, stared through the sight at the door as it swung open. He deliberately slowed his breathing, listened. Nothing. Just silence.

Then Sam stepped out. Cautiously, almost as though she expected to have a hole blown in her if she moved too fast. She wasn't wearing the veil anymore. Did they have her at gunpoint?

Something was off. She stood frozen outside the threshold, glancing around her as though uncertain of what to do. Her head turned his way. Through his NVGs he saw her face…

And the abject terror in her expression.

"Shit," he breathed, whole body tensing. "Order everyone to stand down."

"What's happened?" Luke demanded.

"Something's wrong. They must have a bead on her."

Sam took a couple halting steps away from the door, but paused again, eyes swinging wildly up and down the alley.

"I'm coming to you," Rhys said.

Luke issued the order to the others to stand down. "Hold your position until I get there," he told Ben.

"Copy that." He studied her rigid posture, how wide her eyes were. God, she was fucking terrified.

What's going on, Sam?

Had those bastards hurt her? Had they somehow found the transmitter? It took everything he had to remain still while she took a halting step in his direction, her movements wooden and awkward like she was scared to move. He counted her steps. Seven. Eight. Nine. She still hadn't seen him. Twelve. Thirteen…

Rhys came out of the alley behind him and crouched at his side. "What's wrong with her?" he whispered, voice barely carrying over the still air.

"No clue." But whatever it was, it was bad.

Luke's voice came over the radio, quiet and sure. "Let her pass you, then follow and see where she goes."

"Copy that." Ben tensed as she came abreast of him. Her breathing was ragged, eyes glassy with unshed tears but she kept walking, didn't even glance his way.

Rhys placed a hand on his shoulder and squeezed once, almost a gesture of reassurance. They followed in her wake, concealed by the darkness, their NVGs lighting up the night with a neon green glow. Twice she stopped and glanced around her, and Ben swore he heard her choke back a sob. He almost broke his cover, but reminded himself he had his brother and Luke to think about, and for all he knew, she was leading them all into an ambush.

Minutes ticked past. Nothing disturbed the silence but her sobbing breaths.

She moved like an old woman. Had they beaten her and now she could hardly walk? More time slipped by. Ben tamped down his rising irritation. How the hell long were they going to have to wait before going after her? Clearly something bad was going down.

Luke's voice came over the radio at last. "No other contacts reported. Move to intercept her."

Finally.

He and Rhys hauled ass around the back of the next building to head her off, and when she maintained her course, Ben stepped out in front of her. She jerked to a halt, one hand going to her throat.

"Hey, Sam," he said, keeping his voice low and calm as he pushed the NVGs up onto his helmet.

She gave a jerky shake of her head, appearing anything but happy to see him. "N-no." Her arms came up, hands splayed outward as though to ward him off. "Get back!"

He didn't. He kept coming at her at a slow pace,

never taking his eyes off her.

"Stop!" she hissed in a loud whisper, backing up fast. "For God's sake, Ben, don't…" Her voice broke.

Everything in him screamed that he should grab her and haul her to safety. "Tell me what's wrong, Sam."

"If they s-see me or hear you, they'll…rem-mote detonate the b-bomb."

He froze. Rhys cursed in his ear over the radio.

Christ. "What bomb? Where?"

She continued scrambling away from him, and now he could see she was trembling so hard her teeth were chattering.

"Where, Sam?"

A sob hitched in her throat, hitting him square in the chest.

For a moment, he thought she wouldn't answer. Then she stopped and stared at him with swimming eyes. "H-here."

His eyes darted around. "Where?" In a building? Hidden in a pile of garbage? He looked back at her, ready to take her down and shake it out of her if necessary.

She trembled as she faced him, her expression impossibly sad. Resigned.

A shiver of unease rippled over his skin.

"Here," she whispered.

He sucked in a breath. *What the—*

She lifted the hem of her blue robe and drew it up over her pants, revealing the white canvas suicide bomber vest wrapped around her torso.

His heart stopped. "Oh, shit, Sam…"

Chapter Ten

Sam's legs shook so badly she could barely stand up. Every muscle in her body quivered with the knowledge that whoever held the cell phone with the remote detonator would push a button at any time and turn her into a human shotgun, killing her and anyone within a fifty-foot radius. If she had to die, she did *not* want Ben or the others to go because of her.

"Oh, shit, Sam..."

She wanted to bawl. Ben's face said it all. She was doomed. Looking away from his stricken gaze, she searched for a place to hide that might contain the explosion if the vest went off.

"Sam, sweetheart, don't move."

God, he was coming toward her. "No!"

She had to get away from him, for his own protection. She frantically scanned the street for a dumpster, a cement wall... A flash of silver caught the light. A bumper? Straining to see, she made out the shape of a car parked in the next alley. Without glancing at Ben, she tore towards it and skidded to her knees between it and the wall, huddling into a shaking ball, expecting to be blown to pieces at any moment.

Please God, don't let me feel it. Don't let it hurt anyone else.

Running footsteps got louder as they approached, and she huddled down with a whimper locked in her dry throat. "I told you, stay *back*!" Why wouldn't he listen to her?

In seconds, Ben appeared next to the bumper and got down on his haunches, meeting her terrified gaze.

"Get away from me! They're going to blow it. I don't want you anywhere near me when they do." She choked on another sob and squeezed her eyes shut, pressing into the still-warm brick wall to make herself as small as possible.

"Shh, Sam." Not only did he stay, he got down right next to her and took her face between his palms.

The physical contact jarred her, and she tried to twist away.

"Please, Ben, just g-*go*…"

"No." His grip was gentle, but implacable. "I'm not leaving you."

She couldn't hold the tears back. "No-o-o…" If he stayed, he would be blown to pieces. She wouldn't let that happen.

Ben wiped the tears away with his thumbs, and she became aware that he was speaking to her softly.

"Dammit, you have to go!" She tried shoving him with the heels of her hands, but he didn't budge. "Do you want to die?" she finally yelled. "Get the hell out of here!"

He got right in her face. "Look at me."

Her eyes squeezed shut. "*Please*…"

"Look at me."

He wasn't going to leave. Not even to save himself. It broke her heart and made her want to hit him. But she met his pale gaze. "Ben… Go while you s-still can."

"Shh. We're going to disarm the thing, okay? Just stay still and look into my eyes so you know I'm not going anywhere."

She tried to stop shaking, but it was impossible. Blind terror had hijacked her body, turning her into a mass of adrenaline and instinct. God help her, but she loved him more in that moment than she'd ever loved anyone else. Even after all that had happened, even though he had reason not to trust her, he was risking his life to stay at her side.

Luke suddenly materialized out of the darkness and took the situation in with a single assessing glance. "Hey, Sam."

More tears blinded her. She hitched in a sob as everything clicked into place. Of course. They'd done this to kill Luke. They'd manipulated everything to end it this way. Tehrazzi knew Luke, probably better than anyone. He'd known Luke's honor would never let him desert her. And the vest was the perfect weapon of choice, wasn't it? Who knew more about explosives than a Navy SEAL? They'd known he would come out of hiding to help diffuse the bomb. "This is w-what he w-wants."

"No doubt."

"Leave m-me." Her jaw quivered so hard her teeth chattered. "D-don't let him win."

His eyes were dark and steady. Fathomless. Full of resolve. "We won't."

She couldn't believe they were staying, risking their lives to try and save her. How could anyone be that brave?

"Ben said they're using a remote detonator."

"Y-yes," she managed.

"Let's see what we've got, okay?"

His voice was so damn calm, and his demeanor even more so. Like he dealt with this situation every day. A shudder ripped through her. She could feel the seconds passing, imagined someone's thumb poised over the button that would blast her into a red mist so that someone would have to hose her remains off the buildings and street.

"How long have we got?"

"D-don't know."

He pulled up her robes. “Let’s get this thing off.”

“H-hurry.” If they weren’t leaving, she wanted the thing off. Now.

Luke pulled out a penlight and held it in his mouth as Ben cut the robe off her, exposing the hideous vest with its intricate webbing of wires attached to the C4 explosive and its shrapnel of ball bearings. Her breath hitched in, and she turned her head away, unable to look at it a second longer.

“Stay real still,” Ben instructed, tossing the ruined robe aside and getting on his knees before her. “Hold onto me, Sam.” He took her icy hands in his and gripped them good and hard. “Now look into my eyes.”

Clenching her fingers around his, she swiveled her head and hesitantly met his gaze. He was so beautiful and brave and strong it brought a rush of fresh tears.

Ben’s gaze bored into hers, holding her with the force of his will.

“Stay right here with me and breathe. Don’t look anywhere but my eyes. We’re going to get you out of this. You’re going to be fine.” The low timbre of his voice brushed over her.

God, how she wanted to believe him, but it was hopeless. “I d-don’t want you to die.”

“No one’s going to die, Sam.”

She didn’t see how they could survive. Luke had lots of experience with explosives, especially from his time in the Teams, but even he had to see how dangerous this was. They had no control over when the bad guys set off the bomb. Staring into the green depths of Ben’s eyes, she spoke to Luke. “If you don’t think you c-can do it, don’t t-try. Just leave me. Please.”

“Nope,” he said around the penlight.

Ben tightened his grip, jerked her attention back to him. “Right here with me, Sam.” She refocused on his eyes. "Slow your breathing down to match mine." His voice was calm, but she noticed the sheen of sweat forming on his upper lip as he glanced over at Luke to check on his progress before meeting her eyes again. "Almost there."

Please, God, please don't let us die.

Somehow she found the strength to hold Ben's gaze. If he was brave enough to face this, then she owed it to him to not look away. Was this the last time she'd look at him? Here in this dark alley, with her heart pounding against the explosives that would kill them all?

The faint illumination from Luke's penlight washed over Ben's dark hair and bearded jaw, covering the cleft in his chin she loved so much, and made his eyes glow an unearthly shade of green. In the ebony depths of his pupils, she could see her reflection, face pale and pinched. Terrified.

I love you.

She almost blurted it out, but somehow held the words in. It was enough that she knew. At least she had that to hold onto for whatever time she had left. Could be seconds.

A clipping sound made her muscles seize. A faint tug pulled at her as Luke adjusted his grip on the vest to cut something. If he got the wrong wire... Well, she'd never know about it, would she?

"Breathe, Sam," Ben ordered softly.

She maintained the eye contact, the most intimate of her life, and commanded her shuddering lungs to even out her breaths. *I love you, Ben. I always will.*

"Stay real still. Small, shallow breaths."

She gave herself a mental slap. *Stop shaking. You have to stop shaking.*

"Rhys and Davis reported the warehouse is empty," he told her. "The CIA team is following the targets, but so far no remote detonators have been recovered."

"C-cell phone."

Ben's eyes sharpened. "Copy that, Rhys?" After a second he nodded. "He heard you."

Luke shifted beside her. "Hold this thing for me," he said to Ben. "I need a better angle."

Ben took both of her hands in one of his and kept looking into her eyes. "I'm just going to hold the light steady."

He'd warned her because he wouldn't be able to maintain eye contact anymore. "O-okay."

Once the penlight was in the right spot, Ben kept his eyes riveted on whatever Luke was doing. In any other circumstance, she might have been able to help with advice on the wiring, but she was too far gone with shock and fear, and it took all her focus to keep her eyes on Ben's face rather than the vest.

Another quiet snip of the wire cutters from Luke's jackknife, and she flinched.

In the hush, her heart pounded like a bass drum in her ears. Her body's pump, full of desperate hope, frantic to live, racing so fast it made her freezing cold and raging hot at the same time.

Then Ben stiffened and raised his eyes to Luke's. The alarm in his face kicked her in the gut.

Her blood pressure plummeted.

Luke's sharp words into the squad radio broke the awful stillness. "Anyone with a cell phone you shoot through the neck."

Sam bit her lip until it bled. A shot high up in the neck would sever the spinal cord and instantly paralyze the victim.

So they couldn't push a button on a cell phone.

God, they must have engaged the enemy. Was someone's finger hovering over the number that would end their lives right now?

Ben squeezed her icy hands. Sweat trickled down her temples. "Hey," he said. "It's all right.

Almost done here."

The shaking started up again, with a vengeance. "You c-can still leave." She forced the words out. "I'll und-understand."

"Already told you, sweet thing. We're not going anywhere."

Her muscles quivered like she was having a seizure.

"You gotta hold still, Sam," Luke growled.

At her breaking point, she closed her eyes in desperation and clung to the last thread of control she had, concentrating on the feel of Ben's hand curled around hers and the faint evergreen scent of him rising up to her in the still, warm air.

Another snip. Then another.

"Watch their hands, Rhys," Ben urged. "If they so much as flinch, take the bastards out."

Visions swam in her head, of Rhys and Davis sniping off the arms dealer's men, chasing them through the darkness and taking aim at anyone holding something in their hands.

Two more cuts, in quick succession. Luke paused.

He and Ben were motionless. Something must be happening over the radio. Seconds ticked past. Luke held the wire cutters poised over the vest.

Then, "Is he down?" His voice was full of urgency.

A beat passed.

"Shit—" Tension poured off Ben.

"Take him out—"

Someone had the remote trigger. A scream formed in her belly, rose up her throat.

"*Do not let him hit that button—*"

Snip.

"Christ," Luke snarled. "One more, just—"

Snip.

"Clear!"

The vest was ripped off her, and someone swept her off the ground. She dared to open her eyes. Ben had her, was running flat out, Luke barking orders behind them. The horizon dipped and tilted, her mind struggling to grasp that she was alive and the vest was gone.

I'm not going to die.

Her body didn't seem to believe her. She was quaking in Ben's arms like she was dying of hypothermia. And she felt just as cold. Her hands dug into his BDUs, fingers sinking into the hard muscles in his shoulders. A truck raced up beside them, skidded to a stop. Ben threw open the door, and set her on the floor of the back seat. Rhys was behind the wheel.

"She okay?" he asked.

"Yeah." Ben slid into the front passenger seat, and the truck sped off.

Huddled on the floor, Sam wrapped her arms around herself. She wasn't okay. She wanted to scream and throw something and cry until the tears were gone, somewhere private where she could be alone and let it all out.

"Talk to me, Sam." Ben reached back and sought her hand. He wound his fingers around it, but her joints were too stiff to squeeze him back.

"I'm…f-fine." The engine roared as they sped through the darkened streets. The few lights they passed created shifting bars across the back of Ben's seat. She stared at them, transfixed.

"You're safe now, sweet thing."

The words sounded far away. She'd almost been blown up, would have died without him and Luke.

Ben swiveled his head to look at her. "Cold?"

She nodded, feeling like her bone marrow was frozen.

"We'll get you into a hot shower as soon as we hit the hotel."

A shower. Such an ordinary thing. The insane urge to laugh seized her, but she held it back with a shudder. The pitch of the truck's engine held steady for a while, then dropped as they slowed and turned a corner. She closed her eyes and fought the adrenaline crash taking its toll on her body. She could barely hold her head up.

Hold on. Just a little longer.

****

Holding Sam around the waist, Ben kept her tight beside him and checked inside the hotel room before ushering her across the threshold. She was in shock, her eyes blank, face white as paper, but at least the shaking seemed to have stopped. She followed him like a sleepwalker to the bathroom, stood there while he ripped back the curtain on the tub and fired up the shower.

When it began steaming he faced her, hesitating. "You okay for me to leave? Or do you need me to get your clothes off and lift you in?"

Sam blinked at him like an owl, almost catatonic.

Ben let out a breath. He had no problem getting her undressed, but once she regained her senses, she might be embarrassed about it. And with how jacked up he was right now, having his hands anywhere near her naked skin wasn't a good idea. Facing and conquering death had the very human reaction of making you realize how fragile life was, which made you want to... Well, it made him want something he shouldn't, plain and simple.

"Sam," he tried one last time, "can you get into the shower by yourself or not?"

Her glassy eyes focused on him, her throat undulating as she swallowed. "Yes." The word came out a scratchy whisper.

He was doubtful, but giving her some privacy was the best thing for both of them under the circumstances. "I'll be right outside the door if you need me."

She nodded once.

Closing the door behind him, Ben leaned his head against it and closed his eyes, taking slow, deep breaths. Christ, it had been so close tonight. For a minute he hadn't been sure he was capable of sticking it out with her. But he had, and he was glad. And once she was calm enough, she had some questions to answer. Like what the hell had happened to the transmitter she'd made. It'd been working fine in the first meeting. They'd heard everything with crystal clarity. Then in the second meeting, all of a sudden, nothing. Just dead air. He'd ask her what had happened and report it to Luke.

A low sound came from the bathroom. A hiccupping moan, followed by a sharper sound. Then a burst of sobs.

Sam was crying her heart out in the shower.

For a moment he debated going in after her, but decided to grant her the privacy she needed to get it all out of her system and hope it would give her some level of relief from the fear and realization of how close she'd come to dying. He almost envied her the release. He never cried, and the only form of release his body wanted involved her naked under or over him, with his cock shoved as deep in her as it could get for as long as she could take it.

He'd learned long ago to let the adrenaline run its course, so he dropped down onto the carpet, put his head in his hands for a few minutes and let it do its thing. His racing heart gradually slowed and his stomach unclenched, but then the awful burn started up again under his breastbone, worse than it had ever been. When the sweat popped out on his brow, he focused on deep breathing to push the pain away. Once his respiration rate normalized he sat up, but he couldn't get the image of Sam wearing that vest out of his head. It made him want to take the men responsible to pieces with his bare hands.

Scrubbing a hand over his face, he pushed to his feet. He grabbed a couple of Tums and crunched them down, then took his pack of Big Red off the table to give him something to chew on while he paced around. When Sam came out of the bathroom, he needed to be one hundred percent in control of himself so he could do whatever it was she needed of him to make her feel safe. This went beyond the urge to shelter and protect her. What he felt was way deeper than that, something primal and territorial, and it wasn't something he was prepared to deal with right now.

He glanced around, looking for options to distract them both, and his gaze fell on the laptop sitting on the coffee table. It was late September, and the Red Sox were about to clinch a spot in the playoffs. Sam was a card carrying member of the Red Sox Nation, just like him. Resolved to finding a game online, or even highlights, he booted the thing up and surfed around the net. Perfect. Third inning of a live game back at Fenway. They'd have at least a couple hours of baseball to watch and help settle them.

A live feed of the game came on the screen, and the moment the Green Monster appeared in the picture, a sense of nostalgia hit him. His adopted dad had taken him and Rhys to lots of games over the years. Ben made a promise to himself that when he got home he was going to take them all there.

The bathroom door opened a minute later and Sam poked her head out with her hair wrapped up in a towel, the rest of her concealed behind the faded wood. Her eyes were swollen and red. "I don't have any clothes."

His heart swelled, but sent most of his blood rushing to his groin. "Hang on." He got up and rummaged through his duffel, pulled out a black Sox hoodie and a pair of boxers and brought them to her. She took them without meeting his eyes.

"Thanks," she murmured, and shut the door. A minute later she came out running her fingers through her damp black hair and stopped when she saw he'd put the game on the laptop.

The plan was to act normally, and not even bring up what had happened. If she wanted to talk about it, that was fine, but he wanted to make sure she was okay first. He'd get to the questions later. "Haven't seen a game in a while, so I thought we could watch it together."

"I'd love that."

Some of the tension in his muscles dissipated. He held out an arm. "C'mere."

She padded over and slid onto the couch beside him, his hoodie hitting her at mid-thigh, and scooted under his arm so that she was snuggled up against him. Ben felt every inch of her delectable curves imprinted on his body. More blood went south. He did his best to ignore it, but the fact that he'd cheated death and she was naked beneath his clothes and pressed up against him were damned big distractions from the ballgame. The clean scent of shampoo and soap rose up from her skin and hair. She felt so good resting against him, all soft and warm. It made him feel that much bigger and masculine, which strengthened the instinctive urge to comfort her.

And get inside her as fast as he could.

He steeled himself as she burrowed closer, tucking her hands between her up-drawn knees, and allowed himself to lean down and kiss the top of her head. The moment he did, she sighed and turned into his body. Her face pressed into the hollow of his throat and her breath feathered over his suddenly violently sensitive skin. A tremor rippled through her.

His body leapt with urgency, but he held himself in check. “Okay?”

Sam nodded, rubbing her cheek against his shoulder.

Before he could stop himself, he brought his other arm around her and stroked his palm over her damp hair. She’d been so goddamn brave out there—had even hid behind that car to shield him and anyone else in case the explosives detonated, and begged him to leave her so he wouldn’t be killed. How the hell could he not admire her? Coupled with her sweet personality and brains, that kind of courage completely melted him. He only wished he knew if he could trust her with all that had happened. He needed to hear her side of the story, but couldn’t bring himself to dredge it all up when she seemed an inch away from going to pieces.

He fumbled for something to say to fill the void. “Been a long time since I was at a Sox game.”

“I’ve never been,” she said quietly, though her voice was rough. “My dad loves the BoSox. Guess that’s why I do, too.”

“Mine used to take us to Fenway a few times a year when we were growing up.”

“You grew up in Boston.”

“Yeah.” In the roughest section of south Boston. *Keep talking. Give her something to occupy her mind so she doesn’t think about what almost happened out there.*

“In Southie.”

He hid a smile. “Oh, you know it?”

“I went to MIT,” she reminded him. “Was it hard for you?”

Their neighborhood had been full of pimps and gangs and drug dealers. “You sure you want to hear this?”

“Yes.”

Not a topic he would have chosen under the circumstances, but at least Sam was interacting with him, focusing on him instead of tonight. "Well, let's see. By age eight, I could hot wire a car and drive it around until I got bored and decided to ditch it. Probably had a bad case of ADD going back then. Cops caught me a couple of times, but nothing ever came of it." He toyed with the damp ends of her hair. "Then Rhys and I started earning extra money by delivering drugs for a local dealer to help supplement the family income." Their mother had sold her body to put food on the table, such as it was, but after a while most of the meager funds she brought in went to sustain her drug habit to allow her an escape from her life. Them included. "Our mom was a crack addict, so she wasn't around much."

Sam gave a sympathetic murmur. "Is that why you ended up in foster care?"

"Yeah." He hated talking about it because it made him remember how alone and scared he'd been. Plus, it was no one else's biz. But he somehow didn't mind telling Sam. "At one point she had us living in a beat-up 1984 Pontiac when we were ten." The only regular meals they'd gotten were at school. They'd spent many a hungry night on the floor in front of the TV, salivating at the scents of cooking coming from the Italian neighbor's apartment next door.

"Our teacher finally found out what was going on and reported us to social services. They took us away that night." He swore there'd been relief in his mother's drug-dulled eyes. Not because her boys had been saved, but because she didn't have to look after them anymore. "They dumped us into the system, and we stuck together through foster home after foster home, while adding a new list of credits to our juvie records."

"How come you turned out so well, growing up like that?"

"My parents."

"The Sinclairs?"

"Yeah. If they hadn't taken a big chance and adopted us both as teenagers, for sure I would have either been in jail or dead by eighteen."

Sam nuzzled his chest with her cheek. "They turned you around."

"Them and my martial arts instructor." Master Joe had taught him the value of hard work and discipline, but he'd struggled with his emotions the whole way through, envious even then of Rhys' self-control. "Then when we were old enough, we enlisted in the army." Sounded so simple laid out like that, but it was for the best. He didn't want her knowing how bad it had been for him, and didn't want to dwell on it anymore. He was Ben Sinclair now, a completely different person from that scared, angry little kid.

"Your birth mother—she lied to you, didn't she?"

His hand froze on her back. "Why do you say that?"

"I know you hate liars. From what you just said, I guessed it must have been because of her."

Yeah, mostly it was. But until the Sinclairs had taken them in, life had taught both him and Rhys not to trust people. That way you didn't wind up disappointed, and it hurt less when you realized words and promises didn't mean anything. "It wasn't so bad."

"Makes my life look like a Disney movie."

Her hair slid through his fingers in soft waves. "Where'd you grow up?"

"Ohio. My mom died when I was little, so my dad raised me."

"And he named you Samarra after his first dig."

"Yep. Taught me Arabic, too. When he was away

I stayed with his sister. That's why Nev and I are so close."

"Because you were practically raised together."

She nodded and grew quiet. With the thread of conversation used up, the silence expanded and filled the whole room, save the audio from the game. Ben resumed stroking her hair. He really should ask her about the transmitter. Instead, he searched for something else to say that might distract her a little longer. "Want me to turn the game up?"

"No." Her hand crept up to grip the front of his t-shirt. "I've got exactly what I need right here."

His heart squeezed. She needed comforting, but given what they'd just gone through and the fact they were alone, he should put some distance between them now, before the temptation to go further overwhelmed his good intentions. But when she wrapped both arms around his neck and trembled, he didn't have the heart to push her away. Instead, he returned the embrace, locking his arms around her back to let her take whatever solace she could from him. God knew, he needed it as much as she did.

"Tighter," she croaked.

Ah, sweetheart. Upping the pressure, he closed his eyes. As he held her, what started out as an attempt to comfort her began to soothe him as well. She did that to him. With her warm weight settled in his lap and her heart beating against his, some of the tension melted out of his muscles.

Sam burrowed in even closer with a shuddering sigh and laid her cheek on his chest, her arms straining to hold him tight. Ben turned them, shifting on the couch so he was stretched out the length of it and she followed him down to lie grafted to his side, her face turned toward the laptop. His body reacted instantly to the feel of her thigh draped across his groin. He did his best not to react any more than that, focusing hard on the batter taking a ball inside to make it full count in the bottom of the fourth. If Sam noticed his erection, she didn't show it. She pulled in a few deep, slow breaths and released them, growing pliant in his arms as he continued the gentle caresses over her hair and back. Damn, she felt good.

Way too good.

As though reading his thoughts, she lifted her head and looked at him.

Busted.

He strove for something light to say, anything to maintain a sense of normalcy. "Better?"

Her thigh came up to tuck between his, pressing against the aching length of him. He sucked back a moan. Her red-rimmed eyes darkened with longing before dropping to his mouth, inches beneath hers.

Shit. He wanted her so badly he didn't know if he could say no if she started anything, and knew for sure he wouldn't be able to stop once it did.

She met his gaze again, and surprised him by asking, "Why did you stay, Ben?"

His hand ceased its rhythmic motion on her back. "What do you mean?"

"You know what I mean. Before." She settled more fully atop him, making his hands bite into her waist to hold her still. "You would have died with me if Luke hadn't disabled the bomb."

Swallowing, he fought not to kiss her. He wanted in her, even if it was only his tongue in her mouth. "But we didn't. And there's no way I could have walked away and let you face that alone." As it was, he'd remember the terror in her expression until the day he died.

Sam pressed her lips together a moment, as though fighting not to cry. "Thank you," she whispered.

Ah, damn. "Anytime."

She laid her palms against his bearded cheeks, freezing him. Ben's heart started a slow thud. He had plenty of time to avoid the kiss he knew was coming, but couldn't make himself move. Her lashes lowered as she dipped her head toward him, and he even raised his head to meet the brush of her lips against his. The sweet contact hit him like a fist, and had him opening to the tentative caress of her tongue, then winding his hands into her thick hair to hold her closer.

She surrounded him with her warmth, following as he dropped his head back against the cushion, her lips gentle as she explored him, the glide of her tongue erotic as hell. She gave a soft murmur and moved deeper, gaining confidence with each slow twirl. When her luscious breasts pressed against the wall of his chest, he groaned and arched his back, helpless to stop as pleasure swamped him. One of his hands went down her back to grasp her butt, holding her tight against the aching length of him, ready to burst at the thought of pushing into her.

The sharp knock at the door saved him from caving completely.

Sam jerked back and scrambled to her knees, her face flushed and her breathing unsteady.

"Don't worry," he soothed, stroking her cheek as he got up to answer it, snagging his gun from the table before checking the peephole. "It's just Luke," he said, and unlocked it.

Their boss strode in, eyes sweeping over Sam's huddled figure on the couch, then to him. He raised his brows in a silent question.

"Haven't talked to her about it yet," Ben said in a low voice. "She's still upset."

If Luke sensed that anything had happened between them, he didn't let on, and crossed the room to sit on the corner of the coffee table. "How you doing?" he asked Sam.

"Okay."

Ben took a seat on the couch next to her, but not close enough to touch her. He braced himself for what was coming. Sam had some tough questions to answer, and he desperately wanted her to be innocent of any wrongdoing.

"I'd wait to do this if I could," said Luke, "but we don't have time. We captured two of the arms dealer's men and questioned them." His dark gaze settled on her. "I want to know what really went down out there tonight. In the second meeting."

Sam curled sideways on the couch, hugging her arms around her waist, but otherwise didn't seem upset or surprised by his demand. "The transmitter stopped working, didn't it."

God, she knew? Ben's hands clenched into fists.

Luke nodded. "As soon as you went through that second door."

She sighed, dragged a hand through her mussed hair. "I was afraid of that." She fidgeted with the hem of his hoodie. "I just wasn't sure if it was that, or if you'd decided to leave me there after all."

Christ, Ben thought as his stomach tightened. She'd really thought that?

"The building was concrete. I don't know how thick, but I noticed the acoustics were different. Dampened. So I thought maybe it was reinforced somehow. It must have blocked the frequency, and then when they put the…the vest over me," her voice thickened for a moment but she regained control before finishing. "It muffled anything you'd be able to pick up when I left." She lowered her eyes and toyed with the cuff of his hoodie. "Sorry I lost contact. Guess the design wasn't very good."

Luke exchanged a glance with Ben that said it was possible. Then he leaned back and folded his arms across his chest. "So what happened in there?"

She took a deep breath. "The arms dealer took

the money and put it in a safe." Her head came up. "I need a pen."

Ben grabbed one, slid it and a piece of paper to her and she began sketching on it with quick sweeps.

"Remember in Paris when I was searching through that database and pulled up a hit on a group working in the tribal region on the Afghanistan-Pakistan border that used the symbol of a black scorpion?"

"The Islamic Resistance."

"Yes. He was putting the money into the safe and when his sleeve pulled up I saw this symbol tattooed on his forearm." She spun the paper around for him to look at.

Ben studied the drawing of the black scorpion. He'd seen that before, too, during his job as security chief for Daoud in Beirut.

Luke's expression sharpened. "You sure?"

"Yes, because he said he'd been warned I was more intelligent than most, and then told me he worked so well with Tehrazzi because they only used messengers like me once." She glanced at Ben. "That's when they put the vest on me. I tried to fight them off, but..."

His eyes trailed along the bruise marking her jaw. "Is that how you got that?"

"Yes. I nailed him with a shot of pepper spray, though."

From her hair clip. Good for her. "Hurting?"

"No, it's fine." She seemed uncomfortable that he was bringing attention to it, but it looked sore. Her head was probably pounding because of it.

The bruise had him wondering what other injuries she'd suffered. But what he hated most was knowing she'd been in there questioning whether they'd abandoned her. That's what had been going through her head while she'd tried to fight them off, and while they'd put that fucking vest on her.

Sam took a deep breath, then laid a hand on Luke's knee. "Is that where Nev and the others are? In the northwest region with someone from the Islamic Resistance? It fits with the police reports that she was taken in that direction."

"Could be." Luke cocked his head. "Anything else?"

"No. Just...thank you, for getting me out of...that thing."

When she repressed a shiver, Ben had to hold back from scooping her up in his arms again.

Luke waved her thanks away. "Nothing to thank me for."

"Yes, there is."

Luke got to his feet and pulled out his phone, dialing as he went to the door. "Be ready to leave by first light, and get some sleep if you can." His eyes cut to Ben. "I'll update you when I know something further."

"'Kay." After Luke left he turned the deadbolt and threw on the safety latch, then gathered his thoughts for a moment before facing Sam.

She was staring hard at the paper, tapping the pen absently with her brain no doubt searching through its endless data files trying to remember anything about the Islamic Resistance she'd seen or heard about.

He took her a bottle of water and uncapped it. She barely glanced up at him when he offered it to her, a trait he now recognized as meaning she was concentrating on something.

"Thanks." She tipped her head back and drained half of it, and then closed her eyes with a sigh. "Looks like we're going to the tribal region, huh?"

"Looks that way."

She rolled the bottle between her hands, back and forth, the plastic crinkling and crunching.

"Guess it's too late for me to back out now."

When he didn't answer, she stopped and met his gaze. Damn, he wanted to tell her she didn't have to go, but they didn't have a choice with Tehrazzi using her as the contact. That fucking sucked. "Yeah."

Sam rubbed her fingers over her eyes as though she was exhausted. And she had every right to be.

Did she have the strength to keep going after what had happened tonight? He almost scooped her up again, but something held him back. "You should get some sleep. We could be leaving in a matter of hours."

"Yeah." Her fingers slid around the back of her neck and squeezed as she rolled her head from side to side. "God, what a day."

Tell me about it. Luke had interrupted the only good part of it.

She sighed again, and stretched her neck as she rubbed her jaw gingerly.

"Being hit in the jaw can give you a wicked headache. Believe me, I know, having been smashed in the face a few times." Mostly by his brother. He nudged her hand out of the way and sat next to her, kneading the taut muscles. Her soft groan was the best compliment he'd ever received. Steeling himself, he kept up with it until she squeezed his hand by way of a thank you and stood up without looking at him.

"Guess I'll hit the rack."

"Sure." He knew damn well she wouldn't sleep after what had happened, but he wasn't going to tell her that. Nor was he going to go after her. Not so very long ago he would have, and gotten her naked and in bed without thinking twice. But he'd changed. He wouldn't let his emotions get in the way, and the proof was in his ability to ignore the urge to go over and draw her into his arms again. If she wanted comfort, she'd have to come to him. And then heaven help them both.

"Night."

"Night."

Somehow he stayed where he was while she went into the other bedroom and shut the door behind her.

Chapter Eleven

Sam lay in the darkness, huddled deep in Ben's bed. She could hear the shower running on the other side of the wall, imagined his tall, muscular body under the flow of water. Every cell in her body cried out for him. Flopping over, she hugged the pillow to her chest to stem the ache of longing the image evoked. She wanted him so badly and suspected the feeling might be mutual, but he hadn't made a single move toward her after Luke had interrupted them. Was it because he was dealing with his own emotions about what had happened out there tonight? Or was he still hung up on Bryn and she didn't make the cut?

Not that Sam could blame him. That woman was something else—a terrifying cross between Xena, warrior princess, and a Victoria's Secret model. She wouldn't have needed the pepper spray tonight. No, Bryn would have kicked their asses with her bare hands and feet, and might even have made it out before they'd put the vest on her. She was fierce.

Sam sighed. The only fierce thing about her was her brain, and even that hadn't saved her tonight. Covering her eyes with her hands, she blew out a shaky breath. It had been so close. Without Ben and the rest of the team...

She shoved the morbid thought away. Dwelling on that was a waste of energy, plus it would only upset her all over again. What was done was done. Right now, she had an overload of adrenaline and longing to deal with, and the object of her desires was in the shower in the next room.

They were going into the tribal region with the rest of the team in the morning, and she was smart enough to be afraid of what would happen out there. The moment they touched down in that chopper, they were walking targets. Might as well pin a bright red bull's eye to their backs. Trying to find, and then extract, Neveah and the rest of the hostages was going to be every bit as dangerous as tonight's operation that had almost killed her. And Ben... He and the others were going into harm's way because of her cousin, so if anything happened to them, it would be Sam's fault.

Don't go there. Think positive.

She had to look at the important things. She was alive. Ben and the others were alive. For the moment, they were all safe. They had at least one last night on earth. Her fingers fidgeted on the bedspread. God, if anything happened to him or the others she'd never forgive herself. Her feelings for Ben were so intense, she couldn't even handle the thought of him being wounded. He could have died tonight. All three of them could have.

The shower quit.

Sam bit her lip in hesitation. She had two options: pine for him alone in her bed, or spend the night in it with him. Did she have the guts to ask him? Because he wasn't coming to her, she could tell that much. If she wanted him, she was going to have to go after him. Right now, before she wasted what could be her last chance. Her heart sped up. He might push her away. She wasn't experienced with the casual sex thing, and hadn't ever been the aggressor before in terms of luring a man into her bed. Mind you, she'd never been motivated to take on the role before now.

Ben Sinclair was all the incentive she needed.

She'd never wanted like this in her life, and had never dreamed she could feel like this about anyone.

When the bathroom door opened a minute later, her newfound courage fled as fast as it had formed. She listened to him moving around the other part of the suite, all the while scolding herself for getting cold feet while the clock kept ticking. Rhys probably wouldn't be back until morning. They were all alone, so if Ben rejected her, only the two of them would know about it. Wasn't the chance of being with him worth the risk of being shut down? No one had ever died of humiliation. If he said no she'd handle it like an adult, get over it and do her job tomorrow like a professional without missing a beat.

The sliver of light coming under her door went out as he turned off the lamp. Was he stretching out on the couch? All that lean, sexy muscle laid out like a mouth-watering banquet. She didn't hear the TV, though he was a considerate guy and would have kept the volume low or on mute so as not to disturb her. Maybe he didn't realize he disturbed her just by existing. To the point where she couldn't breathe without wanting him on top of her, inside her.

For crying out loud, he's right outside this room. Get up and go to him.

Something held her back. Pride, fear of rejection maybe. She made herself sit up and throw back the covers. She'd just survived a plot to blow her up. God, she was afraid to make a move on a man she lusted after, and she was about to go on a military op in hostile territory?

That did it. She was no wimp. Worst he could say was no. She would recover from that.

Sam stood up, took a bracing breath to slow her racing heart, and padded to the door. Her hand closed around the knob, turned it slowly and pushed the door open a few inches. The suite was dark, quiet. No flickering glow of light came from the other room, so he wasn't watching TV. Was he asleep? Her steps faltered.

"Sam?"

She jerked at the sound of his voice, and pressed a hand to her galloping heart as his shadowy silhouette appeared in the far doorway. "Hi."

"You okay? I thought you'd be fast asleep."

"I..." She had no reply to that. *I can't sleep because I want to have sex with you* was a little too bold for her, even under the circumstances.

He came toward her, a giant shadow in the darkness. "Thinking about tonight? Or worried about tomorrow?"

"Both."

"It'll be okay. We'll get her out. And about tonight... It'll get better with time."

She froze in surprise when he stepped close and drew her into his arms. His palms slid over her spine. A tremor ripped through her as she fought to keep from throwing herself at him. His hands stopped moving on her back.

"Sam? Talk to me."

The concern in his tone undid her. She raised her head to stare into his eyes. He brought a hand up to sweep her hair away from her cheek. Moving without conscious decision, she wound her arms around his strong back and went up on tiptoe to kiss him.

****

Ben froze for an instant, caught off guard by the frantic hunger in her kiss. Sam made a soft whimpering sound and pressed her lush curves closer, urging his lips open. A thrill shot through him as her satin tongue slipped into his mouth and stroked his. In reflex his arms tightened, one hand sliding up to the back of her neck. The skin there was warm and soft as silk against his palm.

His whole body hardened, heat roaring through

him. She felt incredible and tasted even better, a combination of mint and vanilla. Her hands slid down his chest and under the hem of his t-shirt, up over his bare skin. He groaned into her mouth, head spinning. Jesus, the woman could kiss, but the desperate need he sensed threw him. With the two functioning brain cells left in his head, he made himself break the kiss.

"Sam—"

"Don't say no," she begged, leaning up for another brain-melting kiss. "Please."

Ben struggled to hold on to his control and set her a few inches away. "Tell me why, then."

"I want you."

The need in her eyes ripped through him, but he held back. "Why now, Sam?" If this was about what had happened tonight she would probably regret it later, so the kindest thing he could do was say no. Even if it killed him.

She stopped struggling closer and tipped her head back to look up into his face. The blood pounded in his ears, but he distinctly heard her hard swallow. Was she nervous? "I…have feelings for you."

It took a moment for that to register, for him to grasp what she was telling him and notice the sudden stillness in her. Ben sensed the quicksand under his feet. Part of him balked at the idea of emotional entanglement with Sam. One false move and he'd be up to his neck, maybe even get pulled under. He cared for her, a lot, but he didn't know how much farther it went than that. And if he was falling for her, he didn't want to let her in until this was all over.

The faint light from the streetlamps spilling in between the curtains revealed the vulnerability in her wide brown eyes. His thumbs brushed over her cheeks as he stared into her face, at a loss for words.

She was so damn beautiful, wide open and hoping he wouldn't reject her.

It was a piss poor idea, but he couldn't stop himself. With a rough sound, Ben lowered his head and kissed her, hands moving with barely contained urgency over the shape of her luscious curves concealed in his boxers and hoodie. He skimmed over the fabric covering her stomach, higher over the firm, generous slope of her right breast, drinking in her gasp as he brushed lightly over the tight nipple. She moaned and leaned into his touch, demanding more, pressing her hips against the raging erection pushing at his zipper. He cupped her breast, molded his hand around her incredible softness as she struggled closer. Not enough. He wanted to be inside her.

His hands closed around her lower back and lifted her against the wall so he could wedge his hips between her thighs. She made room for him instantly, wrapping her legs around him, and threw her head back when his erection made contact between her thighs. Capturing her mouth with his, he slid his tongue deep and rubbed his hips against her in tight circles. Her fingers clamped around his shoulders as she increased the friction, waves of heat pouring off her.

Somehow he managed to wrench his head away before things got totally out of control. "Condoms?"

She stared up at him in surprise. "I—no." She sounded heartbroken.

"Be right back." He went to the bathroom, grabbed a couple from his shaving kit and came right back to find her waiting in his bed. Even though it was dark, he could see she was already naked. The amazing curves of her body stood out in shadowed relief, making him lightheaded. He tossed the packets on the nightstand and sank down on the mattress.

Sam didn't give him the chance to reach for her, just straddled his hips and grabbed the bottom of his shirt, pulling upward. He helped her peel it off, then met her lips in another kiss that had him desperate to push into her. She sucked in a breath when he grasped her waist, letting her feel some of his strength as he lifted her and eased her full length against him, lying down on the cool sheets.

Another throaty sound came out of her as her heavenly weight pressed down on him. Her palms slid all over his sensitized skin, biting her lower lip again when he found her nipples and rubbed. She arched like a cat and kissed him harder, rubbing her pelvis against his aching cock. One of her hands grabbed the waistband of his shorts and tugged them down. He lifted his hips to accommodate her, content to let her have her way with him. In his wildest dreams he'd never imagined Sam being so aggressive, but he loved it.

Her hand wrapped around the length of him. The breath froze in his lungs. His heart threatened to implode. Ben groaned and grabbed the back of her head to kiss her hard, letting her know exactly how much he enjoyed what she was doing. Sam squeezed and stroked, making his head kick back into the pillow. He grabbed her hips, fighting the urge to roll her onto her back beneath him. The way she caressed and sucked his tongue made his eyes damn near roll to the back of his head, but he let her have control, holding on by a thread. Her skin was so warm, so smooth, her beautiful hair falling around them like a fragrant curtain.

Then the kiss changed, slowing and drawing out the minutes as she stroked him with her palm. Heart pounding, Ben followed the lazy movements of her tongue, reveling in the shivers that coursed through her. He wanted to touch her all over, slide his hand between her thighs and inside her. Wanted to dip his head down there and make her come against his mouth. God, he was so close already. He had to pull back and make sure he pleased her before he lost it completely.

He felt her lean to the side, heard the sound of foil tearing and then Sam was smoothing the condom down on him. Already? he thought in surprise. He'd barely touched her.

Still kissing him, she shifted her weight and brought the head of his swollen penis against her, pushed just enough to bring the tip of him inside. He growled low in his throat, closed his eyes as he absorbed the feel of her, hot and sleek, hugging him. He wanted in so bad he was shaking. "Sam..."

She made a murmuring sound and rocked forward a little, then back, sinking down lower, taking more of him into her body. Breathless, enthralled, Ben lay helpless beneath her and gave himself over to her. Her slow rhythm was hypnotic.

In the darkness he couldn't make out more than her outline, but his hands followed every supple curve and hollow, spellbound by the sexual energy blazing out of her. Her body squeezed and released him, over and over. Sweat popped out over his forehead and chest as he fought to hold on. Above him, Sam rocked and undulated, her breathing becoming choppy and shallow.

Oh, hell yeah. He could lose it just looking at her and listening to the mewls of pleasure bubbling up from her throat. She strained above him, thighs tightening on his hips. God, he wasn't going to last, not with her looking like she was about to explode. His hands clenched her hips, fighting to hold her still. "Sam," he managed, his voice rough, "I'm gonna come if you don't stop."

In answer, she leaned over, threaded her hands into his hair and slid her tongue into his mouth. *Jesus.* He wrenched his head to the side, sucked in a breath. Was that what she wanted? He didn't want to get this wrong. "Do you want me to come?"

She purred and nibbled at his mouth, tongue blazing a wet path down his throat as her hips pumped, gaining speed. Again her breath shortened, and when he brought his hands up to her face, he found her eyes squeezed shut. She was straining, reaching for release, but if she didn't stop he couldn't hold on much longer. He went to grasp her hips again, but she pushed his arms away and kept rocking.

"Sam—"

Too late. Too far gone now. The orgasm barreled toward him, his body taking over as he thrust up hard, once, twice. With a hoarse cry he came, pumping into her, hands locked on her hips to keep her tight to him. When the wrenching pulses finished, his head hit the pillow on a groan.

Sam was still above him, breathing fast as she stared down at him. She jerked a little as she slid off his softening erection. Her legs trembled. Ben grabbed her by the waist. "Hey, where are you going?"

She tried to push his hands away, but he refused to let go. Her reaction confused him. He'd given her ample warning to stop and she hadn't, so she couldn't be upset with him, right?

"Come back here," he said, wanting to take care of her.

"It's okay." She tried again to scramble off the bed. "I'll get you a washcloth."

Washcloth? What the hell did he care about a washcloth when she was still shaking with need? His cock might be finished, but he wasn't. Not by a long shot, and from here on out it was going to be all about her. "Sam, come here." Ignoring her protests, he sat up and gathered her close, heart squeezing at the way she trembled and lowered her head. Was she embarrassed? He tipped her chin up with one finger and touched a tender kiss to her lips. "Let me take care of you."

"No, it's fine—"

"You were close before, weren't you?" He stroked the silky skin of her back with his fingertips, trying to take some of the tension out of her.

"I… I think so."

She thought so? She'd seemed pretty damn close to him. "So let me make you feel good."

"You don't have to."

"I *want* to." She had no idea how much.

Before she could argue he pulled her down and kissed her, letting his hands wander, finding the underside of her breasts and grazing the pads of his fingers up lightly. She shivered in his arms and softened with a moan.

He took care to unravel her gently, slowing the kiss down until she squirmed in his lap. He toyed with her sensitive nipples, swallowing the broken sounds she made, then slid one hand down over her flat stomach, across that expanse of petal soft skin. She held her breath and burrowed in closer as he moved lower over her thigh and back up the inside, stopping short of his goal. While he nibbled and kissed the side of her throat, his fingers smoothed up to brush over the damp heat between her legs. She lurched against him with a soft cry as he traced through the delicate folds to her swollen clitoris and circled it.

The note of vulnerability in the sound pulled at him. "Sweetheart," he murmured, and cradled her closer as he kept touching her, then slid two fingers into her slick core. Her spine arched like a bow, her whole body shuddering. She cried out again, and another tremor racked her. Almost like she was frightened.

It turned Ben inside out. He hadn't thought of it

before, but maybe she'd been surprised by what she'd been feeling when he was inside her. There hadn't been much foreplay for her, so it was a miracle she'd felt much of anything, let alone get close to orgasm solely from him penetrating her. The thought that she might be inexperienced flooded him with tenderness.

"Sam." He nuzzled beneath her ear, hand moving slowly to draw out her pleasure. "Ease down on me." She hesitated a moment, then sank down, adding pressure to his searching fingers. Her muscles clenched around him.

Oh yeah. So beautiful. Ben carefully rubbed her clitoris with his thumb as he stroked in and out.

She gasped, arms clinging to him, struggling toward release with a frustrated whimper.

He shifted her away a little and nibbled at the slope of her breast to slow her down. "Take your time, sweetheart," he coaxed. "I'm not going anywhere."

Her tiny sob of relief tugged at his heart. He raised his head to sweep his tongue back and forth over one ripe nipple. Her fingers dug into his hair. She panted, moving harder against his hand. Close now. The muscles in her arms and legs tensed, her breaths came faster. He closed his mouth around the puckered nipple, sucking tenderly, all his attention focused on her response, her pleasure.

Her hips rocked faster. Low moans tore from her throat.

He closed his eyes, savoring her response. "Mmm, perfect," he murmured against her breast, wringing another shiver from her. He wished he had more light so he could see her better.

"God, Ben I need..."

He took over instantly and flipped her onto her back. No way in hell was he going to leave her hanging. Keeping his hand where it was, he lowered his head between her creamy thighs.

"Wait—"

He kissed her there. Gently. Sam hissed and went rigid. Sliding his other arm beneath the small of her back to anchor her, Ben licked her softest flesh. She lurched and moaned, fingers digging into his scalp. God yes, he thought, and began to lap at her with lazy sweeps of his tongue. Within moments she was a wild, trembling mass of pleasure beneath him. He loved every second of it. Her hips mimicked the tender rhythm of his hand and tongue until she was sobbing breathlessly.

She kept moving with him until finally her head fell back and she cried out, her orgasm coursing through her sweat-dampened body. Ben waited until the last ripples faded before softening his mouth and stopping his hand. When she collapsed in a quivering heap against the bed, he gathered her as close as he could and lay down, pulling the covers over them. She felt like heaven in his arms, all warm and satiated, fitting perfectly into his body. Like she'd been made for him. A contented smile spread across his face. Who'd have thought such a fucked-up day could end so well?

"Thank you," she mumbled sleepily against his chest.

He laughed in the darkness and kissed the top of her head. "My pleasure, sweetheart."

Chapter Twelve

Next morning Sam helped load some of their gear into a Black Hawk helicopter and climbed aboard to sit bedside Ben. After what he'd done to her the night before she'd crashed hard into a dreamless sleep. She was still shocked by the unbelievable pleasure he'd given her, and relieved there was no awkward tension between them this morning. She'd braced herself for it but, in fact, she detected the opposite vibe coming from him. Waking up curled against him, he'd nestled her tight into his body for a few minutes and simply held her as though he didn't want to let her go. She'd expected him to roll her onto her back and pick up where they'd left off, but he'd just cradled her, and in doing so had cemented the fact that she was in love with him. Not that she planned on telling him, but she couldn't change how she felt.

The rotors sped up, creating a wash of dust and grit across the ground as they lifted off and rose above the buildings of Kabul. The aircraft angled forward as it sped away and then banked to the east, and Ben automatically braced her against his body. She peered out the door as the endless expanse of desert passed beneath them, a wasteland of mud-colored rock and sand, like the surface of the moon.

She'd almost died out there last night. The knowledge numbed her out. Maybe it was her brain's way of coping with it. For the best, since she didn't have time to dwell on it. Luke and Ben seemed unaffected by it, even though they had to be jarred on some level. If they could set it aside, she could too. It was just a matter of focus. She was good at focusing and compartmentalizing data. For now she'd file that horrific experience away until she had time to analyze it later.

Gaining its cruising altitude, the chopper veered toward the rising sun and into much more dangerous territory. The few roads they passed cut through the unforgiving terrain like scars, and Sam found herself thinking what a miracle it was the people of Afghanistan could eke out an existence in such a harsh land.

When they finally reached the landing zone and touched down to unload their gear, the first thing she noticed was how much thinner the air was. She had a distinct sinking feeling when the chopper lifted off and soared skyward, leaving them behind.

The boys shouldered their massive rucksacks, stuffed with sleeping bags, ammo, medical supplies, water and food. Each carried at least eighty to a hundred pounds on their backs, while her pack, full of water, com equipment and other odds and ends, weighed under forty. She slung the shoulder straps in place and secured it at her waist, mentally groaning at the added weight. It was going to be hard enough climbing over the rough terrain at the increased altitude, let alone under the burden of her ruck. Considering the distance they had to travel, she worried she wouldn't be able to keep up with the rest of the team. Luke would make allowances for her lesser stature and strength, but she didn't want to slow them down or be a burden anymore than she already was.

"Ready to roll?" Ben asked, shifting the weight of his rucksack, looking like a Sherpa beneath the mountain of equipment.

"Ready." She'd keep telling herself that as the hike progressed.

Luke seemed pale as he swept his gaze over her. "Speak up if you need to stop. If I don't hear anything from you, I'll assume you can keep going."

"Okay." She'd say something, but only if she was about to drop. She was determined to show she could handle this and earn back some of the respect she'd inadvertently lost in their eyes. Her pride was at stake.

Luke took point, then Rhys, whom she followed, and Ben positioned himself a few steps behind her. They picked their way between rocks and boulders up the side of the ridge and within ten minutes the thin air and extra forty pounds of weight were already sapping her strength. Her heart rate was elevated, partly from anxiety that she'd be forced to stop them, and partly from the exertion. Climbing higher, she had no idea how the guys did it. She knew all of them had gone through rigorous programs in the military, and that they were all used to forced marches with heavy rucks, but it still amazed her how strong they were. After another fifteen minutes, her back and face were soaked with sweat and she was panting to keep her breath. The others didn't seem affected at all.

She gritted her teeth and concentrated on taking one step at a time, following in Rhys' wake, envious of the ground his long legs ate up, but then he was a foot taller than she was. If she allowed herself to think about how much farther they had to go, her mind would give up. But when they reached a steep incline and began ascending, her legs trembled with fatigue partway up. Determined to make it, she doggedly leaned her weight forward to help propel her up the slope, and grabbed hold of the rocks to anchor her and take some of the strain off her screaming thighs.

"You okay, Sam?" Ben called from below her.

She managed a nod, trying to hide the fact that

she was gasping. Already a dull headache throbbed in her temples and the shoulder straps dug into her skin mercilessly. *You can do this, Sam. Slow down a bit if you have to—slow and steady, pace yourself.*

Forcing her body onward, she kept it up for another ten minutes or so, but by then an ever-increasing gap had opened up between her and Rhys. No way could she keep up with them. The muscles in her legs shook. Oh, God, she was going to collapse if she didn't stop. When her foot slipped on some loose sand, she threw her arms out to catch herself, but couldn't get her exhausted legs to take her any further. She held her position in misery for a few seconds, her face burning more with humiliation than exertion.

"We need a halt," Ben called to Luke, well ahead at the top of the rise.

Instantly, Luke and Rhys stopped and hunkered down with their weapons held at the ready in a defensive position. Sam shut her eyes and fought not to cry when she heard Ben's boots crunching over the gravel as he climbed up beside her. His rucksack hit the ground with a thud, and then he was pulling hers off her back. A wave of blessedly cool air hit between her shoulder blades, and her wobbling legs sighed in relief.

"Sit down," he ordered, and she did, butt hitting the dirt hard. She tried to mask her harsh breathing, but it only made her lungs burn more. He handed her a canteen. "Take a few sips. Get your breath back."

She took a couple swallows in between pants, but still couldn't bring herself to meet his eyes. Instead, she scanned the empty horizon and the comparatively dismal amount of ground they'd covered. Had she left them exposed by stopping here? What if a militia found them and they got into a firefight because she was too weak to keep moving?

She blinked fast to keep the scalding tears at bay. What good was crying going to do anyone?

"Sorry," she managed, vowing to get herself together as fast as possible and get back on the trail.

Ben took the canteen back. "It's okay. The altitude was bound to get to you sooner or later."

Yes, but way sooner than she'd dreaded. And alone out here in the middle of hostile territory, she was both a danger and an impediment to the others. The weak link.

"How long does she need?" Luke called down.

Sam glanced up briefly, cringing at how feeble and helpless she must appear.

"A few more minutes," Ben answered.

She nearly laughed. A few more minutes wasn't going to cut it. Hell, an hour wouldn't do it. She needed to be a hell of a lot stronger than this. Her mind and heart were willing, but her body wasn't, and there was nothing she could do to change that. Her gas tank was empty. Staring out at where they'd come from, she wondered if they would be better off to call the chopper back to pick her up and return her to Kabul.

But then Nev will die.

"Sam," he interrupted, and tilted her face up with a finger under her chin. She met his gaze reluctantly. "You need to speak up if you're tired. You're no good to anyone collapsing on the side of this mountain, because we can't carry you on top of the load we're all hauling."

Sam lowered her eyes and nodded, dismayed her breaths hadn't yet evened out. Ben wasn't even breathing hard.

He released her and pushed to his feet to peer up the hillside. "We need to slow down for her."

Luke answered instantly. "Negative. We're too exposed here. She'll have to tough it out until we can find better cover."

Her throat tightened, but she got to her knees and reached for her pack. Ben helped her slide it on, and pulled her to her feet.

"We'll stop as soon as we can," he soothed. "Just do your best. I'm right behind you, and I won't leave you, but we've got to keep moving."

She nodded, not wanting to waste precious oxygen with a reply that would probably come out as a sob anyway. He would stay behind, even if the others went ahead, and he would remain there for as long as it took to watch over her. And if some hostile force attacked, he would die protecting her. That's the kind of man he was. She loved him for it, but didn't want him risking his life for her anymore. Once was more than enough. Grimly, she started up the hillside while Luke and Rhys moved on, up the steepening slope toward the top of the ridge. As promised, Ben stayed on her like a shadow, pushing her to keep moving.

After a few minutes, her legs began shaking again, her lungs heaving as though she'd never taken a break.

"Move it, Sam," Ben ordered curtly when she faltered. "One foot in front of the other—let's go."

Her eyes narrowed in response, but she was too tired to snap at him, and she dragged herself a few meters higher, sweating and shaking. *Come on, come on…*

"Move your ass, Sam," he ordered, relentlessly driving her forward.

A sob hitched in her throat, but she'd rather have died than let him see her crying like a baby. His sharp words pushed and prodded her, ruthlessly forcing her past her limit. God, how much further? If she didn't pass out first, her heart and lungs were going to explode.

"Almost there, Sam," Rhys called above her.

"Come on, Wallace," Luke barked from

somewhere overhead. "Don't you dare quit."

They were trying to motivate her, but Sam wished they'd shut the hell up. She was done.

Ben shoved her up the last few meters with a hand planted on her butt, and Rhys hauled her up over the lip. Shaking and nauseated, she fell to her hands and knees, sucking in air. Someone pulled her rucksack off and she rolled to her side, past caring about the spectacle she presented. Ben knelt next to her and dropped his own load, then cradled her head in the crook of one arm to get some water down her. She choked and sputtered, letting her eyes close as her head hit his arm, his strength the only thing keeping her upright.

"You did it, sweet thing," he murmured, pushing her soaked hair away from her face. The endearment made her want to cry.

Panting, she forced her heavy lids open. She was shocked to see him smiling down at her.

"Proud of you."

The genuine warmth in his gaze made her heart catch. He was so good to her, despite the way she'd just jeopardized them all. "I hate…all of you…right now," she managed.

He laughed and laid her head on her pack so she could rest. She had no idea how the rest of them were standing up. Amazing bastards.

Luke came over to peer down at her, hands on hips, the bulge of his biceps revealed below the sleeves of his snug t-shirt. The man was fifty fricking years old and he was pure muscle, in better shape than most men in their thirties.

"See?" he said. "You're stronger than you thought."

Not really.

"We'll give you a half hour to rest, then move to someplace we can set up camp for the night. Give us a few hours to acclimatize before we make the next climb."

She groaned and tried to sit up, but Ben had to help her. She dragged her pack closer, pulled out her own canteen and drank half of it. Her feet were soaked. She had to change her socks, make sure she treated any blisters before they got going again. At least if she had something to keep her mind busy, she wouldn't be able to think about how much further she would have to go today. Digging out some duct tape, she stuck small squares of it over the raw spots she found on the balls of her feet, then pulled on a fresh pair of socks.

Ben watched her, grinning as he swallowed some water. "For a tenderfoot, you know your stuff."

Sam dug through her supplies for some of the wet wipes she'd brought, shrugged. "I read a lot."

"I'll bet," he chuckled, gazing at her fondly while she wiped her face and neck, under her arms, then sealed it in a Ziploc bag she'd brought for that purpose.

She held out the package. "Want one?"

"Is that your way of saying I stink?"

"Just being polite. Take it or leave it, I don't care." She handed him one, waited while he washed his face, neck and chest, and held out the Ziploc for him. "Better, right?"

"Yeah." Once she had her boots back on, he pulled her to her feet. "Eat something, then go lie down in the shade for a bit."

She glanced around. Shade? The only shade she could see was a thin slice between some boulders, so she headed for it, dutifully chewing on a protein bar. It dried her mouth out some, but she had to conserve the rest of her water until they got more at the base camp Davis had gone ahead to set up. She couldn't wait to get there and crawl into her sleeping bag for the night, especially if Ben was beside her. Obviously there wouldn't be a repeat of last night, but at least she'd be able to cuddle up and hear him breathing next to her.

While the men held a pow-wow, she found a spot amongst the rocks and lay down in a bit of shade after stomping around to scare any scorpions or snakes she might have missed.

At first she was too wired to go to sleep. Her body was heavy with fatigue, but her mind kept spinning. Were they headed in the right direction with this? Hank Miller back in Kabul had seemed so sure about the location, but being up in these mountains was an eye opener. They were so vast and inaccessible. The villages were remote and sparsely populated.

Her gaze strayed to Ben. He was propped up with his back against a boulder, choosing small pebbles lying around him and throwing them at Rhys, who was talking to Luke. The first one hit him between the shoulder blades. The second bounced off his shoulder. The third caught him on the back of his neck and he still didn't react. But when the fourth one pinged off the back of his head, Rhys finally got pissed off and whipped an apple-sized rock at his brother's head. Ben ducked as it sailed past his ear and smashed into a boulder with a solid thunk and broke into pieces. He even had the gall to snicker. The display made Sam thankful she'd never had a brother.

After that Ben gave up and tipped his head back, resigned to his boredom, and things got quiet again. With her head pillowed by a wad of socks she let herself drift. All too soon Ben woke her. She blinked up at his tall silhouette, backlit by the brilliant mid-day sun, and stifled a sigh of disappointment that her nap was over.

"Time to go, sweets."

Oh, God, already? Mind over matter, she told herself, and shrugged on her ruck. Instantly her neck and shoulder muscles shrieked in protest. Rolling her head didn't relieve the strain, so she settled for slipping her thumbs beneath the cushioned straps to ease the way they cut into her flesh.

Luke waited ahead on point, and as soon as she got into line behind Rhys, he started off. They had to be at least nine thousand feet up by now. Her pounding headache could have been from the onset of altitude sickness, but when she'd researched it, she'd found most instances didn't show up until between eight hours to two days after surpassing eight thousand feet, so she'd have to attribute it to the weight on her shoulders and possible dehydration.

To their left, the terrain dropped away sharply, while the mountains reached skyward on the right. Was Neveah up there somewhere? Is that why no one had found the hostage camp yet? The area was so vast, so rugged. How would they ever find her in time? She kept thinking of bin Laden and that the US military, with all its powers had been unable to find him in these same mountains.

They'd hiked along the ridgeline for another hour when all of a sudden Luke made a sharp hand signal, waving his palm at the ground as he dropped to one knee. Rhys instantly followed suit, and so did she, but Ben came up to her in a crouch and squatted down, eyes trained in the distance. In the sudden silence, all Sam could hear was the pounding of her heart and her labored breathing. What had Luke seen? He was staring through a pair of high-powered binoculars, in a north-easterly direction if she was reading the location of the sun properly.

Luke lowered the binoculars and glanced at them, lifting two fingers to his eyes, then holding up his index finger. One contact approaching. A scout? The head of a group of fighters? She swallowed, turned her head to see what Ben wanted her to do, ready to dive for cover or make a run for it back the way they'd come to that group of boulders they'd passed a ways back on the trail. They'd make good cover if a firefight broke out, and from there she could whip out the radio, crank it up and call in help if they needed it.

And then hope the hell the cavalry got there in time to help.

"Get your burqa on," Ben said in a whisper that barely reached her.

Without hesitation she threw off her ruck and dug inside for the voluminous blue garment, tugging it over her head with shaky hands. The hooded veil was the worst part, because it made her feel suffocated, and the air was already thin enough. Through the stillness a few minutes later, the musical chime of tiny bells reached her ears, growing louder with each passing moment. Then Luke snapped his fingers at her.

Get over here.

A startled instant passed in which she fought the urge to look over her shoulder for someone else. Surely he didn't mean her? But Ben nudged her with his arm.

"Go," he whispered.

Staying low, Sam got to her feet and made her way to Luke, who hauled her upright despite her rigid muscles. The shoulder straps gouged into her flesh, sweat forming beneath the pack across her back. She sucked in air through her nostrils, trying to stay as quiet as possible, praying whoever was out there would pass by without noticing them. It wasn't to be.

In the distance, a smooth-faced adolescent boy emerged on the trail ahead of them, driving a herd of goats. He was tall and thin, dressed in flowing pants, a tunic and vest, with a round hat on top of his curling black hair. He scrambled over the lip of the ridge and paused to dust himself off while the animals bleated and milled around him, the bells tied around their necks tinkling. When he caught sight of them he froze, his hand halted in mid-motion on the front of his vest. His eyes widened, and he glanced about as if wondering whether he should run or not.

Sam bit the inside of her cheek, watching Luke. What would he do? If he captured him, they had nothing to tie their prisoner to, so unless he wanted to hog-tie the kid using duct tape that wasn't a viable option. She doubted Luke would kill him, though, and not because he cared about her psychological well-being. Even a suppressed shot would make noise that would echo down into the valley below, and sooner or later the goats milling about would give away the body's position and everyone in the goat herder's village would know enemy soldiers had killed him. Then they'd have every Taliban fighter within a hundred miles or more scouring the mountainside for them, day and night. It was the night part that scared Sam the most.

Her best guess was that Luke intended to use her presence to convince the boy to believe whatever story he was concocting in his formidable mind. She hoped it was a good one.

While the twins hunkered in their hidden positions, Luke left her, approaching the boy and calling out in Pashto. The goat herder stopped his instinctive retreat and remained where he was, regarding them warily. Sam could only pick out a word or two, but his attention seemed riveted on Luke, as though trying to make up his mind whether or not he was a threat. His black eyes swept over her and back to the towering man in front of him, but so far Sam didn't think he'd spotted the twins frozen still as boulders further down the trail. In answer to Luke's questions, he gestured down into the valley, speaking in a low, respectful tone. He glanced her way again, his expression full of curiosity, and Sam wondered how in hell Luke had explained their presence way up here at 9,000 feet.

Then again, a woman shrouded in a burqa and loaded down like a pack animal wasn't a threatening sight, and maybe that's exactly why Luke had brought her forward. Then a wide grin broke over that smooth, pre-pubescent face when Luke produced something from his pack.

After conversing for another few minutes, the boy inclined his head and shook the hand Luke offered, then went on his way, glancing over his shoulder once to wave farewell as he herded his goats back down the hill away from them. When he'd disappeared from view and the bleating and tinkling of bells faded in the eerily still air, Luke came back.

"That was Karim," he said. "A local from a village a few miles from here, under protection of a warlord I had dealings with in the Afghan-Russian war. Said he hasn't heard anything about American hostages in the area, but he'll keep his ears open."

Sam frowned, running her gaze over his neatly trimmed beard and sharp, obsidian eyes. Battle weary eyes. "Did he guess you were American?"

"Probably, after I dropped the warlord's name, but that seemed to impress him enough to agree to be our informant. Then I sealed the deal with a Hershey bar."

Coming up behind her, Ben laughed. "Helluva lot cheaper than a wad of cash."

"Hey, whatever works. And I promised guns, of course."

"Oh, that goes without saying."

Sam wasn't convinced this was a happy turn of events. Even now that kid could be running to the closest Taliban scout and betraying their position. If that happened, the hills would be swarming with radical warriors bristling with AK-47s and the conviction that Allah had prepared a place in paradise for their sacrifice. The automatic rifles were only part of their worry, and they all knew it. But Sam wanted it straight from the horse's mouth, from the one who had trained the enemy they were now moving amongst.

"This warlord," she said to Luke. "Was he one of the tribal leaders given Stingers in the eighties?"

His enigmatic gaze warmed a fraction, as though she secretly amused him. "Christ, you read too much, Wallace."

Yeah, and so she knew all about the accounts of CIA operatives sent in to buy back the heat-seeking anti-aircraft missiles that had so decimated the Soviet Air Force.

"Maybe the Agency should think about making you an analyst instead."

Not in this lifetime. "So did he sell the ones he didn't use up to the Agency for a ton of money, or does he still have a few lying around?" If they got into serious trouble and needed air support, the heat-seeking Stingers would cause a major problem for any rescue aircraft coming in to save their asses. And if the warlord had sold the weapons back to the US, God only knew what he'd used the cash to replace them with.

"Not sure. I don't remember being at that meeting."

Uh-huh. Good to know they were deep in enemy territory with no reinforcements, surrounded by people who'd been at war for generations in this harsh land, and were armed with US weapons that included Stingers, land mines, rifles, and ammunition. Not to mention the Chinese AKs and RPGs. See what reading stacks of books on counterterrorism did for a girl?

At least the introduction to Karim had ended peacefully and now they might have an ally out here in the middle of nowhere. Shouldering her pack though the straps dug cruelly into her muscles, she got in line and trudged out behind Luke and Rhys.

"Nerd," Ben teased in a whisper.

She cast a glare at him. Like he was any better? He knew more than she did about the things going on behind the scenes in this war, and worried just as much about things he had no control over. Hence all the Tums he thought nobody knew about. Tossing her head, she extended her middle finger and kept going. His deep chuckle followed her.

****

Hours later, Luke led them down a steep but short face of shale and over a narrow trail to a cave hollowed out in the side of the mountain, to find Davis sitting on a boulder at the mouth of it, lounging with his back against the sun-warmed rock as though he didn't have a care in the world.

As a former Green Beret, he'd had extensive training in FID, foreign internal defense, so it was no wonder he was comfortable out here. He'd spent most of his adult life infiltrating hostile villages in hot spots throughout the Middle East, earning the peoples' trust to gather valuable human intelligence and then training the villagers how to conduct their own fight against insurgents. From the reading she'd done, she'd learned Green Berets were teachers as much as they were soldiers. Davis' fluency in Arabic, Pashto and Farsi, paired with his chameleon-like ability to blend into other cultures, made him an ideal field operative. They were lucky to have him on their team.

"Hey," he said, removing his wraparound sunglasses, a smile crinkling the corners of his ebony eyes. "Glad you guys could make it."

Ben glanced around and snorted. "You've been up here for what—two days? And this is the best digs you could set up?"

"Yeah, well, the interior decorator I hired must have gotten lost, because she never showed up. I hear that happens a lot up here."

This was all too bizarre. It was like they'd arranged a camping trip together and were just about to crack open a few cans of Budweiser around the fire. Only too happy to get the backpack off, Sam set it down with a groan and rubbed at her aching neck and shoulders. The cave was about four or five times deeper than its width, and littered with broken crates. "Taliban use this place before?" she asked Davis.

"Them or Al Qaeda. But don't worry. They're long gone since all the carpet bombing and JDAMs the Air Force sent in here a couple years back."

So strange, to be staying in a place once occupied by the enemy. At least the climb was over. Now she'd have at least a few hours for her body to acclimate and get everything set up the way she wanted so she could work with maximum efficiency. She pulled her laptop and equipment out, then got to work getting it all up and running while the guys set up their perimeter and went over logistics. She was linking up with a secure CIA database when Ben came over and hunkered down next to her. Every nerve in her body went haywire, including the ones in her brain.

"How ya doin', sweets?"

"Good." She ignored the invisible pull he exerted on her and kept watching the laptop screen, determined not to let him or any of the others know how much he affected her. Nobody else needed to know what had happened between them last night.

"Everything's secure, so you can get some sleep once you're done."

"Thanks, but I want to dig into the files the Kabul office sent over. Their intel on the Islamic Resistance goes back at least six years." She typed in a command, accessed the secure link and brought up the encrypted files. "Hopefully we'll find out who's been active in this area recently, and then hear some chatter about Nev."

Her head was killing her. The pain shot straight up from her burning shoulders to her neck and landed in her temples. She rubbed the back of her neck with one hand to ease it, and thought about taking some ibuprofen.

Ben nudged her hand away as he'd done the night before to squeeze and knead the stiff muscles with his strong fingers. Helpless to resist, she closed her eyes and moaned in relief.

He chuckled. "You should take something. As glad as I'd be for an excuse to get my hands all over you, I don't want an audience for that."

She laughed, blushing to her hairline. "I've got some meds in my pack."

"I'll get them."

"It's okay—"

"I said I'll get them."

She scrolled through some old e-mails about the militant group's operations in the tribal region of Pakistan along the Afghan border, but her concentration splintered because Ben was rifling through her stuff. She opened her mouth to protest, but bit her lip. He already thought she was an uptight freak, and she didn't want to give him the satisfaction of proving he was right. But it drove her nuts.

He rummaged through the bag without any regard for the care she'd taken in packing it. It irked her enough that she stopped reading and aimed a disapproving frown at his back. She'd specifically organized everything in there to maximize space, and so she'd be able to find any given item fast. He was ruining it all.

He paused and turned his head to see her. "Where is it, at the bottom?"

Her eyes remained on the pile of once carefully wrapped and folded things lying in a heap in the dirt next to the bag. All her clothes, her deodorant, the little finger toothbrushes and dry shampoo she'd packed.

"You think we were spending the week pleasure camping or something?"

She raised a brow. "Just because we're in the middle of nowhere on a mission doesn't mean I can't keep clean."

He rummaged even deeper, scowling. "Christ, Wallace, where the hell are they?"

"They're in a Ziploc bag." She had to restrain the urge to push him out of the way and do it herself.

He dug deeper, gave the works a shake. She flinched. "Labeled with a P-touch I'll bet."

She glared. "So?"

Grinning, he turned back to her with a gleam in his eyes. Then he stuck his arm in up to the elbow and wiggled it around.

She narrowed her eyes. *Jerk.*

The smile widened. "You can't stand it, can you?"

No. She set the computer aside and leapt up, reaching for the bag but he held her off with one arm. "Just give it to me," she demanded, "I'll do it myself."

Smothering a laugh, he held up his other hand. The Ziploc was already in it. Which meant he'd been riling her on purpose.

She snatched it from him. "God, you are such a pain in the ass."

"Yeah." He handed her a bottle of water while she took three tablets. "And you're way to tightly strung." The glint in his eyes turned wicked. "I'll work on your knots later." Leaning close enough so his chest brushed her shoulder with an electric tingle, he murmured, "I'm going to love unraveling you, sweetheart."

Her mind went blank from the wave of erotic heat spreading over her skin. God, the memory of his hands on her naked skin… She couldn't believe she'd let him distract her like that. Face burning, she brushed past him and headed for her laptop. "Don't you have work to do?"

Chapter Thirteen

Davis had done a good job choosing their location, Luke noted with approval. The cave was large enough to accommodate the team and their equipment, but the terrain surrounding it was steep, and the trails narrow. An enemy force would have a hell of a time getting up here, and if they did, they'd have to stack up almost single file on the approach and that would make them easy targets. Not that it would stop them. They'd keep on coming until every last one of them was dead.

He knew firsthand the resolve of the Pashtun people. He'd spent years crossing back and forth over the Pakistani-Afghan border, had lived in a cave much like this one for months at a time as a guest of the mujahedin while on covert missions for the CIA. If it weren't for the pain in his head and the subsequent dizzy spells, he might have stepped back in time.

At first he'd thought the increased severity might be from altitude sickness, but he couldn't see why it would affect him now when he'd never experienced symptoms at this elevation before. The headache felt the same, though, a sickening pounding in his temples. Altitude sickness would also explain his nausea and lack of appetite. Sleep disturbances were another common symptom, but it's not like he'd notice those. He only slept in quick snatches when he was out in the field.

He covered a wince as a shock of pain exploded in his skull. Could be he was just getting old. Shit, he was fifty. On the downswing from his prime. Maybe that's why he wasn't healing up like he used to. He'd suffered all kinds of injuries and wounds over the years, but the most he'd ever been laid up by a concussion was two days on his back, and that's when he'd been blown out of his clothes by a mortar round that landed too close. This should have run its course by now, but it was getting worse and starting to affect his vision. The doctor in Basra hadn't said as much, but maybe he really did have something wrong with his brain. The initial tests had shown some bruising and swelling, but he'd left AMA before they could do more. Could be he had a bleed somewhere, and the altitude was making it worse.

It was all for shit now anyway, at over nine thousand feet up in the Hindu Kush deep in enemy territory. If things deteriorated he'd approach Ben, the resident medic, and much as Luke hated even thinking about it, he might have to stand down from any operations. Things out here were dangerous enough without him losing his edge and getting someone killed.

"Luke?"

He nodded to Sam and headed to where she was hunched over her computer. Hard, dedicated worker, that one, and she'd been through hell the past few days. "What's up?" He crouched next to her.

She gestured to the screen. "E-mail just came in to your account."

She was checking his e-mail way out here in the middle of nowhere?

"I didn't read it, but it's from your son."

All Luke's muscles tensed. He nodded at her to open the file and read it, then waited a few seconds while she did. "An emergency?"

"No, it just says they've moved the wedding up by a few months to mid-November so Christa can make her training camp."

He withheld a sigh. Perfect. It meant he'd probably miss his only child's wedding. But hey, on the bright side, at least they'd invited him. As little as six months ago he wouldn't have been. Peering over Sam's shoulder, he scanned the message, tensing further when he got to the postscript at the bottom.

You might want to talk to mom ASAP.

Not likely. Not after that disaster the last time he'd talked to Emily over the phone. But why Rayne would tell him that could only mean bad news. This wasn't a "Hey, Dad, you should talk to Mom about the arrangements". Uh-uh. The only reason his son would have e-mailed him in the first place was because he couldn't reach him on his cell. Up here, they had to use satellite phones and that wasn't a number he gave out, even to his family.

An unreasoning fear pooled in his guts. Was something wrong with Emily? The urge to make sure she was okay was so strong he nearly grabbed the satellite phone sitting next to Sam, but he held himself back. If something was wrong, Rayne would have said so, and talking to his ex was a distraction he didn't need right now.

"Everything okay?" Sam asked, going through some electronic files. Obviously she sensed something was wrong but wasn't looking at him because she knew it would make him uncomfortable.

"Yep. Fire one back saying I'll be in touch when I can."

"Sure." Her fingers flew over the keyboard and finished with a flourish on the send button. "Done." She studied a fingernail. "Do you, uh...want to send anything else?"

He cast her a sideways glance. She'd spent time with Bryn in Baghdad. Since Bryn was his son's best friend and tight with his ex-wife, she had more dirt on him than the CIA ever would. How much did Sam know about his past? "Maybe later."

"Okay."

In true Sam style, she buried her nose back in her work and tuned him out completely. He could have been standing there stark naked and she wouldn't so much have glanced at him. Now, if Ben was in his birthday suit next to her, that might be a different story, but as far as the power of concentration went, hers rivaled the best Luke had ever seen.

"I'm going down into Karim's village to do some recon. Can you get me a transmitter?"

She stopped scrolling and finished reading a line before replying. "Got one right here." She dug in her bag and pulled out a plastic film case. Popping the cap off, she pulled out a micro transmitter. "Anywhere near the head should be fine. Let me code it in." Her slim fingers danced over the keys again, connecting the device with the radio link. "Voilà. You're good to go." She held it out to him, about the size of a pea.

"You're a gem, Wallace." He peeled off the backing and fixed it to the back of his cherished St. Christopher medallion. Em had given it to him over thirty years ago, and he'd never taken it off. Not once.

Waiting for the heat in his thumb to warm the adhesive, he finally let it go. "Test, test."

She gave a satisfied nod. "Clear as a bell."

He crossed the cave to get a pistol, and shoved it in the waistband at the small of his back under his wide-legged loose pants that men wore in these parts, and decided on an AK just in case. Next, he grabbed a wad of cash and stuffed his pockets full of candy bars. Whatever it took to grease the wheels. "You up for a little visit, Davis?" Tehrazzi was in these mountains. Luke was going to hunt him down.

Davis' dark gaze slid over to him from where he

was going over a topographical map with the twins and eyed the hardware Luke was carrying. “Friendly one?”

“Of course.” He patted the automatic rifle. “We’re all friends in these parts.”

Trouble was, you didn’t know for sure who your friends were out here. In Afghanistan, defecting wasn’t cause for shame. You could buy an informant one day, and the next he might change allegiance if a better offer came along. The trick was setting yourself up to look like the better deal and hoping it stuck, while never giving them information that could be used against you. And then you’d better grow eyes in the back of your head, else you’d get a permanent crick in your neck from constantly looking over your shoulder. That was the only way to avoid getting shot in the back in these mountains.

****

After working through much of the night to get everything set up, Sam had slid into her bivy bag between the twins and fallen asleep in less than a minute. By the time the sun’s glow touched the edge of the valley beneath them, they’d all been up and at their appointed posts. Sam and Rhys were monitoring the computers for new intelligence, Luke and Davis were out scouting the area, and Ben was guarding their location. Early in the afternoon, Sam’s head came up when Rhys swiveled around.

“Got something,” he said, and turned back to his own computer.

Without wasting time asking what he’d found, she ran outside to get Luke, who was talking to Karim. His head came around when she appeared, his dark eyes watchful.

“Something’s come in on the link,” she said, dread and excitement swirling through her.

Luke murmured something to the boy in Pashto and the youth sat in a patch of shade to wait, licking his lips as he tore the wrapper off another Hershey bar. Had the CIA ever bought information so cheaply before? The kid was a total chocolate addict. Luke followed her back into the CP.

"Where's Ben," she asked.

"Right here."

They glanced over their shoulders as Ben came striding up the slope, M4 in his hands. Her heart quickened.

"What's Rhys got?" Luke asked.

Sam shook her head. "Not sure." Had to be important, though. Rhys wouldn't have bothered announcing it if it wasn't.

They pushed aside the blanket flap covering the cave entrance and crowded around the computer screen. Ben came up behind her, close enough that she could feel his body heat and catch the scent of cinnamon as he chewed his gum.

Rhys ran his fingers over the keyboard, bringing up an e-mail file, but she couldn't read most of it because it was in Pashto. "You have failed to meet our demands," he translated in his deep voice, "and the first deadline has passed."

Her stomach went tight as a fist. Ben laid a hand on her shoulder. She grabbed it without thinking.

"This video will give you further instructions regarding our agenda."

"Formal for a ransom demand, don't you think?" Luke remarked. Then his keen gaze cut over to her. "I think you should step outside."

She shook her head, her neck stiff with tension. "I want to see Nev."

The seconds ticked past as his eyes bored into hers. Then, "Go ahead, Rhys. Fire it up."

Rhys tapped a few keys and brought up the video clip.

She stared at the icon flashing on the screen as

it loaded, heart in her throat. Was Neveah safe? Had they hurt any of the hostages?

The image of two masked men dragging a middle-aged man in front of the camera came up. He was swearing and struggling, his eyes bulging with terror. Sam swallowed hard.

"That the oncologist?" Luke asked.

"Yes," Rhys answered.

The balding doctor was still fighting. "Let me go! You fucking crazy zealots, let me—"

One of his captors kicked him in the ribs and he cried out, doubling over. Sam winced, bit her lip. *Please God, don't let them hurt him.*

Ben tightened his grip on her shoulder. "Maybe you should wait outside," he murmured.

She shook her head, mute as she stared at the terrified man on the screen. She needed to find out what they'd done to Neveah and wasn't moving until she knew.

The doctor started bawling as they bound him to a thick wooden beam and taped his hands behind his back. They bound his feet, too. Then a tall, masked man entered the frame. He wore a knife sheath on his hip. Something about him was familiar.

Sam sucked in a breath, guts clenching. "Oh, shit," she breathed. "It's him. It's Tehrazzi's bodyguard." She knew his posture, his stance. She couldn't take her eyes off the handle of the knife. He wouldn't use it, she told herself. He would only threaten the hostage, not kill him. What good would it do to kill a hostage?

Even as she thought it, she knew he might. She knew all about his reputation and had looked into his reptilian eyes when he'd pinned her to that brick wall in Baghdad. They'd been soulless. Full of simmering hatred.

"Sam," Ben said. "Go outside. Now."

She shook his hand off her shoulder.

On screen, the bodyguard stepped in close to the prisoner and drew his knife. A matte black blade, military issue like the ones Ben and the others had. The point appeared razor sharp.

"No!" the prisoner screamed, trying to wrench away. "Fuck you, no!"

As she watched in disbelief, Tehrazzi's bodyguard seized a handful of the hostage's hair, then wrenched his head downward.

The prisoner sobbed uncontrollably, thin shrieks of hysteria ripping out of him. He continued his futile struggle, tears streaming down his face.

Sam's heart pounded. He won't do it, she kept telling herself, gaze glued to the knife. He wouldn't do it, because—

But he did.

He brought the blade down against the nape of the man's neck and started cutting. An inhuman scream ripped through the cave.

Sam whirled away with a horrified cry, clapping her hands over her eyes as though she could block out the sight of that knife slicing into human flesh.

Ben grabbed her by the shoulders and propelled her out of the cave, the doomed prisoner's bloodcurdling screams following them. The bodyguard was still cutting him. She let go of her eyes and covered her ears with her hands, but the sound of his unimaginable agony bled through anyway. Oh Jesus, what had they done to Neveah? Bile rose up her throat. *Not my cousin, please not my cousin…* She couldn't bear the thought of that knife touching Neveah's soft nape, and wanted to scream in anguish.

"Sam. *Sam.*" Ben gave her a shake.

She opened her eyes and looked up at him, still covering her ears. He tugged her hands away and held them tight in his.

His pale green eyes bored into hers. "Breathe,

Sam, just breathe."

She sucked in a ragged breath, realized she was shaking from head to foot. Her teeth chattered. "Jesus," she gasped. "Oh Jesus, Ben..."

"I know." He pulled her into his arms, tucked her face into his shoulder. "Just hold onto me."

Her arms locked around his waist, thinking of that poor victim. Was it over yet? What a horrific way to die. God, his screams. A shudder sped through her muscles.

Ben squeezed her tighter. "Shit, I wish you hadn't seen that."

Yeah. That made two of them. She would never get the sight of that out of her mind. "How can he d-do that?" she whispered. How did a person have the ability to do that to any living thing, let alone another human being?

"No idea, except that he's a sick mother fucker."

"D-do you think Nev—"

"No. She's still okay. We're going to get her out, Sam. Count on it."

She pressed her cheek against his hard chest, seeking more of his reassuring warmth and prayed it was true. She had to believe it was. She couldn't deal with the thought of Nev dying, let alone being murdered like her colleague.

****

When Sam was as settled as he could get her, Ben went back to the CP. Rhys stood outside the entrance.

"Is it over?"

Rhys nodded and gave a hard swallow. "Yeah." His voice was gravelly, and he looked like he was fighting not to puke.

A wave of dread swept through Ben.

Rhys didn't get rattled. Ever. He was calm, level headed, cool under pressure. Always. He'd had to be, since they were kids. The hairier things got, the calmer he became. That's why he'd made Delta in the first place, and why he'd done so well there. But after seeing the video link of the hostage execution in real time, he looked ill.

Ben frowned. "You okay, man?"

"Yeah."

That was Rhys. About as open as the vault at Fort Knox. Ben guessed it was the thought of Neveah going through the agony they'd just seen that was to blame. Rhys hadn't said as much, and he wouldn't admit to it, but she mattered to him on a personal level. That only upped the stakes for everyone involved.

"Anything else I need to know?" Ben asked.

"Yeah. There's more."

Shit, more? He followed his brother back inside to the laptop, ignoring the way Luke and Davis stopped going over their maps to watch him with grim expressions. Rhys started the video again, picking up just as the murder had finished. The victim's headless body lay in a spreading stream of blood. Ben folded his arms across his chest and steeled himself for whatever came next. To his utter revulsion, Assoud bent down and picked up the severed head by the hair with one hand and raised it up for the camera. The victim's sightless eyes were half closed, his mouth still open in a soundless scream.

Ben's skin crawled.

An evil smile spread across Assoud's face, pulling at the scar in the center of his chin. In English he said, "Let's go see what the rest of our guests thought of the performance."

"Oh, shit," Ben breathed, thanking God Sam wasn't here to see this, and held his breath while Assoud stalked toward the back of the room to a crude wooden door. Someone followed him with the camera, catching every second of the grisly footage.

The door creaked open. Assoud flicked on a flashlight, aiming the high-powered beam into the stygian darkness beyond. Its light revealed Neveah huddled against a mud wall on a dirt floor, arms wrapped around herself. Her tormented expression made it obvious she was struggling not to show how terrified she was. The other two hostages, both men in their fifties, were dragging their hands through their unkempt, filthy hair and doing their best to hide the fact they'd been crying despite the tear tracks glistening on their cheeks in the beam of the flashlight.

Assoud's low, oily laugh bubbled up in the quiet. Ben clenched his jaw as Assoud raised that goddamn head up into the light so the hostages could see it. Neveah's horrified cry had Ben squeezing his fists so tight his hands went numb. Beside him, Rhys was stiff as a bronze statue.

Assoud swung the head to and fro, obviously enjoying his audience's reaction. "Would you like to say goodbye to your friend before I toss him down the mountain for the vultures?"

The only answer was Nev's quiet sob.

"No?" Assoud continued. "Then I wish you pleasant dreams. I'll be back again tomorrow for whichever one of you draws the short straw."

Rhys stopped the video, but Ben couldn't look at him. He spun around and headed outside for some air. When he'd calmed down enough, he looked over his shoulder at his brother. Rhys' deep blue eyes were filled with steely resolve. He flicked a glance in Sam's direction. "How is she?"

"Shaken, but not as much as she would have been if she'd seen the rest of it."

"Yeah. Assoud made sure it wasn't a quick death, but the rest..."

Christ. Ben's stomach rolled in response, threatening to bring up the MRE he'd eaten a half hour ago. All he could think about was Sam's reaction and what she'd said about her cousin.

Neveah had to have heard the execution from that filthy room. She must have listened to her doomed colleague's bloodcurdling screams as Assoud sawed the victim's head off.

The timer on the video said his death had taken at least a minute, maybe more. He must have screamed right up until the stroke that severed his spinal cord in the middle of his vertebrae. He must have felt every slice of that knife until then. No way would he have bled out in that amount of time. He'd been conscious and aware of everything right until the end.

Ben rubbed a hand over his own nape, thinking of the anatomy back there. Multiple layers of muscle tissue, tendons galore and a whole wad of tough ligaments to saw through. Christ. He could still hear the sound of that knife slicing, like a butcher carving up a side of beef.

The muscles in his jaw went tight, salivary glands working overtime, flooding his mouth. He swallowed repeatedly, and realized he was seconds away from throwing up for the first time in memory.

Calm down. Take a second. Puking's not going to help anyone.

But Jesus, if they'd done that to a middle-aged man, what the hell would they do to Neveah, a young, five-eleven knock-out? Rape? Torture? The possibilities turned his blood cold as ice water.

After sucking in a few more breaths, Ben glanced over his shoulder at Sam. She was chalky white but watching them anxiously, eyes huge and glittering with tears. Christ, he wished she hadn't seen any of that video. If it had been up to him, he'd never have let her in the cave, let alone watch it along with them.

Gut check time. This was exactly the kind of shit

he and Rhys had trained for, had executed ops and rescues for. Hostage extraction might be Rhys' specialty, but he didn't have his Delta teammates with him now. Out here in the ass end of Afghanistan, they didn't have anything more than the equipment they'd carried in, plus whatever strings Luke could pull, and that would most likely be in the form of chopper extraction, maybe some sort of air support. If they were lucky.

So here they were: a former Ranger with a hothead reputation he'd battled all his life; a former Delta member that was attached to one of the hostages; one out of action former SEAL that should still be in his Basra hospital bed; a CIA spook who Ben had never seen in combat; and a civilian female communications contractor. They were going to take on the ruthless terrorist cell that had just decapitated one of their valuable hostages with a K-Bar knife.

Go, team.

Thinking about what Neveah's death would do to Sam, Ben's eyes burned with rage as he faced his brother. "Tell me we know where they are."

"Wish I could."

His jaw muscles flexed. "Then Luke needs to send Sam home. She can't take this, and it's fucking cruel of him to make her stay here."

Rhys let out a slow breath. "She won't leave. Not unless we get her cousin."

"You think I care if she wants to leave voluntarily or not?" Ben shook his head. "I have no problem tying her up and personally hauling her ass onto the next transport out."

"Luke thinks we need her."

Ben's spine stretched taut. "Fuck him. We already did this with Bryn. You want Sam to go through more of this? Maybe wind up dying out here just because we told her to hang around in case we needed her?"

"Don't underestimate her. She'll do what needs to be done."

"I don't *want* her to hang in there. That's the whole point!" He dragged a hand through his hair. "Dammit."

"At least she'll be with Luke at the CP and not on the op."

Ben threw him a nasty look as he walked past. "Yeah? Well, gee, what the hell am I so worried about?"

Chapter Fourteen

Sam couldn't sleep. She lay on her side, huddled in the fetal position under Ben's bedroll. All alone, because the others were outside discussing their options to give her some privacy.

The wind gusted outside the flap in a mournful, desolate moan. She couldn't get warm. Not since she'd seen that horrific execution. How did one human being do that to another? How did someone have that little humanity to be able to do something so hideous? She shivered, staring at the weave of the blanket in front of her. It was almost dark now. Less than eighteen hours until the next deadline. What if they couldn't pinpoint the cell in time and the bodyguard killed Neveah? Sam didn't know how she would go on if that happened. Death was awful enough in any form, but to be hacked to death like that while you fought and twisted and screamed for mercy…

A tear rolled down her cheek and plopped on the sleeve of her jacket.

The satellite phone beeped next to her head. Wiping her face, she sat up and grabbed it. "Wallace." Her voice sounded surprisingly normal.

"It's Miller."

Her lips thinned. "Guess you heard the news."

"Yeah. We've verified the killer to be Assoud."

No news flash there. "Any idea where they are?"

"I just sent a cable to the Pakistanis. The ISI's going to assist us in locating them so long as we do the dirty work once they find them."

She toyed with the corner of her bivy bag. "What's the…the thoughts on Neveah's chances?" Saying it out loud was hard. "Are they saving her for last?"

"We think so. More bang for their buck that way."

His callous phrasing made her clench her hands into fists. "Is that right."

"Just telling it like it is. She might be your cousin, but you're a CIA employee. You need to take your emotion out of this if you want her to get out safely."

"Don't worry about me and my emotions."

He chuckled. "Hutchinson said you were tougher than you look."

"That's right."

"Then tell me one thing. If it came down to choosing her or one of our guys, who would you save?"

She thought of Ben, and how he might be hurt or killed going in for Neveah once they located her. Sam bit her lip. During the op, she'd be the one watching the satellite feed and directing the team. Would she be able to function if Ben was hit? How would she ever be able to trade one of them for the other and live with herself afterward? But that's what Miller expected her to say, wasn't it. He expected her to go to pieces when tough decisions had to be made. Well, damned if she'd give him the satisfaction of being right.

She gripped the phone until her knuckles ached. "You know what they say. Blood's thicker than water."

"Good to know. Have Luke contact me."

In the midst of hanging up, the flap lifted and Ben's head and shoulders appeared in the opening.

"*Ben.*"

Yanking the cover down behind him, he came

down on his knees in front of her and hauled her right into his arms. She clung to him, face scrunching in her grief, her fear. He didn't say anything, just held her tight and pressed his face against her hair. His strength soothed her a little, his body heat wrapping around her in another kind of hug. She rested her head on his hard shoulder and tried to focus on him, struggling to forget what she'd seen for a little while. He stroked a hand over her back, up and down, offering her the wordless comfort of his embrace. "Who was that?"

"Kabul." She didn't want to discuss it.

He gathered her tighter. "I'm worried about you."

Ben. God, she loved him. She didn't want him going after the animals that had Neveah. She wanted him safe and warm, next to her like this, but back home and far away from anyone that could hurt him.

He kissed her temple, then leaned away for a second. "Brought you something to drink."

She sat up, wiped at her cheeks and waited while he poured something hot into a mug from a thermos. "Tea," she whispered, perilously close to tears again. He pressed the cup into her hand, wrapped her chilly fingers around it.

The feelings in her chest were too full to be contained anymore. The timing sucked. It was all wrong—Neveah being held captive, the rest of them hunting through the tribal region of Afghanistan, racing against the clock. It didn't seem to matter to her heart, though. The video had given her a pointed reminder of just how capricious and cruel death could be. How fleeting life was.

She gazed up at Ben through tear-blurred eyes and put her hand against his handsome, bearded face. This was the least romantic place she could think of, but she couldn't help how she felt and wanted to say it out loud in case she never got another chance. She blew out a ragged breath and took the plunge. “I really love you, Ben.”

Even in the dimness, she saw the shock on his face. She winced inwardly. Not the reaction she’d hoped for. “Sorry. I’m not trying to put you on the spot, but I didn’t want to keep it to myself anymore. You know, in case something goes wrong out here.”

Ben took her face between his broad palms and held her gaze in the half-light. “Damn, honey, you sure know how to yank the rug out from under a guy’s feet.” He leaned his forehead against hers. “You know I care about you, Sam.”

She couldn’t take his rejection right now. “It’s all right—I don’t need you to explain. I just had to say it.” To spare them any more awkwardness, she leaned up and kissed him, showing him how she felt instead. He wrapped her even closer, opened her lips and stole into her mouth with his tongue. She melted.

At least he wanted her. That was something for her to hold on to.

He broke the kiss and pulled back, rubbing his hands over her arms. “You’re freezing, aren’t you? Come here.” He undid his jacket, lay beside her and pulled the sleeping bag over them. Then he tucked her into the warm curve of his body and closed his jacket around her. “Better?”

She wiggled closer with a sigh. “Much.”

The wind buffeted the flap and rattled the fasteners. She soaked up the comfort of his warmth and strength surrounding her, savoring every point of contact between them.

He kissed her forehead. “Sleep for a while, sweetheart.”

“Okay,” she said to placate him. No way was she going to be able to sleep. Not when she saw the knife sawing through that man’s neck every time she shut her eyes. Pain lanced through her when she thought of Miller's question about who she would save. Would she have to decide between her cousin and Ben? Sam didn't know how she would live with herself if she was forced to make that choice.

****

The next day everyone was quiet and grim as they went about their business. Ben kept a watchful eye on Sam, who was working on less than four hours of interrupted sleep.

Through the night she'd woken up several times from nightmares, but being in the cave with his brother and Luke didn't give him the privacy to offer any other way to comfort her than curling around her in his sleeping bag. She'd turned into him without a word, and he hadn't spoken because he didn't want to embarrass her by drawing attention to the fact she was afraid, even though he knew Rhys would have pretended to be fast asleep. Instead, his twin had thoughtfully moved closer to her on the other side so she was sandwiched snug between them. Ben hoped that had given her some measure of comfort.

Watching her now, her face pale and pinched from the strain she was under, Ben was powerless to lessen the burden for her and he hated it. He crossed the cave and knelt beside her. She didn't look up at him, but he hadn't expected her to while she was in work mode. "See anything?"

He raised a hand to stroke the back of her head. Her hair was shiny and clean from the dry shampoo she'd brought along, her need for cleanliness and order just as strong out here in the field.

"Nothing." Her voice rang with frustration. "Davis is sending in all these coordinates, and not one of them has turned up anything."

Yeah, well, the odds of finding the hostages in these mountains were nil without some kind of tip from the locals. "If anyone can find them, Luke and Davis can."

Sam pressed her lips together, still staring at her screen. After a moment she said, "But will it be in time?"

That was the kicker, wasn't it?

"Ben."

He looked over his shoulder at Luke, standing in the entrance.

"We're meeting Karim at eleven hundred."

He gave Sam's shoulder a squeeze and climbed to his feet. "Be back in a few."

Her eyes swung up to his, shadowed with worry. "Be careful."

"I will." He gathered his gear and followed Luke.

They hiked down to the edge of the valley where Karim's village lay and waited in the shade of a small copse of trees for the kid to appear. He showed up alone within ten minutes of their arrival and spoke with Luke for a few minutes in Pashto while Ben kept watch, then took his payment of chocolate and medicine and left for home. He scampered down the trail into the valley with the sure-footedness of one of his goats. Ben watched him go, wondering how reliable the intel they got from him was. Kid seemed earnest enough, but his village couldn't want him helping Americans, even with Luke's ties to one of its elders. When Karim reached the valley floor, he and Luke started back to the command post.

"Someone in the village had heard about captives being held high up in the mountains in an abandoned fort used during the war with the Russians," Luke said. "He gave a fairly detailed description of the area from the warlord, so we'll see what Sam can find using the satellite."

Ben prayed this was the break they'd been waiting for. Time was running out, and they had nothing to go on yet. It frustrated the hell out of him, not only because he wanted to get the hostages out and nail Tehrazzi, but because each day that passed without finding the location was killing Sam.

He paused to let Luke climb up a steep incline, and didn't like what he was seeing. His boss was moving unusually slowly. When he stopped at the top to rest, Ben ran his medic's eye over him and noted the lines of pain bracketing his mouth under the beard. "You okay, man?"

"Fine."

He wasn't fine. "Head bothering you?"

"I'm good."

He wished they weren't wearing shades so he could see Luke's eyes. They would tell him things their owner wasn't willing to. "If it keeps up, let me know so I can give you something." Like an assessment and something to combat the symptoms so he could function at an optimal level.

Luke ignored the comment and pushed past. Ben withheld his sigh and followed, knowing damned well the guy was hurting from the diminished pace he kept. By the time they reached the cave in mid-afternoon, only a few hours remained until the next deadline. Sam was still at her station, but Rhys was hunkered beside her with an arm around her shoulders. He looked up when they entered, and Ben's heart sank at the grave expression on his twin's face.

"What's happened?" he demanded, going straight to her and pulling her into his chest.

She pushed away and turned the screen so he could see it. "Tehrazzi just sent me this."

The name started a slow burn on Ben's temper. He read the encrypted e-mail file she'd opened. *Time grows short. You alone can save the others. Give me your teammates and I will release the hostages. Their lives are in your hands.*

"Bastard," he snarled and motioned to Luke. He

came over and read it, his expression inscrutable.

"Want me to ignore it?" Sam asked in a ragged voice. Ben rubbed her back. She couldn't take this much longer. He was surprised she'd held out this long after everything she'd gone through.

"Yeah," Luke answered. "Don't let him mess with your head."

Too late for that, Ben thought with a pang of dread as Luke walked away. Sam had to be right on the edge. Tehrazzi piling that kind of responsibility on her was beyond cruel. Ben would have done anything to take that weight from her shoulders.

"Got some new intel from the village," Luke said, and gave her the coordinates.

If he'd meant it as a distraction, it worked. In the blink of an eye she was back in work mode, but Ben worried about how much longer she was going to be able to bury all the stress and fear before it shut her down. Or gave her an ulcer. He stayed next to her while she diligently searched the area, but nothing came up. Another dead end, and the clock was ticking.

The remaining time passed without any new intelligence on the hostages' location, and as the second deadline approached, the tension in the cave mounted perceptibly. He and Rhys were fiddling with a couple of headsets when Sam started getting twitchy. She left her computer and emptied her backpack, folding and re-organizing its contents to kill time. Then she got up and started pacing. Ben tried to think of something to say that might take her mind off what they all knew was coming.

"Sam—"

A sharp shake of her head told him she wanted to be left alone. He did, but only because he didn't know what else to do for her. And when the laptop sitting next to him chimed with an incoming e-mail, everyone's gaze flew to it. Ben's whole body clenched as he read the sender's name. The hostage takers. He turned his head to look at Sam, and the instant their eyes met she whirled and left the cave.

He didn't go after her. He was glad she wasn't going to see what was on the video. Once was more than anyone should have to witness.

Rhys nudged his shoulder. "As soon as we're done here, Luke and I'll leave so you two can have some privacy," he said quietly. "I think she's gonna need some after this."

They both were. "Thanks, man."

Luke came up beside them. "Let's get this over with," he muttered.

Ben didn't want to see the second hostage get hacked to death, but it had to be done. Sick to his stomach, he opened the video file and hit play.

****

Hostage location, late evening

The air was clear and cold as the snow began to fall. Like a natural purification, which was fitting considering what had just happened on this desolate mountaintop.

After disposing of the headless body and changing his bloodstained clothes, Tehrazzi's bodyguard knelt on his prayer mat next to him for evening prayers. In unison, they leaned forward to touch their foreheads to the soft nap of the carpet to give proper respect. Thanking Allah for His grace and mercy, Tehrazzi rose and returned to the relative warmth of the hut. Inside, Assoud strode past him. Tehrazzi hid a sneer of contempt, knowing Assoud wanted to see the remaining two hostages and witness their terror of him and his knife before he ate his supper. Assoud pushed open the door at the rear of the hut and Tehrazzi braced himself against the stench of foul waste coming from inside.

The hostages sat still against the far wall,

blinking their squinted eyes as the light hit them. The place smelled worse than a sewer, far worse than the hellhole Assoud had been thrown into at Guantanamo could ever have.

From his position outside the door, Tehrazzi studied the interaction between Assoud and the hostages carefully. The American man kept his head down, afraid to look upon him, but not the woman. Her eyes met Assoud's squarely, and her bravery surprised Tehrazzi. She *wanted* Assoud to see the hatred and rage burning there.

"Take that bucket outside," Assoud snapped to her. Her defiant expression remained. Assoud let his hand settle on the hilt of his knife. Her eyes followed, and Tehrazzi caught her involuntary swallow.

"Now."

She got up and did as Assoud had told her, and when she returned he gave her a shove that sent her sprawling before slamming the door shut.

Returning to his place with the others, Assoud resumed his evening meal, and set his plate of rice and mutton down when Tehrazzi stared at him. "What?"

Tehrazzi glanced past him to the others, then back. Assoud's light brown eyes regarded him shrewdly. "I see you still have your appetite."

His bodyguard grinned as though he'd just received the highest compliment. "Less than eighteen hours until the next deadline. Shall I kill the man or the woman next?"

Tehrazzi's mouth thinned in distaste. "Are you so eager to destroy the only currency we have to bargain with the Americans?"

Assoud's lip curled. "We do not bargain with unbelievers."

No, they did not. But using the hostages as a ruse to attract his teacher was their goal. If things kept going as they were, Assoud would ruin everything. Over the past few years his bodyguard had built a reputation of ruthlessness that sent shivers down people's backbones. He'd already become a rich man because Tehrazzi paid him well for his services. No one dared to cross them because they feared reprisal from Assoud's knife.

"You have fed them?" Tehrazzi asked.

"Of course. We need them alive for me to kill them."

For the time being. Within a day one of them would be dead anyway. A kindness, really. They were both ill with a foul bowel disorder, their weak American bodies unable to tolerate the food and water they were given. Left alive, the sickness would eventually kill them both. Either way, they were both going to die. It was Allah's will. A punishment for their wickedness. Still, something had to be done about Assoud's unquenchable bloodlust.

"The woman will be the last, and not harmed until I give the order. Now, walk with me."

Assoud paused at the unusual request. "Now?"

"Now."

Assoud glanced at his knife sheath, sitting on the table where he'd left it after honing the edge.

Tehrazzi gestured to the other around his waist. "Leave that here."

Assoud's hands tightened into fists. After a moment, he unstrapped the sheath from his belt and laid it on the table. He gave him a hard smile. "Better?"

Much. "Let's go."

Assoud followed him outside into the darkness.

Tehrazzi thought of that favorite knife back on the table. Not that Assoud needed it to kill him if he wished. He could do it easily enough with his bare hands.

"Where are we going?"

The note of suspicion in his voice pleased Tehrazzi. "I wish to speak with you where no one else can hear."

Their feet made swishing sounds in the thin layer of snow as they moved away from the hut at the edge of the deserted village and up the slope of the ridge overlooking the valley. Assoud kept glancing around them and behind them as though he expected to find snipers hidden amongst the boulders. He might be a danger to the operation, but he was not stupid.

Not a sound broke the stillness as they ascended the hillside. Halfway up, Tehrazzi slipped on some loose gravel and lurched down to steady himself with his hands. When he glanced back, Assoud's gaze had fixed on his ankle, positioned inches in front of his hand. Tehrazzi read the intention there. One tug. That's all it would take. One hard pull, and Assoud could send him down the rocky slope to smash against the boulders below.

No one would see. It would look like an accident.

Tehrazzi froze in place, waiting to see what he would do, using Assoud's distraction to retrieve the pistol hidden beneath his vest.

The fingers of Assoud's right hand flexed. He stretched out his arm. Brought it so close Tehrazzi could feel the warmth of his palm against his skin.

Their gazes locked. A heartbeat passed. Then two. Tehrazzi let him see that there was no fear in him, no realization of Assoud's intention as he stared back. Just eerie stillness and a building rage.

Perhaps something in his eyes held Assoud back, because he withdrew his arm and made it look as though he'd been about to offer a supporting hand. Tehrazzi concealed his weapon, and they resumed their climb.

Once they reached the top, they both stood breathing heavily. In the darkness, the valley spread out before them, a vast sea of snow-covered dust and rock. Barren. Desolate. A faint breeze picked up, swirling snow up around their legs. Nothing moved on the hillside below them. No sound disturbed the silence except their mingled breathing and the thudding of Tehrazzi's heart as he prepared to do what must be done. Assoud had sealed his fate long before what had just passed between them on the mountain.

"You should have killed me when you had the chance."

Assoud whipped his head around, eyes widening when he saw the nine-millimeter SIG Sauer aimed at his head. "No—"

"You have become too unstable, too unpredictable, and I no longer trust that you will wait for my orders to kill the woman. I cannot have you jeopardizing my operations."

Assoud pulled his lips back in a sneer. "You are weak," he spat. "I should have gone after Hutchinson myself."

"You would have failed. My teacher is far more lethal than you will ever be."

He laughed bitterly. "You think you can kill him yourself? That you can do away with me, and him, when you couldn't kill any of the others?"

"Yes."

"You *need* me."

"Not anymore."

Tehrazzi watched the knowledge of impending death dawn in his victim's eyes. His bodyguard must die, and he had to do the killing. It was his responsibility. Like a farmer putting a favorite herding dog down because he'd gone rabid.

He curled the fingers of his right hand tight around the grip of the automatic pistol and maintained his aim, precisely in the center of his former bodyguard's forehead. Through the falling snowflakes, an expression of disbelief entered Assoud's eyes, a mere flicker in the black pits. Tehrazzi's index finger tightened around the trigger.

Assoud pivoted to flee.

Tracking him with the pistol, Tehrazzi held steady when Assoud gathered himself and leapt to his left. He caught only the blur of movement as Assoud's arm shot upward, felt the slight whir in the air and instinctively ducked as he pulled the trigger. A sharp crack rent the air. As the gun retracted in Tehrazzi's hand and the barrel recoiled, something hit him hard in the belly. It drove deep with a blaze of fire.

Pain arced through his organs. He gasped and hit the ground with his knees, doubling over. His hands came to rest on something protruding from his abdomen. His eyes traveled down his chest to the black knife handle sticking out of him. A wash of scarlet stained his once-white robes. The pain was hot and vicious, stealing his breath. He raised his head.

Assoud was struggling to his feet, cradling his right shoulder. The fingers of his left hand were stained with blood, dripping from the bullet wound to the snow beneath him. Their eyes locked. Assoud coiled to strike, springing forward with his powerful legs to dive at him. Tehrazzi clenched his hand—

The gun was gone.

He glanced down. There. Beside his foot. He pushed past the agony to bend and snatch it up, gritting his teeth against a cry of rage and pain. He raised it. Pulled the trigger an instant before Assoud's weight smashed into him, sending him flying backward. The impact of their bodies drove the knife deeper still. Tehrazzi screamed and grabbed at the blade, wanting to yank it out, but even through his suffering his will stopped him. If he pulled it, he would hemorrhage and die. His only chance was to leave it in, no matter if it felt as though a flaming torch was thrust into his insides, and find medical help. But to survive, he must kill Assoud first.

Sending up a prayer, he forced himself to go limp as the heavy weight lifted off him, hoping for that one instant of hesitation in his opponent to think he might be dead or unconscious. Then he would strike to kill.

Assoud's breathing was choppy when he pulled back. A mix of warm, iron-tinged blood and bitter cordite filled the cold mountain air. Scents from Tehrazzi's childhood in these same mountains another lifetime ago.

"You are dying," Assoud sneered, boots scraping on the rocks as he climbed to his feet. Tehrazzi slit his eyes open to stare up at the man towering over him. "I know where the Americans are, and while I hunt and kill them, you will lie here and bleed on the soil of your precious ancestors knowing Allah has chosen *me*." He raised his foot.

The sole of the black boot poised over Tehrazzi's wrist, inches from the still-loaded pistol. Like the braggart he was, Assoud waited a moment to savor what he considered to be his victory.

Tehrazzi let his eyes open, showing his contempt as he met that hateful smirk, then snatched the gun in his cold fingers and jerked it up for the killing shot. He fired as the boot hurtled down at his wrist. The shot exploded.

Assoud screamed, his body arcing backward, giving Tehrazzi enough time to struggle to his knees and level another shot. But his victim rolled and flipped to his feet, bleeding from the side of his head where most of his left ear was missing. He shook his head like a wet dog, spraying blood, and charged at him.

Before he could get another shot off, Assoud hit

him in the chest with a well-aimed kick that sent him tumbling down, skidding across the slippery bits of shale toward the edge of the precipice. Tehrazzi threw out a hand and caught the edge of a boulder to stop his momentum. The pain in his abdomen was making him light-headed. He could barely feel his lower body now. Already he was beginning to notice the chill of blood loss.

He might be dying, but he was not going to let Assoud live. Gathering his waning strength, he braced himself for the next blow, fighting to bring his arm up to fire another shot.

Assoud roared and kicked him again, catching him in the shoulder. Tehrazzi spun toward the edge. God would not forsake him. “Allah-u-aqbar,” he whispered hoarsely, twisting as he fell. *God is great.*

Aimed at his killer’s heart, the gun went off, kicking in Tehrazzi’s hand as he fell over the edge into oblivion.

****

Back at the command post, Sam jerked awake in complete darkness with her heart tripping. She was surprised she’d fallen asleep at all, but what had woken her?

Strong arms tightened around her ribs.

Ben.

“‘S only the wind,” he murmured, tucking her in close.

She stared toward the flap at the cave’s mouth, willing her heart to slow down. *I’m safe. Ben’s got me.* She pulled in a deep breath of cool air. God, he felt fantastic up against her like this—her own blast furnace against the cold. He’d zipped their sleeping bags together when he’d crawled in beside her sometime after midnight, and hadn’t let her go since.

What time was it? It wasn’t pitch black anymore. They were alone, so the others must still be out doing more surveillance. The faint impression of light came in through the edges of the blanket at the cave's entrance. Had to be close to dawn. That gave her only a couple of hours at most to be alone with Ben. Or to see him at all, if they found the hostage location.

Because he might not come back from the op.

Stop. It. Sam squeezed her eyes shut, desperate to keep that voice in her head quiet. Her ears perked up, trying to make out anything other than the wind. Was anyone out there?

Then Ben started nuzzling the back of her neck and she was glad. She needed the distraction, anything to keep her from thinking about her cousin and the murders.

Against her nape, Ben's lips were warm and soft, moving so slowly she forgot everything else. Her eyes drifted closed, all her attention now focused on the feel of his lips trailing over her skin, leaving goose bumps. She wanted him, and it didn't matter they were in a cave out in the middle of hostile enemy territory in the tribal region of Afghanistan. It didn't matter if he hadn't said "I love you." Didn't even matter that the others might be close by. All that mattered was that Ben was safe lying wrapped around her and he wanted her.

He shifted his hips closer, pressing the rock hard length of his morning arousal against her buttocks. She pushed back with a sigh, already melting inside. With a little hum she tipped her head back, giving him better access to the side of her throat, rolling a bit so the hand he had tucked under her ribcage could come up to cradle her breast through the jacket. She squirmed, trying to get closer to that hand.

Answering her unspoken demand, Ben pulled the sleeping bag up higher to shield them from the cold air and slid his hand under the bottom of her jacket, beneath the sweater and Gore-Tex underwear layers to her bare skin. His fingertips smoothed over her stomach to her waist, traced up her spine and then back down, over the rise of her hip and thigh, slid down to her knee and back up the inside of her legs, brushing between them for an instant before stealing underneath her jacket again. God, he knew exactly how to touch her. She moved and stretched like a pampered kitten, eating up the trails of heat his fingers left behind, basking in the care he took to arouse her so thoroughly.

So slowly she had to bite her lip to keep from moaning, he eased his hand up until the pads of his fingers brushed the lower slope of her left breast, toying there a minute before lightly skimming up over her distended nipple. She sucked in a quick gasp, the heat of arousal pounding through her. She wanted him inside her, as deep as she could get him. But when she tried to roll to face him, he threw a leg over hers and tightened his arm, pinning her in place.

"Like this," he whispered against her shoulder. "Want to hold you like this."

He could do whatever he wanted with her. She sighed and stretched out, enjoying his languorous exploration too much to argue. She loved being spooned up in the cradle of his body, loved lying here enjoying herself while he lavished pleasure on her. She only wished it could be happening in her bed back home in Virginia.

Ben's knowing fingers swept over her nipple, gently squeezed and tugged until she groaned and pushed back, begging for more. He nipped a tendon at the back of her neck. "Shh. Sound carries a long way up here." He began rubbing his hips against her in a slow rhythm calibrated to make her crazy.

Sam reached around and dug her fingers into his ass. "Stop teasing," she whispered, breath uneven.

"Haven't even started, sweetheart." To prove it, he removed his leg and used it to push her top one forward, sliding all the way forward until his erection pressed between her cheeks and his thigh was snuggled against her throbbing core. Her breath fragmented, but she remained still, dying to know what he'd do next.

The hand toying with her sensitized nipple left despite her moan of protest and ventured down her stomach to the waistband of her pants. She went to undo the fastening but he pushed her hand away and made leisurely work of getting the button undone and the zipper down. His fingers dipped low over her abdomen and brushed over her panties. Her legs parted eagerly but he ignored that too, and pulled her cargo pants and underwear down over her hips and thighs, leaving them wadded at her knees. Then she felt him moving behind her, undoing his own pants, shoving them down, heard the sound of a condom wrapper being torn open.

Oh, thank *God*...

The stroke of his fingers over her bare hip made her breath catch. They moved up to the top and down over the flat plane of her pelvic cradle, into the tangle of hair between her legs. She was so wet already, she wanted him inside her *now*. She grabbed for him but he held her in place with a low sound of negation. Sam huffed out an impatient breath. He chuckled against her hair.

"Slow this time," he whispered. "So slow..." As his fingers played with her, touching her everywhere but where she needed it most, she couldn't help but writhe and whimper in his grasp. Finally, he stroked gently over her throbbing flesh and she bit back a cry, spine arching, slick and desperate for him. Ben hummed in approval and kept caressing, his erection hot against her naked buttocks.

Just when she thought she'd go mad, he fitted

himself against her. She groaned in relief and pressed backward, only to have him stop her with a firm hold on her hip. He pushed the head of himself in and stayed there, fingers searching out her damp heat. Gasping, she wiggled back, trying to push him deeper. He wouldn't budge as he nuzzled her nape, then pressed a warm, tender kiss there. She swallowed, trembling in his arms, ready to beg.

"Give me control, Sam." His voice was yet another layer of sensation on her body, a velvet caress on hypersensitive nerve endings. "Let me make it good for you."

Good? Already way past good—she was half-crazy. Her breath came on a pant and left in a shivery wheeze as she clung to her control, trying not to cry out so everyone in the camp could hear. Then he pulled out, and she couldn't stop the whimper of distress that tore out of her, or the way she grabbed at him.

In reply he pushed forward again, lodging the head inside her and then retreating, pulling almost all the way out before sliding back in. Over and over, and all the while his fingers swirled over her most sensitive spot. Sam gripped the fistfuls of sleeping bag she held, fighting to move toward him, shove him further inside, but the pants tangled around her legs kept her immobile, restricting her movement. She could barely manage a wiggle, let alone part her legs like she needed to.

In and out, in and out Ben slid in a lazy rhythm, his fingers moving patiently, the other hand slipping around from beneath her to steal under her jacket and go after her right breast and nipple.

Oh God, too much. She couldn't bear it.

"Ben..." It came out a strangled whimper, loud in the charged silence.

"Mmm... Good?"

His deep murmur, on top of everything he was

doing, made her eyes roll to the back of her head. Her whole body shivered, the orgasm already building, sensations growing more intense with each shallow thrust. He still wouldn't speed up.

Mindless, she grabbed his thick forearm. His corded muscles moved under her fingers as he caressed her. "God, Ben, please..."

With a low purr, he pressed his hips and belly tighter to her, then thrust a little deeper before pulling almost out. Again. Again. Four...five...six times. Her thighs started shaking, her body straining to clamp down around the hard length stealing inside her, needing the release he was making her work so hard for.

He wouldn't give it to her, though, just kept up with the gentle, shallow thrusts and the caressing until she ground the back of her head against his collarbone with a feral cry. The nipple he was tormenting sent streamers of sensation down to where he was touching between her legs and moving inside her. Erotic overload hit. The orgasm hovered maddeningly just out of reach, and she jerked her hips in desperation, biting down on her lips to keep the scream of pleasure in her throat.

Ben's mouth found another sensitive spot on her neck and sucked gently. "Shh. Enjoy, sweetheart." He picked up his rhythm, thrust faster until his strokes became a continual barrage of erotic friction. His touch on her breast and between her thighs remained slow and steady. Too much. Clapping her hand over her mouth to stifle her scream, the orgasm slammed into her, making her come so hard her eyes teared up. As the pulses tore through her, Ben moaned against the side of her neck and shoved deep, sending her up on another wave as he joined her with a deep growl, his arms locking around her.

Crashing back to earth, her head hit the bedroll like it weighed as much as a boulder. She was panting, sweating, gasping for air, too weak to even open her eyes. Behind her, Ben's sigh of deep satisfaction had a weary smile stretching her lips. He pressed a kiss to the top of her head and withdrew from inside her, but kept her cradled tight against him as he wrapped her back up in his arms. Strong, protective and caring arms, even if he didn't love her.

"Go back to sleep," he murmured drowsily.

Too exhausted not to, she dropped her heavy lids and let sleep wash over her in a dark wave.

Chapter Fifteen

When Sam awoke next, Ben was gone and the cave was quiet. Since the light slanted in through the flap from high above her, it had to be close to noon. How had she slept so late? Swearing, she whipped back the top of the sleeping bag and grabbed her boots, turning them over and banging them in case any spiders or scorpions had somehow found their way inside. She shoved them on her feet, yanked her hair back into a ponytail, and stumbled from the tent, rubbing the sleep from her eyes. The air had a nip to it. The sky was clouding over, thin veils trying to obscure the sun. She glanced around. The site was empty. Why hadn't anyone woken her?

As she rushed out of the cave, she spotted a piece of paper wedged under a rock and a thermos sitting next to it. She sighed. *Ben*...She turned the note over.

Hey sleeping beauty. Guess I must have worn you out. Have some tea, then drag your lazy butt over to the CP so we can get some work done.

Suppressing a grin, she uncapped the thermos and poured herself a cup of the steaming tea, touched by his thoughtfulness. She drank two cupfuls and wolfed down a Power Bar, then washed her face and brushed her teeth with some bottled water and headed to the lean-to tucked into the face of the hill.

From a few dozen yards away she made out the male voices rumbling from inside. Pushing open the flap, she found Ben and Rhys studying some maps laid out on the folding table. They looked up at her when she entered. "Morning. Sorry I slept so late." She smiled at Ben, heart doing crazy acrobatics. "Thanks for the tea. I appreciate it."

His warm gaze brushed over her. "Figured you could use the caffeine."

To help disguise the blush in her cheeks, she nodded to the map. "Any new intel?"

"Yeah. Luke just got word from Karim about a remote camp in the hills about thirty miles from here."

Hope and adrenaline surged through her. "Is it Nev?"

"Davis is digging around."

"Is he telling the truth, or has someone turned him?"

"We'll know soon enough."

A second later, Luke walked in behind her, talking on a headset using the satellite phone, speaking in rapid Pashto. He went straight to the laptop in the corner, pulled something up on the screen, and bent to write on a pad of paper he pulled out of his pocket. She tilted her head to read it. *Yes.* Coordinates. She watched him, grasping only a word or two of what he was saying. House, maybe dwelling. Foreigners. Her fingernails dug into her palms. Was it them? Close now. They had to be close.

Luke disconnected and met her eyes. "I need a satellite image of these coordinates."

She took his place and brought up the link, entered the longitude and latitude positions. A few seconds later an image came on the screen. A cluster of rocks in the midst of a parched wasteland. Her heart sank. She'd been expecting a village or compound of some sort.

"Zoom in here," he said, pointing at the cluster of rocks in the corner.

She did, increasing the resolution and tightening the focus. Blurry images became clear. Huts and the ruins of huts. Men walking around. She went in closer. Armed men, dressed in Pashtun clothing. Sam searched around for any sign of her cousin.

"This it?" Ben asked, jaw working his gum.

Luke studied it a moment longer. "Looks like."

Sam's eyes went to the largest hut, sandwiched in the center. Her heart drummed in her ears. Nev was in there. Had to be. Staring a hole in the screen, hot tears scalded her eyes.

Ben slid a hand under her hair and squeezed the back of her neck. "All right?" he whispered.

She nodded and pressed her lips together, unable to look away. She wasn't a violent person, but if she'd been able to fire a missile at those bastards she wouldn't have hesitated. The hatred rose up in a thick cloud that threatened to choke her. She wanted them all to die for what they'd done. Every last one of them.

The pressure against her nape increased. "Take a breath, Sam."

She let out a shaky exhalation, had to get up and walk away for a moment.

Luke spoke. "Let's do regular headcounts and make sure we know what we're going up against."

"Tonight, then?"

Ben's question made her go rigid. They'd be going out in the dark after all those soldiers on the screen. Just the four of them. She cleared her throat and found her voice. "AWACS imaging is calling for snow this afternoon and overnight. Could get up to six inches."

"It's gotta be tonight," Luke said firmly. "Third deadline's in a few hours. I'm sure the other hostage would appreciate it if we went in before then."

God, if that wasn't the understatement of the

year. She rubbed her damp palms against her pants. Ben was going out there to get her cousin in a few hours. Her eyes swept over him, loving every detail. If something went wrong and he was injured, or… A lump wedged in her throat.

As though sensing her gaze, he turned his head, offering a smile. She couldn't have smiled back at him for anything.

"Hey, don't look at me like that." Ben came over and gathered her up for a hug.

She choked back a sob and wrapped her arms around his back, squeezing as tight as she could.

He pressed his cheek against her hair. "We know what we're doing. And they won't know we're coming."

She nodded.

He tilted her chin up with one finger. "We'll go in hard and fast. It'll be over before you know it, and you'll be in contact with us the whole time."

"That's just it. I don't know if I can do my job this time."

"Sure you can," he said, steering her away from the others so they could have a little privacy. "You're a pro, Sam."

Outside, the clouds were thickening and the air was noticeably colder than it had been. Their breath misted from the chill in vaporous puffs.

"With us and your cousin out there, are you kidding? You'll be at the top of your game. You're too anal to accept anything less."

That forced a watery laugh out of her. "Yeah. See? My anal retentiveness does come in handy sometimes."

"In this instance, yes, but the rest of the time? You gotta loosen up." He waggled his eyebrows. "Stick with me, sweets. I'll teach you how."

She played along, if for no other reason than to support his effort at lifting her spirits. "Could take a long time. Years, maybe forever."

His eyes gleamed. "I got time. Maybe you haven't noticed, but I can be pretty determined when it comes to getting something I want."

"I did notice that." She laid her palm against his scruffy cheek. He turned his lips into it before leaning into her touch. Her heart clenched, full to overflowing. "Be extra careful out there."

"Yes, dear."

"Don't joke about this. I can't even hypothetically think about something happening to you."

"Good, because worrying isn't going to help any of us."

Unfortunately, that was one of the few things she wasn't going to be able to control about herself.

From behind them Luke cleared his throat, and she pulled away from Ben.

"Davis is coming back in. All intel says we've got the right place. Briefing's in five."

Grappling to get herself under control and back into work mode, Sam lifted Ben's hand and kissed the back of it on her way past him. He was right. Worrying wouldn't help. She had to be professional, more now than ever before.

And if she had to make a tough call along the way, well... She'd just have to deal with that when the time came.

Chapter Sixteen

Near hostage location, late evening

He heard voices nearby. Disjointed at first, then clearer over the pounding in his ears. Gasping in shallow breaths, Tehrazzi fought to open his eyes. He was still alive. But how could that be? His hand moved painfully to his belly where the knife remained embedded deep in his flesh. The burn was hideous. All consuming. He forced it to the edge of his consciousness.

When he glanced around in the dimness, he discovered he was on a shallow ledge a few meters below the edge where he'd fallen. His teeth chattered in the cold. He tried to sit up, had to use his legs to push himself into a semi-reclining position against a rock. Its cold edge dug into his back. The voices drew nearer, coming closer as though they knew he was there.

"He fell there, where the blood is," a man said.

The other murmured something he could not decipher. Were they speaking of him, or Assoud? His gaze climbed up the side of the cliff. Had he killed Assoud? He'd shot him in the chest.

"Wait," one of them said. "I saw something." Scuffling footsteps. Then, louder, "Can you hear me?"

He closed his eyes, took a deep breath. "Yes," he called softly, not wanting to raise his voice because the added pressure would make him bleed faster. He might still die. These people were his only chance.

A minute later, two grizzled faces peered in at him. One of the white-bearded men swept his hat off, and Tehrazzi recognized him as the elder from one of the nearby villages he sponsored.

"Allah be praised, you are alive."

The two men lifted him and carried him down the mountain while he ground his teeth together to keep from screaming as the wicked blade shifted with each step they made. He lost consciousness partway down and woke to find himself on a litter nearing the village walls.

They rushed him into one of the huts that reeked of piss and goat dung and summoned a doctor, a man his own age who was visiting from Jalalabad. He examined the wounds and proclaimed they should get him to a hospital where he could operate. That could not happen. Tehrazzi could not leave while his teacher was so close.

"Is it mortal?" he gritted, sweating as he fought to keep the pain at bay, gripping the bloodstained folds of his robes in white-knuckled hands.

"I do not know." The doctor probed at the knife, muttered to himself.

White-hot pain shot through Tehrazzi's belly. He faded a bit, but came to when he overheard a snippet of conversation in the room.

"It is said the bodyguard is hunting for the Americans."

Tehrazzi's whole body tensed. Assoud was alive?

"One of the boys saw him limping down the mountain. He questioned him about their location."

He licked his dry lips. "The boy…"

The man jumped, staring at him with wide eyes. Had they thought he was dead?

It hurt to speak. "Does he…know where they are?"

"Yes," one of the men answered. "Karim said the wounded man is going there tonight."

To kill his teacher. Unacceptable. A tide of anger rose from his racing heart. "Bring the boy to me. He must take me there immediately."

The man patted his shoulder. "You cannot go tonight, nor for a very many nights."

But he must. It was Allah's will. He glanced down at the knife hilt, then back to the doctor. He couldn't go anywhere with the blade embedded in his gut. "Can you remove it?"

The physician met his eyes. "Perhaps. But it has perforated your bowel. You could bleed to death before I was able to sew you up, and even if you didn't you'll likely develop a serious infection."

Tehrazzi had to get to the Americans before Assoud did. *He* must be the one to finish it. "So be it."

****

Back at the command post, Sam used the time before the briefing to check and recheck her equipment, making note of which satellites she could access and for how long they would be able to transmit images.

Beyond the cave's shelter, snowflakes began to drift down from the leaden sky. They seemed to dance in the air as they fell, scattering over the ground in fluffy white tufts.

Footfalls outside alerted her that Davis had returned for the briefing. He greeted her and went straight to where Luke had set everything up, his nose and cheeks pink from the cold. Ben came over to help her up and brought her over with a steely arm draped across her shoulders, completely uncaring that the action announced the claim he'd stamped on her. It warmed her to her toes.

When they'd all gathered around him, Luke stared at the operations area map he'd prepared. "Okay, y'all, let's get down to business," he announced. "First things first, I'm gonna have to sit this one out."

Total silence met his words. They all gawked at him. Unease rippled over Sam's skin. Something had to be very, very wrong for him to stay behind. She looked at Ben, but he seemed as surprised as she was.

Luke tapped his thumb against the LZ he'd marked on a small plateau east of the hostage location and pointedly avoided everyone's gaze. "I think it's best for all of us if I stay here and help Sam with the coms."

A cold knot twisted in her belly. Was it his health, or was he staying because he didn't trust her on her own? Did he suspect something?

"Everyone else will execute the operation as discussed, with Rhys as leader since he has the most experience with hostage extractions." Without pausing, he outlined the logistics for the raid, established contingency plans, alternative LZs and extraction points. He went over entry points and what level of resistance to expect. "Could be as many as two dozen militants guarding the location," he finished, then raised his eyes and gazed around their circle. "Questions?"

Yes, she had a few. "I don't need you to stay behind. I can take care of this myself." She knew what she was doing, and didn't need a babysitter. If having Luke at the hostage site guaranteed Nev's safety, then she wanted him to be there.

"I know, but that's how it's going to be."

She bit the inside of her cheek to keep from saying something she might regret later. When no one else had anything further to add, the boys geared up and got ready to move.

Outside, the sky was nearly dark now. The snow was already a few inches deep and the battery-powered lamp inside the cave showed the large flakes falling thick and fast. Sam wrapped her arms around herself and suppressed a shiver. When they inserted from the chopper, they'd leave tracks a blind man could follow.

Following her gaze, Ben walked up and slid his arms around her waist from behind, gazing out into the night over her shoulder. "Come outside with me for a minute."

Dread settled heavy in her stomach. This was it. He'd be leaving any minute, and she might not ever see him again.

Holding her hand tight, Ben led her behind a rock outcrop and turned back to her. He set his hands on her shoulders. "You gonna be all right?"

"Sure. I've even got a babysitter to look after me."

"You know that's not why he's staying."

Yes, she did. In fact, she'd bet her last dollar it was because he didn't fully trust her more than it was about his injury.

"Well, *I* feel a hell of a lot better knowing he'll be with you. At least now I can focus on what I'm doing instead of worrying about you being alone here."

Rubbing a thumb over his cheek above the soft ebony beard, she gazed deep into his eyes. "No matter what happens, remember that I love you."

A frown pulled at his brows. "That sounds a lot like a goodbye."

Praying it wasn't, she shook her head. "Just in case."

He cradled her face between his hands and lowered his mouth to hers, brushing softly. Not nearly enough. She took over and grabbed the back of his head, opening her lips so she could slide her tongue into him, gliding and caressing, pressing her body as close to his as she could. He responded with a low moan and matched her urgency, holding her with bruising force for a few moments, then easing the pressure and making love to her mouth until she wanted to weep. He was a living, breathing miracle to her. So big and overwhelming but so skilled and tender, bringing her body to blazing wakefulness and taking up space in all the secret corners of her heart. Still clinging to him when he broke away, she flung her arms around his neck.

"Ben," Rhys called out, "let's go."

He squeezed her hard one last time and stepped back. "It'll be all right. See you in a few."

Unable to speak, Sam laid a trembling hand over her lips to stifle a sob and watched him walk away to meet the others. From her vantage point near the cave entrance, she kept her eyes on him until he disappeared from view, but not once did he look back. "Goodbye, Ben," she whispered.

Chapter Seventeen

Insertion site, near hostage location

The whir of the MH-60 Pave Hawk's rotors tore across the silent hillside as the pilots went into an in-ground hover and held their position. At the door, the crew chief tossed out the rope and checked the altitude, then gave the thumbs-up for them to fast rope in while the gunner stood ready to open up with his fifty cal. Rhys went first, then Davis, dropping out of sight from the aircraft and into the inky darkness. With his NVGs on, Ben grabbed the rope with his left hand and swung out, gripping below him with his right to let the rope slide between his gloved hands in a quick but controlled descent. The instant his boots hit the snowy ground he swung his rifle off his back and ran for cover where the others waited. The helo lifted off and gained altitude, steadily climbing into the black sky. Within minutes, the throb of the rotors had disappeared, leaving them in a vacuum of silence.

Nothing moved in the stillness. The only disturbance was a light wind rushing down the hillside from the peaks of the Hindu Kush rising above them. The green wash from the NVGs outlined their craggy peaks in the snowy air like the spires of a great city. Ben glanced at his watch. Just under twenty minutes until the satellite moved out of range. Then they'd have another blackout until the next one came on line.

Rhys spoke into his mike. "What's our status,

Luke?"

"All clear," the report came back. "You're good to go."

Ben had an image of Sam at her work station next to Luke, peering at the laptop screen as she monitored the com links to the satellite and radios. For some reason it comforted him to know she could see and hear him. She could concentrate harder than anyone he'd ever met, and he'd seen it time and again when he'd worked with her in Baghdad. Rhys had commented on it when he'd told Ben about the op they'd worked in Paris together. Her gaze never wavered from the screen, constantly maintaining vigilance to protect her teammates from unseen threats. Plus, she was steady under pressure. That alone made her a natural communications operator. Her voice never betrayed any signs of stress or nerves, stayed calm and collected even when the bullets started flying.

Except a whisper of doubt slid into his mind. That last e-mail from Tehrazzi bothered him. And he'd heard what she'd said to Miller on the phone. Would she really choose her cousin over the rest of them if it came down to it? He shoved that mental baggage into a vault and slammed the door shut. He had more important things to worry about right now, and he had no control over her decisions on the other end of the radio.

He glanced at his brother, six and a half feet of lethal menace, dressed like the rest of them in desert BDUs, face covered in a black balaclava, black Nomex gloves on his hands and NVGs attached to the mount on his helmet. Ready to rock. A tingle of anticipation spread through Ben's bloodstream, like it had back in the day when he'd served with his Ranger battalion. He had absolute confidence in his twin, both as a leader and a soldier. When it came to getting hostages out, you didn't get any better than

Rhys Sinclair. Those terrorist mother fuckers up the mountain were uttering their last prayers right about now, and they didn't even realize it.

"Ready?" Rhys asked him and Davis.

"Hell yeah."

"Okay, let's do this."

Rhys took point, running up the trail with surefooted stealth. Ben covered him with his M4 while Davis brought up the rear. They moved as a unit up the steep slope, hunkering down behind cover at regular intervals to scan in all directions, but everything was still. They resumed their climb and soon hit the main road where the kidnappers had driven up.

"You're coming up on their vehicles, seventy-five meters at your two o'clock," Sam said over the radio.

Sure enough, three dilapidated pickups sat at the bottom of a sharp rise where the road petered out. They slipped past them, taking the hillside as fast as stealth would allow. Nearing the top where the land flattened out into a rocky plain, they slipped behind cover to reconnoiter their objective.

"We have a visual of the target," Rhys said in a low whisper.

A series of crumbling huts lay before them, probably once used by goat herders, but all the other surrounding buildings lay in piles of stone across the plateau. Intel placed the hostages in the largest one, sandwiched in the middle of the ruins. Two sentries sat on boulders near the entrance, speaking quietly to each other. Where were the others? Their team had been told to expect moderate to heavy resistance in the area, but so far these guys were the only ones they'd come across.

Ben concurred with hand signals that he'd only spotted the two sentries.

"Confirm two targets outside the first hut."

"Roger that," Sam answered. "Infra red imaging

confirms two guards outside, and two hostages in the center building with three more hostiles."

"Copy that."

Only five? That couldn't be right. Tehrazzi was a lot of things, but stupid wasn't one of them. Why the hell would he have gone to the trouble to kidnap Neveah and lure Sam out here if he wasn't going to bother protecting his hostages adequately? It didn't feel right. The acid churning in Ben's stomach confirmed it. What the hell did that slippery bastard have up his sleeve that they didn't know about? When they went in, they were going in hard and fast. They had to expect anything, and everything from booby traps to explosives.

Rhys motioned to him, signaled he wanted him and Davis to take out the guards without firing their weapons. Ben gave him a thumbs up, then he and Davis split up and circled around the enemy position behind cover. Coming up from the rear, they gave another signal once they were in position.

Palming his knife, Ben charged up behind his unsuspecting victim and clapped a hand over his mouth, wrenching his head back hard and driving the blade deep, severing his vocal cords and his major blood vessels with one slice. A gurgle of air escaped from beneath Ben's hand, but the man went down silently. Ben lowered the body to the ground and glanced at Davis, who'd dispatched the other sentry to Allah and was wiping his knife on his pants.

"Sentries down," Ben whispered.

Covering Rhys as he dashed over, they got in position to take the main building. Ben and Davis were going in first. They'd take out the tangos while Rhys covered their six and then went in to extract the hostages.

Sam's clear voice reached him again. "Three remaining targets in the exterior room closest to the entry. Hostages are in the room to the rear."

Ben hunkered in position. The hair stood up on the back of his neck. There had to be more out there somewhere. Rhys tapped him. *Ready?* Ben nodded. On the three count, he stood up and smashed his boot into the flimsy wooden door, sending it crashing inward.

Three men scrambled to their feet, shouting, grabbing for their weapons as he fired double taps into two of them. Davis plugged the third. All three were dead before they hit the rug-covered floor. "All targets down."

Rhys tore past them to the interior door and crouched to check for detonators or tripwires while Davis guarded their perimeter and Ben rolled each dead man over with his boot to ID them.

Ben's jaw clenched. "Assoud's not here." Shit. If he wasn't here, he had to be somewhere nearby. Did he have an army of tribesman waiting to ambush them just out of satellite range? And where the hell was Tehrazzi?

"Copy that," Sam replied.

Ben stepped over the bodies to join Davis and peered out into the night. Nothing but empty space met his eyes.

He shook his head, every muscle keyed up as the adrenaline raced through him. "Doesn't feel right, man."

Davis grunted. "Tell me about it."

Going back to guard his brother, Ben stayed by the back door as Rhys burst through it. When his brother froze and lowered his weapon, Ben couldn't help but peer past him into the dimness. The reek of the place hit him hard, but the sight of Neveah seized his muscles.

She was crouched on the dirt floor staring up at Rhys with wild eyes, hair matted, teeth bared through lips peeled back as she let out a feral snarl of warning. She held a chunk of stone she'd pried from the wall in one hand, her arm raised threateningly. Her fingers were bloody. Her other hand pressed the only remaining male captive behind her.

She had placed herself in front of the other doctor to protect him, and was squaring off against Rhys with nothing but a stone in her scraped, bleeding hand, prepared to kill to save her friend.

Ben's heart twisted. Rhys removed his helmet and peeled off his balaclava, then backed up a step to give her some room while Ben fought not to gag at the smell.

"Neveah," he said softly, "it's Rhys." He crouched, as though trying to make his size seem less threatening.

She went still. The snarling stopped.

"It's Rhys," he repeated in a low tone, as though calming a wild animal. "Sam's friend. Do you remember me?"

The hand clutching the rock slowly dropped to her lap, but she didn't relinquish her grip on her weapon. Her lips closed over her teeth. She was shaking.

"I'm here to get you out."

Her eyes flooded with tears, but she nodded. "Rhys." Her voice sounded hoarse from crying. Or maybe from screaming.

"Yes." He hunkered down and set his gun aside.

Ben exchanged a glance with him. Jesus, she looked feral. "Can we come in?"

She swallowed convulsively and nodded, her eyes losing some of their wild gleam.

Rhys edged in slowly, so as not to startle her, and reached out a hand, palm up. The rock tumbled from her grip. She hesitated, but finally laid her trembling fingers in his. "You're going to be okay, Neveah. I'm going to take you away from here."

Her fingers clamped around Rhys' hand in a desperate grip. "I w-want to g-go home."

Ben's heart twisted. He hated knowing Sam was hearing this.

"You will go home," Rhys vowed. "What about your friend there? Can he walk?"

"N-no. In sh-shock."

Yeah, and so was she.

"It's okay. Help is coming. We'll carry you both out."

Her eyes darted past them into the other room and Ben could almost smell her terror. "Th-the others..."

Ben pulled off his own balaclava so she could see his face. "All dead," he told her, deciding it was better to tell her the truth. "None of them can hurt you anymore."

A small sob escaped her. She bit her lip and lowered her head. Ben saw the fat teardrops falling into the dirt beneath her.

"You're safe now," Rhys murmured.

Still crying softly, she leaned forward and lifted her arms to wind them about Rhys' neck. Rhys gathered her close, and to Ben's surprise, ran a hand over her snarled, matted hair. Jesus, she was filthy. The whole place reeked of shit and the oily sweat of terror.

"I'm going to pick you up now, okay?" Rhys said.

She nodded against his shoulder, hiding her face.

Rhys scooped her up like a child and carried her outside where Davis was waiting. He went to his knees in the snow and sat her down, but Neveah pressed close against him and he kept running his hand slowly over her hair and down her back.

Feeling like he was interrupting, Ben came out with the pediatrician over his shoulder and laid him on a blanket, then covered him with another. The guy looked like hell, his face gray, eyes sunken from dehydration.

Rhys bundled Neveah up to get her warm and bent his head to her ear. “We need to get some IV fluids into you.”

At her nod, he lifted her and stretched her out beside her friend. Her eyes seemed a bit clearer as she looked up at him. She hadn’t let go of Rhys’ hand, and he didn’t seem like he was in any hurry to pull away.

“Let me get this line in,” Ben said. He swabbed the back of her hand with alcohol and tightened the tourniquet before slipping the armed IV into her vein. She didn’t even twitch. He taped the thing down and started the drip, then handed the bag of fluid to Davis.

Climbing to his feet, he looked out into the still night. “I don’t like the feel of this,” he said, scanning the barren terrain through his NVGs. “Makes me twitchy that the bastard’s not here. It’s like they wanted to draw us up here so they could get away.”

Rhys nodded and stepped away to take his own look. “Any word from command on the other frequency?”

“Yeah. Helo’s inbound, ETA eight minutes.” A shitload of time to kill if Tehrazzi and his bodyguard were in the area with an unknown number of Taliban fighters.

“How is she?”

Ben glanced down at Neveah, lying so still and pale against the rough blanket. “Dehydrated, but not injured.”

Well, not physically, so far as he could see, anyhow. Psychological damage was another story. Being held in that shit-hole while listening to your friends being slaughtered and wondering if you were next would wound anyone’s mind.

Neveah turned her head and looked at him. Her

eyes were alert. “You look like Rhys. Are you brothers?”

“Yeah, I’m his twin, Ben.” He gave her a reassuring smile. “Sam’s beside herself about you, and said to say hello.”

“She did?”

“Yep. She’s waiting back at the command post right now.” He checked the IV one more time and did the same with the pediatrician, but couldn’t help noticing how Neveah kept watching his brother.

“Hey, Rhys,” Ben called. “I need you over here for a minute.” He nodded toward her.

Rhys came over and got down on his haunches next to her. “Hey,” he said. “Feeling any better?”

She nodded, and Ben was glad he’d called his brother over because the lines of exhaustion and strain around her mouth and eyes seemed to lessen. Still, she was so pale she looked translucent. Neveah’s hand crept over to Rhys’, her fingers curling around to grip his palm.

Her unspoken plea for comfort made Ben’s lungs ache. He sent Rhys a sharp look. *Come on man, say something to her. Or better yet, pick her up again and hold her.*

“I’m here,” his brother answered instead.

She tried to smile in reply, but the effort fell way short of convincing. “Yes, thank God. Sorry, I must smell pretty ripe, but I don’t want to let go of you right now.”

Rhys actually smiled at that. “I don’t mind. We have some time until the chopper comes in anyway. Close your eyes and let yourself go for a few. I’ll stay right next to you.”

But she didn’t close her eyes. She kept looking straight at Rhys, and Ben gazed pointedly elsewhere.

“Thank you for coming for us,” she said.

Her gratitude made Ben uncomfortable, and

Rhys muttered, “You don’t need to thank us.”

“Thanks just the same. You said Sam’s here?”

Ben nodded. “Yeah, with our boss. She’ll be glad to see you.”

Nev shook her dark head. Her long hair was greasy and matted, coated in dust and God only knew what else. Jesus, how could someone have mistreated her so badly?

“Damn that girl. She’s almost as stubborn as I am, coming out here.”

“Almost,” Rhys agreed, and laid his fingers over her eyes so she’d close them. “Rest for a while.”

Ben ran his gaze over her. She seemed so fragile without her eyes revealing her razor sharp intelligence and fierce will to survive.

Rhys stayed where he was, trusting Ben and Davis to guard his back as he knelt beside Neveah, holding her hand. A few minutes later, the clap of rotors in the distance broke the silence and then the Pave Hawk came into view, its distinctive chin mount silhouetted against the starry sky.

When it landed, two Special Air Force Pararescue Jumpers leapt out and ran over with stretchers. Half commando and half trauma paramedics, they operated behind enemy lines to rescue downed pilots and other high priority targets. The fact that the higher ups had sent PJs on the mission told Ben just how important rescuing Neveah and the other doc was to the US government. While Davis provided cover, he and Rhys helped load her and the pediatrician into the chopper, expertly handled by its famous Night Stalker crew.

With Ben and Davis manning the doors with the PJs as they lifted off, Rhys sat next to Neveah and maintained the connection with his hand on hers.

Once they cleared the hostile area, Ben relaxed his vigilance and glanced over at them. Part of him had trouble believing what he was seeing. His steely twin knelt on the helo's deck holding Neveah's hand, his eyes never leaving her pale face.

They touched down at a rendezvous point about fifty miles from the CP, a spot predetermined to be free of Taliban fighters and one of the few places the bird could land and take off safely amongst the unforgiving canyons and sheer faces of the Hindu Kush.

Rhys was supposed to go on to the CP to get Luke and Sam, but Ben hated like hell to take him away from Nev when she so obviously wanted him with her.

Before Rhys could withdraw his hand from hers, Ben stopped him with a nod.

"You stay with her and Davis. I'll go back for the others."

"You sure?"

"Yeah, why wouldn't I be? Looks like you'd be doing her a favor, anyway," he said of Nev, who was awake and listening to them. "Or are you worried I can't handle it?"

"No. I know you can."

About goddamn time, Ben thought with a smile. Together they offloaded their human cargo, and Rhys stayed close while the PJs took a closer look at Neveah and her friend.

Ben started back to the helo with a grin. "Sam's going to be real happy we got her cousin out okay."

A wry smile spread across Rhys' face. "You're so done, man."

Ben held up his middle finger. "Bite me, tight ass. Your time will come."

Rhys made a face. "No thanks. Say hi to Sam."

"Will do." He climbed aboard.

The whine of the rotors got louder, the wash getting stronger as the engine fired up and the chopper lifted off the ground.

As it soared through the sky, Ben found himself smiling.

Yeah, his uptight brother could be a pain in the ass, but you know what? Ben kind of liked that about him.

Chapter Eighteen

Command post

Watching Rhys tend to her cousin on the screen had tears burning Sam's eyes. Nev was right there, alive and whole. The mission had been an unqualified success so far.

Nev was safe.

She did her best to hide the fact she was wiping away tears as she stared at the blank screen in front of her. She'd seen her cousin in Rhys' arms when he'd carried her out of the hut, hadn't taken her starved gaze off Nev until they boarded the helo and took off, taking them out of the range of the satellite. They'd gotten her out, just as Ben had promised they would, and no one on the team had been injured. Pretty goddamn miraculous considering the group they were up against. And now it was all but over. In a few minutes, Ben would come for them and take her to the RV point, and then she'd get to throw her arms around Neveah. Within an hour of that, they'd be back in the relative safety of Kabul and the morning after that, they'd be going *home.*

Wiping her face, she pushed that all aside and focused on the task at hand. With a few typed commands she accessed another intelligence satellite to survey the surrounding area and make sure no one was coming after them.

"How're we looking?" Luke asked beside her. He placed a hand on the rock wall and leaned in for his own assessment.

"Still clear." Her heart raced with excitement. Almost over now. Just one last task to complete. Luke walked away, dialing someone on his phone. *I promised I'd find a way to save you, Nev.* And she had.

The instant the lone figure appeared running over the open ground on the screen in her lap, Sam zoomed in with the satellite link. Behind her, Luke was speaking to someone in Pashto on his cell phone, and she signaled for his attention. He set the phone against his shoulder and laid a hand on her shoulder as he peered at the screen.

"Karim?"

"Yes," she replied, fingers racing over the keyboard to bring the picture into higher resolution. "But what he's in such a hurry about I have no idea. Think everything's okay?" Unease crept in.

"We'll find out soon enough. He alone?"

"As far as I can tell." But the satellite wouldn't be in range for too much longer, and once it swept past, they'd have no way of knowing who else was out there. Her muscles tightened.

"What's his ETA?"

She glanced at the computer image map. "About three minutes if he stays at that clip."

Luke ended his call, then got busy getting a rifle and pistol out of the gun locker.

Her gaze jerked to him. "Expecting trouble?" They were alone out here. Ben was still any number of minutes out, and the others were too far away to get to them if they needed help.

"Not particularly. Just taking a few precautions."

If that's what you called an M4 and a loaded Glock with two extra clips. A tingling of alarm touched her. If something happened and they had to defend themselves, she wasn't going to be much of a help. Her firearms training was almost nil, and even if she remembered how to load and fire a weapon, the chances of her hitting what she was aiming at were less than that. If things got ugly, Luke would have to hold the enemy off while she called in for air support and prayed it got there in time to do them any good.

Don't overanalyze. Nev's safe, the guys are safe. Ben's coming for you.

An instant later, Karim burst around the corner of their hiding spot. He was flushed and sweaty, panting in great gusts of air, bareheaded from losing his hat in his haste.

"Salaam, Karim," Luke said.

"Tehrazzi," the boy blurted, doubling over to catch his breath.

Luke's face transformed into an expressionless mask and he demanded something in Pashto.

Karim wheezed in a few more lungfuls, divided his gaze between her and Luke before answering, but Sam didn't understand anything except "village."

Frowning, Luke handed him a bottle of water as he asked something.

Karim nodded, chugged half the bottle. "Many thanks." He took a deep breath, wiped his sleeve across his upper lip. Then he continued with something about Tehrazzi.

Luke's breath caught and he looked at her. "Tehrazzi's been wounded."

She gasped. "By whom?"

"His bodyguard."

What? Sam held Luke's gaze for another instant, then said of Karim, "Is he sure?"

"His father heard it from an elder." Luke folded his arms and asked the boy something else. When Karim answered, Luke translated for her. "There was a fight. Tehrazzi was stabbed in the stomach." The tension in Luke's muscles had gone up perceptibly.

"When? Tonight?"

"A few hours ago. The villagers have taken him in."

Sam sucked in her breath.

"Where," Luke demanded, grasping the boy's slim shoulders. "Which village?"

Sam couldn't make out Karim's answer.

Luke looked at her. "They've called in a doctor visiting from Jalalabad. Transmit that to Kabul and Langley."

Damn right. She scooted over to the first laptop, typed in a couple of commands and finished the e-mail as fast as she could. They were so close to nailing Tehrazzi. He could be mere miles from their current position. Certainly within helicopter range, and if he was as badly wounded as everyone thought, the only way he could move would be by vehicle or aircraft, both of which could be tracked. If they could get any clear intel on his location, Tehrazzi would be in US custody by morning. A hard smile stretched her mouth. After what she and Nev had been through, Sam would love nothing better than to put that jihadist asshole in the deepest, darkest hole on earth and leave him there to rot.

Movement from the computer screen on the far right caught her peripheral vision. She turned her head, some instinctive warning making her skin prickle. Shadows. Four of them. Four men, creeping into range of the satellite.

"Luke," she said, and he followed her gaze.

"Shit."

The soft expletive made her stomach drop like a rock.

"How far out are they?"

She calculated the distance. "Less than a mile." But they were coming up a steep hill. Moving fast, she zoomed out with the satellite to see if there were more. "Looks like just the four of them." She swiveled around. "What do you want me to do?"

"Can you ID any of them?"

She increased the resolution as much as she could, but the picture remained grainy at best. "That's all I can get."

Karim spoke up. "Assoud." His eyes were round.

How could he tell that? Unease settled around her heart. Did he know something they didn't?

"Yeah, I think it is," Luke said, and then said something in Pashto to Karim.

The boy hesitated only an instant before scrambling out into the open.

Sam swallowed. What were the chances Assoud and his buddies were out on a night-time recon mission, and not hunting for their location? "They must be tracking Karim's route through the snow." Fear began to creep in. "And we've got another problem—the satellite is only within range for the next three minutes. After that, we'll be without eyes for over twenty minutes before the next one comes on line."

"We'll just have to make due."

How could he be so calm? She tried to reassure herself that if he was this calm, then they couldn't be in mortal danger. Which was crap. Luke had served in almost every hellhole on earth, so four guys armed with rifles, and—Oh my God, was that a—

"That's an RPG, and the others have AKs."

Yeah, and that's just what they could *see*. They didn't have a clue what else was hidden beneath their loose robes, or how many others were waiting out of range. Jesus. Her heart started to pound, but doubted Luke's had even sped up. Four guys with RPGs and automatic Kalashnikovs weren't something he was going to get his tail in a knot over, but it was enough to turn her stomach into concrete.

The rattle of metal on metal broke her

concentration, and she looked up to see Luke slinging a sniper's rifle over his shoulder. She stood up in alarm. "Where are you going?"

"I'm going to head them off," he answered, checking the firing mechanisms.

But his head injury...he wasn't in any condition to go on sniper detail, let alone by himself at night without a spotter or backup of any kind. "What about your—"

"Get the others on the radio, update them and send another chopper in to get one or two of them for backup in case we need it. Once I'm in position, I'll signal you."

"But the satellite will be out of range by the time you—"

"Stay here until one of the others comes for you."

She opened her mouth to protest, but he was already out of the flap, moving to engage the enemy on that flat, open ground.

****

Ben settled back against the bulkhead of the chopper and closed his eyes, imagining the ecstatic expression on Sam's face when she saw him. Things had gone far more smoothly than he'd ever dreamed. It still made him edgy as hell, some part of him convinced it just couldn't be this easy. None of them had a clue where Tehrazzi and his bodyguard were.

The Irish in him was waiting for Murphy's law to take effect.

The radio crackled to life in his headset. "Ben?"

The undiluted fear in Sam's voice brought him bolt upright. "What's wrong?"

"Assoud is coming for us. We picked him up on the satellite."

"Wha—"

"He wounded Tehrazzi in a fight and now he's coming for us. Luke's gone out to intercept him, and I don't want to abandon the coms, but he's alone and injured, so if he needs help I'm going to have to go after him..."

Fucking Murphy. "Shit, Sam, just stay there." He frantically checked his watch. "I'm inbound, ETA—"

"I know. I just wanted to make sure you knew what was going on when you came in and that there could be a firefight." She paused a second. "Be careful."

Urgency hummed through his veins. "Stay put. Let us handle this."

"Have to clear this frequency now."

"Sam—"

"I'm out."

She'd effectively hung up in his ear. Christ, she wouldn't really try and go out there, would she? He didn't want to believe it, told himself she was smarter than that, that she wouldn't race out into the darkness after Luke. But his gut said otherwise. And his gut was never wrong.

"God dammit," he snarled, banging the back of his helmet against the bulkhead out of pure frustration. He made his way over to the cockpit. "LZ just got warm," he yelled over the rotors. "Be advised, we may be going in hot."

"Roger that."

Helpless to do anything more, Ben clutched his weapon and prepared himself to ride out the rest of the flight. "Don't you do it, Sam," he muttered, afraid it was already too late.

The hell of it was, there wasn't a goddamn thing he could do now but wait to find out what she'd done.

Chapter Nineteen

Out in the darkness, silhouetted by the thin covering of snow layered over the peaks of the mountains, Luke crept on his belly toward his quarry. Slowly. Silently. He wished to hell the snow had held off so the darkness would give him some cover. Being backlit on a stark white background in this desolate escarpment, with no place for concealment, made him feel like he was maneuvering in the glare of a goddamn spotlight. He inched forward a few feet then stopped, put his head down and waited a few minutes to find out if anyone had spotted him. He turned his gaze so he could see behind him.

Shit, his tracks stood out like he'd lit up the path with a flare. It made his progress painfully slow, but it was either that or commit suicide by enemy sniper. Anyone with any training at all would be able to pick him out if he moved any faster. As it was, he wasn't too optimistic about his chances of sneaking up on Assoud, let alone remain unspotted for much longer. He'd just have to be that much faster and more accurate than his enemy.

Sam spoke into the radio earpiece in his left ear. "He's at your one o'clock, about three hundred meters out."

Luke didn't dare raise his head to look or get his rifle in position. Against someone as deadly as an assassin who could have possibly killed his boss, a man who gave most of the folks back in Langley nightmares, Luke would only have one chance of nailing the bastard. One instant to swing the sniper rifle up and get a killing shot off before he was noticed sticking out of the snowy plain like a gator at a garden party.

Hooyah, Hutchinson. SEALs never surrendered. And they never quit. Not even when they were mostly blind and thought their skull was going to fracture apart at the seams, and they were dizzy and trying like hell not to gag because any sound would get their ass blown clear off the side of the mountain back to Bagram Air Base out on the Shomali Plains.

He had to eliminate this threat before they got to him, because Sam was back at the CP undefended. But damn, the ground here was every bit as bad as he remembered. He'd trained the teenage Tehrazzi in these mountains back during covert operations in the Afghan-Russian war. Now, twenty years later, Luke had come back to kill the prodigy that had served the American purpose so well in defeating the spread of Communism, because Tehrazzi had evolved into something that posed every bit as much a threat to America and the entire western world. Maybe more.

That all ended here and now. Once the bodyguard was taken care of, Tehrazzi was next. Luke would finish what he'd started, right here where it all began.

****

Sam didn't know if he'd make it. Watching Luke struggle over that brutally exposed terrain had her heart in her throat. He was hurting way worse than he'd ever let on. That's the only reason he'd stayed behind for the hostage rescue, and only because he knew he'd be an impediment to his men. Period. Once a SEAL always a SEAL, or so he'd told her. Which meant if they'd needed him, he'd have gone in to get Nev and the other hostage, even if he was shot all to hell and bleeding from a dozen bullet wounds.

If Luke had the strength to lift a gun and fire it, he'd keep going, until they killed him.

Seeing him crawl his way toward Assoud via the satellite link brought tears to her eyes. He shouldn't be out there. But he was not going to sit back and let that crazy bodyguard take their position, their equipment and the coordinates to the rest of the team and the hostages they'd pulled out. No, he was going out there to kill Assoud to defend his teammates, or die trying.

From what she was seeing on the monitor, Sam feared he might do just that, and didn't know how she'd bear it. She glanced at her watch. Only a few minutes had passed since she'd made contact with Ben, but it seemed at least an hour ago. He and the helo crew wouldn't be able to offer any support until they got here.

Something moved on screen.

Her eyes shot toward it. The breath caught in her throat. Men were moving toward her position, coming up the mountain. Swearing, she grabbed the radio.

****

The shuffle of footsteps drew nearer but Luke kept moving, focused on his task. He ignored the blinding pain in his head and the way it radiated down his neck into his spine, gritted his teeth, and fought the waves of dizziness that grew with every meter of ground he covered. Goddamn concussion was the worst he'd ever had, but he had to wonder if the altitude was making it worse. His body should have compensated for it by now, but the symptoms were getting worse. Clammy sweat beaded on his forehead.

For a split second the world turned on its axis. His stomach pitched sickeningly, saliva pooling in his mouth. He fought it, blinked fast to restore his vision, but now black spots swam before his eyes.

Shit, he had to clear his head so he could see what the hell he was aiming at. The footsteps came closer, hushed voices floating down to him. Arabic instead of Pashto.

"Luke, we've got a problem." Sam on the radio.

He froze, waited.

"Satellite picked up an enemy force approaching from the southwest."

Shit.

"So far I've counted fifteen of them, but there could be more coming." Her voice was still calm, but he knew she had to be terrified. "The satellite will pass out of range in another few minutes. Can you advise?"

Not without getting blown to hell.

He ran through his options. Sam was bright. She might understand Morse code if he tapped it out against something for her, but he still couldn't risk the noise. He'd have to kill Assoud and his pals and then haul ass back to the CP, and pray Ben got to her before the Taliban fighters did.

He dragged himself forward, the black spots obliterating his vision. Christ, he didn't have time for this. Neither did Sam.

Swallowing, trying to calm his racing heart and slow his breathing, Luke stopped and allowed himself a few seconds of rest. He had to do this. Sam's life depended on it. He couldn't risk trying to reach her over the radio, and even if he did, there was nothing she could do for him until Ben got here with the helo. Dammit, he had to keep going, but he couldn't see. Cold air brushed over his sweaty face. He wasn't going to give in to his body's weakness. Fuck that. But as he pushed up on his elbows to resume crawling, a lightning strike of pain bolted through his skull. It paralyzed him. He couldn't see, couldn't breathe. A wave of blackness rushed at him. He fought it back, struggled to hold on, clenching one hand around his rifle and the other into a jagged rock hard enough to make him bleed, using the pain to center him.

"Luke?" Sam's voice held a fearful note, but he couldn't reply.

Panting like a dog, he raised his eyes to the swirling horizon and pushed forward with his legs. No good. He tried again, laying his face against the snow so the cold would shock him back to alertness. His vision dimmed, going hazy and gray. He shook his head, bit down on the inside of his cheek. That awful ringing started up in his ears, horribly familiar.

Don't you fucking pass out. Don't you—

The black tide came back and hit him like an avalanche, burying him alive as it took him under.

****

He wasn't moving.

"Oh, God." Holding her breath, Sam divided her attention between the approaching enemy force and Luke, sprawled face down in the snow and fought the urge to panic.

"Luke," she said again, forcing her voice to remain calm. Had he been hit? She hadn't seen or heard a shot. Her muscles vibrated with tension. "Luke, can you hear me?" He didn't stir. Didn't even twitch. God, was he unconscious? She waited another few seconds.

"Luke, signal if you can hear me."

Still nothing. Fear almost choked her. Snatching up the other radio, she contacted Ben using the other frequency. "Luke's down. I don't think he's been shot, but he appears to be unconscious, and now we've got soldiers coming up the mountain from the southwest." Her voice shook on the last few words.

"Shit. Are you all right?"

"Yes, for now, but you're still too far away. What

should I do?" If she ordered a Medevac, they wouldn't make it here until after Ben arrived, and the soldiers were closing in from the west.

"Call in air support."

"They won't get here in time—"

"Call it in." Ben's voice was firm, commanding. "Sam, I want you to get out of there. Take a med kit, a weapon and some ammo and go to Luke quick as you can."

She faltered, heart in her throat. "And do what?"

"Just hold on until I get there."

Assoud and his crew would see her way before she reached Luke. They'd shoot her down like a dog without hesitation. Her muscles cramped. "Ben, I haven't fired a gun since—"

"Just move, Sam. Right now, and keep this frequency open."

"Ben…" She was fighting back tears now.

"Go, Sam. I'm coming."

Fueled by adrenaline, she dumped the radio. Racing to the medical kit, she stuffed it in her pack along with a pistol from the gun locker and some full magazines, then wrenched a Kevlar vest on and secured the Velcro straps around her ribs, the whole time trying to come to terms with the fact this really was happening. Yanking the pack on, she grabbed a helmet and a pair of NVGs. She was already sweating when she abandoned the CP and scrambled through the falling snow up the steep bank to the flat plain Luke had gone out to.

Breathing hard as she reached the top, Sam crouched and scuttled her way toward a group of snow-covered boulders to get her bearings. Staring out into the empty space, she tried to figure out where Luke had gone, and found the faint tracks he'd left in the snow that the storm was rapidly erasing. She took a step away from her cover, and realized with a start that she'd left the laptop running, with the scribbled series of coordinates written on her scrap of paper beside it. Shit. Should she go back? If one of the bad guys got there first, they might be able to find the rest of the team. She cast a hesitant glance over her shoulder. The cave was too far away now, and she couldn't afford to waste time getting to Luke. Just please, please let her get there in one piece and in time to be able to help him.

Screwing up her courage, she tore out at a full sprint across the open ground to Luke's position, terrified she'd be shot down at any moment. She'd never felt so alone or so exposed as she did then, moving at a dead run while trying not to stay in a straight line in the hopes it would make her a more difficult target to hit. Her knees were like jelly, lungs pumping, boots pounding over the layer of snow and shale covering the ground, dodging rocks and boulders, eyes riveted on Luke's shadowy form in the distance. After a few minutes, a new voice took over.

Get down.

Without thinking, she dove to the ground and stayed there. Shaking, she lay on her belly, face pressed into the dirt, afraid to move. But she had little choice. The only option was to keep moving, and hope they wouldn't see her. Her breaths came in shallow pants, every instinct yelling at her to stay still and hide like a hunted animal, when she knew damn well she couldn't. The enemy had to be close now. She had to get to Luke before they spotted their position and let loose with a hail of tracer-lit automatic fire.

Get up. Move.

It went against every instinct she had. Her body shook. She didn't dare raise her head. Levering up on her forearms, she crawled forward on her belly, desperately gazing around for some cover, but there was nothing to hide behind. She had to keep going, knowing that when she got close enough, the shooters were going to have Luke in their sights as well. She inched closer to Luke and sent up a prayer, trying to reach him over the radio. No response.

Her fingers curled into the loose, snow-covered shale and dragged herself onward, scraping her arms, hips and legs over the sharp edges of rock. In her racing mind, she went over the procedure for loading and firing the pistol. It was only good for short-range targets, but she had a better chance of hitting someone with that than a rifle. She had to get to Luke and build up some sort of protective wall for them, and hope the hell he came to in time to pick off the bad guys, or that Ben came in hot with the helo in record time.

Moving as fast and low as she could, Sam wound her way to Luke's position, called out his name softly when she got within earshot. He moved. Her heart leapt.

"Luke," she urged again, coming up behind him on her elbows to grab his ankle and shake him.

"I'm okay," he muttered, his voice slurred.

Wasting no time, Sam clawed her way up beside him and started piling rocks on top of one another, grabbing whatever was within reach to give them some cover. He raised his head slightly, and even in her terror she recognized the pinched expression on his face. "Still four of them," she whispered, frantically building their barricade. "They must be close now, but I don't think they've seen us yet."

Luke struggled up onto his elbows, rifle held in a death grip, eyes trained on the horizon before them.

"Are you hurt?" she demanded.

"No."

Jesus, this was not the time to keep up the alpha male image. "I brought a med kit. Do you need anything?"

"No."

"Don't tell me there's nothing wrong—you passed out, I saw you!"

His jaw flexed. "I can't see," he said finally.

"What?" She couldn't help the note of hysteria in her voice. Did he mean he couldn't see the enemy? That his vision was blurry? Or did he literally mean he couldn't *see*? For him to have said anything at all spoke volumes. God, nothing in the medical kit was going to be able to help that, and no medical advice from Ben was going to change anything.

Luke didn't elaborate any further, but when she stole another glance at him, she saw beads of sweat dotting his face, and knew they weren't there because he was overheated. He was scared. She'd never, ever seen him anything but one hundred percent in control at all times, and the knowledge that he wasn't sent a tidal wave of fear crashing through her. She forced it down. "Can you shoot?"

"Yep." His eyes never strayed from whatever it was he was staring at. Her only comfort was that she knew he'd never quit. He'd stay and fight it out no matter what, to the death if necessary. That's how strong his will was, and why he'd made the SEAL Teams.

She spoke in a whisper to distract herself. "Ben's on his way, should be here in a few minutes." The rock wall was as high as their heads now, tall enough to duck behind, but not enough to give them good protection. "I've got a pistol, but—"

To her horror, Luke turned his head and gagged repeatedly, vomiting into the snow. The sour stench of bile rose up, making her own stomach twist.

"Luke," she whispered, close to falling apart as she grabbed his shoulder to steady him. He was way worse off than he'd ever admit, but he pushed her away and propped himself back up on his elbows, laying the barrel of his rifle on the rocks she'd put up and aiming through the scope. She bit her lip to hold back a sob of fear and fumbled to get the pistol out, jamming a magazine into it and taking the safety off before loading a round in the chamber with a metallic clink. Her hands were shaking like flags in a windstorm.

Beside her, Luke sucked in sharp breaths through his nostrils, the SEAL in him fighting through the agony to hold his position as they waited for the enemy to find them and start shooting. Minutes passed in eerie stillness. Sam squeezed her eyes shut and prayed for Ben to hurry.

She jumped when the first bullet slammed into the boulder beside her, instinctively throwing herself to the ground as a second whizzed past her shoulder.

"Stay down," Luke rasped.

He needn't have said anything. She'd already flattened herself into the dirt, mind racing through the sudden spike in fear. AKs weren't very accurate. Luke had told her that once. They tended to fire up and to the right, and Taliban fighters tended to hold their weapons at waist level. Risking a glance up, Sam turned her eyes to the sky as a line of bullets arced over them, the tracers glowing green through the lenses of her NVGs. Another bullet pinged off a rock to her left, close enough she saw the sparks and a quick sting hit her jaw.

Biting back a gasp, she wiggled deeper into the loose soil and touched the spot. Her fingers came away wet, the metallic scent of blood hitting her nose as her brain processed what had happened.

A ricochet.

She kept praying for the sound of the rotors, hoping Ben would get there before the attackers improved their aim. Nothing came back but the rasp of her shuddering breaths and the slam of her heart in her ears.

Luke hadn't budged, and hadn't fired a shot yet. Could he see the enemy? The tracers must have given their positions away. Either way, she and Luke were fighting for their lives with every heartbeat.

Chapter Twenty

Near command post

"Can you stand without us?"

Tehrazzi ignored the whisper and stepped out of the truck on his own, fighting the debilitating weakness assailing his body. Covering a wince, he slung his sniper's rifle over his shoulder, sweat breaking out on his upper lip as the layers of stitches holding his innards together strained with each movement. Hooking the fingers of one hand through the strap, he left the three other men in the vehicle and began the steep climb up the trail to the place they had decreed to be the best vantage point for his mission.

He'd refused the opium they had offered him. The pain was bad, but he used the hatred within him to devour it, using it to center himself and focus his mind on what he needed to do. He could not fail, no matter what the circumstances. Any weakness would cost him the position of power he'd struggled his whole life to attain. Here, in these barren mountains, he'd struggled and starved in the most brutal poverty on earth, a kind so desperate it never left him, not even with all his millions of dollars and properties around the world. That kind of stain on your soul never left you. It followed you throughout your life and into the next, and only God could erase it.

Fighting back his fatigue, Tehrazzi started uphill, leaning his body weight into the incline, distracting his body from the pain by thinking of those pivotal days that had led him to this very place, at this exact moment. A circle completed.

His grandmother had grown up here. As a boy, he had visited her poor relatives after spending some time in Kabul where she'd been born. He had seen how they struggled to survive and felt a mixture of pity and contempt, hating them for how little they did to advance themselves. But he had also seen the steely core of the Pashtuns, the strength of will bound by the blood of generations reaching back for thousands of years and the strict code of conduct that held the fabric of their culture together. And he had known even then they would always remain. They had survived the Indians and the British, and when the Soviets invaded during his teens, he had watched the news reports back in Syria and known they would prevail. Because they were survivors, just as he was.

He had joined the resistance as a teenager, and there he had met his teacher. And when the Soviets abandoned their tanks and their attack jets in the airfields of Kabul and Bagram Air Base, the Americans had deserted the Afghan people. Without military or financial aid, the country fell into chaos until the Taliban took control and implemented the true rule of Islam. Now that the great Islamic warriors had driven a sword into the belly of the great Satan, the United States, the whimsical tide of American politics had turned. Its leaders and people had taken a sudden interest in Afghanistan's plight, and used it as an excuse to bomb its villages and mountainsides to protect themselves from the very people they had considered so insignificant as to not warrant helping after the Russians left.

Americans and their western allies were self-serving, corporate pigs who only took their snouts out of the trough if a better opportunity came along, or if they were in danger.

Well, they were all in danger now, and none of them had the will or determination to win this war. Their impatience was yet another advantage to their enemies. The American public expected immediate victory, and had no stomach for suffering casualties. To defeat them, all an army had to do was inflict steady casualties and hold out until the next election, making the war so unpopular that the next president would pull out. The Americans had done the same in Vietnam, and though that war was only a few decades past, the memory had somehow faded from the public perception until recently. But the Pashtuns had been waging war in these mountains since their ancestors had settled here. They understood what resistance meant. Every man, woman and child would die defending their homeland if necessary. America would never win this war.

Tehrazzi's feet slipped on the loose dirt and rock covering the snowy trail, but he propelled himself upward step by step, being careful to make as little noise as possible. He was skilled, but even he couldn't match the locals with their surefootedness and stealth. Once, back during the anti-Communist jihad, he'd seen a band of tribesman sneak up and slit the throats of an entire Russian platoon before any of them could scream a warning.

His heart beat fast as he neared the top. Dropping to his hands and knees and ignoring the hot tear in his belly, he reached the outcrop and crawled forward, putting the scope to his eye. Appearing momentarily from behind the clouds, the thin moon gave him enough light to see as he scanned the plain before him, followed by gunshots—the distinctive report of the Kalashnikovs, and the deeper note of a rifle. And another, higher pitched. More rapid. A pistol.

Whoever had fired it must be in desperate shape.

There. There they were. His teacher and the American woman who'd brought him here, pinned down by Assoud and his men. Praise be to Allah.

The hair on Tehrazzi's arms stood up. He tightened the focus on the scope, soundlessly loaded a round into the chamber. The bolt clicked into place. Balancing the barrel on a boulder, he lined up the crosshairs on his target's head, caught in an odd mixture of elation and sadness as he set his finger on the trigger. He curled his first knuckle around the curved edge and tightened it a fraction, his gaze never wavering from his unsuspecting victim. One shot would finish it, and then he would disappear down the mountain and vanish with the help of his fierce Pashtun brothers.

One shot, he thought with a grim smile. He tightened his finger, preparing to squeeze the trigger.

****

"How much ammo do you have?" Luke asked above the din.

Sam searched in her pack. "Three more magazines for the pistol." He didn't reply, and she didn't expect him to. The pistol was useless to them. It was only accurate for close range targets and could never reach Assoud and the others at this distance. Unless Ben got here and opened up with the Pave Hawk's M60s, they were in deep shit.

"Keep firing," he directed.

Not about to question his reasoning, she slammed another mag into the gun and pulled back the barrel to load it, propping the muzzle on top of the rocks to fire, squeezing the trigger repeatedly. The steady pop-pop-pop of the pistol added to the noise, but she wasn't optimistic it would keep the bad guys away for long. Another bullet slammed into the rocks, making her snatch her hand back in reflex. She had the passing thought that if she held up her fingers, they'd all be shot off. Then a battle cry rose up. The eerie howl flowed over her crawling skin as it grew louder. They were charging down at them from the ridge. She cast a frantic glance at Luke. He hadn't moved, his finger still poised on the trigger. She shut her eyes.

The rifle cracked.

Her eyes flew open in time to see the rifle butt recoil against Luke's shoulder.

"One down." He was breathing fast, but his hand seemed steady as he drew back the bolt and loaded another shot.

Crack.

"Two down."

Driven by self-preservation, she reloaded her pistol and added her own firepower, shooting randomly into the open to try and slow their advance. Still no sound of the chopper. She keyed her mike. "How long, Ben?" Her voice was shrill to her own ears.

"Two minutes. You both okay?"

"Just hurry," she begged, hands shaking as she loaded her last clip.

Luke fired again. This time when she glanced at him for confirmation of a hit, his complexion was gray. He squinted out into the snowstorm, blinking fast. "Winged'm."

Still two alive, then.

A second later Luke gagged and turned his head away, dry heaving.

The yelling grew louder as the enemy approached, until she swore she could feel the vibration in the ground from their pounding footsteps. "Can you get them?"

Luke didn't answer, only nodded, pulling himself up and aiming with brute determination.

"Want me to take the rifle?"

He shook his head, and the fact that he was unable to speak scared the holy hell out of her. Tamping down the rising panic, she risked a split second's peek over the pathetic barricade. Two of them, at least a hundred yards out. Could she hit them at this range? Assoud hung back, his accomplice still racing toward them. Taking deliberate aim this time, she got down as low as she could and peered through a gap in the rocks, picking the moment where she thought the pistol might reach him. Seventy-five yards.

Her hands clenched around the icy grip.

Over the swirling wind, the faint throb of rotors reached her. "I can hear you," she said into the headset. "Can you see us?"

"Any second."

Sixty yards. Assoud had stopped. He raised his rifle to his shoulder, sighted down the barrel. Her stomach did a terrified back flip.

The other soldier kept running, screaming at the top of his lungs in defiance of death. She squeezed the trigger. The gun bucked in her hands. The man kept coming. She fired again.

A bullet smashed into the rocks in front of Luke. Her eyes shot to him. He was panting, eyes closed, his cheek pressed against the rifle stock.

"Luke."

His lids lifted a fraction.

Shit. "Ben, Luke's going under."

"Hold on, Sam. Any second now…"

She didn't have that long. Raising her eyes, she focused on Assoud, still poised in position, aiming right at them. Through the veil of snow, she could see the blood from his fight with Tehrazzi staining his clothes. The other man sprinted at her. Sensing his victory as he closed in.

Fifty yards. The rotors came nearer.

She was on her own. No one could help her

defend them. She had to do this herself.

A surge of power rushed through her body. Goose bumps rippled over her skin.

Forty yards. In the kill zone now.

As though detached from herself, Sam felt her body shove upward. She gained her knees, then her feet, driven up in an almost euphoric haze. Gripping the pistol, she vaulted the barricade. Her feet hit the snow-covered ground with a thud. Adrenaline blasted through her, fueling her thighs to eat up the distance. The man's mouth was open. She saw nothing but the fanatical expression on his bearded face. He raised his weapon. Her heart slammed against her ribs. He fired. The shot whizzed past her right shoulder.

A scream of rage and power tore out of her throat. She leveled the pistol and squeezed the trigger. Once. Twice. Over and over. He jerked backward. A look of astonishment transformed his face. She kept firing. His left arm flew up. Blood erupted. The rifle fell. She fired again. He arched back. A dark hole bloomed in his chest. She fired again, still screaming. He toppled over. Lay still. His hate-filled eyes stayed on her, and then turned glassy.

She stopped running. The screaming died away. He was dead. She'd killed a man.

Her entire body started shaking. Her stomach heaved and twisted as she stared at the pool of blood spreading from the body.

"Give me status, Sam."

She couldn't answer Ben. The chopper must be close.

Then something slammed into her chest, hard as a sledgehammer, and threw her off her feet. She crashed onto her back in the snow, unable to breathe as the snowflakes swirled down to land on her face. A bullet. Her hands grabbed at the burning pain in her chest as she struggled for air.

"Sam?" Ben's voice registered through her earpiece.

Her frozen fingers touched the Kevlar vest.

"Sam!"

Air raced into her starving lungs. She tried to raise her head. Not dead, she thought, lifting her eyes.

Assoud lowered his rifle. He smiled.

I'm not dead, you son of a bitch.

Her fingers closed around the pistol.

She struggled onto her elbows. He raised the gun.

The rotors were loud now. Her eyes fixed on the end of the rifle's muzzle. She'd never hit Assoud at this distance. She raised her weapon anyway.

Lifting her gaze, she stared into Assoud's eyes, and prepared to fire.

A second later the front of his head blew out in a bloody mist. She jerked, paralyzed as she watched him topple forward. As he hit the ground, the report of a rifle echoed through the stillness.

****

"Sam? Sam!" Ben shouted into the radio aboard the Pave Hawk. He'd heard that gut-wrenching cry enough times to know she'd been hit. Fear grabbed him by the throat. God dammit, he was moments away from being in range to help her…

Fighting back his panic, he held on until they cleared the last ridge.

"Got 'em," the co-pilot announced.

His heart was beating so fast he was almost hyperventilating.

"Three targets down."

Fuck! He grabbed a med kit, closed his eyes and prayed he'd get to her in time to save her.

"Fifteen seconds."

Ben counted down to three, and made ready to

jump. The rotors sent up a spray of snow that obscured his vision. The instant the wheels made contact with the ground he leapt out and sprinted out into the open, rifle aimed. When he finally saw Sam, his heart tripped. She wasn't moving. No shots came. Two bodies lay bleeding into the snow in the distance. He flung his rifle down.

"Sam!" he yelled, tearing over, afraid he'd find her bleeding out.

She rolled to her side and struggled up on all fours, dragging in thin breaths. He skidded to his knees beside her, yanked her up to flip her over. She grabbed his wrists. No blood, but she could have internal injuries. He grabbed the front of her jacket, ripped it open. Froze.

A silver dollar sized hole in the Kevlar vest met his eyes.

"Ben."

He raised his head, met her tear-filled gaze. "Are you hit?" Ripping the thing off her, he passed a hand over her sternum. It came away clean. The vest had saved her. Hauling her up into his arms, Ben buried his face against her and rocked her back and forth, letting the shakes roll through him. "Shit, shit, I thought you were dead or dying."

She clenched her hands into his jacket. "N-no."

He pulled back and took her face in his hands. She was white as the snow, pupils constricted despite the darkness. "Oh, sweetheart." He tucked her tight into his body and held her against his slamming heart.

"She all right?"

He looked up to see Luke standing there, supporting his weight with his rifle. "Yeah. You?"

The older man nodded, and sank down onto one knee. The front of his BDUs were covered with vomit. "Was close."

Way too fucking close. Ben nodded toward the

dead men. "One of them Assoud?"

"Yeah. Wasn't me who got him, though."

He glanced at the top of Sam's head. "She did?"

"No. She got the other one."

Ben frowned. "So who—"

"The shot came from behind him."

He turned his head to search through the falling snow. Whoever it was must still be out there. "Let's move." He started to lift Sam into his arms.

"N-no." She pushed away and stood on her own. "Help L-Luke to the ch-chopper."

"I don't need help," Luke argued, starting for it himself.

She swayed a little, and Ben took her by the shoulder. "Help him."

"You first," he said. "I'll come back for Luke afterward."

But she shook her head. "No. More soldiers coming. Have to get the equipment from the CP."

"I'll get it."

"No, I have to be there."

Screw it. He dragged her up and hauled ass to the helo, setting her down gently on the deck before going back for Luke and giving him the same treatment over his growled protests. The co-pilot was checking Sam over when they arrived. They'd never be able to land by the CP, it was too steep and there wasn't an area wide enough to set down. "We're going to have to go on foot," he told her, searching her eyes. "Just tell me what you need and I'll go."

"No. I'll come."

He didn't think she was in any condition to go anywhere after what had just happened, but her eyes had fire in them and her color was better. "We've got to haul ass."

"Okay." She hopped off the deck and started jogging in the direction of the CP. Staying close while scanning the horizon for threats, he led the way with his weapon ready, matching his pace to hers, admiring the way she pushed herself up to a sprint despite how weak she must have felt. The snow was dying down and visibility was increasing. "The fighters are coming in fast," he warned.

She didn't answer, just tore down the mountain, slipping and sliding her way behind him. When they reached the ledge the cave was located on, he stopped dead. Two sets of footprints tracked through the snow, one moving toward the CP, and the other leading away. The treads were covered with a dusting thin enough to tell him they were made recently enough that the snow had been petering out. He pushed Sam against the cliff and approached the entrance with his rifle up and ready, burst inside and swept around with his NVGs. Empty.

He stuck his head out. "Hurry."

****

When Sam tore into the CP and flipped on a battery powered light, the first thing she saw was the crumpled candy bar wrappers lying on the ground. Her eyes automatically shot to her computers, all up and running except the one that had been monitoring the rest of the team at the rendezvous point. It was missing.

Her heart lurched. Had she moved it? She couldn't remember. Dropping to the ground, she shoved gear around, searching for it. Nothing. "One of the computers is missing."

Ben frowned. "Missing?"

"It had sensitive stuff on it, intel and e-mails."

"Must be here someplace." He didn't sound hopeful, but squatted beside her. "What do you need?"

She didn't look at him as she raced to gather up the remaining equipment. "The laptops, radio and batteries. The rest we can replace." At least, she hoped they could. Where in hell was that damned laptop? She searched around for it and the pad of paper she'd scribbled the coordinates on, but couldn't find either of them. "The meeting point location," she blurted, yanking out wires and stuffing equipment into her pack, "it's missing too. I wrote it down—"

"You *what*? Why the hell would you write it down?"

His anger made her heart beat even faster. "There were too many for me to remember, and—" Her eyes fell on a piece of paper lying on the ground near her feet. As she bent to retrieve it, her stomach grabbed.

"What?" Ben demanded, hurriedly jamming electronic gear into another bag.

She stared at the Arabic handwriting. "It says, 'You owe me your life, my brother.'" Cold began to seep into her skin. "The candy bar wrappers... Karim must have come back and taken the laptop and coordinates, then left this." But that didn't make sense. Karim was an uneducated peasant, and only spoke Pashto. He couldn't have written that note. So who had?

"Shit." Ben's face tightened. "Come on, let's get out of here."

They gathered up what they could carry and Sam shut off the light before running with him out of the cave. Rounding the bend on the approach to the embankment, someone suddenly leapt out at her. She screamed and lunged back, falling on her butt in the snow. Ben hurtled past her to intercept the threat. He let out a vicious snarl and caught the attacker in a flying tackle. A deep grunt as they hit the ground told her it was a man.

Ben was both beautiful and deadly as he grabbed the assailant's arm and whipped it up and back. She'd never seen anyone move so fast. The man screamed and lashed out with his foot. Ben blocked it and twisted up, throwing him over his shoulder. The guy hit the ground with a thud near her feet, and Sam did a fast crab-walk to scramble out of the way. The enemy rose to his knees and drew a knife. She swallowed a shriek, but Ben smashed into the guy's wrist with a high kick and dove on top of the attacker, pinning him down.

"Don't look," Ben bit out. He grabbed the knife.

Sam shut her eyes and turned her head away. A wet slice and a gurgling yell were all that met her ears. A second later, Ben grabbed her arm and hauled her to her feet. There was no body. Ben must have thrown it over the edge. Her terrified gaze ran over him and the blood staining his clothes. Was he hurt?

"Run," he snapped.

Swallowing the bile in her throat, she did. On autopilot, she struggled back up the slippery hill, but he kept her from falling and dragged her up onto the flat expanse where the helo waited.

Luke appeared at the threshold, gray and grim. Gasping for breath, she thrust the note at him and scrambled aboard with Ben. Her head spun. She had the detached thought that her brain was about to short out. The engine powered up. She watched Luke pale even more as he read the paper.

"Tehrazzi," he snarled, crumpling it in his fist. His eyes burned with deadly purpose. "Fucking with my head, as usual."

Tehrazzi had killed Assoud? He'd had Luke in his sights and taken out his bodyguard instead? She scrambled to make sense of it. A gasp stuck in her throat. Oh, shit, the missing paper. "H-he knows where the team is. He's got the coordinates."

"What?"

"He—I left a piece of paper with them on it when I came after you, and he got one of the laptops..." The sudden rage in Luke's eyes scared her so much she backed away. Her useless apology stuck in her throat.

Scalding her with that lethal gaze for another moment, he turned away and rushed to the cockpit to order the pilot to do a search of the area. "He's got to be close, and the snow will make it easy to track him." His residual anger was palpable.

"Alert the others, then let's nail the bastard," Ben muttered, manning the door.

Right. Focus. Get to work. The mist in her brain cleared. Having a task to complete brought her back like a bucket of ice water in the face. Braced against the bulkhead, Sam opened up the laptop and waited for the satellite link to get a visual on Nev and the others. When it came on, relief slid through her. The screen filled and she zoomed out on their location, the infra-red sensors illuminating the four of them, either Rhys or Davis out front in a defensive position to guard Nev and the pediatrician. She zoomed back out, checking the perimeter. Then more movement caught her eyes. Six bodies were climbing up the mountain toward them.

Oh God, no… She gasped and sat up so fast Ben glanced over at her. She met his eyes. "Taliban are coming at them." Damn, how had they'd reacted so fast?

Ben was up and looking at the screen in a heartbeat. "How many?"

She zoomed out further, revealing another twelve men. "Eighteen so far."

Luke came over, took in the situation with a single glance. "Call in close air support," he instructed her.

"We've got to extract them," Ben argued.

"We won't get there in time; they need an air strike to clear them off the mountain."

Sam's gaze darted between them and settled on Luke. He wanted Tehrazzi. Her chest iced up. He wouldn't leave the rest of the team there, would he?

Ben got in his face. "The team gets first priority."

A tense standoff ensued where they stared each other down. Then Luke relented. "Get them moving," he snapped.

Sam frantically zoomed out and increased the resolution, searching for a possible escape route to send them on. The terrain was rough, the only flat spot was the LZ chosen to set down the chopper, otherwise everything was steep and rocky, hard enough to navigate without carrying hostages. Then she remembered something.

"There are trucks," she announced, bringing their heads around, "two of them at the bottom of the gulley a few hundred meters below their position." She pulled it up and let them see, then got on the radio and patched through to Rhys to bring him up to speed. "They're like the ones you passed before," she told him.

"Roger that."

She eyed the fighters coming in. Calm. She had to stay calm. "You've got ten minutes, tops, before they come within range."

On the screen, Rhys broke cover and took off down the mountain, sliding his way down the steep incline toward the waiting vehicles. Ben hovered over her shoulder, tracking his brother's progress with unblinking eyes. The tension in him was palpable. Rhys finally hit the bottom of the trail. "How'm I doing?" he asked her, breathing fast.

"You're good. Six minutes left. Can you see the trucks?"

"Affirmative." He ran straight for them, tried the door of one, and it must have been locked because he smashed the driver side window with the butt of his rifle, then wrenched it open, and within seconds had it running. "Where to?"

She directed him to what looked like the best route up to the others, guided him over the whine of the engine coming through the radio.

"Two minutes," the pilot called out. "Get ready."

Ben readied his weapon, threw a hand out to steady her when the helo banked sharply, giving her a bird's eye view of the desolate landscape hundreds of feet below the open door of the aircraft.

The soldiers were almost to the ridge now. *Come on, Rhys, drive!* The old Toyota lurched and ground its way up the incline as he followed her instructions to a fork in the trail. She hesitated. Sending him right was less steep, with fewer impediments. But the left was the most direct route to the others.

"Which way, Sam?" he demanded, voice tense.

"Left."

She held her breath as he made the turn, muscles strung tight as wires across her bones.

"Coming up on position," the pilot announced.

They banked hard to the right and decreased altitude.

"How long until air support gets here?" Luke asked.

She glanced at the time display. "Three minutes." The truck continued its steep ascent up the trail, the enemy almost within range—

The truck exploded into a ball of fire.

Chapter Twenty-One

Sam cried out. She gripped the laptop in white-knuckled hands as horror swamped her. Rhys was trapped in the flaming interior of the truck.

"What was that?" Ben demanded, grabbing the laptop. The instant he saw the burning wreckage of the truck, he tore the headset from her numb hand. "Rhys? Rhys, answer me... Fuck!" His eyes cut to her, and the awful rage burning there chilled her blood. "What did you do?"

She couldn't speak. *God, Rhys...* An aching knot seized her throat.

Her mind whirled for an explanation. Couldn't be an IED. Not up here. Hadn't been an RPG or a Stinger. That left—

"A-a mine..." She shrank from the accusation in those green eyes and the knowledge she'd just watched Rhys die. "I'm sorry—oh, God!" She covered her mouth with her hands, reeling with shock.

"We're going in hot," Luke shouted over his shoulder, manning the door with his M4.

A thousand words of denial, of apology crowded her throat, but she couldn't get a single one out. Rhys was burning in that truck because she'd sent him over a goddamn mine.

Face tight as a mask, Ben threw her one last scathing look and whipped around to man the other door with one of the crew members. Sam dropped the headset and covered her face with her hands, as if that could block out what she'd just seen. She couldn't bear to look at the screen again. A whimper crawled up her spasming throat. She wanted to wake up and find out this was only a nightmare. It couldn't really be happening.

Pop-pop-pop. Pop-pop-pop-pop.

She jerked when the big 50 cals started firing from the open doors, and grabbed onto the seat as the helo tilted hard to the right. Ben and Luke fired from the open doorways at the enemy on the ground closing in on the team's position, probably drawn by the burning truck. Closing her eyes, Sam had an awful image of Rhys burning alive in the twisted wreck. She fought down the surge of nausea.

"Incoming!"

Her eyes flew open at the co-pilot's shout, and the next thing she knew, Ben had knocked her to the deck, pinning her with his body. The Pave Hawk rose and banked tight, then plunged nose-first toward the ridge top, still hurtling forward at top speed. A scream locked in her throat. The pilot swerved again, and only Ben's weight kept her from slamming into the bulkhead.

Lifting her head, she made out the streak of a missile as it shot past and slammed into the ground with an explosion so big it shook the chopper and everyone in it. Heat seeking missile. Had to be. One of the Stingers the CIA hadn't gotten back. When the pilot righted them and regained altitude, Ben lifted off her and went right back to his post at the door, firing at the approaching Taliban troops.

Grabbing the radio, Sam dove for her computer, praying Rhys had somehow gotten free. His radio was still working. She could hear the fire crackling and popping in the background.

Oh God, please be okay…

A glowing figure showed up on the screen, running to the burning truck, reaching it as Rhys fell out and hit the ground with his jacket on fire. Sam bit the inside of her cheek to keep from sobbing.

Rhys was on *fire,* burning before her eyes.

Whoever it was next to the truck dove at him, swatting at the flames on his back and throwing armfuls of dirt and snow to smother them. Agonizing seconds passed before the flames were extinguished.

"Rhys?" Sam said hoarsely above the din of the big fifty caliber gun Ben was firing, hoping he could hear her despite his injuries. "Rhys, answer me!" Nothing.

Whoever was helping him turned him over, and Sam was stunned to hear Neveah's voice, telling him to lie still.

Then his deep voice made her jump. "I'm hit," he said clearly.

Sam gripped her earpiece. "Rhys!" He was still alive. She caught Ben's grim stare.

"Jesus, oh Jesus," Nev was saying. "Rhys. Rhys, stay with me… No!"

Oh my God, he's dead, Sam thought, stricken. She was so deep in shock she barely noticed when someone dropped down next to them on screen, and Davis' voice came over the radio. "We need an emergency Medevac," he said.

Sam gazed around the chopper. They had limited medical supplies on board. Nev was a surgeon, but she might not have the equipment they needed. And even if she and Ben could stabilize Rhys… They might not get him to the hospital in time.

Bile rose in her throat.

"Chopper will be here any minute," Davis was saying.

Sam's throat was too tight to answer.

"He's still b-breathing," Nev answered, and Sam sagged, tears spilling over her cheeks. "Pulse thready. How long?"

"Too long," Davis muttered.

"How *long*?"

"Once we're on board...it's a twenty minute flight to the nearest hospital."

Pain welled up in Sam's heart. Almost half an hour. Rhys'd be dead by then.

Staring down at the three glowing figures on the screen, she wanted to scream at the horrific irony of their situation. Nev was a trauma surgeon, but there was nothing she could do for Rhys out here. For now, all Sam could do was silently join in Neveah's fervent prayer for Rhys.

"Stay with me... Stay with me..."

Alone, numb, Sam sat on the vibrating floor of the helo and bit her lip until her teeth punctured through. Coppery blood filled her mouth. She couldn't help any of them anymore. She'd had one job—to get Rhys and the others out safely. Her choice had doomed Rhys, and maybe her cousin if they couldn't fight off the attackers.

She raised haunted eyes to Ben, his profile lit up by the muzzle flash of the machine gun he was firing. Every feature was stamped with resolve. Her heart broke as she realized he was fighting to go in and save his brother. He would never accept that his twin was going to die before they got him out.

****

The Pave Hawk made a fast descent, and as the ground rushed up to meet him, Ben leapt from the helo and dropped the last few meters. He hit the ground hard and rolled, his left thigh screaming with the impact, but he barely felt it. Nothing mattered but Rhys. His sole purpose was to get to his brother, lying prostrate on that frozen escarpment, his life's blood flowing into the barren Afghan soil beneath him.

His boots pounded over the loose shale as he tore across the space that separated them, an animal scream of denial clawing its way up his throat when he saw the terrible wound in the side of his twin's skull. He fought down the panic flooding him as he flung the medical supplies to Neveah and skidded to his knees beside Rhys, taking his brother's bleeding head in his hands.

Shrapnel had ripped a ragged baseball-sized hole in Rhys' right parietal bone, and blood was still flowing out of it despite Neveah's attempt to slow the loss. Ben had no idea how far the fragments had penetrated into his twin's brain, but they had obviously torn into his parietal lobe, and maybe gone further than that. Any brain injury was bad, but this… How was he still alive?

"Christ," Ben cried, almost a sob. He held Rhys' head and neck steady while Nev rummaged through the kit and pulled out the equipment to intubate him. Nothing was happening fast enough. They were losing too much time.

Nev's expression was set as she threaded the instrument into Rhys' airway. If there was swelling in the throat she'd never be able to get the tube in, and the only thing left was a risky needle cricothyrotomy—

"I'm in," she said finally, and Ben let out the breath he'd been holding. The two Air Force PJs came running up with a stretcher and lifted Rhys onto it.

"Warthogs inbound," one of them shouted. Neveah pulled out the instrument and grabbed the other equipment from him. Her hands fumbled a bit.

Ben's heart slammed against his ribs, hands itching to rip her out of the way and do it himself. "You've got to hyperventilate him—"

"I know." She attached a bag to Rhys' mask, began pumping.

A shriek rent the air overhead. The two A-10s roared past, and seconds later an ear-shattering explosion shook the earth. He ducked and sheltered Rhys as best he could while the concussion ripped into them. When it was safe to look, he glanced over his shoulder at the carnage behind him. The entire hillside where the enemy had been was gone, earth and smoke rising up in a huge cloud.

"Let's move him," Nev said.

About goddamn time. Holding his brother's head steady, Ben ran to the Pave Hawk with the other crewmembers and hauled him aboard. Nev stayed at Rhys' shoulders, continued to bag him. The helo's twin engines howled as the pilots powered up and shot them into the night sky for their race to Kabul.

Please, God, oh, please… He prayed enough oxygen would reach his brother to reduce the pressure in his skull. How far had the bone and metal fragments penetrated his brain? How much damage had they done? All of a sudden Rhys arched up, muscles going rigid in rhythmic waves. Ben's heart almost stopped. "Shit, he's posturing. Put him out, Nev!"

"I'm trying!" she snapped, fighting to hold down Rhys' muscular arm to get a line in. Ben immediately took over ventilating him and pinned the arm with his knee. The spasms almost threw him off.

Fuck, oh, fuck…

When Nev got the IV in, she pumped it full of meds. In seconds, Rhys went slack and fell back to the helo's deck. "Ativan and a little morphine," she said, sitting back on her heels and wiping an arm across her glistening forehead. Her eyes met his. "How long to the hospital?"

Too fucking long.

"Pilot says fourteen minutes," Sam said hoarsely.

He looked over his shoulder at her, pale and misty eyed as she stared at Rhys.

She crawled over, sparing a glance at Ben as though seeking permission, then took his brother's hands.

Her eyes squeezed shut and her lips moved. Praying.

Staring down at his brother, Ben closed his lids and joined her.

Chapter Twenty-Two

The remainder of the flight took forever. When they finally touched down at the American-run hospital, Ben and Davis rushed Rhys in with Nev running alongside, shouting orders at the waiting staff. The pediatrician stumbled after them. Sam clambered out of the helo on wooden legs, the rotor wash beating at her clothes and kicking up a stinging spray of sand on her skin. She was surprised she could feel it. Inside, she was completely numb. Frozen by that single accusing look Ben had aimed at her.

So much death. So much violence. She'd killed a man. She'd watched him fall and seen the blood spilling from his wounds.

Oh, but wait. That wasn't the only murder she'd committed tonight, was it?

A cry of anguish rocketed up from her chest. She smothered it so it came out a strangled whimper.

Behind her, the pitch of the engine changed. She looked over her shoulder at Luke.

His face was gray, his eyes bruised underneath. Like a sleepwalker, she raised her hand, thinking he needed help getting out.

He waved her away. "Go!"

She couldn't move. He needed a doctor. "W-where are you going?"

"Where do you think?" He moved deeper into the belly of the helo as it lifted off the ground.

He was going after Tehrazzi. Rhys was dying and Luke was badly injured, but he was going out again anyway. He wanted Tehrazzi bad enough he was willing to die for the chance to get him. Her remaining strength drained away. She was too tired to care about his death wish anymore.

The chopper flew away, leaving her in a sudden vacuum of silence. Her neck felt like it was a rusted cable when she turned her head to look around. She was alone, standing in the dust. The only one here without a purpose anymore. And now she was no better than Fahdi. She'd just killed one of her teammates with a bad decision. Her stomach pitched.

Somehow, her feet carried her into the hospital. The door banged shut behind her and she blinked in the sudden sterile brightness. Several people looked at her in alarm. She knew why. She must look like a mad woman. Her hair was snarled, her clothing torn, she was spattered with blood and pale from shock.

"Are you all right?"

Sam turned her head and met a nurse's concerned gaze. Was she? Her heart hurt so much she almost wished she could die. Just drop right there on the scarred linoleum floor and never wake up again.

Rhys was dying, and Ben blamed her for it.

A wave of grief rushed over her, so strong it tore a sob out of her. She slapped her palm over her mouth to stifle it.

"You're hurt," the nurse said, tugging on her arm. "You need treatment."

Sam shook her head. No amount of medicine was going to help her.

"Sit down."

"N-no." She at least wanted to find out about Rhys, and as stupid as it was, she wanted to stay close in case Ben needed her. Right now, though, she wasn't sure she could face him again. "The

American. He just came in. Where is he?"

"In surgery. You won't be able to find out anything for a while yet."

Was he already dead? Nev was in there, fighting for his life with her own hands. Where was Ben?

"The others are in a private waiting room. Let me get those cuts cleaned out, and I'll take you to them."

Cuts? Sam glanced down at herself, frowning at the tears in her clothes and the blood on her jacket. Was she bleeding?

"Come on." The nurse wouldn't take no for an answer and towed her into an examination room. After pushing her onto a table, she gathered some things and began swabbing at Sam's face.

The burn of antiseptic melted away some of the ice encasing her. She clenched her hands into fists and focused on the pain to center her.

"You don't need stitches," the woman was saying, examining the cut on the side of her jaw, "but I'm going to bandage a few of the deeper ones. Head and facial wounds bleed a lot."

Sam remembered the blood seeping out of Rhys' head from beneath Ben's hands, despite the fact his fingers had been white from the pressure he'd used to staunch it. A fountain of tears erupted, and she turned away to curl into a ball of misery. Was it her fault? Should she have somehow known that road was embedded with mines? The nurse's words of comfort went unnoticed through her haze of pain. Rhys would probably die, despite Nev's best efforts. He would die, and it would be her fault, and Ben would blame her. He already did. And if by some miracle Rhys did pull through, he would likely be a vegetable.

How could she bear knowing she'd caused a friend's death? She sobbed harder, falling into a bottomless well of grief. The agony stabbed at her like shards of steel, left her gagging and dry-heaving. When it was over, she lay staring at the wall with swollen, aching eyes. She wanted Ben to tell her it wasn't her fault. Needed his arms around her.

Like that was ever going to happen again.

Get over yourself, Sam. Ben's waiting alone, knowing his twin is dying.

She dragged herself into a sitting position, glad she had privacy so she could compose herself. Ben might not want her around, but the least she could do was make sure he wasn't alone through this. She owed him that. And if he told her to drop dead? She'd just have to take her medicine like a big girl.

It wasn't hard to find him. The hospital was small, and when she worked up the nerve to glance through the window of the waiting room she saw him in a plastic chair with his head buried in his hands. Her chest ached. Steeling herself for anything, she turned the knob and opened the door a crack. He glanced up, and the agony in his eyes was like a knife in the heart. She couldn't move, couldn't breathe. Davis pushed away from the wall he was leaning against and came over to her. He laid a hand on her shoulder, and she met his eyes briefly. The empathy in his dark gaze almost made her cry, as did the comforting gesture.

"I'll go see if there's an update," he said quietly and shut the door behind him, leaving her alone with Ben, who dismissed her by dropping his head back into his hands.

The ticking of the clock seemed loud as gunshots in the suffocating silence.

She didn't dare speak. Couldn't have even if she'd wanted to because her throat was so tight she could hardly breathe. Afraid he might come out of that chair and unleash the volatile emotions she could see churning in the taut lines of his back and shoulders, she slowly crossed the room and sank to the floor in the corner, never taking her eyes off him. He didn't move. Not a single shift in position, just the ridge of his shoulder muscles straining under his shirt and the fingers clenched in his hair.

Minutes passed. Sam remained frozen like a frightened animal in the corner with her knees drawn up to make herself as small as possible, which was stupid. He knew perfectly well she was there. Was she making it worse for him? She wanted so badly to comfort him, but she had no idea what to say or do, and saying she was sorry was totally inadequate. The second hand tracked around the clock in slow motion. She wished Davis would come back so she could leave. What had she been thinking, coming in here? He'd made his feelings about her crystal clear back on the helo.

The tension increased until she had her fingers wound so tightly around each other they went numb. Ben was a proud man, and as stubborn as they came. No matter how much he was hurting he wouldn't let go, wouldn't let himself cry or scream even though he needed to. God, how she wanted to slide her arms around him and absorb some of his pain. Even if he vented it all at her, it would be better than him holding it in.

"It's been an hour."

Her eyes shot to him, but he wasn't looking at her so she stayed silent, hoping he'd keep talking.

"They must know something by now."

He was looking for reassurance. Surprised he was even speaking to her, she swallowed and carefully considered her words. "Nev will tell you something when she can."

He dragged his hands through his hair and surged to his feet, making her flinch instinctively. But he merely paced on the other side of the room, his gaze on everything but her.

Please look at me, she thought, watching him.

As though he'd heard her, Ben stopped and raised his eyes to hers. A sheen of tears glistened there. "Tell me you didn't know that road was mined."

Her breath whooshed out like he'd kicked her in the gut. She blinked up at him, brain struggling to process the words. "W-what? I don't—"

"Save it," he snapped. "Just keep your mouth shut and maintain the shred of respect I still have for you."

My God, he thought she'd done it on *purpose*. She started to shake. He's not thinking straight, she told herself, but then he pinned her with a single, accusatory glance that made her feel like he'd just driven a dagger straight through her wounded heart.

Words failed her. Scalding tears slid down her face. Please let this just be his anger talking, she thought. She could forgive him that. "You *know* I would never hurt him," she whispered, almost paralyzed by the hateful expression on his face.

Ben squeezed his eyes shut for a moment, then locked his gaze on hers. "God damn, I wish I knew if I could trust you."

The bottom of her stomach dropped out. "You think I would have sent him there if I'd known?" she said in a stricken whisper. It killed her he would even think she was capable of it.

"You had access to the satellite feed for hours before we went in."

"For God's sake, Ben, that mine could have been there since the Afghan-Russian war."

His eyes were frigid. "Or it could have been planted a few hours ago because somebody knew we were coming."

"You think I leaked intel to them?" Her brain spun as she tried to understand his suspicion, a million thoughts tumbling through it like ricochets pinging off rocks. Rhys was dying. She'd told him to take that truck. She'd told him to take that route. But it hadn't been intentional. How could Ben think that of her?

His gaze never wavered. "Someone did."

"I would *never* have sent him that way if I'd suspected it was mined."

"No?"

She set her jaw, shook her head. Anger bubbled up over the hurt.

"Then explain to me why you would write the fucking coordinates of their position down and leave them in plain view so that the enemy *you knew* was coming could find them?"

It was too much. "I'd just written down the new coordinates and memorized them, then *you* told me to go to Luke. I didn't exactly have time to clean the goddamn office before I left!"

"And what a coincidence that Karim happened to be lurking nearby to leave a note and somehow knew to grab the one piece of paper that would lead the bad guys to our team."

She narrowed her eyes. "He left that message from Tehrazzi *after* he'd killed Assoud, not before." Fighting back her temper, she waited for him to admit he was being completely illogical and a total asshole, even if he was upset about his brother. It didn't happen. He kept glaring at her.

"My cousin was out there too, you know. You said yourself I wouldn't jeopardize her safety, so why wouldn't I do everything I could to guarantee Rhys got them out?"

"Maybe you'd brokered a deal where they'd turn her over to you once you helped them kill the rest of us."

She jerked as if he'd slapped her. In truth, she would have preferred it to his bitter words. For him to believe that of her, he must not care for her at all.

No. Worse than that. He'd have to hate her guts. Her voice broke as the tears came faster. "How could you say that to me?"

"I read Tehrazzi's last e-mail to you, that's how." He turned his back on her and seemed to battle getting his anger under control. "There's too many goddamn things that went wrong for them to be coincidences, and nobody's that unlucky." He faced her. "I warned you never to lie to me."

A cold wave washed over her.

"*Didn't* I."

"Yes, but I—"

"I'm going to find out what really happened out there, and if it turns out you've been lying to me this whole time..." He stopped and pulled in a sharp breath, seemed to struggle with himself before he regained control. The rage and pain swirling in his eyes frightened her. "You almost had me," he mused, and the suffering in his face tore her apart. He shook his head. "When you said you loved me, I actually believed you."

His eyes were so full of buried rage. Sam took a step forward. "I do love y—"

"Fuck. You."

She recoiled.

His derisive laugh broke the taut silence. "Blood's thicker than water, huh, Sam."

Despair swamped her. "You heard me talking to Miller."

"Oops." A sneer distorted his face. For the first time, he was ugly to her. "Guess you didn't want me to overhear that, huh?"

"You misunderstood." Tears thickened her voice. She forced the words out between panting breaths, panic making her heart race and her lungs burn. "You can't really believe I'd want anything to happen to you or anyone else just to get Nev out."

"Like hell I can't."

He's angry and in pain, he doesn't really mean it. Yet his actions told her he meant every word.

Her heart cracked wide open, and it hurt so bad Sam wanted to die. For a moment, she wondered if she would. But her heart kept beating somehow. She stared helplessly at Ben's broad back through the agonizing silence that followed, wanting to prove her innocence, but not knowing how. Maybe she should go and let him have some space for a while. Whatever pain she was in, his had to be a thousand times worse. She glanced at the door, wondered if her jellied knees would get her that far.

Something stopped her.

To hell with her agony and her pride. This wasn't about her anymore. It was all about Ben. If she didn't get through to him now, she risked losing him forever. "I swear to God I didn't make any deals with anyone." How was she still able to speak with this pain in her chest? "I do love you. I care about Rhys. Deep down, you must know that." She had to swallow twice to force the lump down. "Whatever evidence you've built up against me, your heart knows the truth."

His angry green gaze sliced her like a blade. "My heart? My fucking heart's the problem! My whole life Rhys tried to get me to use my head instead of my gut reaction, and he's dying right now because I didn't listen!"

Tears blinded her. "That's not true. It's not your fault." It was hers. But not in the calculated way he meant.

The misery etched in Ben's features seared into her bones. He covered his face with his hands and swung around. She wanted to hold him so badly it made her bleed inside.

While she watched helplessly, Ben struggled for control. His harsh breaths were awful to hear. A full minute passed before he spoke, and it came out a ragged cry. "I can't lose him."

She bit her lip, trying to stop crying and search through the words for a deeper meaning. Was this his apology? His way of saying he hadn't meant those terrible things?

"I just—Christ, I can't even think about…"

About Rhys dying.

"He's always been there," he rasped, pacing again, rubbing the back of his neck. "Always. I…I can't…" He stopped and whirled to face the opposite wall, covered his eyes with his hand. His shoulders shook. "God, if he dies because I trusted you..."

Uncaring of anything except easing him, she leapt up. "Ben," she whispered.

He shook his head and walked away, the choked sound he bit off making her chest feel like it would split open.

She laid a hand against his trembling back. He flinched at her touch, rejecting her presence and fighting to hold on to his control. This grief was too deep for words or anger. Maybe her love could still reach him. She laid herself against his spine and tentatively slid her arms around his waist. Ben took a shuddering breath, tipped his head back as he blew it out and scrubbed at his eyes with the heels of his hands. She held on, offering the only comfort he allowed her to give. *I'm sorry*, she cried silently. *I'm so sorry I caused this.*

But then he pulled her hands from his stomach and stepped away. Physically and emotionally cutting himself off from her.

She stared at his broad back for a moment, reeling from the implication of his gesture.

She'd just lost him.

It was more than she could bear. She withstood it for another few moments, but he didn't acknowledge her presence. The door opened a second later and a nurse poked her head in.

"Sir," she addressed Ben. "The doctor wants to see you."

Sam inhaled sharply. Was Rhys dead?

Ben rushed past her without so much as a backward glance. In the silence that followed, the nurse looked at her quizzically. "You family?"

"N-no." She was nothing to Ben anymore.

She wanted to scream in agony. Swallowing her tears, she choked, "I'll be outside if he..." She almost said "needs me", but caught herself just in time and left. The door shut behind her with a thud. Alone in the hallway, the sound was as hollow as the empty hole in the middle of her chest.

****

A few hours later as dawn lit the horizon out the hospital room window, Ben was keeping vigil next to his brother's bed when Neveah popped her head in, her damp hair telling him she was fresh from a shower. He leaned back in his chair and forced a weary smile even though his face felt like it might crack from the strain. "Hey."

"Hey. Can I come in?"

"Sure." He scrubbed a hand over his shaggy face and blew out a weary breath.

Beside him, Rhys' chest rose and fell in an eerie rhythm set by the machines he was hooked up to, the right side of his head left wide open under the bandages to accommodate the swelling in his brain. A ventilator inflated and deflated his lungs in that artificial rhythm. His eyes were so badly bruised and swollen his bearded face was distorted. They had him propped onto his left side because his right shoulder, back and part of his neck had second and a few third degree burns on them. Every inch of that skin was singed except where the tattoo below his right shoulder blade lay, the mirror image of the one Ben had inked into the left side of his own back. Eerie, how that spot was the only place left untouched by the fire. Ben had teared up when he'd seen it, that lone patch of skin like an island in a sea of raw and blistered flesh. How Rhys was still alive was anyone's guess.

And yet, Ben kept expecting him to wake up and look at him. Say something stern and irritating, like, "What the hell are you staring at?", or, "Quit gawking at me, punk." Anything. Any sign that he was going to make it.

No, that wasn't quite true. The one thing he didn't want was for Rhys to come out of this a vegetable. If he'd suffered that kind of brain damage, then it was best if he never woke up. Without a doubt, Rhys would rather die than waste away like that, drooling and shitting all over himself. The thought of his brother ending up like that made Ben want to cry.

Nev edged her way in, checked the profusion of monitors beeping and whirring around his twin's still form. "He's holding his own."

For the moment, yes. "If he's still stable in the morning, they're going to transport him to Germany, then maybe stateside." A pang of loneliness hit him.

Ben fought the urge to fidget under Nev's assessing gaze. Had she seen Sam? He hadn't since that awful confrontation in the waiting room, and didn't want to. Not until he cooled off and got the facts verified from someone he trusted. His heart and his brain were still at war with each other over her. The gnawing pain in his belly shot up like he'd been nailed with a welder's torch, making him want to double over. That's what a full blown ulcer did for you.

"Walter Reed," Nev said as she picked up the thread of conversation. "They do great work with TBI patients." She laid a hand on Rhys' gown-covered shoulder, almost a caress, then turned her attention back to him. "Do you have any more questions about what to expect with all this?"

"No." Rhys was a Traumatic Brain Injury patient. The swelling would take anywhere from a few days to a few weeks to disappear. Once that happened, they'd bring him out of the coma and see how much damage had been done to his brain. He could have permanent motor or speech loss, memory loss, cognitive loss. Even if most of those functions were largely intact, he would still have a shitload of physical therapy to go through. The neurosurgeon had said most of the damage was in the right parietal lobe, and that meant he'd almost certainly have lack of coordination on the right side of his body and left-sided weakness. The possibilities didn't make Ben's ulcer or the sick feeling in his stomach any better. "I hear you're on your way home."

Nev turned her eyes on him. Lake blue, a few shades lighter than Rhys'. "I'd rather stay. I told them that, but they want me home to debrief me. Security reasons and all that."

Made sense. He rolled his head around to try and ease the tension in his neck and shoulders. It didn't help. "Sam going with you?"

Nev gave him a surprised look. "She left hours ago. Didn't she say goodbye?"

A hollow sensation filled his burning gut. "No. No, she didn't."

"They came to take her in for some questioning."

More like an interrogation. He closed his eyes. God, Sam… He still had his doubts about what had happened, but in his heart of hearts he didn't think Sam was capable of selling them out. Not even to save her cousin.

There was nothing he could do for her now, and wasn't even sure he wanted to right then. He just needed time to think. But damn, what if it turned out she was clean? The way he'd reacted, and the things he'd said… He scrubbed a hand tiredly over his eyes. He'd been so damn hard on her. Mean, even. He sighed. Wouldn't be the first time he'd done something he'd regretted. One would think he wouldn't even notice this sinking feeling anymore.

"In the morning they're flying her back to Langley for a full debriefing. That's what she told me, anyhow, that it's standard procedure in a case like this." She cocked her head. "Was she telling me the truth?"

The truth? How the hell should he know? "Yeah."

"She's not in some kind of trouble or anything?"

Not if she was innocent. He prayed to God she was innocent. "She's fine."

Relief washed over Nev's features. "She probably didn't want to distract you. She was really upset about Rhys, and made me promise to let her know what happens to him. I'm sure she'll be in touch once she gets back to the States, but I think she'd prefer to hear about your brother from you."

No she wouldn't. A layer of guilt settled over the emptiness inside. "Yeah." God, he'd treated her like shit.

"Sam's the best person in the world." Her gaze traveled to his brother, and Ben recognized the heartache in her eyes. "Well, maybe it's a tie."

He kept his derisive comment about comparing Sam and his brother to himself. Nobody could touch Rhys when it came to character. He was integrity personified, Ben thought fiercely. How the hell was he supposed to go on without him?

"Hey." Nev laid a hand on his forearm. "The doctors won't transport him if they don't think he's ready. Keep talking to him. Some patients can hear their loved ones speaking to them even in a coma."

He nodded, so desperately exhausted he wanted to lie down on the floor and shut his eyes and sleep, but he wouldn't abandon his brother. Not even in that way.

“Get some sleep if you can. You’re not going to do him any good by driving yourself into the ground. He’s going to need you at full strength when they bring him out of this.” Glancing at Rhys, she shook her head with a smile. “God, he’s strong. He shouldn’t have survived the flight here, but look at him.”

He’d been doing little else for the last six hours.

“Well, I’d better go so you can sleep.”

Ben knew he needed some, but he was afraid Rhys might slip away if he closed his eyes. He was terrified that it might break their subconscious connection enough for his twin to stop fighting and let go. “I can’t thank you enough for what you did—”

“Don’t even say it, Ben. Without both of you, I would be dead by now, so if anyone’s grateful, it’s me.”

When she came up to him and opened her arms for a hug, he almost drew back, but made himself endure the quick embrace even though he was afraid the gesture would undo him and turn him into a human faucet. He was that close to losing it. Nev pressed against him and enveloped him in her arms for a moment, and all he could think about was how he wished it was Sam holding him, and that he’d been such an asshole. He’d probably never feel her arms around him again. Nev kept it mercifully brief and withdrew.

Her gaze strayed back to Rhys. “I wish I could stay with him.”

“Don’t worry, he won’t be alone. I’m not budging from here.”

After she left, Ben stared at his silent twin with gritty, aching eyes, and took stock of everything. Rhys was fighting for his life. Sam was gone. His parents were on the other side of the world. He’d never felt so alone in his life.

"You gotta stay with me, man," he whispered, and because no one was around to see it, he reached for the lax hand nearest his and wrapped his fingers around it in a desperate grip. "You keep fighting, you hear me? Don't you let go."

If he lost Rhys, he lost half of himself. The best half.

He held Rhys' hand for a long time while he watched the machines inflate that strong chest. Up, down. Up, down. Up, down. The rhythmic motion lulled him into a trance. When he snapped out of it, it took him a second to realize his cell phone was buzzing against his hip. Without relinquishing his brother's hand, he answered.

"Sinclair."

"Ben, it's Luke."

He sat up a little straighter. "What's up?"

"Heard your brother's doing well."

That depended on your definition of well. "He's a fighter."

"Yes, he is. One hell of a fighter."

He cleared his throat. "Did you get a lock on Tehrazzi?"

A deep sigh came over the line. "No. He's got to be out there, but no. None of the villagers are talking. We think he may have been smuggled over the border into Pakistan in a tanker convoy. Possibly in an empty drum."

So his brother had suffered all of this for nothing? Ben's throat ached with the pressure of unshed tears. "Sorry to hear that."

"Don't worry, we're still gonna nail him. Listen... I thought about waiting to tell you this, but figured you'd want to know ASAP."

"What?"

"About Sam..."

All his muscles tensed. "What about her?"

"Miller and I talked with her, and her side of the

story checks out. Then we brought in Karim and leaned on him. Turns out Tehrazzi used the kid's family as leverage for intel on our team's location. When Sam came after me, Karim snuck back into the CP to drop the note for me, then took the laptop and relayed the coordinates to his village where Tehrazzi was waiting."

Aw, fuck. Ben closed his eyes as a wave of pain engulfed him. He remembered the candy bar wrappers strewn on the ground, and the terrible hurt in Sam's eyes when he'd confronted her. "So she *was* innocent."

She'd been telling him the truth, and he hadn't even listened. He'd opened up on her with both barrels and blasted them at her like a verbal shotgun. Well fucking done. He was torn between bitter laughter and tears.

"Yeah, I know you had your doubts, but she's clean. The locals took Tehrazzi in under *Lokhay Warkawal* to treat his wound and give him protection. Heard of it?"

"Yeah. It means they're honor bound to defend him to the death."

"Right. He received the information about the team's location there."

Which was why the Taliban had been coming up the mountain after Rhys and the others when they arrived in the helo. Christ. The whole thing had been an accident, and he'd blamed Sam for Rhys getting hit. Among other things, like her making a deal with Tehrazzi to kill them off. Jesus. Did he never learn? Why hadn't he trusted his gut in the first place? He swallowed hard. "Thanks for letting me know."

"No problem. They transferring Rhys tomorrow?"

"If he's still stable."

"He will be. And if there's anything you need,

just let me know. You call me, day or night, no matter what it is. Okay?"

"Thanks. I appreciate it." He almost asked Luke how his head was, but thought better of it and left it alone.

"I'll get in touch with you once you're home and things have settled down, give you the report about what's going on here in case you're still interested in a job."

"Sure." Ben didn't care about terrorists at the moment. The job and all the money in the world meant shit to him right now. All he wanted was for his brother to open his eyes and look at him with some sort of recognition. If that happened, then he could think about the rest of his life and figure out how to fix what he'd done to Sam. For now, the only thing he cared about was his brother waking up.

"One last thing."

Ben grunted.

"A word of advice from an old turd who's stepped in it more than a few times in his sorry excuse for a life…"

"What's that," he responded, setting the phone in the crook of his shoulder and pinching the bridge of his nose.

"Apologies that size only work if they're delivered in person."

"Is that right. You an expert or something?"

"Nope. Only done it once. But I've been practicing the most important one for over twenty years. If I ever got the chance to give it… Believe me, I'd do it in person."

Thinking about that cryptic comment after he'd hung up, Ben gazed at his brother's misshapen face. Rhys' father-figure complex had always made him so goddamn mad, but now… Jesus, he'd give anything to get a lecture and some unsolicited advice from him.

Sighing, he squeezed Rhys' limp hand. "You need to wake up, man, because as usual I've fucked up in a colossal way."

Sam was Rhys' friend. If his twin woke up with his brain intact, Ben had better prepare himself for a verbal ass kicking. Since he had lots of time to kill in the meantime, he'd give himself a mental one instead.

Chapter Twenty-Three

Virginia, two weeks later
Evening

Sam returned Nev's call as she pulled into her building's underground parking lot, but got her cousin's voicemail. She tucked the phone into the curve of her shoulder as the electronic beep came. "Hey, it's me. I'm good, so don't worry. I'm about to go up and open a can of soup and then put myself into a chocolate coma for the night. Talk to you later."

She put her cell into its designated pouch in her purse, hating that an image of Ben smirking at her obsessive organizing fetish popped into her head. But what did she expect? He was all she'd thought about the past two weeks no matter how hard she'd tried to stop. If an antidote to him existed, she hadn't found it yet.

Sam was in full comfort mode these days. As soon as she hit her apartment, she was going straight for a hot bath, followed up with her fuzzy robe and slippers and a pint of Ben and Jer—

Oh, crap. Couldn't she even eat ice cream without being reminded of him? Damn, and that's the only kind she had. Fine. No ice cream. Chocolate bar instead. There weren't any Ben bars, were there? She gave herself a mental smack. No more thinking about him. And she was definitely not going to listen to the three messages he'd left on her answering machine, even though she'd stupidly saved them all. She was *not* going to play them just so she could hear the deep, achingly familiar timbre of his voice. She was not going to pull out her pack of Big Red that she'd bought because it smelled like him. She was not going to cry when a Tums commercial came on TV. That was just pathetic.

She was pathetic.

If it weren't for her job keeping her mind occupied, she'd have had a mental breakdown over him by now. As it was, she'd lost weight and barely slept for more than a few hours at a time. She had nightmares about what had happened out there. Sometimes they were about the man she'd killed. His frozen stare as the life drained out of him still haunted her, even though she knew he would have killed her had she not taken the shots. But mostly they were about Rhys burning in that truck and the look in Ben's eyes when he accused her of setting them up to die. Her subconscious tortured her with it even when she was sleeping. Her CIA-assigned psychiatrist said she had a combination of post-traumatic stress disorder and survivor guilt. Exactly the same diagnosis Nev had received. The fact that she wasn't alone in her suffering didn't comfort Sam in the least.

Facing the prospect of another lonely night filled with despair and terrifying dreams made the increasingly familiar pang of grief well up despite her best effort to stop it. Dammit, she missed him. At times she thought she'd die from the pain in her heart, and part of her thought it would be kinder. Living with the loss of him every day was like dying a slow death, and she could neither stop it nor speed it along.

She grabbed her briefcase from the passenger seat and swung the door open with a sigh. At least she could talk to her cousin about it if Nev called later. Sam had no one else to listen.

****

Ben's heart rate doubled when Sam's red two-door compact pulled into the underground parking. He stood in the shadows as she parked and watched her climb out of the car in her black high-heeled pumps, her slim legs bare to the knee, snug black pencil skirt hugging her hips and thighs. Her hair was back to its natural shade of red, he noticed, admiring how beautiful and shiny it was in the overhead lights. She tossed the fiery cascade of it over one shoulder of her pale pink blouse and tugged out her briefcase, shut the door and locked her car, all without glancing around her.

It occurred to him it was the first time he'd ever seen her wearing anything other than robes or cargo pants and an olive drab t-shirt. This new look suited her. A mix of polished professional and feminine sensuality. Ben shook himself. She might be beautiful, but he still wanted to turn her over his knee for not being more cautious when she was alone in an underground garage. Just because she was back in civilization didn't mean bad things couldn't happen to her.

He hadn't heard a word from her in over two weeks, not since that hellish day Rhys had been wounded and gone in for surgery. Ben had stayed with his brother when they transferred him to Germany, then to Walter Reed Army Medical Center in Washington D.C. When Rhys had finally come out of the drug-induced coma nine days after the accident, it had taken Ben a few days to come to grips with the fact that his twin wasn't going to wind up a vegetable, and then a few more before he could dig his head out of his ass and realize Sam wasn't going to return his calls.

And why should she have, after how he'd treated her?

The final kick in the ass came when Rhys, who

couldn't speak until his vocal chords healed from the trauma caused by the emergency intubation, had scribbled something down on a piece of paper. *Spill it,* he'd finally managed to write.

Cringing inside, he'd told Rhys what had happened with Sam and then watched with a breaking heart as his twin struggled to hold the pen and form the letters of the words he couldn't say. The clumsily written response was now burning a hole in Ben's back right jeans pocket, looking like a pre-schooler had printed it.

Stupid punk. You're lucky I can't get out of bed. Go grovel. Now.

Since he at least owed Sam an apology, Ben had decided to take Luke's advice and had driven down to see her so he could deliver it in person. Because he'd been a total prick to her back in Kabul, he wasn't sure what kind of reception he'd get. He wouldn't blame her if she threw something at him or slapped him across the face. He deserved that and more, but he was counting on the fact that she still cared enough to hear him out. Big goddamn gamble, under the circumstances.

Ben watched her stroll away from her car. She still didn't know he was there, and he wished the hell she would pay more attention to her surroundings. He'd have to talk to her about that later. If he got the chance.

Bracing himself, he followed her to the stairs. Sam glanced over her shoulder as she heard him approach, did a double take and stopped dead. The keys in her hand jangled softly. Her dumbfounded expression confirmed that he was the last person she'd expected to see standing there.

His stomach was a giant burning knot below his ribcage. "Hi," he ventured, stuffing his hands into his front pockets while keeping a careful distance between them. He had no idea what to expect from her.

She swallowed and recovered from her surprise. "H-Hi." Her fingers tightened around the handle of her briefcase, betraying her nervousness. She must be unsure of why he was there.

"Just come from work?"

She nodded, still staring at him like she was looking at a ghost.

"I assume you got my messages."

"Yes."

The clipped word did nothing to buoy his spirits. Ben fought the urge to fidget. He had no clue what was going on in her head, and her expression didn't give anything away other than she was wary of him. But that all changed in an instant when he opened his mouth again.

"What do you want?" she demanded.

Ouch. Now her eyes were shooting sparks. "To see you."

"Why the hell would you want to see me? I almost killed your brother, remember?"

"Sam, don't—"

"I have nothing to say to you." She pivoted on her high heels and took a step away from him.

Ben floundered, staring at her back. Had no idea how to fix the mess he'd made, but he couldn't let her go until he'd done everything humanly possible to undo the damage. "Rhys came out of the coma a couple days ago."

She stopped. Faced him.

"Looks like he's going to be okay."

"Yes, I know. I get daily updates from Nev."

"Oh." How did Nev know? He hadn't seen her since the day after Rhys' surgery. Ben rubbed the back of his neck. "Listen, I wondered if we could talk."

She raised one auburn brow in a haughty gesture.

He shifted his feet. "I feel bad about the way we left things—"

Her eyes narrowed. "Excuse me? *We*?"

Damn. This whole operation was like walking through a minefield. Every step could blow his legs off. "Okay, I feel bad about the way *I* left things. I was upset about my brother, but I shouldn't have said those awful things to you." He wished the hell they weren't having this conversation in the middle of the damned garage.

The anger in her gaze was so hot it scorched him. "You thought I'd sent him over that mine on *purpose*."

He winced. "I know. I'm sorry."

The accusation in her brown eyes stabbed at him.

"I was an asshole. I'm sorry."

Still nothing. Just that angry gaze, a little of the hurt he'd caused showing through.

Okay, he was running out of ways to apologize. That familiar burning started in his gut and spread up into his chest, but he wasn't going to show weakness by grabbing the roll of Tums he clenched in his pocket. "Look, you have every right to be pissed, but at least hear me out. Can we go for a walk? Maybe grab a bite to eat?"

He caught the sheen of tears in her eyes before she looked away and shook her head with a hollow laugh. "Is that it? That's what you drove here to tell me—that you're sorry you were an asshole?"

He had nothing else at the moment.

Sam flipped her hair over her shoulder again, a few of the glossy waves clinging to the curve of her breast. Somehow he dragged his eyes up to her face.

"So," she said, "why the change of heart? Luke call you up and say I was telling you the truth?" When he didn't answer, she shook her head. "Well, lucky for me he was there to redeem my reputation."

Her tone dripped with disgust.

Damn, what should he do? Ben felt almost as helpless as when Rhys had hit that mine. "Come for a walk, Sam. Please."

She studied him for several agonizing moments, then relented. "You want me to take a walk so you can try and explain yourself? Fine. But let me take my stuff upstairs first." Without waiting for him, she went into the stairwell. He followed a few steps behind her.

He couldn't help but admire the muscles in her bare calves and the shape of her ass in that snug skirt as they climbed the five flights of stairs. The whole time he berated himself for ogling her he thought about how those sexy legs had felt wrapped around him in that Kabul hotel room. He was here to apologize, beg for mercy if necessary, and shouldn't even be *thinking* about getting her naked. Duly chastened for his wayward thoughts, he trailed behind while she went to her apartment and unlocked it, opened the door just long enough to toss her briefcase inside and grab a sweater hanging on a hook in the entryway before shutting it.

As she faced him and wrapped her arms around her waist in that inherently feminine gesture of self-comfort, Ben wanted to touch her so badly he could hardly breathe. He wanted to hug her, chase her sadness away and cover her face with beseeching kisses until she forgave him.

"Let's go," she said, in a "let's get this over with" tone.

Well, what had he expected? "Sam."

She raised her eyes and arched a brow, an invisible wall between them. A wall he'd slammed up in that Kabul hospital waiting room. He regretted that. He hated the cold front coming from her more than anything. He'd rather she yelled and threw punches. Shutting him out like this put him in knots.

At least she was willing to let him talk. He had that one advantage, so he might as well get down to it. Ben took a steadying breath and maintained eye contact. "I'm sorry I hurt you." He took the shock in her expression as a sign it was what she'd hoped to hear but never expected him to say. "I'd go back and fix it if I could." He thought her lips trembled. *Please don't cry.* His stomach seized with guilt.

Sam's eyes were wet, but she composed herself fast. Her jaw tightened. "You know what? I don't want to do this in public." She unlocked the door and pushed it open. "Go in."

He did, waiting for her to escort him into her cozily furnished, earth-toned family room. On the white traditional mantel were pictures of her and Nev, and the antiqued pine coffee table held a book about Iraq. The room was soothing and cozy, devoid of clutter and neat as a pin. Just like its owner. Ben glanced at her and stood awaiting further instructions. He wasn't going to risk doing something else wrong.

"Sit wherever you want."

She said it as if she couldn't have cared less what he did, including take a leap off the balcony railing out the sliding glass doors behind her.

Ben sank onto an antiqued chocolate brown leather couch. It creaked as he settled his weight into it, and the sound was loud in the hollow silence between them. The roll of Tums in his pocket dug into his thigh. They weren't going to be able to ease his discomfort, because they did dick all for the ulcer he'd been diagnosed with. Hell, at this point even a fire extinguisher wasn't going to be able to douse the flames in his stomach. Rhys' recovery and Sam's forgiveness were the only cure, and he desperately needed them both.

Sam wandered around a bit, her gaze flitting all

over as though she had no idea what to look at. Then she nailed him with the liquid brown eyes he hadn't been able to get out of his head. "You know what? I loved you."

The past tense set off a crushing pain in his chest. *You deserved this*, he reminded himself. *Take it like a man.*

"I loved you, and even though I knew it wasn't mutual, I still thought you might have had feelings for me. Through this whole thing, that was the worst part about what you said to me, because it made very clear the fact that you hated my guts."

"I never—"

"How could you have thought I had something to do with Rhys hitting that mine? Me, Ben? Of all the people in the world, I thought you knew me well enough to know I'd never hurt someone I cared about."

Jesus, he still cringed when he thought about it. He didn't know what to say to make it better. "I'm sorry." A hollow feeling filled his gut. "Is that why you left?"

"Partly." Her gaze bored into his. "Mostly it was because I didn't have a choice. They physically dragged me out of there and took me straight to the CIA station so Miller and Luke could 'question' me," she finished, using her fingers as quote marks. "I realize you were going through hell, Ben, but while you were sitting next to Rhys's bed, did you ever once think about what *I* was going through? Did you ever consider that I'd just gone through the same thing as you, except I'm a civilian? I had absolutely no training to fall back on for that scenario, and I had no way of coping with the fact that I had killed a man and been shot with a rifle round and watched one of my teammates get blown up because I'd sent him down the wrong road. Or did you forget all of that?"

"I—"

"Not only did I have to deal with the fact that you blamed me for everything and hated my guts, I had to answer to my boss and his superiors because of it. And when they sent me to Langley for more debriefing, who did I have to turn to when they hollowed me out like a melon and sent me home when they were done? No one. Not my dad, because he could never even begin to understand what I'd been through. Not even Nev, because she'd already been sent home to New York and had her own baggage to deal with. You were the one I needed to talk to, and I couldn't." She put her hands on her head. "God, do you have any idea what being treated like that feels like, let alone by someone you *loved*?"

Because he didn't trust himself to speak yet, Ben shook his head. God, the pain he'd inflicted on her.

"Well then I'll tell you. Devastating doesn't even begin to describe it. I feel sick to my stomach all the time. I can't concentrate, and I can't sleep. And when I do, I either have nightmares or dream of you. I wake up alone crying *every single night*."

The sorrow in her eyes made him want to drop to his knees and beg her forgiveness, plead for another chance. "Sam…"

He started to rise and go to her, but she cut him off with an angry shake of her head. Ben fought down his impatience and sat back down. He at least owed her the chance to vent and get this all out.

"You know what the most pathetic part of it is? I wasn't going to leave that hospital in Kabul. Not until we cleared everything up between us. I would have stayed as long as it took for you to talk to me. I would have been there for you every second of Rhys' coma and I would have stuck with you through everything that came afterward if I thought there was any hope at all that you cared about me."

He knew she would have. Holding her gaze, he leaned forward. "I wasn't thinking straight that day. That's the only thing I can say in my own defense, and I'm so damned sorry. I shouldn't have accused you and shut you out like that. I just didn't know what to think. There were too many coincidences."

"But you *should* have known what to think. You shouldn't even have had to question my love for you and my loyalty to the team. That's the point."

He sighed. "Just for a second, try and see it from my point of view."

She snorted. "You don't think I have? I was there. I realize how suspicious things must have seemed. I even tried to give you the benefit of the doubt because of all that had happened since Baghdad and because I knew how terrified you were that Rhys would die. The missing coordinates and note from Tehrazzi looked bad enough before Rhys got hurt, and after that I didn't have a chance in hell of defending myself to you. But I still thought you'd come to your senses when Rhys came out of surgery and things calmed down."

"You're right. About everything. I shouldn't have accused you no matter how traumatized I was. Believe me, I regret every stupid fucking word I said to you in that waiting room."

Sam hugged herself tighter, looking so hurt and bewildered it damn near killed him not to hold her.

Then she hid her emotions behind a calm mask before straightening her spine. "Fine, I believe you," she said, turning away as though she was going to leave the room. "Thanks for telling me."

Ben couldn't help but notice she hadn't said anything about forgiving him before she'd dismissed him.

Without thinking, he jumped up and grabbed her arm. Sam froze, jerking her gaze up in surprise. The warmth and firmness of her skin registered beneath his fingers. He wanted to bend his head to kiss each and every freckle on her pretty, straight nose. Her scent reached out to tease him, a mix of fruity shampoo and lotion that made him ache to pull her close and breathe more of it in. He'd dreamed of her, too, along with the nightmares. Did she think he wasn't affected by what had happened out there? He'd woken up alone and aching for her night after night, knowing he had no one but himself to blame for her absence.

Helpless not to, he brought one hand up and stroked his thumb over the petal softness of her cheek. She didn't move, but he caught the shock and flare of physical awareness in her eyes. "Sam…"

"What?" she whispered.

"Tell me what to do to fix it."

She shook her head and closed her eyes as though she couldn't bear to see him. "You can't fix it."

He had to. Failure here was not an option. "Let me try."

"There's nothing there to fix anymore."

"Yes, there is."

Her eyes flew open and she nailed him with a venomous glare. "Why the hell should I listen to anything you have to say after the way you treated me?"

The muscles in his jaw flexed. He'd never felt so exposed, but he'd known this wouldn't be easy. "Because I love you."

It stunned her into stillness. Her mouth parted in surprise. It took a moment for her to collect herself. "You can't say that to me. Not now."

"I just did." Heart pounding, he took her face in his hands, desperate to get through to her. He had to make her believe him. "I love you."

She blinked a couple of times, her eyes flooding with tears. Then she shook her head.

He wouldn't give up. "Why do you think I reacted so strongly? I'd fallen in love with you somewhere along the way, and I thought you might have betrayed my brother to save your cousin. It was a shitty thing for me to think, yeah, but if I hadn't cared about you so much I wouldn't have blasted you like that."

"What, you expect me to be glad about that?" She stifled a choked sound.

"Don't cry," he pleaded, dropping his head to kiss the tears away, his chest tight as a vise. He hated knowing he'd caused her so much pain, would do anything to take it away, even if it meant leaving her. It would tear his heart out, but he'd do it if it was best for her. "Please, Sam. Give me one last chance."

She vibrated beneath his hands. "God, Ben, I can't take this. Not now. I've spent this whole time trying to get my life back together. I need to get over you..."

A flare of panic hit him. "Sam, please let me—"

"*Stop*."

Unwanted tears boiled up. In another second he was going to lose it completely. He shook his head. "I can't," he said hoarsely. "I can't let you go without a fight."

"That's just it, Ben. I don't want to fight, and I'm done with being on the receiving end of your suspicion and anger."

He firmed his grip, determined to get through to her. "I never meant to take it out on you, Sam, and I swear to God I'll never hurt you again. Just please, don't walk away." He swallowed. "Please. I need you."

A moment later, she lifted her head and stared at him with tear-drenched eyes. "I can't do it. I can't open myself up to you like that again. I want to believe you, more than anything, but I don't think I can trust that you won't do the same damn thing the next time something goes wrong."

"Just give me the chance to earn your trust back."

"It's not that simple, and you know it." A terrible sorrow filled her eyes. "I tried to earn yours back, and look how well that turned out."

Ben swallowed. The crushing pressure in his chest almost suffocated him.

Sam's eyes squeezed shut as she battled with herself. Then the lids flipped open. "Even if I did, I don't know if I can forget what happened."

Sensing a softening in her, he leapt all over her indecision. "I don't expect you to. All I want is another chance."

A bitter laugh escaped her. "You've had plenty of chances already. What makes this one any different?"

He pushed, because fighting back was the only thing he knew how to do when his back was against the wall. "Because I love you and I don't want to lose you."

"God, you have no idea how badly I want to believe you."

Ben held his breath. *Please, please…*

Sam studied him a full minute while he sweated out her decision. Then she exhaled a deep breath. "Don't you *ever* hurt me like that again."

Was that a yes? His heart broke open. "I won't. I swear."

"But if I do this, you need to know this is your last chance." Her set expression left no doubt she meant every word of it. The next offense was strike three, and he'd be out on his ass for good.

"Understood." The ache in his throat nearly choked him. Had he done it? Had he won her back? He stroked a hand over her shiny hair. "I'd *really* love to hold you right now. Can I?"

A tear slipped over her cheek. He brushed it away. She hesitated a moment, then tucked her face against his chest and melted into him. Her grip was fierce. The earth seemed to tilt under Ben's feet. He slid his hands over her shoulders and wrapped his arms around her, groaning in relief as he brought her full up against him. A tremor rippled through her.

"Sam," he murmured, burying his face in her soft hair. He'd missed her so damn much.

Raising her face, she gave him a tentative, watery smile. "God, you have no idea how much I've missed you." Then she leaned up and kissed him.

Joy and need raced through him, making him lightheaded. He kissed her back, his arms jealously tight around her, locking her to him as he took over, licking along her soft lower lip until she opened and let him in to caress her tongue with his. She moaned and twined her arms around his neck, her urgency making him burn with the need to bury himself inside her. The realization had him breaking the kiss.

Sam blinked up at him with a confused expression. "What's wrong?"

His throat was as tight as the rest of him when he answered. "This isn't why I came." It seemed presumptuous to tumble her into bed when her trust in him was so precarious. "I promised you a walk."

She smiled. "Later. I want you."

He hesitated. "You sure?" He was so afraid of messing this up.

"Don't you want me?"

What the hell kind of question was that? He was standing in front of her and breathing, wasn't he? "Hell yes, I want you."

A bright laugh escaped her. "We've already lost two weeks together. Don't make me wait any more."

"I don't want to screw this up—"

"Then listen to me." Her eyes challenged him. "You said you love me. Prove it."

He didn't deserve her. All that warmth and strength, all that passion blazing in her eyes for him. Instinct took over. He grabbed her up in his arms, nibbling at the sensitive spot on her neck and inhaling her delicious scent as she fumbled with the buttons on his shirt. By the time he made it to her bedroom and laid her on the soft white sheets of her sleigh bed, he was ready to burst.

Fighting to slow down, he kissed her tenderly while he unbuttoned her blouse and undid the front clasp of her pink lace bra. For a moment, he stared. Her skin was so lovely, all pale and creamy, her nipples a delicate shade of pink, turning to a deep raspberry as they tightened beneath his gaze. Two rosy buds begging for his touch, his mouth.

The instant his fingers stroked over the curve of her breast she bowed up with a guttural moan and clutched him tighter, bringing her legs up around his hips and pulling him into her body. His cock pulsed desperately against his zipper. He sank down with a sigh and lowered his mouth to one nipple, sucking with slow, firm pressure. So lovely.

"Ben," she quavered breathlessly, fingers ripping at the buttons on his shirt and roving over his bare chest, down his clenched abdomen to his waistband. "I want you in me."

He shuddered, pushing against the eager hands stroking over his throbbing erection. She shoved her skirt up and he wrenched her panties down her gorgeous legs, leaving her bare to his hands and mouth. Sam cried out and buried her fingers in his hair when he licked her there and tried to drag him up, but he held her thighs wider apart and loved her with tender sweeps of his tongue, lost in her outrageously sexy response, hungry for the taste of her. He suckled gently, fighting back the need to rear up and plunge inside her when she moaned low and long in her throat. Sam's eyes were glazed with pleasure, the lids heavy, her cheeks flushed, full lips parted. She trembled beneath him, sinking her teeth into her lower lip when he slid a finger inside her.

"Ben..." She moaned and pushed up against his mouth. She was panting, almost there. "Inside me. Please."

Reluctantly, he released her, pausing a second so she could watch him glide his tongue along his lower lip and suck at it, savoring her tangy-sweet flavor. In answer she grabbed him and hauled him up the length of her with surprising strength. He chuckled against her lips as she tore the condom she'd grabbed from her nightstand open and helped him smooth it on. She ate him up like a famished woman, undulating against him and taking his straining cock in her hand with an impatient sound when he didn't move fast enough for her.

Ben let her guide him into her and held her gaze as he slowly buried his length inside her, watching her reaction through the haze of his own pleasure. Her body hugged him so tight. "I love you."

She gasped, her head kicking back into her pillow. Ben groaned and slid his hands beneath her hips, lifting her into his rhythm, kissing her urgently. She made a keening sound and locked her legs around him, begging for more. He shifted forward, changing the angle so he could rub against her clit while he kept his pace. Watching with hungry fascination, he reveled in the way she squeezed her eyes shut with a desperate moan, pumping beneath him, then broke apart in his arms.

Still moving inside her while the pulses of her release faded, Ben's heart lurched with tenderness when she opened her eyes to look at him. They were liquid with tears. She blinked them away, never taking her eyes off him as he rocked in and out. The intimacy was shattering; Sam's whole being wide open and defenseless to him, her loving gaze on him as the pleasure grew until he could barely breathe, muscles straining for release. Trembling, he let himself go with a hoarse shout and hung there, as vulnerable in her arms at that moment as she'd been in his. Lying in the cradle of her body afterward with her hands sifting through his hair and over his dampened skin was the sweetest thing he'd ever known. Tucking her securely beneath him, they dozed for a while.

Later, when he found the will to leave her warmth, he got up and pulled his jeans on, playing with the contents in the pocket for a moment before sitting on the edge of the bed and staring at her in awe. She was so beautiful. He'd never forget the way she looked then. Sated and relaxed, her brown eyes languorous from pleasure, rich auburn hair spilling over her creamy shoulders. Sam gave him a sleepy smile and stretched with a contended sigh, kissing his hand when he stroked her hair.

"Love you," she murmured, reaching out to lay her palm against the side of his face.

Ben sighed and closed his eyes, leaning into her touch. No matter what happened from here, he was hers. Forever.

His fingers tightened around what was in his pocket. Slowly, he withdrew it. Opening his eyes, he watched her face as he held up the diamond ring so she could see it.

Sam pulled in a sharp breath and raised her shocked gaze to his face.

"I bought this the day Rhys came out of the coma," he said, turning it over in his fingers, the gem sparkling like white fire in the light coming through the window beside her bed. "Even though I knew I'd probably lost you."

"Ben—"

"I know I'm not the easiest person to live with, but I'm hoping that won't put you off." Her surprised smile had his heart knocking against his ribs. "And I know I can be a pain in the ass, but I'll always take care of you, make sure you're safe and happy." He gulped down the lump in his throat. "I love you with everything in me, Samarra. I know it's too soon for a ring, but I want you to take it anyway. And when I've earned your trust back and you know in your heart how much I love you, give it back to me and I'll ask you properly." Her stunned expression didn't ease his nerves any. "So... Will you take it?"

She stared at him for the longest time, as though trying to decide if he really meant it.

Ben had never meant anything more in his life.

And when his stomach burned hot enough to make him sweat, she finally sat up and took it from him. Sliding the ring onto a finger on her right hand, Sam wrapped her arms around him. "I will."

Epilogue

Alexandria, Virginia

Sam pushed her apartment door open with her hip and hauled her suitcase over the threshold, setting it down to shut the door as quietly as possible. She was bone-tired after her drive home from New York, but it had been worth it to see Neveah, even though she hated to be apart from Ben, but he hadn't wanted to leave his brother. He went to the hospital every single day to cheer Rhys on and generally annoy the hell out of him in an effort to speed his recovery.

As for her cousin, Nev was defying the odds and coping well in the aftermath of her traumatic experience in Afghanistan. Not that Sam should have been surprised. She'd never met anyone tougher than her cousin. Once Nev made up her mind about something, that was that. She squared her shoulders, stuck her chin out and followed through. So far, it seemed like she was winning the battle of returning to normalcy. And if Sam wasn't mistaken, Nev seemed to have more than just a clinical interest in Rhys' recovery. Wasn't *that* interesting?

Stifling a yawn, Sam unbuttoned her coat. In the light of the Tiffany hallway lamp Ben must have left on for her, her diamond engagement ring sparkled. She'd caved after a month and given it to him while they were at a sports bar watching a Red Sox game. She hadn't expected Ben to propose then and there, but he had. He'd done it like he did everything else—with passion and total disregard for how much it might embarrass her. Over her shocked protests, he'd gone straight down on one knee and popped the question in as loud a voice as he could manage, right in the middle of the seventh inning stretch. He hadn't cared at all about the crowd they'd attracted, and when she'd said yes, the whole place had erupted in cheers. The memory brought a smile to her face. So did the knowledge that Ben's ulcer had cleared up, and that she hadn't seen him pop a Tums since the day they got back together.

She checked her watch. After midnight, and the apartment was silent. Ben must be asleep, she thought, leaving the lamp on while she went through the foyer, the jewel-toned glass sprinkling color over the cream floor tiles. Sam set her keys on the entry hall table and toed off her pumps, then hung her coat in the closet before lugging her bag toward the kitchen.

Flipping on the row of pot lights above the range, she blinked while her eyes adjusted to the sudden brightness. Her gaze instantly fell on the crystal cookie jar she kept on the black granite island. Fixed to the middle of its gleaming lid was a P-touch label, proclaiming *Cookie Jar*. She released her suitcase. Strange. Ben must have done it, but she couldn't fathom why. Since it bugged her to think of that sticky adhesive all over her good lead crystal, she got busy with scraping it off. When her fingernail didn't do the job, she opened the utensil drawer to—

Ben.

Each piece of silverware was labeled, too. *Salad fork. Dinner fork. Knife. Spoon.*

How…thorough of him.

She glanced around the white and stainless

steel kitchen. Sure enough, more labels met her suspicious gaze. *Light switch. Sink. Refrigerator.*

Her left eye twitched as she stared at the big Frigidaire. *He wouldn't…*

That hope died a quick death when she wrenched the thing open. More labels.

Yogurt. Eggs. Cheese. Ben's beer. Girl food on her container of salad greens.

"Ben," she muttered, and slapped it shut. Talk about overkill.

What the hell had possessed him to waste her P-touch labels like that? So she liked to be organized. What was the big deal? She found more labels on her trip to the back of the apartment. *Hall light switch. Picture of weird-ass dude*, stuck to her Van Gogh print on the wall. Across the subject's forehead was *Step 1 in OCD recovery: Admit you have a problem.*

Oh, he was so in for it. She was going to have him scrape them all off and Windex the marks from the glass and stainless steel in the kitchen. Sam found more on the floor. *Floor tile.* Well, duh. *Accent tile*, on a black granite diamond. Then, above the light switch at the bedroom, helpfully labeled as *Bedroom light switch*, was the coup de grace. *OCD Helpline: 1-800-NT-FREAK.*

He was so dead. Her hand made contact with yet another label when she went to open the door. She glanced down. Stuck to the knob was *Gateway to sexual ecstasy. Must be 18 years or older to enter.*

She damn near burst into giggles. It was all just so ridiculous. So Ben. His off-kilter sense of humor might drive her crazy, but it was one of the things she loved best about him. Everywhere they went, he was the life of the party. People loved him, and his completely extroverted personality was good for her, often dragging her out of her comfort zone. He made her studious, hum-drum life fun. An amazing feat.

Turning the stainless steel knob, she pushed the

door open, and the first thing she noticed was he'd left the TV on his favorite sports highlight station. He'd muted it, but she had no idea how he slept with the light from the screen flickering all night. As for the Label King himself, he was stretched out on his back in their ebony-wood king-sized bed, his clean-shaven face turned away from her. He must have shaved for her before turning in for the night.

Sam's heart caught at the sight of him. He was so damned beautiful with his black hair tousled over his forehead like that, the creamy white sheets wadded around his waist so she had an amazing view of his sculpted chest and arms. In the glare of the TV, she spotted another label, this one displayed proudly across the pad of his left pec. She didn't dare guess what that one said. He looked so peaceful she almost hated to wake him. Almost. But he deserved to suffer some sleep deprivation after what he'd done.

Deliberately letting the knob go it released with a click. Ben came instantly awake, lids snapping open, gaze focusing on her with unnerving speed. He was always like that, zero to sixty in the blink of an eye. In everything he did. Ben only had two speeds—stop and go. And usually, it was all green lights. Especially when it came to her.

Her heart sped as his jade eyes met hers and that trademark slow smile spread across his wickedly handsome face.

"Hey," he said in a sleepy rumble and stretched his arms over his head, his body arching and flexing like a contented panther. And every bit as sensual.

"Hey yourself," she replied, coming toward him. "Have fun decorating while I was gone?"

His smile widened, revealing even white teeth in the light from the TV. His eyes were positively dancing with mischief. "You noticed."

Sam snorted. "Why do I get the feeling I no

longer have any label tape in my P-touch?"

"Don't know." He displayed more of himself with the lazy grace that was such a part of his sensual nature. The sheets barely covered his groin now. "How's Nev?"

God, he was temptation personified. "Good. She sends her love. How's Rhys?"

"Relentless and rigid as ever. He's upped his rehab sessions to five hours a day instead of three." Ben cocked his head. "You gonna come over here and give me a real hello? It's been four days, you know."

His eyes said he knew damned well she wouldn't be able to stay ticked off or keep her distance. Wouldn't surprise her if he knew just how revved up her body was becoming simply by looking at him. "You gonna make it worth my while?" she countered.

"Don't I always?"

She laughed. God, he was arrogant. When she was within arm's reach, she finally made out what the label on his chest said. *YOUR MAN*. "Very nice."

She traced it with a fingertip, and his pec rippled beneath her touch. She wasn't the only one affected. It was always like this between them. Ben might seem relaxed and languorous on the surface, but he wanted her every bit as badly as she wanted him. Sam gave him a slow smile of her own. "I like this one. I think we should keep it, unlike all the others which you're going to scrape off first thing in the morning."

"By myself?"

She grinned at the alarm in his voice. "I'll supervise."

The gleam in his eyes turned wicked. "Sure. If you have the strength to move when you wake up."

He sat up, a glorious display of fluid male power and slid his arms around her. His hands threaded through her hair as he brought her down for his kiss, full of leashed heat and yet so tender it made her breath shorten.

"Missed you."

She burrowed in tight. "I missed you more."

"Not possible. I got so bored I had to resort to using your P-touch like I was fricking Martha Stewart just to amuse myself."

She giggled, she couldn't help herself. "God, you are such an idiot."

Ben nuzzled the side of her throat, drawing a shiver out of her. "I know. Strip those clothes off and slide under the sheets with me so I can make it up to you."

She pressed a kiss to the label stamped over his heart. "I think I might."

He pulled her down and settled her full length on top of him, then kissed her some more until her thoughts scattered. When he pulled back and swept the hair away from her face, that devilish gleam was still in his eyes.

"What?" she whispered with a smile.

"Got one more label you might be interested in."

Oh, she could just imagine. "Yeah? Where's that?"

"It's a surprise." He surged upward with his hips, pressing the hard ridge of his erection into her stomach.

The teasing yet loving expression on his face filled her heart to overflowing. She was so lucky to have him in her life. Ben was the rock to steady herself on when she needed it, her unflinching protector who chased the shadows away, and the man who made her laugh and drove her crazy by turns.

She wouldn't have changed him for the world.

Rubbing against him, already bursting with the need to have him inside her, she played along. "What's it say? Give me a hint."

His boyish grin melted her before he raised his

head to whisper against her ear. His warm breath brushed over her skin, sending a delicious ripple of pleasure down to between her thighs. "It's the name of a famous clock in London."

Sam burst out laughing.

A word about the author...

Kaylea Cross has dreamed of being an author since she was a child. A Registered Massage Therapist, this mother of two is an avid gardener, artist, Civil War buff, belly dancer and former national level softball pitcher.

She lives near Vancouver, B.C. with her husband and energetic little boys.

LaVergne, TN USA
26 September 2010
198515LV00001B/1/P